Also by J. Courtney Sullivan

The Engagements

Maine

Commencement

Saints for All Occasions

Saints for All Occasions

J. Courtney Sullivan

Alfred A. Knopf

New York

2017

THIS IS A BORZOI BOOK PUBLISHED BY ALFRED A. KNOPF

Copyright © 2017 by J. Courtney Sullivan

All rights reserved. Published in the United States by Alfred A. Knopf, a division of Penguin Random House LLC, New York, and distributed in Canada by Random House of Canada, a division of Penguin Random House Canada Limited, Toronto.

www.aaknopf.com

Knopf, Borzoi Books, and the colophon are registered trademarks of Penguin Random House LLC.

Library of Congress Cataloging-in-Publication Data
Names: Sullivan, J. Courtney, author.
Title: Saints for all occasions : a novel / J. Courtney Sullivan.
Description: First Edition. | New York : Alfred A. Knopf, 2017.
Identifiers: LCCN 2016048931 | ISBN 9780307959577 (hardback) |
ISBN 9780307959584 (ebook)
Subjects: LCSH: Domestic fiction. | BISAC: FICTION / Family Life. |
FICTION / Sagas. | FICTION / Contemporary Women.
Classification: LCC PS3619.U43 S25 2017 | DDC 813/.6—dc23
LC record available at https://lccn.loc.gov/2016048931

Jacket photograph of Dorchester Heights, Massachusetts, by James L. Woodward via Wikimedia Commons
Front jacket flap image: Godong / Alamy
Jacket design by Abby Weintraub

Manufactured in the United States of America
First Edition

For Jenny Jackson, Brettne Bloom, and Ann Napolitano,
who kept the faith

I exist in two places,
here and where you are.

—MARGARET ATWOOD,
"Corpse Song"

Part One

❧

2009

I

IN THE CAR on the way to the hospital, Nora remembered how, when Patrick was small, she would wake up suddenly, gripped by some terrible fear—that he had stopped breathing, or spiked a deadly fever. That he had been taken from her.

She had to see him to be sure. They lived then on the top floor of the three-decker on Crescent Avenue. She would practically sleepwalk through the kitchen and past Bridget's door, and then down the hall to the boys' room, her nightgown skimming the cold hardwood, the muffled sound of Mr. Sheehan's radio murmuring up from downstairs.

The fear returned the summer Patrick was sixteen, when they moved to the big house in Hull. Nora would awaken, heart pounding, thinking of him, and of her sister, images past and present wound up in one another. She worried about the crowd he ran with, about his anger and his moods, about things he had done that could never be undone.

She met her worries in the same old way. Whatever the hour, she would rise to her feet and climb the attic stairs to Patrick's bedroom, so that she might lay eyes on him. This was a bargain she struck, a ritual to guarantee safety. Nothing truly bad could happen if she was expecting it.

Over the years, there were times when one of her other three consumed her thoughts. As they got older, Nora knew them better. That was something no one ever told you. That you would have to get to know your own children. John wanted too much to please her. Bridget was a hopeless tomboy. They had carried these traits along with them into adulthood. When Brian, her baby, moved away, Nora worried. She worried ever more so when he moved back in.

But it was Patrick who weighed most on her mind. He was fifty now. For the past several months, the old fear had returned. Ever since John kicked things up again. Things she had long considered safely in the past. Unable to check on Patrick on those nights when the feeling arose, Nora would switch on the lamp and shuffle through her prayer cards until she came to Saint Monica, patron saint of mothers with difficult children. She slept with the card faceup on Charlie's empty pillow.

Tonight, for once, she hadn't been thinking of Patrick. Of all things, she was thinking about the boiler down cellar. It had been clanging since just after supper. Adjusting the temperature didn't help. Nora thought she might have to bleed the pipes. As a last resort, she tried saying a rosary to make it stop. When this seemed to do the trick, she went to bed with a fat grin on her face, thus assured of her own powers.

She was awakened not long after by the ringing telephone, a stranger's voice saying there had been an accident, she should come right away. By the time she reached the emergency room, pink flannel pajamas under her winter coat, Patrick was already gone.

The ambulance had taken him to the Carney.

It took Nora forty-five minutes to get from home to the old neighborhood.

They were waiting for her by the door: a doctor and a nurse and a priest about her age. The presence of the priest made it clear. She thought of how they left Dorchester all those years ago for Patrick's sake, but as soon as he was old enough he moved right back. This would be where his life had started, and where it came to an end.

They took her to a windowless office. She wanted to tell them she wouldn't go in. But she followed right along and sat down. The doctor looked terribly young for such a job, but then a lot of people were starting to look terribly young to her. He wanted Nora to know that they had tried to revive her son for close to an hour. They had done all they could. He explained in calm detail that Patrick had been drinking. That he lost control of the car and slammed into a concrete wall beneath an overpass on Morrissey Boulevard. His chest struck the steering column. His lungs bled out.

"It could have been worse," the doctor said. "If he wasn't wearing a seat belt, he would have been ejected from the car."

How could it be any worse than death? she wondered, and yet she clung to this detail. Patrick had worn his seat belt. He wasn't trying to die.

Nora wanted to ask the priest if he thought all her fears had pointed to this moment. Or if they had been the thing to stave it off for so long. She felt that she should confess something. Her guilt. She knew they would think she was crazy if she said any of it out loud. She sat there with her lips pressed together, holding her pocketbook tight to her chest like it was a fidgety child.

After the signing of papers, the nurse said, "We'll give you a minute with him, if you like."

She led Nora to a room down the hall and closed the door.

Patrick was lying on a gurney, a white blanket covering his body, a breathing tube protruding from his mouth. Someone had closed his eyes.

From the hall and the rooms all around came the beeping of machines, the scurry of feet, and low voices. A burst of laughter from the nurses' station. But in this room, everything was impossibly settled, final. Still.

Nora tried to recall what the doctor had said. It seemed that if she could just piece it together, figure out what was to blame, she might still have him back.

She felt overcome with anger toward John. She returned to that moment last May, when he first asked if she remembered the McClain family from Savin Hill. Their oldest son had approached John to run his campaign for state senate.

"They weren't very nice people," she said. "I don't think you should do it."

What she meant was *Don't do it*. But John went right ahead. It had led to that terrible fight at Maeve's confirmation. Patrick and John hadn't spoken since. Patrick hadn't been himself.

Nora had seen another article in the paper just yesterday, a slight agitation taking root in her chest, as it did whenever she saw Rory McClain's name in print.

There was a photograph of Rory looking every bit the politician, that face so familiar to her, all black hair and toothy smile. His wife stood by his side, and three teenage boys, lined up according to height. Nora wondered if beneath the collared shirts and school picture day haircuts they were as wicked as their father and grandfather had once been. It seemed to her that a duplicitous nature must run in a family, like twins or weak knees.

She hadn't read the article. Though she knew John would call to make sure she had seen it, Nora turned the page.

She took in a deep breath now and told herself to put these thoughts aside. There wasn't much time left.

Patrick had had a horrible mustache for the last two years, despite her begging him to shave it off. She let her hand hover in the air just above it, so as to hide the proof, and then she looked at him. She looked and looked. He had always been handsome. The most beautiful of all her children.

After a while, the nurse knocked twice, then opened the door.

"It's time, I'm afraid," she said.

Nora pulled a small plastic hairbrush from her purse and smoothed his black curls. She checked his pulse, in case. She felt as if a swarm of bees were darting around inside her, but she managed to let Patrick go, as she had on other occasions when it felt impossible. When he was five and frightened about the first day of kindergarten, she slipped a seashell into his pocket as the yellow school bus came into view. *To get you through,* she said.

In the fluorescent-lit hallway, the priest placed a hand on her shoulder.

"You're in better shape than most, Mrs. Rafferty," he said. "You're a tough cookie, I can tell. No tears."

Nora didn't say anything. She had never been able to cry in front of other people. And anyway, tears never came right away at a moment like this. Not when her mother died when she was a child, and not when her husband died five years ago, and not when her sister went away. Which was not a death, but something close to it.

"Where in Ireland are you from?" he asked, and when she stared back blankly, he said, "Your accent."

"County Clare," she said.

"Ahh. My mother came from County Mayo." The priest paused. "He's in a better place."

Why did they send the clergy at times like this? By design, they could never understand. Her sister had been just the same. Nora pictured her, in full black habit—did they even wear those anymore? She would wake up this morning at that tranquil country abbey, free from all attachment, free from heartache, even though she had been the one to set the thing in motion.

All the way home, unable to think of how she would tell the children, Nora thought of her sister. Her rage was like another person sitting beside her in the car.

When the children were young, Charlie was always telling stories about home. The one they liked best was about the Bone Setter.

"Did I ever tell you who came when you broke a bone in Miltown Malbay?" he would ask.

They would shake their heads, even though they'd heard it before.

"The Bone Setter!" he'd cry, clasping the closest child in his arms, the child squealing in delight.

"You didn't go to the doctor unless you were dying," he said. "No, if you broke something, like I did—my ankle—this fine man would come to your bedroom and snap you right back into place with his hands, as good as new." Charlie made a popping sound with his tongue. "No drugs. Didn't need them."

The children went green when he told it. But then they begged him to tell it again.

As usual when he spoke of home, Charlie left out the worst bits. The man had set his ankle slightly off. It led the rest of his body to be out of balance so that eventually, his knees bothered him, and later, his back.

The lies they had told were like this. The original, her sister's doing. All those that followed, an attempt on Nora's part to try to preserve what the first lie had done, each one putting Patrick ever more out of joint. She had accepted it as the price of keeping him safe.

John always complained that Nora favored Patrick. Bridget said that until she was five years old, she thought his name was *My Patrick*, since that's all Nora ever called him. She had thought that someday they would understand, they would know the whole story, though she could not imagine telling it. Patrick had asked, but she could never bring herself to answer.

She hadn't even told them that she had a sister.

Her mind wandered again to the abbey. Those women outside the world, capable of casting off everything, even their own names. Nora had realized long ago that the walls the nuns used to keep others out could just as easily wall a person in, imprison her with her thoughts. Let her sit with this, then. The weight of it. It wasn't right that Nora should have to carry it on her own.

As soon as she reached the house, she went to the junk drawer and found her old address book. She called the abbey for the first time in more than thirty years. She told the young one who answered that her name was Nora Rafferty and she needed Mother Cecilia Flynn to know that her son Patrick had died late last night, in a car crash, alone.

Outside, she could hear the first of the commuters driving down the hill, headed for the highway that would take them to the city, or else to the ferry, where they'd drink a cup of coffee as the boat cut a course across the darkened harbor.

Nora took a notepad from the counter and made a list. She brewed a pot of tea in case company should arrive sooner than expected. She sat down and wept, her elbows on the table, her face cupped in the cool palms of her hands.

Part Two

1957-1958

2

THEIR FATHER HIRED A HACKNEY to drive them as far as Ennistymon. From there, a bus would carry them the rest of the way to Cobh.

At six in the morning, he stood smoking by the kitchen window, tapping his foot, waiting for Cedric McGann's black Ford to come chugging up the road.

Nora hadn't slept. While the house was silent, by the light of an oil lamp, she made certain they had everything they needed. She checked three times to be sure. Now, their suitcases by the door, she sat at the table, hoping he might tell her not to go. But her father wouldn't look at her.

"Are you all right?" she managed to ask.

"Right as the mail," he said.

An hour ago, she had fixed him a boiled egg. It was still on the plate, untouched.

In one of his letters, Charlie said his father's cousin in Boston was a marvelous cook, that Nora had never seen the likes of her food. Nora had told her father that the woman was strict so he wouldn't worry, but in fact Charlie reported that she barely noticed the family members who came to stay. Girls lived on the second floor, and boys on the third, and as long as you minded your manners, Mrs. Quinlan didn't bother you.

Charlie said they wouldn't live in her house for long. Once they were married, they would get their own apartment. *What about Theresa?* she asked him when she wrote. *She can come with us if you like,* he replied. *Or she can stay on at Quinlans'. We won't be going far.*

Nora watched her father at the window. She felt like there had been a death, that mix of sorrow and anticipation that arose to fill the space when someone vanished.

Her sister came bounding into the room, giddy, wearing her nicest dress.

Nora was about to tell her to have some porridge, to fill herself up for the journey.

"Oh!" Theresa shouted as she reached the threshold. "My hat!"

She ran out as quickly as she'd come in.

"Quiet," their father called after her in a hush. "You'll wake Herself."

Their gran had said her good-byes the night before. She said she couldn't stand to see them go. Didn't want to hold the memory of it.

When the taxi arrived, Nora thought that she would simply not leave. How could your legs walk someplace when you had no desire to make them? Yet here she was, placing one foot in front of the other, body betraying mind, exchanging a long embrace with her father and a quick one with her brother, who slunk out of his room at the last minute, head down. Martin had been protesting their leaving ever since it was decided upon, ignoring his two sisters, as if rehearsing for a life in which they no longer existed.

Her father's eyes were glazed with tears that threatened to spill over but wouldn't. He looked tired, he looked old, his face brown and leathered from the sun.

He had terrified Nora when she was a girl, once her mother was gone, his temper raging over a cup of spilled milk as if his children were a punishment. They ran screaming, they hid from him in corners of the house he could not reach, behind heavy furniture, or under their grandmother's bed, a meaty, menacing hand coming toward them.

A child had no choice but to forgive. And he could be kind in his way. He took them fishing, taught them how to pull a trout from the water with their bare hands. Every summer, he brought them to the Miltown races and gave them each a penny to bet on whichever horse they chose.

He liked that Theresa was bold. He didn't discourage her. Only Nora did, trying to teach her how to behave properly, the way their mother would have done. But Theresa and Martin hadn't known their mother long enough. She didn't get the time to shape them as she had Nora.

Before she died, she told Nora that the younger ones were her responsibility. Maybe she only said it so Nora would have something to hold on to. So she wouldn't feel as lost. But Nora took the job seriously, even though they didn't mind her most of the time. She wasn't firm, forceful, like their mother had been. She could never quite convince them of her authority.

As she grew, Nora feared her father less. She became more like his equal in the house once she started earning. They'd talk over breakfast, about the farm, and the girls at work. Her father laughed easily, recounting the story of some barroom brawl back in his youth. She saw that he was not such a large man at all. He was slight by most standards, his fair hair and eyebrows making him look almost boyish when he grinned. She learned that he was not the same man after a given hour, after he poured himself a whiskey, then a second, then a third. She liked her father best in the morning, when she could be certain of him.

From the front hall, he turned his head now and said, "Theresa! Where are you? Come on."

Nora looked to see her sister standing in the doorway of the bedroom they had shared for seventeen years, since Theresa was born. The bedroom walls were a bright, bright blue. They framed Theresa in the morning light like a portrait of the Virgin. She and Nora had all the same features—the same wide blue eyes and thin lips and brown curls. But Nora thought that somehow they were arranged in a more pleasing manner on Theresa's face than her own.

When she was very young and afraid of the dark, Theresa would crawl into Nora's bed in the night and cling to her. Nora would moan and pretend to shake her off, but in truth she liked the warmth and the comfort. She knew Theresa's body as well as she knew her own. Better. Nora had bathed her as a girl, brushed the knots from her hair. When Theresa fell, Nora was the one to dab iodine onto her scrapes as she roared the house down.

"I can't find it," Theresa said. "Help me. You know the one. It has a pink silk flower at the brim."

"Leave it," Nora said. "It's half six."

Their father handed them each a bit of money. Theresa slipped hers into her coat pocket and kissed his cheek. Nora thanked him and then put the bill into the toe of his empty boot by the door when he wasn't looking. He would find it later, and need it. He was always making gestures he shouldn't be. Offering to buy a round of drinks at Friel's when they didn't have enough money for sugar and flour; donating to someone's charity fund when in fact they needed the charity themselves. Even the hackney was a luxury he couldn't afford, but there was no other way to get there with the luggage. She had already determined to send the fare back to him on top of whatever else she could manage.

She had told her brother to watch him, to make sure he was careful. But Martin was only nineteen. Who knew if he had any sense about him?

The men carried the bags out. Nora and Theresa followed.

Cedric McGann stood by the car. He was the brother of a girl she had known at school. She had seen him at the dances plenty of times. But still, she felt her cheeks go red when he said, "Morning, Nora."

A week ago, she had vowed never to blush again, something she did at the most ridiculous times, moments when any other woman wouldn't feel in the least bit flummoxed. She blushed when she went into Jones's market and had to stand at the counter and ask Cyril Jones for the tea. She blushed when Father Donohue looked her in the eye as he placed a Communion wafer on her tongue.

Charlie had said you could make yourself over in America, leave behind all that you didn't like. Yet here she was, not yet to the front gate, and already it was clear that Nora was stuck with herself.

"Hello, Cedric," Theresa said, a teasing note to her voice as if they had some secret between them, which Nora knew for a fact they did not.

She was grateful anyway that Theresa had taken his mind off her.

"What was the final score in the football last night?" her father said.

"Twelve to two," Cedric said. "I got knocked about some, but it was worth it."

"Thatta boy."

Her father's tone was light, as if Cedric were only here to drive the girls to a dance in Lahinch and home again.

Nora looked back at the low stone walls separating one farm from the next, cutting a jagged line down the green hills for miles, until the green faded into sea and sky. In the foreground were the barns that sheltered the cows, the donkey, the pigs and hens, animals Theresa had named, though their father told her not to.

She looked at the stone cottage. They were all born in this house. Their mother had died here. Nora set her eyes on her grandmother's bedroom window to see if she was peeking out through the yellow curtains for one last look at Theresa, her favorite. Everyone's favorite. But the curtains were still.

Nora wished her father would hug her once more, even if it had to be in front of Cedric.

"Be brave, my girl," he said instead.

She knew he said it because she was not brave, not in the least.

"I will," Nora said.

"And look after Theresa," he told her, instructions that had been given to Nora every day since memory began.

"I will."

On summer mornings from the time they were small, Nora led her brother and sister across the fields and went to the sea with all the other kids in town. There was often a moment when Theresa swam out so far that Nora's chest tightened, watching, waiting for her head to break through the surface of the water. Just as she began to panic and got to her feet, Theresa emerged, laughing.

She was the youngest, born without fear. It wasn't quite right to say that Theresa was bad, though she could be. She was simply the *most*. The most brave and beautiful and brash and clever. Even the most devout, in her way. As a child, she had memorized the lives of the saints. Now she was a flirt, devoting all the attention she had once given to the martyrs to the boys of Miltown Malbay.

While Nora went to the Holy Hour each day, Theresa snuck off to go walking with Gareth O'Shaughnessy. Plenty of girls did the same, but only Theresa was bold enough to ride right up to the church gates afterward, perched on the handlebars of Gareth's bicycle, asking, "Who said the rosary? Come on, tell me quick, before I see Daddy and he asks. I'll be killed."

Whatever age Theresa was, Nora had been there already. Theresa always managed to get more out of things, to do it better somehow. Nora had been a day pupil at the convent school until her father couldn't afford it any longer. She never got beyond the tenth grade. At fifteen, she went to work at the knitwear factory on the edge of town. Theresa earned a scholarship and graduated with the highest marks. The nuns said teaching was a calling, a vocation of sorts, and Theresa had it. If they had the money, she would be on to Limerick by now for her degree.

As it was, she had joined Nora at the factory. For years, Nora had worked eight hours a day on her feet at the pressing machine, hot steam rising up into her eyes, her fingertips singed red by the end of the week. She had never considered the job beneath her. She felt lucky to have it, when so many people she knew had no work at all. But she hated to see Theresa there, watching the clock for the ten-minute break like everyone else, sitting in a row of girls at their sewing machines, a ladies' cardigan or jumper on the table in front of her, something they themselves could never afford, which would be shipped off to Penneys or to Dunnes with all the rest. Old Ben Dunne himself, president of the store, visited the factory to thank them every year. Nora had always thought it was quite an honor. But when he came and she saw him smile at her sister, she thought of how he had no idea of the potential in her. Theresa stayed up late every night reading books lent to her by an old teacher, a nun. This pleased Nora, though she told her to get to sleep, that she'd be exhausted in the morning.

In the backseat of the car now, Nora reached for her sister's hand and held it tight without a word, without a glance. They drove the mile into town. She was used to traveling this road on foot, or on her bicycle, dirt puffing in clouds at her ankles, staining the ruffled edges of her white socks.

Passing by the Rafferty farm, she imagined Charlie's parents and his brother, sitting down to breakfast. She felt pure spite in her heart, though she would never say so. If it weren't for their decision, she wouldn't have to go.

Nora had expected her life to take a certain path. She and Charlie would be married and live on the farm beside her father's. She could look in on him and her brother each day. She thought her children would grow up as she had, knowing the names of every wildflower, climbing, three or four of them on a single bicycle, coasting down the hill to Spanish Point.

Nora told herself to let this be the last of her protestations. She would soon be Charlie's wife. Though the fact of it felt more impossible than the ocean crossing.

She had run into an old school friend on a recent Sunday, while walking home from church with her sister. Aoife, newly fat and bouncing a baby on her hip.

"Soon it will be you, Nora," she said. "I hope Charlie's a better father than my George. He's gone off to wet the baby's head at the pub every day since he was born."

Nora felt sick to her stomach, imagining her first child born in Boston, a place she'd never been. A city full of strangers. Charlie more or less one of them now.

"I'm afraid I'll have another before long," Aoife said, and laughed. "The things they never told us in school."

"What did she mean?" Theresa asked after they'd parted.

"Never mind it," Nora said. She herself only knew because her best friend, Oona, had explained things, after an older cousin explained them to her. Someday Nora would tell Theresa. When it was time for her to know.

It was just after seven when they reached town. On Main Street, the pubs and the parish hall and Jones's grocery were shut, and would be for another hour yet. She had never seen it so empty. Most of the houses scattered around the area were low and built of grey slate. The row of shops on Main Street offered the only color. The butcher's was a pale yellow. Jones's was bright green. There were pubs and hotels painted white or gold, light blue or pink.

Once a month, on a fair day, this road filled with farmers selling cabbages and cows, their voices shouting out a price, an exclamation of disappointment or of victory, depending. The next morning, the street would stink to high heaven, the gutters clogged with manure. The shopkeepers would grumble and you'd think the town would never be put right again. But a day or two later, it looked like nothing had ever happened.

In the spring, when the bishop came for confirmation, orange bunting was strung from one high window to another across the way, all up and down the road. Classes at school were suspended for weeks so the students could study their catechism. The bishop asked them each three questions. Most children stood before him, sweating, trembling, hoping to get an easy one, praying they knew the answer.

When Theresa was twelve and her turn came, she stood up straight and confident. She met the bishop's eye. He asked, "How many sacraments does the church recognize?"

"Seven," she said, and went on to deliver them from memory.

"What happens if you die in a state of mortal sin?"

Again, the answer came straightaway. "You go to hell," Theresa said. "But a mortal sin can be forgiven through the sacrament of penance."

Nora could see he was impressed.

For the final question, he asked, "What happens at the sacrifice of the Mass?"

Theresa said, "The bread and wine are changed into the body, blood, soul, and divinity of Jesus when the priest repeats the words of consecration spoken at the Last Supper. In this way the sacrifice on the cross that Jesus offered on Calvary is made present again so that we can join in offering it to the Father and receive its benefits."

"Well done," the bishop said.

Afterward, Nora overheard him say to her father, "You've got a very bright child there. Are all your others as sharp as that?"

"Heavens no. We don't know where she came from."

It didn't hurt Nora to hear him say it. She had lived in her younger sister's shadow most of her life. She had never much minded it there. Nora scolded Theresa all the time. She grew exasperated by her every day. But if you were shy and quiet, mere proximity to someone so sparkling did something for you. In Theresa's presence, she became less terrified of everyone and everything. Her sister spoke for her when she was too afraid to speak for herself.

They reached the intersection at the center of town. If they turned right from here, they would come to the church and the cemetery and onward into twenty miles of farmland. To the left was the national school and then farms beyond, eventually spilling out to the beach.

Cedric went straight, onto the Flag Road, toward Saint Joseph's holy well, where Nora's gran used to dip bits of cloth into the water, hoping they might heal her only daughter.

Nora closed her eyes. She didn't want to see the third farmhouse on the left up ahead, the white stucco with red flowers in the window boxes that belonged to her best friend, Oona Coogan.

Oona Donnelly, now.

Theresa had loads of friends. Nora had Oona and wouldn't have traded her for all the rest of them combined. They had spent every day together at the convent school as girls, and at the factory these past six years. Oona was one of nine children, and like Nora, she was the oldest.

For years, she had been on and off with Conall Davis, but months ago, without warning, Oona's father had forced her to marry an old farmer with a good bit of land.

Oona didn't meet the man until two days before the wedding. That morning, as her mother rushed around hanging rosary beads from trees and delivering eggs to the Poor Clares to ward off rain, Oona cried bitterly to Nora, up in her bedroom, wearing her white dress. After the wedding, she told Nora how the farmer barely talked to her. He hated Oona's cooking, her heavy footsteps, the pitch of her voice. She dreaded evenings, when he came in for his tea, and she dreaded what he expected of her after they'd gone to bed.

"I don't know how I'll manage when you leave," Oona told Nora. "I'll have nobody."

Now Theresa said, "Stop, Cedric. Stop the car."

Nora opened her eyes to see Oona standing at the edge of the road. She climbed quickly from the car and they embraced so long and hard that she thought perhaps they'd miss the bus, and then the boat in turn.

Oona had made them a sweet cake for the journey.

"I'll write to you every day," she said.

"I'll do the same," Nora said.

As they pulled apart, Oona pressed a note into her hand.

"For when you get lonesome."

Back in the taxi, Nora said a prayer for her friend. It was hideous what Oona's father had done. Nora supposed her own parents had been a made match, but that was the fashion then. It shouldn't happen to a girl anymore.

Then again, maybe her situation wasn't much different. Charlie was not a bad man. But theirs was no great love story. From an early age, Nora had understood that the farm would go to her brother, that she and Theresa were expected to do their part. To marry, to vanish. There were things that were never discussed. This was why her father would not meet her eye.

What would there be to remind her now of all that she had known? Her memories were here, ignited by the sight of a specific shop or house or corner.

Her melancholy led her down a road that ended at her mother. Nora felt the absence of her, total in some way now.

She began to cry.

Theresa said, "Come on, so. We'll be back before long."

Nora wondered if her sister believed it. She tried to picture Miltown Malbay as a bird might see it from above, tried to press every bit of the town into her memory. She supposed Theresa was doing just the opposite: soaking up what was around them right this moment. The scent of Cedric McGann's cologne and the grumbling engine and the houses up ahead, coming into view.

The bus to Cobh smelled of herring. A man in the second row had brought it for his lunch, and the odor traveled ten rows back to where she and Theresa sat. Outside the window, the sun shone over vast cliffs as they traversed the coast. In two hours, Nora saw more of Ireland than she had seen in her twenty-one years.

They came to villages where an electric light shone out through the odd kitchen window. One by one, they were wiring the small towns. Miltown Malbay could have had electricity a year ago, but everyone in a parish had to want it unanimously, and Mrs. Madigan on Church Street had refused to pay. She said her sister in Roscommon had gotten electric lights and now she could tell that her house was full of cobwebs no matter how she cleaned.

"You're so quiet," Theresa said. "Are you thinking about Charlie?"

From across the aisle, an old woman looked up from her knitting and stared at Nora, awaiting her response.

"No," she whispered.

"Liar," Theresa said.

"Really. I wasn't."

They exchanged a glance. They laughed. She suspected Theresa knew something about how she felt, though Nora had never told her.

When she was eighteen, Charlie Rafferty kissed her as they were walking home from a dance. From then on, they were an item. They met for walks down on the beach, and at the dances, though they pretended not to be there just for each other. Nora didn't fancy him, particularly. Charlie was silly. When they were young, at Christmastime, he ran around with the Wren Boys, going house to house in masks, singing carols, his brother Lawrence on the tin whistle. They wouldn't leave a person alone until he'd paid. Nora's father said he'd have whipped any one of his children had they joined in with that bunch.

Charlie was older now, but he still told horrible jokes and pulled pranks on his friends. He laughed too loud, embarrassing Nora, as if the sound was coming out of her mouth instead of his. She knew why he had chosen her, when there were more outgoing girls, prettier girls. She had wanted him for the same reason.

Nora had never been a romantic like her sister, her head full of fantasies. The one thing she and Charlie had in common was practicality. They wanted the same sort of life. She could tolerate his quirks, endure his manner for the sake of getting to see her father, her gran, her sister and brother, her best friend every day. Their farms stood side by side. Joining the land would be good for both families. A husband didn't matter that much, compared to all the rest. Most of the married couples she knew hardly seemed to interact, especially after the children came.

The Flynns and the Raffertys had helped each other down through the years, the friendship between them stretching back to the town's founding and solidified in 1888, when the pub owners and shopkeepers boycotted the local landlord, Moroney, refusing to serve his people. The shopkeepers were thrown in jail, including Miles and Henry Rafferty, Charlie's great-grandfather and his brother, who ran the butcher shop in town but were needed home on the farm at the weekend. The pair was imprisoned for the better part of two years. It was John Flynn, Nora's great-grandfather, who vowed to help keep the farm alive in their absence, going over each day with his three brothers after working their own land.

Years later, Henry Rafferty went to America. Once established, he began bringing relatives over from home. Now, as most young people in the town headed to Liverpool or London, the Rafferty children went to Boston. Charlie's sister Kitty and three of his brothers had been there for years.

Charlie had no intention of joining them. He thought America was crowded, hectic, morally corrupt. Kitty had run off and married a Protestant from California, a man she barely knew. The episode caused Charlie and the rest of them no end of heartache. *They get there and they think it's a dream,* he said. *They get there and they just run wild.*

Until a year ago, the only Rafferty children left in Ireland were Charlie and his oldest brother, Peter, who spent most afternoons on a bar stool inside Friel's. It was Charlie who did the work, devoting himself to the family land like it was his birthright. More than once, his father had said, "Someday this will be yours."

Nora turned nineteen, twenty. Then Charlie proposed down on the beach, on bended knee and all. A pointless gesture. They both knew they couldn't be married until the land was passed to him. Nora waited. She did what she could to help her father, but she knew he couldn't go on with three grown children in the house much longer.

She gave him most of what she made at the factory, but it wasn't enough. She hung back at the dinner table, going to bed hungry some nights, though she didn't let anyone see. Once a year, her father shot a pig, or her brother, Martin, did it. Theresa would cover her ears to block out the animal's scream. Dinner was always a single rasher cut down for each of them, the salt rubbed off, the rest fried in a pan and served with brown bread and turnip. As a year wore on, the rashers got smaller and smaller to make them last.

One Sunday morning after Mass, Nora found Charlie waiting for her in the churchyard. From the look on his face, she thought someone must have died. She knew her gran was inside, hoping to get her face seen by the visiting monsignor. Who then? His father. Her father.

"Who?" she asked.

"My father said last night that he's getting tired," Charlie said slowly, precisely. "He's ready to hand down the farm."

"Charlie, that's grand."

She pictured herself and Oona hanging curtains in his mother's sunny kitchen. Herself and Oona drinking tea in the garden.

"He's decided Peter will get it. He says Peter is the oldest and that's how his own father did it."

"But Peter will—"

"It doesn't matter," he said. He looked like he would cry if Nora went on, so she stayed silent, even as her head filled with questions.

His father had told him he should go to America.

That was it, she thought. He had come to break it off with her.

But Charlie said he had worked out a plan. He would go ahead to Boston and get them situated. When he was ready, he would send for Nora.

"We'll be back before long," he said. "With enough money to buy a farm of our own, bigger than our two fathers' farms combined."

She was stunned that he wanted the two of them to carry on. She didn't know what to say.

Nora had never given much thought to America. Only when she was seven, and Oona received a talking doll for Christmas from her aunt in Chicago. It was the first talking doll anyone in town had ever seen. Nora wished then that she had an aunt in America. She had even lied and told Oona that she did.

Her strongest urge was to tell Charlie they should end it. She knew people who had lost a boyfriend, a girlfriend when someone went away. Charlie had to go, and that was that. Nora went with her family more than she did with him. She loved them more, owed them more. But Charlie wanted to stay together. He was one to get used to things. His brothers had married their first sweethearts and he would do the same.

At home that evening, she told her father what Charlie had said. Nora assumed he would tell her she was needed here. She thought he would forbid her to leave.

But instead he said, "You'll have to go with him. You're engaged to be married."

Nora thought of Theresa. She couldn't let her sister end up the woman of the house, working in the factory, waiting on the men for the rest of her life. Their father didn't have a clue how to raise her. And for all her flirting, Theresa didn't know a thing. Nora had protected her as best she could.

She recalled how Father Boyle came to lecture to the first-year class at the convent school each year. He liked to lean over a girl from behind while she was seated at her desk, doing the reading. He'd hover there, looking left and right, howling at anyone who dared to lift her eyes from the page. They all stared down, though they knew just what was happening. The girl he singled out could feel his breath in her ear. Ever so lightly, he'd place a hand on her shoulder and run it down, down into her dress, making no sound, cupping her breast, his cold and clammy skin against hers, soft and warm. He'd leave his hand there for an agonizing moment before drawing it away, shouting, "Now. Girls. What have we learned?"

He always chose the prettiest girl. In Nora's year, it had been poor

Oona. Oona never told a soul besides her. She said her mother would have blamed her. You didn't question a priest. Whatever he did was justified by God, by his position. Nora knew her own father wouldn't believe such a thing was even possible.

When Theresa had to go into his class, Nora couldn't stomach the thought of what he would do to her. She made a bodice out of cloth and feathers, a pillow, to the thickness of a slice of bread. It clung tight to Theresa's chest, bound to her skin from waist to collar. When Father Boyle tried his old trick, he found that there was no way into her. She wore a soft suit of armor beneath her clothes.

"I could never go to Boston without my sister," Nora told Charlie before he left.

It seemed to her like a barrier he could not overcome. But he said he would save enough for both their passages. He told Nora she could come first, and in time they would bring Theresa.

Nora told him she would wait until they could travel together. It came to her then, a reason to go. In America, Theresa might become a teacher, as she was meant to. A woman their mother would be proud of.

Charlie's mother thought they should be married before he went away. She said it wasn't proper for a girl to cross an ocean based on only a promise. But Nora said there wasn't enough time. Charlie's father's cousin in Boston, Mrs. Quinlan, said she'd never had anyone but family come to stay. As it was, her guest rooms were always full. But she agreed to take Nora and Theresa in for a short while, as long as Nora and Charlie were married soon after they reunited.

While they were apart, Charlie wrote her letters, and she did the same. The letters took a week to arrive. The conversation was disjointed. He told her about the city, about the job he'd gotten, painting houses with his cousins. He said it was easy work most days, compared to what they had to do on the farm. Sometimes, holding a thin blue envelope in her hand, Nora imagined it contained a message telling her that he had found someone else, that she wouldn't be going after all.

It took eleven months for him to save the money and make the arrangements. He wrote then and told her to prepare. He said the timing was good. Another relative had just moved out. There was an empty room in the house for Nora and Theresa. Mrs. Quinlan had helped Charlie secure jobs for them both in a dressmaker's shop.

Charlie promised it wouldn't be forever. He said Nora would like Boston, for as long as they were there.

I'll never get used to how different it is. You turn a knob on the kitchen sink and hot water flows right out. There's no carrying water from the pump, or boiling it in the kettle to clean the clothes. That's just one of a million little miracles that everyone here takes for granted. You won't believe it, Nora. I can't wait for you to see.

The town of Cobh was busy and bustling. Brightly colored shops and houses were crowded into the hillside, a grey cathedral looming over all.

They sat on a bench by the pier for hours, watching the fishing boats and the ships passing by. Nora felt exhausted already and the real journey hadn't yet begun. Six days at sea, and on the other side of it, a world she couldn't imagine, a man she could barely recall. She hadn't seen Charlie's face in a year.

As night fell, she saw Theresa smile at a young brown-haired man passing by with his friends.

"You girls on the eight o'clock?" he asked.

"Yes," Theresa said. "You too?"

"Come have something to eat at the Commodore while you wait."

Theresa opened her mouth to reply, and Nora said quickly, "No thank you."

"But I'm hungry," Theresa said as they watched him go.

Nora took Oona's sweet cake from her bag and handed it to her sister. "There."

When it was finally time, they lined up to board a tender that would take them to meet the ship. Nora's heartbeat seemed like it might rip a hole in her dress at the sight of the thing, floating in the distance, massive, lit up against a black sky and sea.

Once, a circus had come to Miltown Malbay. Everyone gasped as an elephant ambled down the Flag Road. Nora thought then that it was the most extraordinary thing she would see in her life, but she had been mistaken.

3

THEIR CABIN WAS BELOW the waterline, four narrow bunks with a private toilet. Nora had brought a light yellow blanket from home, crocheted by her grandmother. She spread it out on one of the bottom bunks first thing. The sight of it made her feel better.

At first, they thought they might have the room to themselves. But before long, a lady and a little boy entered, lugging a trunk covered in stickers in a language Nora couldn't read. German, she thought. They smelled like they hadn't bathed in days. They didn't say a word.

Theresa widened her eyes.

The woman opened the trunk and began to place items of clothing directly on top of Nora's blanket.

Her chest tightened. She didn't know what to say. She looked to her sister.

"Excuse me," Theresa said. "That bunk belongs to her." She pointed at Nora.

The woman looked confused. Nora thought perhaps she didn't speak English. Theresa said it again, gesturing toward the blanket. The woman took the items back and placed them on the bed opposite.

"Sorry about that," Nora said.

She showed no reaction.

The woman who did not speak snored louder than seemed humanly possible. The little boy slept right through it, but for the entire first night, Nora and Theresa were kept awake by the sound. Theresa kept throwing the top half of her body down over the rails into Nora's bunk, sighing audibly, daring to shoosh the woman every hour or so, though it made no difference.

Nora lay there, worrying about what was to come. She had been so busy that she hadn't had much time to think. She knew it was an indulgence. When she stepped off this ship, she would have to accept her life as it was. She imagined them sinking to the bottom of the sea, all her worries for nothing.

She wondered where the woman and the boy were headed, who would meet them on the other side. Were they leaving a husband and father behind or going toward one?

She thought of her mother, wondered if she hadn't died, what she would advise Nora to do now. But if she hadn't died, this moment might never have come. Nora might have ended up more her own girl. She might have gone off to Dublin like some of them did, become a nurse, met a man whom she hadn't known every second of her life.

Most of all, she thought of Charlie. Every hour, she felt a heavier sense of dread, that much closer to him.

When the sun rose, Theresa said she would go mad if she couldn't get out and take a walk before breakfast.

"Come with me, the air will do us good," she said.

But Nora couldn't move. Her body ached.

"What's wrong?" Theresa said.

She couldn't explain it. Charlie had warned her that she might feel ill if the ship passed through a storm. But this wasn't that. The waters were calm.

"I'll be better in a few hours," she said. "I just need sleep. You go on without me."

But it seemed like a permanent state. She imagined the ship docking in New York, with her unable to get off. Maybe she could ride all the way back to Ireland, her sister safely chaperoned to her new American life.

All morning, the room was silent. The woman sat in her bunk writing letters, as her child tried to make his plastic soldiers stand up straight on the floor. Each time a wave rocked the ship, they toppled, and he began all over again.

Theresa didn't return until early afternoon, throwing the door open, giving them all a start. She was flanked by four other girls. They piled into the tight quarters, as if, having found one another, they could not bear to be separated for even a minute. The German woman looked up as Theresa introduced them by name like they were all one—*Anna-and-Madeleine-and-Helen-and-Abigail*, she said.

She rooted around in her suitcase at the foot of the bed, and Nora pulled the sheet to her chin.

"Anna heard a rumor that Jean Simmons is in first class!" Theresa said. She looked like a child whose birthday cake had just been carried in on a platter, even though Nora didn't think Theresa had particularly strong feelings about Jean Simmons, one way or the other.

"We're going to find her and refuse to leave her alone until we get an autograph," one of the girls said.

Another, a tall blonde in glasses, came right over and pressed the back of her hand to Nora's forehead as if they'd known each other all their lives.

"Theresa said you were sick. Do you have a fever?" she said. "Maybe you need the nurse."

"No," Nora said. "I'm all right. I just want to lie here a little longer."

"Well, I can see why. On account of it being so luxurious and all," the girl said with a smile.

"Abigail's going to be a teacher in New York," Theresa said, gesturing toward the blonde.

"Ninth grade math," Abigail said. "Saint Hugo of the Hills High School. I know it sounds like it belongs in the countryside, but my cousin assures me it's just a big ugly building in Queens. She's held the position until now, but she got a new job and she put me up for her old one. She's been trying to get me to come over for ages."

"You've already had your teacher training?" Nora said.

"Yes," she said. "In Dublin."

Nora wondered why she would want to leave home when she could get a good teaching job in Ireland.

The other girls were all going different places. Anna said she was bound for Cleveland, where her brother and his wife were. Madeleine would take a train from New York to Virginia. Helen was going to Philadelphia to live with a great-aunt she'd never met.

"In her day, you could take the boat straight there," she said.

"A friend of my mother's flew over in forty-four," Anna said. "The plane landed in Nova Scotia and they gave everyone breakfast while they refueled. Then they were straight on to New York. Now that is the way to arrive in America."

They all talked as much as her sister did. How did girls like this always find one another? It was so easy for Theresa to make friends. Nora never felt comfortable around new people. She couldn't think of what to say. Even at sea, they were themselves.

She wished the girls would stay for a while. Sit on the bed and tell her stories. But a minute later, they were gone.

They came back to fetch her for dinner, but she said she couldn't eat.

Madeleine said there would be a dance tonight, and Nora ought to try to come.

"I don't think I can," she said.

"I've never been to a dance anywhere but home," Theresa said, twirling in place. "In our town, they still stop the dances for Lent. It's as backward a place as can be. I heard they've had dances during Lent in Galway for years."

Nora gave her a look. Theresa was talking too much. She was showing off.

"That's how it is where I grew up too," Abigail said. She turned to Nora. "We'll bring you back some soup. Are you sure you're all right?"

"She'll feel better tomorrow," Theresa said, and stroked Nora's head like she was a cherished pet.

"Be good, Theresa," Nora said. "Behave."

"See? You sound like your old self already."

Nora heard them laughing as they went down the hall. Girls who hadn't been allowed to go into town in the evening unaccompanied, sent across an ocean to a world they'd never seen. None of them seemed in the least bit afraid.

She had sworn to herself that she would save Oona's letter for as long as she could. It was far too soon. But still she found the paper, unfolded the page. She felt a pang, seeing the familiar handwriting.

When we meet each other next, I wonder what you will have seen. You will have had such adventures by then. If you ever feel scared, picture me by your side. With you always, Oona

Nora wanted to be sitting in Oona's warm kitchen, or even just picking her up in the early morning for the long walk to work. She looked down at herself, curled in bed, and felt embarrassed, as if Oona were watching her from another room.

The thought was enough to get Nora to her feet. She would take a short walk, breathe the fresh air, like Theresa had said.

She went down the narrow corridor, her legs not used to the rhythm of the waves.

Once on the deck, Nora looked out over the ocean. It was an astonishing sight. No land in any direction.

There weren't many people around. She supposed most on board were eating their supper.

After a few minutes, she was done. That was adventure enough.

As she turned to go back to the cabin, she crossed paths with a boy about her age. He wore a brown flat cap. When she reached him, he removed it, nodded at her.

"Evening," he said, and smiled.

Nora saw his face go red.

She pictured Oona there beside her.

"Hello," she managed to say.

After that, she made a promise to herself. Two short walks a day, no matter what. She only ever went as far as she had that first night, as if there were an invisible rope tying her to her bed. She spent most of the day there, pretending to read or write or sleep, but mostly just stewing over what lay ahead. She still couldn't eat. The thought of food made her ill. Theresa brought her cups of water, and tea, and buttered rolls. She stroked Nora's hair and sang to her, songs that Nora had sung to get Theresa to sleep when she was a baby.

Most of the time, Theresa was off exploring with her friends. Every so often, the girls would stop in and tell Nora all that was going on outside the room. There was a swimming pool at the bottom of the boat. In the afternoons, they went for a dip. They watched movies in the theater and sat around in the smoking lounge hoping to meet boys. They reported that there were cables to hold on to in the ballroom, and it was great fun trying to dance around them. Nora felt like her own invalid grandmother. She felt like they were telling her about some faraway place, not the world on the other side of the door.

On the fourth night, she woke from a nap suddenly famished.

She put on a plain cotton dress, walked out into the hall alone.

The dining room was crowded. She searched for her sister, but Theresa wasn't there.

Nora sat alone.

The food was all American—fried chicken, gravy, mashed potatoes, and sirloin. She had never seen so much food.

A waiter asked the boys at the next table how many inches thick they wanted their steak.

"Three inches!" one of them cried out.

"Four," another said.

The waiter said he would bring them five. A challenge. They left half of it behind, bloody on their plates.

Nora was considering this when she heard someone behind her say, "Mind if I sit down?"

She didn't think the words were directed at her. But then she felt a hand on her shoulder, and the same voice, a young man's, said, "Is this one beside you taken?"

She looked up to see the boy in the cap who had smiled at her two nights earlier.

"Go ahead," she stammered. "Sit. I was about to leave anyway."

"Oh," he said. "Stay a minute. Please?"

She pretended she wasn't blushing. But he was blushing too, and that made her like him.

"All right," she said.

"Cillian," he said as he sat.

"Nora."

He told her he came from Coachford and laughed when he saw her face.

"Never heard of it," he said. "Guess I'd better get used to that."

He said he was bound for New York and homesick already.

"I've been wearing my father's old cap just to have the smell of him near," he said. "Doesn't that sound sappy?"

She thought of her grandmother's yellow blanket.

"No," she said.

"And you?" he said. "Where are you headed?"

"To Boston. With my sister."

She didn't say any more than that, didn't add that she was going there to meet the man she would marry.

"You're lucky to have your sister along," he said. "It's a lonely voyage, being on my own."

"You don't seem shy," she said with a smile.

"Well, I am. This is the first conversation I've had in days."

After he finished his chicken, he walked her to her room.

"Nice chatting with you," she said, and before she knew what was happening, he was kissing her softly on the lips.

"And you," Cillian said, and walked on.

A few hours later, there was a loud knock at the cabin door. She was sure it was him. Nora lay in her bed, stock-still.

Another knock, and this time the door just opened wide.

The woman in the other bed pulled a blanket over her head and her child's both.

A porter stood there, with Theresa and her friends behind him. He had caught them sneaking into a party in first class and brought them to Nora, like she was the mother of them all. They collapsed on the bed around her, giggling, before he'd even gone.

"They were all so handsome!" Theresa said.

"That one in the blue sure liked you," Abigail said.

Nora didn't like something in her tone. She had lost control of herself and her sister all in one night.

"Theresa, get hold of yourself," she said sharply. "Start acting right or I'll send you home. I'd do it, too, you know. Not another word."

The other girls slunk out of the room. Nora could tell Theresa was embarrassed. She got up and washed her face in silence and then climbed the ladder to her bed. Nora thought of her sister, reading anything she could find back home. Theresa hadn't picked up a book since they came aboard. She prayed she hadn't made a mistake.

In the morning, over the sounds of snoring, Theresa whispered an apology.

"It's all right," Nora whispered back, too worried about her own bad judgment to argue.

"Come to breakfast with me, just us two."

"I can't."

Nora's appetite had returned. She was hungry. But she didn't dare go into the dining room, for fear of seeing him.

"You're too skinny, Nora," Theresa said. "Abigail says she doesn't think there's anything wrong with you. She thinks you're just sad."

"Is that right?"

"It happens to a lot of people. Abigail knows these things. I think she's wonderful. Isn't she wonderful?"

"I don't know her," Nora said.

"Her boyfriend's American. She showed me a picture. He's lovely. She met him in Dublin. He was just there on holiday, and there she was in a shop when he walked in. Can you believe it? She thinks I'll find a handsome American too before long."

"Ahh."

"It's not hard," Theresa said. "Abigail has a friend from Cork who met a big shot banker on the boat ride over. She never had to work a day. Lives in a mansion on Central Park and does nothing but go to lunch and read magazines."

Nora wondered if it was true.

"You do remember that the whole point of your coming was to go to school."

Theresa ignored the comment. "She asked me what your Charlie does, and I said he's not as impressive as all that. He paints houses. And she said, 'Well, you can't help who you fall in love with,' and I said, 'Oh, Nora's not in love with him. She's not like that.'"

"Theresa!" Nora said.

"Are you really going to marry Charlie Rafferty?"

"Of course. Now let's please keep our business to ourselves and not go blabbing to strangers."

"Abigail's not a stranger!" Theresa said. She sighed. "I think I would have been alone forever had I stayed. There weren't many left to marry. All the good ones had gone off to their relations. Speaking of, I hope there will be a handsome American cousin or two among your new relations."

"They're not my relations," Nora said. "I've never met them."

"They will be, soon enough," Theresa said. "I can't imagine marrying any boy from home now."

"With all the worldliness of five days away. I suppose you think you'll marry a film star and live in Los Angeles."

Theresa grinned. "Well, why not?"

When the Statue of Liberty came into view the day they arrived in New York, it seemed every person on board was lined up at the rail to get a look. Nora wondered if the boat might tip right over. She regarded the people around her, the Americans returning from vacations with Irish lace and crystal in their suitcases. Heading home to familiar houses. As the ship sailed up the Hudson River to Pier 54, she looked for Cillian. She half wanted to see him and half prayed that she would not. She couldn't find him in the crowd.

They waited in line to disembark, taking in the sight of a high-roofed pavilion at the end of the gangway, the words CUNARD and WHITE STAR printed above the entrance.

Charlie was meant to borrow his cousin's car and drive from Boston to meet them at the boat. Nora hadn't imagined there would be so many people.

"What if he can't find us?" she said. "What if he has to turn back?"

"He wouldn't leave you," Theresa said.

They waited hours in a line marked FOREIGNERS. They shivered in the early morning cold. Nora could smell her own sweat coming through her clothes. There was a small washbasin in the private bath but no shower or tub. She had cleaned up as best she could, but still she felt filthy. She wished she could sink into a bath before talking to anyone. Theresa had borrowed perfume from one of the girls and sprayed it all over to try to cover her scent. But this only made her smell worse.

She wouldn't shut up. Nora wished she could have just a moment's peace to sort herself out, as if there hadn't been enough time to think on the boat.

At some point, she caught sight of the familiar black trunk, the stickers she'd been staring at for days, wondering what they said. There was the little boy, crying. His mother, exasperated, alone. Nora wanted to go to them, but a moment later the crowd had shifted and they were lost to her. She hooked her arm through Theresa's, held her close.

Charlie was right there waiting when they got to the other side, just as Theresa said he would be.

He tried to kiss Nora. She felt herself harden but attempted a smile.

She wondered if he could sense her misdeed on her skin.

"It's good to see you," she said.

In the car, Theresa couldn't stop talking about the girls on the ship, the music in the ballroom. Charlie told them the story of a man he'd met, who took the boat from Cobh to Quebec. He rode second class, and he and his brothers had drained the ship's bar by the end of the journey.

"They were as drunk as anything when they pulled into port," he said. "The first thing they saw was a billboard that read *Drink Canada Dry.*" With each of the three words, he thrust a hand into the air in front of him for emphasis. "These guys turned to one another and said, 'Don't mind if we do!'"

He laughed at his own joke, chortling on and on.

Theresa laughed too, but Nora felt uneasy, bashful, like he was a stranger.

Her sister was so familiar, the one familiar thing. Nora couldn't stop looking at her. She could not imagine if it was only herself and Charlie here.

When they stopped at a restaurant for tea, the most elegant girls she'd ever seen filled the booths, pretty and polished and made up. They wore bright new dresses, the colors of springtime, gathered at the waist and wide at the bottom. Nora looked down at her simple dress, a thin white cardigan buttoned over the top.

Charlie pointed to a girl passing by in the highest heels she'd ever seen. He said loudly, "It's a wonder she doesn't topple right over."

"Shh," Nora said.

"I think they're beautiful," Theresa said.

The waitress brought over three china cups of boiling water, perched on white saucers. A tea bag and a lemon slice rested on each plate. Nora took the bag from her plate and tore it open, shaking its contents into her cup.

Charlie laughed. "What the heck are you doing?"

She looked down to see the tea leaves floating at the water's surface.

"The bag is meant to be dunked straight in," he said. "Like this."

As he demonstrated, Nora felt her face grow hot. "Oh!"

During the war, when tea was rationed, one of the Raffertys sent tea bags from America home to Charlie's grandmother. She had shared them with Nora's gran. None of them had ever seen a tea bag before that. Her grandmother ripped the bags apart and shook the leaves straight into the pot as Nora herself had just done.

She thought she might cry and blinked to keep the tears back. What a ridiculous thing to cry about.

When Theresa went to powder her nose, Charlie said, "It's just me, Nora. The same old Charlie."

"I know," she said. "I'm sorry."

"For what?"

He reached across the table for her hand.

She felt seized by a desire to run. For a year, she had been corresponding with a ghost, a void. Now here was the flesh and blood man in front of her. If she loved him, she wouldn't have talked to a stranger that way. She wouldn't have let him kiss her.

She felt too frightened even to look at Charlie.

"I know it's a lot to get used to," he said. "We'll go back home as soon as we can. But it's good for us to earn some money while we're young. See new places. And Mrs. Quinlan has a lovely home. You'll see."

She didn't believe him, that they would go back for good. She had staked her life on a plan that would never come to pass.

The whole ride to Boston, Nora only wanted to arrive, to know how it would be. But once they were there, she felt nervous. It was dinnertime. She counted eight people sitting around the table. Their chatter quieted when she and Theresa entered the room.

Mrs. Quinlan got up and gave them each a stiff hug. She was a thin woman, bony, with an angular face. She carried herself tall and confident.

"Charlie, leave their things by the door for now," she said. "I'll show them to their room after we eat."

Nora was surprised to hear an American accent. She had imagined her being from Ireland. But now she thought she remembered from Charlie's letters. Mrs. Quinlan was one of the first in his family to be born here.

She guided Theresa to a chair beside an old lady with a large silver crucifix around her neck and then motioned for Nora to sit in the empty spot between two women who might have been thirty or forty, older than her, but not old.

"My nieces," Mrs. Quinlan said. "The two Elizabeths."

The women said hello.

"How was the trip over?" one of them asked.

"Good," Nora said.

They smiled, nodded. It seemed they were waiting for more, but she couldn't think of a thing to say. An idea would come to her and she would reject it, try to come up with something better. She wanted to ask if they were married, but it seemed rude. She wondered how long they had been here but didn't want to pry.

The two Elizabeths returned to their conversation.

Nora noticed the wallpaper. It looked like green velvet, with a print of ivy swirling this way and that. There was a bowl of oranges on the sideboard and an electric chandelier overhead.

Theresa was chatting with the old lady. Laughing already.

From across the table, Lawrence Rafferty grinned. "Hello there," he said. "Remember me? Do I look handsomer in this American light?"

Of course she remembered Charlie's older brother. Half the time back home, he wore a Pioneer pin in his lapel, a tiny image of the Sacred Heart, a sign that he had taken the pledge to abstain from alcohol, with the good Lord's help. The rest of the time, Lawrence was the one falling out the door of the pub, landing in the street, where they'd still be stepping over him the next morning.

"Meet my bride-to-be, Babs McGuire," he said. He leaned over and kissed the cheek of the woman beside him. She swatted at him with her napkin and laughed.

"The future Mrs. Lawrence Rafferty!" he shouted, and Nora wondered if he was half drunk now or merely energized by the prospect of matrimony.

"If you play your cards right," Babs said. She winked at Nora to let her know that she was joking. "So nice to finally meet you."

Nora tried to remember what Charlie had written about them. Lawrence was a bus driver now. Babs was from Tipperary. She cleaned houses. She lived in another town but came often for dinner without warning, a habit Mrs. Quinlan said she could do without.

Lawrence would be her brother-in-law one day, Nora thought, trying it on. This girl, Babs, would be her sister-in-law.

On Lawrence's other side sat a man of about the same age, whom she didn't think she had met before. His bald head gleamed like marble. He smiled to reveal the most enormous teeth Nora had ever seen in a person's mouth.

"Bobby Quinlan," he said. "Welcome to Boston. Hope the car ran okay."

"My son," said Mrs. Quinlan. "And there's my husband, but don't be thinking you'll be getting any conversation out of him. Lord knows I haven't in the last thirty years."

Nora glanced down to see an open newspaper at the head of the table, held aloft by an unseeable man. The fingers on one hand wagged hello.

"And I'm Aunt Nellie," said the old lady by Theresa's side. "I guess I have to do everything, even introduce myself."

"My mother," Mrs. Quinlan said, as if she were just receiving the bad news. "Now, shall we say grace? Show our new arrivals that we're not a pack of heathens?"

They did, joining hands before they ate. Nora pretended to close her eyes, but she couldn't help herself from squinting, trying to get a good look at Mrs. Quinlan. Charlie's brothers Matthew and Jack, and his sister, Kitty, had lived in the house too when they first arrived in this country. Lawrence had been here two years. He would leave as soon as he was married, just as Nora and Charlie were meant to.

She wondered if Mrs. Quinlan liked all the company, the comings and goings of relatives she didn't even know, or if she merely saw it as a duty. Nora knew they all paid Mrs. Quinlan something, whatever they could afford, but even so. She herself wouldn't have been able to stand it. She felt guilty in a way she hadn't before, for staying here. She and Theresa weren't family. Charlie had joked about the inconvenience of Babs coming unannounced to dinner. Imagine what they said about strangers who just showed up and stayed.

There were bowls of turnips and carrots and peas on the table, and a platter of white fish. For dessert, Mrs. Quinlan gave them each a baked apple with vanilla ice cream on top.

She scooped the ice cream from a cardboard drum right there in front of them, and when she reached the bottom, she sent her son to fetch more from the icebox. Nora had never known anyone who kept ice cream in the house. It seemed a luxury beyond imagining.

"Tomorrow I'll take you both to meet my friend Mrs. Byrne," Mrs. Quinlan said. "I've sorted something out for you with her. She's the busiest seamstress in Dorchester. She can use your help. The Irish still teach needlework to girls in school, don't they?"

"Yes ma'am," Nora said. "Thank you."

"I hope to find work as a teacher," Theresa said. "A friend of mine is going to be a teacher in New York."

Conversations around the table grew quiet. Nora stared at her sister, her own face going red. Theresa ought to have said thank you and left it at that. The audacity of her.

Mrs. Quinlan was dismissive, cool. "That would take a lot more schooling than you've had, I'm sure."

Now the old woman, Aunt Nellie, spoke up. "I worked in the mills when I was young. My husband, God rest his soul, swept up peanut shells at Fenway Park in summer and shoveled coal into the furnace of the hospital up the road in winter. He dug subway tunnels and was happy for the work. I swear he died from whatever he breathed in down there."

Nora knew what the women were trying to say. They didn't think Theresa should want so much so soon. She agreed with them. But this was the only good reason she had for being here.

She looked over at Charlie. He was chewing his dessert with his mouth wide open.

It took every bit of courage Nora had to say, "My sister was recommended to the teacher's college in Limerick. She's finished secondary school."

"Is that right?" Mrs. Quinlan said. She looked impressed. "I was a nurse for years myself. But I know a lot of teachers. Maybe I can talk to a few people. You could earn your certificate in the evenings. If you've gotten that far already, it wouldn't take long."

Nora smiled, with gratitude big enough for them both, since Theresa wouldn't know there was anything to be grateful for.

"Thank you," Nora said. "That would be grand."

4

WHEN THERESA FLYNN was a child of seven, she mistook the *Lives of the Saints,* with its green leather cover and golden lettering, for a book of fairy stories. She spotted the thick volume on a high shelf in her grandmother's room and read it straightaway. She fell in love with Saint Cecilia, a noblewoman who became the patron saint of musicians, among the most famous of the Roman martyrs. In the year 180, she was stabbed three times in the neck with a sword but lived for three more days, time enough to ask the pope to convert her home into a church.

Theresa loved Saint Seraphia, a devout orphan who refused to marry, sold all her possessions and gave the money to the poor, then sold herself into slavery, eventually converting her master. When they threw her into the fire for her faith, she would not burn. Theresa loved Saint Catherine Labouré, a French nun in the nineteenth century, who had a vision of the Virgin Mary telling her, *God wishes to charge you with a mission. You will be contradicted, but do not fear; you will have the grace to do what is necessary. Tell your spiritual director all that passes within you. Times are evil in France and in the world.*

How often had Theresa read those words to her uninterested family. Again and again, she told them how Saint Catherine woke one night and heard the voice of a child calling her to a chapel. There, the Virgin presented herself in an oval of light, standing upon a globe, surrounded by stars. She instructed Saint Catherine to ensure that the image was placed on medallions that would bring good graces to all who wore them. These became the Miraculous Medals, the oval trinkets carried or stowed in a drawer by every woman they knew. Theresa was awake many nights thinking about Saint Catherine's incorruptible body, so holy that it never decomposed after her death.

She paid no attention to the male saints. She cared only for the women, the way most girls loved the princess in a story and hardly noticed the prince. As she read, Theresa saw how many of these brave and righteous women had been nuns.

An older cousin of hers, Mary Dolan, was a nurse with the Sisters of Mercy in Dublin. Theresa knew that under Mary's wimple lay a mass of thick brown curls, which were somehow more beautiful to her in their invisibility than anything her eyes could behold. Mary came home only once, for her sister Annabelle's funeral. Theresa just gazed at her as if she were a film star.

"I'm going to be a nun too one day," she said.

As she grew up, she noted that most of the nuns she met were nothing like the ones in her stories. The nuns at the convent school had foul breath and saggy arms. They would sooner sprout wings than endure flames or stab wounds in the name of devotion. When Sister Florence thwacked Theresa across the head with a rolled-up copy of the *Clare Champion* for talking in class, there was nothing saintly in it.

Magdalene nuns ran the orphanage in Cloonanaha. Their father had threatened to send them all there on some occasion or another. And so, from a young age, Theresa was terrified of the place.

Later she read about the scandals throughout history. About the ancient aristocrats who moved their daughters into the convent only because it was a more affordable alternative to a dowry. About poor Arcangela Tarabotti, forced into monasticism like many others in the seventeenth century because she was disabled. About the Medicis, and the lay nuns called skivvies, who were made to be servants to the dowried nuns.

But it was none of this that deterred her. Only that at some point, Theresa discovered boys. She tucked away her dream then, as if it were any other childish thing, a stuffed toy or a soft baby blanket, designed to be cherished and then forgotten.

With her gran's permission, Theresa brought the *Lives of the Saints* to America. She kept the book by her bed in the room she and Nora shared on the second floor of Mrs. Quinlan's house. It was a simple space with three small beds, one of which remained empty. There were two dressers, a closet. The walls were painted a plain cream color. Nora said it would be rude to ask whether they could hang anything.

Babs McGuire had laughed when Theresa told her this. Babs was her favorite person in Boston. Theresa adored her from the start. On one of the first nights they met, over dinner at the house, Babs told Theresa that she worked as a lady's maid for a well-to-do family in Chestnut Hill. Every winter they went to Florida and Babs got to go along.

"I just do the nice work," she said. "I don't have to scrub pots and clean up the way a scullery maid does. The women of the family treat me like one of their own."

"The only one of their own who happens to work for a living," Lawrence said.

Babs ignored him. She said most of her friends worked in grand houses in Newton or Brookline. They made good money cooking and cleaning. Instead of having to pay room and board, they lived with the families they served.

"It's the best job a girl can have. It gives her a skill. She gets her independence, no one looking over her shoulder every minute, telling her what to do."

"It sounds lovely," Theresa said.

"An awful lot of rich people have live-in housekeepers, a cook, a lady's maid. I'm sure you could get hired on by someone."

"Theresa's going for her teaching certificate," Mrs. Quinlan said. "In the meantime, she has a fine job already."

Theresa would have loved to be a maid in the meantime, but like everything else, her job was decided for her long before she arrived.

She spent her days in a small seamstress's shop, sewing hems or stepping behind the curtain to measure bulging waistlines and pale legs covered in blue veins. She listened to women complain about their achy backs and their useless husbands and tried not to die from boredom. She sometimes missed the factory back home, where at least there were so many girls her age to talk to. All of them lined up at their machines in long white coats. They weren't supposed to talk while they worked, but they had the lunch hour in the canteen to gossip and chat and buy biscuits and tea. At the end of a shift, they all got on their knees and said the rosary together.

Theresa told Babs about the great highlight of her short career at the factory, when they were given the task of making blouses for the Aer Lingus hostesses in Shannon. All she did was wind the yarn that would be placed in the knitting machines, but as she did it, Theresa thought about those young women who flew through the air, the life of adventure they led. The way the wool in her hands somehow bound her to them.

She told Babs how she envied the way women dressed in Boston. Everyone here seemed to have piles of clothes. In Ireland they only had a few different changes. She had arrived in America with just a small suitcase.

Babs brought over a bag containing a few of her old things.

"If you have two skirts, you're in business," she said, spreading an emerald green one out on Theresa's bed. "You can wear them again and again, and if you change the blouse, no one will ever be the wiser."

Babs brought forth a pink flowered shirtwaist with a convertible collar, a grosgrain ribbon belt. Theresa had seen her wearing it once and told her how much she loved it.

She squealed. She hugged Babs tight.

"Would you believe I got that at Filene's Basement, half off?" Babs said.

Theresa said, "I'm putting it on right now and wearing it forever."

She had never owned a dress that wasn't handed down by her sister. And Nora's taste was nothing like Babs's. Nora liked a dress that would last. Something sensible. She didn't care what they were wearing in the magazines.

"We girls who come here alone must stick together," Babs said. She lowered her voice. "How do you think your sister's getting on? She's so quiet, it's hard to tell what she's like. I want to get to know her. I guess we'll be family soon."

"I don't know about that," Theresa said.

Babs frowned. "What do you mean? They're engaged, aren't they?"

"I suppose."

Theresa thought Nora was too serious a girl for Charlie Rafferty, too special. Going together was one thing. But marriage! He wanted to be married the minute Nora stepped off the boat. Mrs. Quinlan was always pushing them to book the church. But Nora kept finding reasons to wait. Theresa didn't believe she loved him.

Nora was only fun when she wasn't nervous, and since they arrived in Boston, she was nervous all the time. The best version of her appeared when they were alone in their bedroom in the evenings, and even then not very often. She bossed Theresa no end. She always had, but it was worse now than ever.

Nora chastised her for wearing lipstick and for traipsing over cobblestones in heels. When Theresa mentioned that it seemed like Mrs. Quinlan's husband didn't do much but sit in the parlor and read all day, Nora hissed, "Don't go repeating that."

"I wasn't going to repeat it, I only told you. Who would I repeat it to?"

Nora got flustered when she asked too many questions. At home Theresa's precocious inquiries were indulged, even encouraged, especially by her father when he was in a particular mood. But here she was a guest. Her sister liked her to remember it.

"A girl's first Dudley Street dance is a rite of passage," Babs declared over dinner a month after they'd arrived. "How have we not taken you yet? We'll all go on Thursday."

Theresa was delighted. She counted down the days. Even Nora seemed to pep up some when Thursday came.

"Try this lipstick," Theresa said before they left. "You'd look good in pink."

"I wouldn't," Nora said. But then she ran the color over her lips.

"Beautiful!" Theresa said.

"It is nice, isn't it?" Nora said, as if it had been her idea.

Thursday was maid's night out. It thrilled Theresa to see the girls pouring from the train station in their skirts and blouses, in groups of three or four. She envied them their friendships and their freedom. She didn't know another girl her age in all of Boston. She missed her friends from home and the girls she had met on the boat.

After that first time, Babs took them to the dances every week. There were three halls to choose from on Dudley Street. Theresa was partial to the Intercolonial. They played some rock and roll, but mostly the songs were Irish. Accordions, fiddles, banjo, uilleann pipes. The first waltz started promptly at eight. Couples floated in a circle around the room, the crowd of dancers growing denser as the night wore on. By eleven o'clock, you could hardly move.

Back home, Theresa cycled two miles to a dance in the parochial hall and paid five shillings to see all the same boys she had seen there the week before. She had enjoyed those country dances when she didn't know any better. But after Dudley Street, she couldn't imagine ever going to one of them again.

On her fifth visit to the Intercolonial, she met Walter McClain. He had a face like Clark Gable. A mischievous smile. Hair so dark black and shiny that it could have been patent leather. After she danced with him once, Theresa felt sure she would marry him. The light touch of his fingers on her back filled her body with delight. He was twenty-four, seven years older than she was. He was a junior executive at the Boston Edison plant, not far from where she lived. He said he had never been to the Intercolonial before that night. His friends at work had tried to get him to Dudley Street in the past, but he refused.

"It must have been written in the stars," he said, and she felt so grateful, to God or to chance—imagine if he had come sooner, met a different girl.

"That one looks like trouble," Nora said, which made Theresa like him even more.

He wasn't there the next time or the time after that. Theresa danced with other boys, and with her sister, but she had her eye on the door. Sometimes Charlie and Lawrence and their brother Matthew came along, or Bobby Quinlan, with those big white teeth that put her in mind of a cartoon shark.

On what would be their last visit, it was just the girls—Nora and Theresa and Babs. Theresa watched as a handsome young sailor spun her sister around the room, Nora's brown hair flying behind her. She had forgotten what a good dancer Nora was. She hadn't seen her sister dance since Charlie went away.

That next weekend, Lawrence and Babs got married. After passing out cold at his own wedding, Lawrence found the local chapter of the Pioneer Total Abstinence Association.

Nora said Lawrence had tried it before, back home, and failed. Babs told Theresa in confidence that she hoped he'd fail again, and soon. Lawrence wouldn't let her go to the dances anymore. She was only allowed to go to PTAA table quizzes and talent shows with him, where the women sipped apple juice and talked about the Lord.

That left Nora to accompany Theresa to Dudley Street, but Nora refused no matter how she begged.

"We can't go, just me and you."

"Why not? You had fun."

"I don't have time for that nonsense."

"Why?"

"Theresa, please stop asking me about it."

"You just want me to be miserable. A miserable old crone," Theresa said.

Nora's voice turned sharp. "Not everything is about you."

She could tell then that there was something Nora wasn't saying, but she knew that, as with most secrets, her sister would keep it to herself.

Theresa missed every last lovely thing about the dances. Handing her fifty-cent admission to the doorman, climbing the two flights up to the hall. The girls in their skirts and sweaters lined up on benches along one wall, and the boys standing against the opposite, hands folded behind their backs. For a while, they'd just stare across at one another, the air buzzing with hope and fear and possibility. Theresa's stomach was full of jitters as she wondered whether one of those boys might cross the room and ask her to dance. She would dance with anyone, if he was handsome enough. Even though her heart was with Walter.

She tried to behave. To fill her evenings listening to *Fibber McGee and Molly* on the wireless, or studying her books. She sometimes sat beside old Aunt Nellie after dinner, as she spread her prayer cards out on the dining room table, deciding who needed which one tonight. Theresa's grandmother had a similar collection, each printed with an oil painting of a saint or a religious scene on one side and a prayer for a particular worry or hardship on the other.

Aunt Nellie's cards came in a bright blue box, the words *Saints for All Occasions* printed in gold foil on the cardboard cover. Theresa flipped through them, memorizing each one. Prayer for a Pet. Prayer for Widows. Prayer in Time of Economic Hardship. Prayer for a Safe Return Home. Prayer for Grace. For Students. For Patience. For Divine Mercy. Prayer to a Guardian Angel.

Her class met every Monday and Wednesday night. She loved watching the teacher, a skinny American in a sweater and a dark suit jacket, tell them how important a job it was, to teach, to mold young minds. Her grandmother's grandmother had taught in a hedge school in Miltown Malbay a century ago, giving the children of the town their lessons in secret when it was forbidden for them to go to school, a dozen of them gathered in a barn. Her gran had told her that teaching was her destiny, and the nuns at the convent school had agreed. Now finally, her chance.

Theresa studied for hours. She went to the library near the house and took out as many books as were allowed each week. This in itself was a thrill, since there was no such thing as a library back home. She read and read. She was excited to one day have students of her own. Sometimes she taught a pretend lesson in front of the bedroom mirror when Nora wasn't home.

But much of the time, she was restless, bored. It was particularly hard at the weekend, when she'd see groups of girls out laughing in the streets. She missed Walter, wondered who he was dancing with now.

One evening when she got home from work, Mrs. Quinlan handed her a letter, postmarked New York. It was from Abigail, her friend from the boat ride over. They had exchanged addresses and Theresa had written first. She sent a postcard with a picture of Boston Common in the snow.

Abigail wrote that Theresa must look her up if she ever found herself in Queens.

"Let's go for a weekend!" she said to Nora that night.

"She's only being polite, she's not inviting you," Nora said.

The next day before breakfast, Theresa mentioned it again.

"We could borrow Bobby's car maybe. Charlie could drive."

"Stop," Nora said. "I don't want to hear another word about New York."

"I'll drop it if you'll go to the dance with me."

Theresa smiled. She thought Nora would relent then, but her sister's face was humorless, cold. Nora turned and went down to the dining room.

On a Tuesday in late September, as the first autumn breezes came through the windows, Theresa could wait no longer. Nora was out with Charlie, over at Lawrence and Babs's place for supper. Theresa was sore that they hadn't invited her. Babs, newly pregnant, said she was too fat to be seen out anywhere. She seemed able only to socialize with other dull, coupled-up types.

Mrs. Quinlan sat in the parlor listening to Bishop Sheen on the wireless, drinking the one Tom Collins she allowed herself each night. The bishop's talks were the bright spot in her week. She said he had a voice like honey, the voice of an angel. Everyone in the house knew to be quiet or get out while she was listening.

In her room, Theresa put on the green skirt Babs had given her. She tucked in her white blouse and slipped Nora's white cardigan over the top. She added a black leather belt that Babs said made her waist look impossibly small and a pair of black pointed pumps, on loan from Babs. Nora said she looked like a child learning to ice skate when she tried to walk in them, but they were so beautiful, Theresa didn't care. She brushed her hair gently so the curls would stay put. She walked down the stairs and out the door without anyone noticing. The cool air brushed her bare calves. A group of boys played ball on the green. They stopped and watched as she went by.

She felt wonderful, riding the train alone for the first time.

But once she reached the hall, her confidence faded. The doorman asked, "Aren't you with anyone?" A group of girls glanced over, making their disapproval known. Still, Theresa climbed the stairs to the second floor. When she stepped into the room, she felt the same excitement as ever.

No one spoke to her for the first half hour. She shuffled back and forth, feeling a fool, as if everyone were looking at her, even though they weren't. But then a redheaded girl said, "I like your skirt."

"Thanks," Theresa said.

"I'm Rose. This is my sister Patty."

They were twins, with red hair and freckles and bright green eyes.

"Did you come alone?" Patty asked.

"I did," Theresa said, feeling vaguely ashamed and remembering now how many Irish people in Roxbury and Dorchester Mrs. Quinlan knew personally. For all she knew, here were two of them. They might tattle on her. Then Mrs. Quinlan would tell Nora, and Theresa would be killed. Murdered.

But Patty only said, "That was brave of ya."

At home, she never would have dared go to a dance alone. But life in this place didn't feel quite real, like anything that happened here existed in a dream and would disappear when she woke the next morning.

The twins went to the bar to get a soda and invited her along. Theresa was grateful. She stood chatting with them, until at last Walter walked in. Handsome in his jacket and tie, his hair slicked back. It had been weeks. She wondered if he would remember.

He noticed her right away and came over.

"Where have you been?" he said.

They danced for an hour, never even considered dancing with anyone else. Theresa wanted to stay until the band finished and the lights went up, but she knew she had to beat her sister home. Walter rode with her on the train. He asked her to meet him again the following week. She promised she would. He kissed her at the corner before letting her go on alone to the house.

Theresa had been kissed exactly seven times before. Six of them were with Gareth O'Shaughnessy, a boy whom everyone in Miltown Malbay called Bottle, because his skin was so pale you could nearly see through it. Gareth was sweet, but he had enormous, awful lips that seemed to want to reel her in like a fish on the line. When she pulled away, her chin would be all wet.

She had once kissed a jobber in town for a fair day. Theresa's whole family had been up early, getting the cattle ready to sell. At four in the morning, her grandmother splashed holy water on the cows, then sent her son-in-law and his children to town. Hours later, the jobber, having gotten a good price for his boss, had celebrated with several pints at one of the pubs on Main Street. He came upon Theresa alone just after. He said hello and next she knew, he was kissing her, the earthy taste of beer still in his mouth.

Her first American kiss was something of a different order.

Theresa glided down the hall on stockinged feet. In her room, she pulled the pins from her hair one by one, letting her brown curls fall against her shoulders. She hung her skirt and sweater in the closet.

She felt a chill standing there undressed. She slipped into her nightgown and flopped onto her bed. She went over each moment of the evening in her mind, uninterrupted.

Before leaving home, Theresa swore to her gran that she would say her prayers every night in Boston, as she had in Ireland. Though her eyes ached for sleep, she got to her knees. The prayer she always started with was the one Nora said their mother had recited over them in their beds when they were babies:

> *Angel of God, my guardian dear*
> *to whom God's love commits me here.*
> *Ever this day be at my side*
> *to light and guard, to rule and guide.*
> *Amen.*

Whenever she said it, Theresa thought of her family and her whole body hurt for missing them. She understood that it might be years before she could afford to go back. Years before she would hear her brother's voice or the sound of her father laughing along to *Living with Lynch* on Radio Éireann. She thought of the worried frown on his face when he waited for the weather and the football results. She might never see her dear old gran again. Theresa pictured her, singing softly as she cooked dinner over the open fire. It must be quiet there now, with just the three of them.

Boston was far more exciting than home. She liked the people in the house. But they would never be her family.

Theresa even missed the animals. Since they were children, she and Nora had to milk the cows promptly at six o'clock in the evening. When they were young, they'd get a slap if they didn't rise the froth. She hadn't much enjoyed milking cows, but now she craved the quiet conversations she would have with them. She missed the haughty cats that lived in the barn, and the sweet dogs, which she often snuck into the house at night if it rained. She had once been caught bringing a piglet into her bed and gotten hit on the bottom with a wooden spoon. It seemed a grave injustice at the time, but when she thought of it now, she laughed and laughed.

To the usual list of people she prayed for each night—her gran and her father, her sister and brother, her mother in heaven—she added one more. Walter McClain. Her true love, who would be her family one day.

Theresa crossed herself and got back into bed. When Nora came in, she didn't suspect a thing. Theresa lay very still and kept her eyes shut, though she wanted to explode with the story of her night.

She could hear someone walking about in the room upstairs. When she moved into the house, this was the hardest thing to get used to—the strange sound of footfalls overhead. That, and the way people came and went. For a time, there were three small children in the next room, Mrs. Quinlan's great-nieces. Theresa assumed their parents were dead, but when she mentioned this to Charlie, he laughed. "They live in Quincy," he said. "A few miles from here. They've so many children—fourteen, I think, or fifteen—that they sent a couple to live away for a while. A lot of people do it."

"Not any people I know," Theresa said. She felt indignant on the children's behalf. From then on she was nicer to them and gave them what was left over of her cake after dinner.

The following week and the week after that, Theresa managed to see Walter again. He kissed her with such passion when they parted. But then, on two occasions, he wasn't there when he promised he would be, and after that it seemed Nora would never go out. Theresa skipped her class to go to the dance once but felt so guilty, so sure she'd be discovered, that it was hardly worth it.

One night, after they had turned out the lights and Nora started to mumble in her sleep, Theresa slowly got out of bed. She reached into the closet in darkness, felt around for the right dress. She used her bare feet to find the shoes she was after and even dared to take a pair of nylons from the dresser drawer. All of it in her arms, she stood still as a tree and listened. Her sister was asleep.

Electrified by her own boldness, she got dressed in the bathroom and quickly left the house. The dance would be ending soon.

When she arrived, she saw him, laughing, leading another girl across the floor. But when he saw her, Walter came right to her side.

"I thought you'd vanished," he said.

They danced and danced. The night felt like magic, something out of time. She could not believe that an hour ago, she was lying in her bed. That she might have missed this.

Walter pulled a flask from his pocket and took a sip, offered her one.

"Go on," he said.

She took the flask from him, sipped at it.

"That's good scotch," he said. "Have some more."

They danced and they drank, Theresa feeling dizzy in a way she adored.

Walter said, "You're beautiful, you know."

All the boys she had ever met were too shy to say a simple thing like that. She smiled.

"Come with me," he said. "I want to show you something."

He led her out into the hall and down the stairs, his hand on the small of her back. Theresa thought maybe they would go somewhere for a late dinner.

But when they reached the first floor, instead of descending to the ground level, he led her down a corridor.

"What are you up to?" she said with a laugh.

He shushed her playfully, took her by the hand. He opened a door into a large dark closet and guided her inside. Walter closed the door gently behind them. He kissed her. He hugged her tight. In the darkness, he ran his hands down the back of her dress. Theresa stood completely still. The room smelled like cleaning solution. She thought about confession, of how impossible it would be to explain this to a priest.

She could hear him unzipping his pants, the cool sound of the fabric falling to the floor. Walter raised her skirt, pulled down her knickers, and pushed her gently against the door. He came closer and closer until she could feel him pressing against her and then inside her. Theresa gasped, and he laughed, kissing her neck. It hurt for a moment, but he kept going, and after a while it felt marvelous. This became a ritual whenever they met, and it was heaven. Better than any dance she had ever known.

On a Thursday in December, she crept up the staircase, willing her footfalls to be silent. She knew her way in the dark, knew that the fourth stair from the bottom creaked in the middle, that the rug on the final step was worn down to nothing and a person could slip if she wasn't careful.

She stopped halfway up, removed her shoes. The house was silent.

Theresa made it to the second floor landing and stood there a moment, listening. The door to Mrs. Quinlan's room was open a crack. She could tell it was dark on the other side.

Tonight, Walter had told her he loved her.

She was in the middle of a story when he said it. She was saying that she hadn't thought much about being Irish until she came to America. She saw that it meant more to a person here. Mrs. Quinlan had told her that on Saint Patrick's Day, everyone had the day off and the city threw a massive parade. Back home, the men might go to the pub or to the races if they had the money to spare, that was all.

"I thought the people I knew here would be Americans, mostly," she said. "But you're the only one I talk to. I can go days without hearing an American accent, besides the Quinlans'. And you know there are clubs in Boston for people from every part of Ireland. Babs's cousins go to the Tipperary. That's where they're from back home. Friends of theirs go to the Galway. I told Nora that—"

Walter pressed a hand over her mouth. "I think I'm falling in love."

As she remembered it now, she felt the same rush she had gotten right there in the moment. Theresa opened the bedroom door, undressed, and slipped under the covers.

Then Nora shot up in her bed.

"Turn on the light," she said.

Theresa did as she was told.

"Where have you been?"

"Right here, you just woke me."

"I saw you coming up the road. A girl your age has no business being alone on Dudley Street at this or any hour."

"I just turned eighteen!"

"Exactly."

"I haven't been to Dudley Street, I was only out for a walk."

Nora sighed. "Theresa. I have enough of my own worries. Please don't do this to me."

"It won't happen again," she said. "I swear."

"I won't be here much longer," Nora said. "You have to start behaving yourself."

"Where will you be?"

"Once we're married, Charlie and I will move somewhere else. Not far, but still."

Theresa thought it would be ages before that ever happened, if that ever happened.

Her sister kept a closer eye on her from then on, but still she saw Walter as often as she could. She loved him, though he was not the most reliable man. They might make a plan to meet for dinner, and he'd let her sit in the restaurant alone for hours, waiting. But when she saw him again, it ceased to matter. She loved him that much.

One rainy Wednesday in March, Theresa sat down at the crowded breakfast table.

"He's the handsomest man I've ever seen," said one of the two Elizabeths.

"Who is?" Theresa asked.

"Senator Kennedy," she said, as if it should be obvious.

They had all seen him passing by in the Saint Patrick's Day parade the weekend before.

"He'll be president one day," Aunt Nellie said. "An Irish president. A Catholic. Imagine that. I wish my husband had lived to see it."

"Don't count your chickens," Mrs. Quinlan said.

"Why shouldn't I?"

"It's bad luck, for one thing."

"Catholics don't believe in luck."

"I loved his wife's coat," Nora said. "It was beautiful."

"I'll get you one just like it," Charlie said. "I bet it didn't cost much, right? Heck, we'll get two!" He laughed.

Nora glanced at him quickly, then looked away as if she had mistaken him for somebody else.

Mrs. Quinlan said, "Theresa, Nora, you'll be getting a new roommate this weekend."

"A new roommate?" Theresa said, wondering who and for how long but not daring to ask too many questions while her sister was in the room.

"Yes," Mrs. Quinlan said. "Kitty's coming back."

"Kitty?"

"Charlie's sister," Nora said. "You know who she is."

Back in Miltown Malbay, Theresa was only vaguely aware of Kitty Rafferty's existence. They were probably ten years apart.

"Where has she been until now?" Theresa asked.

No one responded.

Aunt Nellie asked for the jam, and someone passed it. As she spread the strawberries across a thick white slice of bread, she looked at Theresa and raised an eyebrow, as if to say there was a fine story there.

Theresa and Nora returned from Mass on Sunday to find that Kitty had moved in her things.

Kitty didn't say much to them. She was gone a lot—out with friends late into the evening and off to work in the morning before Theresa and Nora were even awake. When Kitty got to Boston years ago, she too had worked in Mrs. Byrne's shop, but over time she earned her degree and became a nurse at Saint Margaret's Hospital. Theresa wanted her to know that she was on a similar path, that she wasn't going to be stitching hems forever. But she couldn't say it. Kitty left her tongue-tied.

Before Kitty moved in, Theresa had spent hours in front of the bedroom mirror, turning her head this way and that. Pouting and smiling and laughing. Everyone said she was pretty. But once she had the up-close view of Kitty Rafferty, Theresa realized that she herself was plain.

Kitty was the closest thing to Elizabeth Taylor she had ever seen in real life. She had those sharp contrasts to her face—milky white skin and bright green eyes, though her hair was a gorgeous shade of auburn. She was tall, as tall as her brothers. When Kitty stood, she curved her shoulders forward slightly, as if to take a few inches off.

Under Babs's tutelage, Theresa had purchased one pink lipstick. She could never decide if it looked good on her, but she continued to wear it anyway. She also had a tube of black mascara, a prized possession. Kitty had more makeup than a fashion model. She laid it out on the dresser, pushing aside Theresa's hairbrush and her rarely perused Bible to make room for perfume, for eye shadow and blush, for black eyeliner and two fat white powder puffs in white porcelain jars.

When Kitty was out, Theresa looked through her things. She once dared to spritz a fine mist of Kitty's perfume and then sat fretting for the next hour, afraid of what might happen if Kitty or Nora came in and smelled it in the air.

Kitty came to breakfast one morning in a pair of bright blue Capri pants and a sleeveless button-down shirt, looking like something from a magazine. Theresa vowed to save her money to buy an identical outfit.

Two years ago, Enda Kelly had horrified everyone in Miltown Malbay when she walked into the chemist's with a visiting American cousin— a teenage girl in blue jeans. Theresa hadn't seen her, but her friend Sheila reported that the old ladies in line shook their heads in disgust. Nora said the poor girl probably felt mortified when she realized how out of place she was there. But Theresa doubted it bothered her. She guessed that the American cousin felt superior to them all and went on with her day. That's how she wanted it to be when she went back. She would cause a stir and barely notice.

Theresa begged her sister for the full story about Kitty. Nora told her not to be nosy. But after a week, she relented. The two of them were in their beds, tucked in beneath the covers. Kitty wasn't home yet. Nora was in a rare and lovely mood, light and unguarded, the way Theresa liked her best.

"Two years ago, she ran off and married a Protestant. A doctor," Nora whispered. "No one's heard from her since. Charlie supposes now the doctor's gone and left her and so she's back."

Theresa had never heard of a married woman living without her husband, unless he was dead. "No one says anything about it," she said.

Nora seemed amazed by her surprise. "They wouldn't now, would they?"

"Do you like her?" Theresa asked.

"I don't know."

"You should make friends. She'll be your sister-in-law soon."

Nora didn't say anything.

"Well, won't she?"

"If we get married, then yes."

"If!" Theresa said.

"Charlie's been after me to set a date. Every time I think of it, I want to be sick."

Theresa was thrilled to be let in on her sister's private thoughts. She started to reply, but the door opened then, and Kitty said, "It's only me."

It didn't seem like something she would say. Under normal conditions, she would have barged in as if this were her room alone. And so they knew that Kitty had heard it all, or some part of it anyway. When she turned her back to them, taking hold of a hanger in the closet, Nora widened her eyes at Theresa, then closed them tight as if to erase the moment from her mind.

5

Theresa was on her way to the tub when Kitty Rafferty pushed past her into the bathroom. "Sorry! I need to get in there! I've had a visit from my little friend and I'm headed out the door."

Theresa waited outside in her robe. No matter how she timed it, a bath was never a simple proposition. Thirteen people shared this bathroom. Mrs. Quinlan didn't like them to bathe more than once a week. "Saturday's wash for Sunday's dash will do you fine," she said. But even then, there was usually some complication.

When Kitty came out, Theresa went in and ran the water. She undressed as she waited for the tub to fill. Kitty's mention of her little friend put Theresa in mind of her own. When she first got to Boston, she didn't bleed for three months, but after that, her period arrived just when she expected it. Until recently. How long had it been? She tried to recall as she sank into the bath.

Theresa ran a hand over her stomach. Was there a rise there that she hadn't noticed before, or was she imagining it?

She lay still until the water grew cool, and then she added more.

A thought crossed her mind.

There was a pounding at the door. She shot upright.

"While we're young, Theresa!" shouted Aunt Nellie, who was eighty-five.

She stood and dried off in haste, then pulled on her robe and went to the bedroom.

Aunt Nellie called after her, "I was twelve when you went in there!"

Alone in the bedroom, Theresa let the robe fall to the floor and looked down at her belly. Next moment, the door flew open.

"Sorry, I left my—" Kitty's eyes landed on Theresa's naked body. She slammed the door shut, leaning up against it as if fending off a mob.

"Jesus," she whispered. "Are you pregnant?"

Was it possible to know something fully and yet not know it at all? The truth came to light, and still Theresa said, "Of course I'm not."

"Do you know how babies are conceived?"

Theresa thought she did, vaguely, though no one had ever told her. She nodded.

"Have you—has someone—some man—done something to you?"

"No! Well. Yes. In a way."

"When?"

"It's happened a few times."

Kitty looked almost amused. "That's where you sneak off to." She seemed to catch herself. Her face turned serious. "Have you felt ill?"

"No."

But now that she thought of it, Theresa had been exhausted. Twice, she fell asleep at work. Fasting before Mass had become a hardship. She snuck a slice of bread from the kitchen the previous Sunday. She had blamed it all on her late nights, on the hunger she worked up dancing.

Kitty started pacing the room.

"I'll get a cup at work and bring it home," she said. "I'll just take a sample to the hospital. I'll mark it Joan Doe. People do it all the time. Of course, they'll probably think it's mine." Kitty laughed, considering this.

While she waited for the results, Theresa wanted more than anything to tell Nora. Every day at work, she'd stare at her sister until Nora said, "What's the matter with you?"

She knew Nora would be furious over what she had done. But somehow she still didn't believe it could be true. At night, all three of them in their beds, Theresa bargained with God in her head. If He would just let it not be so, she would do anything. She did not sneak off to a dance even once. She didn't talk back to her sister.

When she found out for sure, Theresa wept. Kitty made her go to a doctor to confirm it. He said she was four months along.

She did not have to find a way to break the news to her sister, because that same day, Kitty told Nora and Charlie.

"I can't be the only one who knows," she said. "I'm sorry."

The four of them gathered in the bedroom, trying to whisper.

It was a relief and it was a nightmare, having her sister know. Nora sat on her bed. She didn't say a thing. She wouldn't look at Theresa.

"He'll have to marry you," Charlie said.

"Do you want that?" Kitty asked. "Could you marry this man?"

Theresa was too fearful even to find the words. "I thought," she began. "Someday."

"It's not the time, Charlie," Kitty said. "She's too young."

"I forgot, we've got a marriage expert present," he said.

"Why are you angry with me? I haven't done anything. We've all made mistakes, haven't we?"

"Some worse than others," he said. "Plenty of girls her age get married here. It's not like at home, where we're forced to wait until we're a hundred. Here, you decide these matters for yourself."

"That's just the point," Kitty said. "She hasn't decided."

"Where is he?" Charlie said. "Where does he live?"

The thought of Charlie and Walter in the same place, discussing this, mortified her. "I don't know."

"You don't know? Christ in heaven."

"It's all right, Charlie. Calm down," Kitty said. "I've talked to a nurse at the hospital who knows someone. It will cost two hundred and fifty dollars. I don't know where we'll ever get that, but I can help a little."

Charlie shook his head, closed his eyes. He breathed in deep through his nose, so all of them could hear. "I knew you would say that. I should have you sent home for even suggesting it."

Kitty laughed. "I'd love to see you try."

"If she won't be married, she'll go to Saint Mary's," Charlie said.

Theresa watched them as if she were watching a play, as if it weren't her fate they were deciding.

"You have no idea what you're asking of her," Kitty said. "My way will be easier."

"Easier until she's burning in hell. Until we all are, since you've brought us into it. I won't allow it. It's a crime. It's a sin!"

Theresa weighed her soul against her freedom—she had only just begun to know it.

"Do you want this decision to be down to you, Charlie?" Kitty asked. "Do you want whatever happens on your shoulders?"

He ignored her.

"Saint Mary's is a nice place, Theresa," he said. "Run by nuns. It's next door to the hospital where Kitty works. You'll go away for the last few months. Then you'll have the baby at Saint Margaret's. No one ever has to know."

"How will she go away?" Kitty asked. She came to Theresa's side. "If you do what I tell you, you'll have a short visit to a doctor's office. It will be like getting your tonsils out. It will all be over in a day or two."

"A doctor's office!" Charlie cried. "It'll be a short visit, Theresa, provided you don't die on the good doctor's table."

Theresa had never seen him like this. Serious, stern. All his humor drained away.

She felt the full force of it now. Die on the table or go to the nuns.

She looked to her sister, but Nora sat staring straight ahead, saying nothing.

"Nora," Theresa said softly. "What should I do?"

"You don't ask me that now," her sister said. "It's too late for that."

"Please don't tell Daddy," she said. "I'm begging you."

Nora closed her eyes. "Is that all you can think of?" she said. "Oh, Theresa."

It was decided that Theresa would go to Saint Mary's at five months and stay until the baby was born. Nora made her swear that she would never see Walter again. Theresa agreed, but she could not leave him wondering. She went to the next dance as planned, met him outside. When Walter reached for his wallet to pay their way in, she put a hand on his and said, "Let's take a walk."

She told him what had happened and felt her body flood with shame, as if they had not done the thing together. He didn't believe her at first. He said she didn't look pregnant, and he should know. But Walter had only ever seen her body in the dark.

Theresa told him her plan, and he nodded along. He said he knew a girl who'd gone to Saint Mary's once.

He told her he loved her. He said, "I'll be here when you come back."

Theresa felt overcome with a deep disappointment she couldn't quite name. Maybe she had wished that he would ask her to marry him, despite what she'd said.

"You can visit me," she said.

"I will, then."

He kissed her good night.

Saint Mary's was a small, unremarkable building, tucked into the shadow of Saint Margaret's Hospital. Theresa must have passed it a dozen times without ever wondering what went on inside.

Charlie and Nora brought her when the time came. They told Mrs. Quinlan they had found Theresa a summer job on the Cape, cleaning in some visiting family's beach house, the job she had always wanted. In the fall, Theresa would start teaching, so nobody minded much when she left the seamstress's shop and went off for what Charlie described as her last hurrah.

"You've done the right thing," he said before they parted ways on the sidewalk. "Remember that."

Nora walked Theresa to the door. The nun who answered had a warm smile. She introduced herself as Sister Josephine.

"Come now, I'll take you to meet Sister Bernadette. She's in charge of intake."

Nora held back, waiting, until Sister Josephine said, "You can come in for this part."

She led them both to an office at the end of a dark hall.

Sister Bernadette had an intimidating bosom, a slight mustache. She rose from her desk when they stepped into the room and stayed on her feet while she spoke, her fingers knotted together as if in prayer.

"You girls are from Ireland."

"Yes, Sister," Nora said.

"And does your mother know about your situation?" She was looking at Theresa now.

"My mother is dead, Sister."

"Your father, then."

"No."

"Where is he?"

"Back home."

"Whereabouts is that?"

"In the west. County Clare."

"I don't suppose you know the O'Rourke family in Killarney. Ailish O'Rourke?" She paused. "No, why would you?"

When Theresa didn't reply, the nun said, "You do realize you've committed a mortal sin. Have you been to confession? Have you told a priest?"

"No, Sister," Theresa said.

Nora straightened in her chair.

"Well. You will while you're here. You'll behave, and you'll be brought back to the path of righteousness. You can get on with your life. Put this behind you. The baby will go to a good Catholic family. We consider it a gift to them, from God."

"Have they already been chosen?" Nora asked.

"Yes."

"Will I meet them?" Theresa said.

Sister Bernadette shook her head.

Theresa nodded, relieved. She envisioned the moment when she would leave this place and finally be herself again. She wondered how soon Walter would come.

"Are we understood?"

"Yes, Sister."

"Good." Sister Bernadette passed a pen and paper across the table. "Sign that," she said.

Theresa did as she was told. She looked at Nora and Nora forced a smile.

Sister Josephine was waiting in the hall. She guided them back the way they came.

"I'll just show you out," she said to Nora.

Before they parted, Nora hugged her so tight Theresa thought her ribs might crack. She didn't want her to pull away.

She watched as Nora slowly descended the stairs to the sidewalk, to Charlie waiting in the car. The door closed, taking the light with it.

Sister Josephine led her up a long marble staircase. At the top, doors on either side lined a wood-paneled corridor.

The nun went to one of the doors and pushed it open.

"This will be your room," she said. "You'll have two roommates—Susan and Mae. These are not their real names. And you're not to tell them yours. As long as you're here, you are Kate. Do you understand?"

Theresa wanted to go home, to undo all of this. But she held back her tears and said she understood.

The bedroom had white walls and three single beds. They weren't permitted to bring anything of a personal nature—photos or makeup or magazines. She thought of the room she shared with Nora, with Kitty, bursting with signs of life. Here, the beds were neatly made, covered in plain white blankets. The room looked like no one had ever set foot in it. The only thing out of the ordinary was the one window, boarded over, with planks of wood nailed into the frame on either side.

Within five minutes of meeting her roommates, Theresa learned that Susan's real name was Patricia and Mae's was Elizabeth. When Elizabeth left the room, Patricia whispered that she was soft in the head. She wouldn't say how she'd gotten pregnant, but Patricia suspected something awful had happened to her. On her first night at Saint Mary's, Elizabeth had tried to throw herself out the bedroom window. Patricia held her back. The next day, a priest came around with the wood and the hammer and nails.

Each day at lunch, they ate stewed tomatoes on white bread. The nuns made them take a water pill to keep from retaining fluid. On Monday afternoons, the doctor examined them. A bell rang and they lined up in the hall. Theresa felt shame course through her when the time came to lie on the table and open her legs. It was unimaginable that those brief moments of pleasure with Walter had led her here.

They attended Mass in the parlor each morning. Afterward, Sister Bernadette spoke to them about their sins and how they might use their free hours to atone. Once, a girl about Theresa's age raised her hand and asked how they should tell their future husbands about all this.

"Don't," the nun said plainly. "No man would want to marry a girl like that."

She thought of Walter, how he wasn't like other men. He hadn't blamed her for being here. He hadn't come to see her yet. She wondered if he was all right. A nagging thought hung at the edges of her mind, but she refused to let it in.

———

In the dark at night, Theresa's roommates cried. They were louder than they might have been if they weren't trying so hard to be quiet. Patricia told her that she didn't want to give her baby up, that she could feel the child kicking, begging her not to go away. She had gotten pregnant by her boyfriend. Her parents made her swear never to tell him what happened. The boyfriend thought she was a counselor at a summer camp in New Hampshire. Patricia said they would still be married one day.

Theresa cried for Walter, not for the baby. But no one could tell the difference. Her breasts grew swollen, foreign, as the weeks passed. Her belly stretched taut like a drum. She didn't think of the thing inside her as a child. It was something happening to her, besieging her, which would pass like any unwanted boil or bruise or flu. She felt horribly lonesome. She thought God had been creative, punishing her for going out to the dances on her own by leaving her truly alone here.

Sometimes late at night, she was awakened by screaming. Girls disappeared and weren't spoken of again. One morning, a blonde let out a yelp in the breakfast room and grabbed her stomach, so alarmed by whatever sensation she felt there that she dropped a water glass, which shattered on the floor. The nuns hurried her out the door, and that was it—they never spoke of her again.

Theresa wrote home to her family, just short notes about the weather. She hated lying to them, and making Nora lie on her behalf. She said a novena for forgiveness.

Nora visited one evening a week, as much as was allowed. She was sometimes stern. She didn't say much. Other times, when Theresa herself was particularly sad, Nora endeavored to make her laugh and whispered that it would all be fine in the end.

Theresa tried not to be hurt when, on Nora's second visit, her sister came in and said, "I have news."

She sounded bashful, embarrassed.

"What is it?" Theresa said.

"Charlie and I were married over the weekend."

"What! Nora!"

"I hated to do it without you. But there was a cancellation at the church and Charlie had been wanting to get it done. It all happened so fast. The priest even waived the banns. We're moving our things into a new apartment. Mrs. Quinlan's helping me fix it up. You'll come and stay there with us when all this is over."

Nora made no mention of what she had said about marrying him when they were alone together. That the very thought of it made her sick.

The girls at Saint Mary's were allowed one outing during their stay. After Theresa had been there ten weeks, Nora and Charlie signed her out. They drove a long way in his cousin's car, nearly an hour's drive. All the way to a town called Hull. A pretty place, right on the ocean. It reminded Theresa of home. Charlie said they wouldn't be seen by anyone they knew there. They could go to a movie if she liked. The Apollo Theatre glowed, massive, welcoming, in the evening light. *King Creole* was showing, Elvis Presley in the starring role.

Afterward, they strolled along beside the seawall. The ocean on one side and an amusement park, all lit up, across the road. Theresa wished they could go inside the gates.

"Wouldn't this be a lovely place to live," Nora said.

She was in a particularly friendly mood, Theresa thought. Marriage suited her, then. Nora walked ahead alone, taking in the scenery.

People smiled at Theresa as she walked at Charlie's side. She thought they must have taken her for a proper wife, a soon-to-be mother. She loved the simplicity of the lie, the purity of it, when the truth had become such an ugly thing.

When they dropped her off afterward, Charlie stayed in the car.

Nora took Theresa to the door.

"There's something I need to tell you," she said.

Theresa could sense that Nora didn't want to say it.

"It's about your Walter," she said, finally. "Theresa, he's married."

"No," Theresa said. "That's impossible."

"Charlie knows people who work at the Edison. They told him Walter has a wife. She had a baby not too long ago."

Theresa's knees began to shake. "Oh."

"It's awful," Nora said. "A married man, a father, behaving that way. The nerve of him. Really, the gall. I'm so sorry, Theresa. He's a snake. I'm glad you're rid of him."

Theresa thought of the nights he hadn't shown up for a date. He had never visited her here. She had forgiven all of it. She had blamed herself.

She had never wondered for a moment if his absences hinted at some deeper transgression. A wife. A child. There was no worse piece of news her sister could have delivered. Walter's love had been the bright light in her thoughts, the one thing she had to look forward to when all this was behind her. She wanted to go after him, to rage at his doorstep, to demand that the truth not be the truth.

Nora put her palms on Theresa's cheeks, holding them there, as if by doing so she might release some of the pain and take it upon herself.

"Don't be too sad," Nora said. "Please."

Theresa felt a sob welling in her chest.

"There's something else I want to discuss with you before I go," Nora said. "It's very big news, in fact." Nora stopped. She couldn't get the words out. She inhaled deeply and then tried again.

"I've thought about it a lot and I've decided Charlie and I will take the baby when it's born. I've worked it all out. I already have everyone thinking I'm pregnant. I wear these big, baggy dresses to work. I send Charlie alone to family parties, with stories about how I'm home sick in bed." She paused. "This way the child will be in your life, Theresa. I know you don't think you care about that now, but you will someday."

Theresa thought of how Walter knew his way to that closet at the Intercolonial. He wasn't discovering it that first time. He was leading her someplace he'd already been.

"Theresa," Nora said. "Don't you have anything to say?"

"I want to go to bed now," she said. "I'm tired."

"This will be the best thing for everyone," Nora said. "You'll see. The baby will stay in the family."

"All right," Theresa said. "Good."

She didn't care about a baby she had never met and couldn't even imagine. She cared about Walter, gone to her now.

All night, she lay awake, thinking of him.

After fifteen weeks at Saint Mary's, Theresa woke one night in what she took for a puddle of blood. She cried out. A moment later, Sister Josephine was at the door, switching on the light.

Theresa saw that it was not blood but water.

Sister Josephine called down the hall, "Sister Bernadette, it's time!"

They brought a wheelchair in. Theresa was wheeled through a long tunnel she had never seen before. On the other side, they emerged into the bright maternity wing of Saint Margaret's Hospital.

Next thing, she was lying on a table, the nuns strapping her wrists down.

"God bless," said Sister Josephine. And they were gone.

Theresa lay alone, screaming, for what seemed like days. Every few hours, a nurse entered the room, checked her, and left without a word. Theresa begged the woman to help her, but the expression on the nurse's face was flat, as if she couldn't hear.

The pain was intolerable, like nothing she had ever known. She stared out the window at a brick wall across the way. She tried to summon the courage of her own mother, who had done this at home three times. But then, her mother was probably surrounded by ladies from town, rubbing her back, telling her stories. Theresa wished she could locate a memory of her face. She screamed for Nora, half expecting her to hear.

She slipped in and out of consciousness. Her head ached as if she had banged it against the table. She couldn't remember seeing day turn to night.

She wailed. She bit down on her tongue until she tasted blood. After several hours, she swore she saw an image of the Virgin Mary flash on the brick wall outside. Theresa thought she must be dying and accepted it willingly if the pain would only go.

A doctor entered the room.

Just before sunrise, her baby was born.

She must have fallen asleep. Next she knew, she was lying there, her arms untied but bloodied and bruised.

Sister Josephine came in holding the child, wrapped in a blue blanket. "Well done," she said. "Would you like to hold him?"

Theresa said she would. She wanted to know if he looked like her.

"You'll have to learn to feed him," Sister Josephine said. "You'll do it for a few days, until he's ready to go home."

Theresa stared down at her son, this beautiful creature with wavy black hair and blue eyes. He was so clearly Walter's boy, the only proof of what the two of them had been.

"Like this," the nun said, trying to avert her eyes and unbutton the top of Theresa's nightgown at the same time. "Go on."

Theresa put the baby to her right breast and nudged his chin up to latch on to her nipple. She had to attempt it three times before he understood. A strange and extraordinary thing, to watch a child so young learn something new.

"I'm going to name him Patrick," she said.

"I think it's up to your sister to name him, Kate."

"My name is Theresa."

They were both silent until the nun continued, "It's such a kind thing your sister is doing. Most girls here won't ever see their babies again. She fought very hard for you."

When Nora visited for the first time, only the two of them and the child in the room, Theresa said, "I want to call the baby Patrick."

"Fine," Nora said.

"You don't need to do what you planned," Theresa said. "I've decided I'll raise him myself."

"How on earth do you imagine you'll do that?"

Sister Josephine came in then. She went to the baby, who had started to fuss in the bassinet. She patted his head, lifted him up.

"I wonder," Nora said, "if we might bring them both home sooner. Today, even."

"I'm sorry, no." Sister Josephine's tone grew curt. "We have a way of doing things. Rules must be followed, even in a situation as unusual as this one."

Theresa wondered what made it unusual. She thought for the first time of the family Sister Bernadette had mentioned that first day. The family who had been chosen to raise her son. She felt overcome by the injustice of the thing. To this good Catholic family, a baby would appear, begotten, not made, like Jesus in the Nicene Creed. Or so it would seem. But no one had spoken of them. Her baby was going to be Nora's now instead.

The next day came, and then the next. Theresa rocked Patrick, fed him, walked the halls with him in her arms to stop him from crying. She could not believe he was what had been inside her all this time.

"I'm sorry I called you a boil," she whispered to him once.

On what was to be her fourth and final night alone with him, Theresa stayed awake past dawn, staring down at his face. The nuns wanted to take the baby to the nursery to sleep, but she begged to keep him with her.

In the morning, they told her, the usual protocol would be followed. Patrick would be taken from her and brought to his new parents in some other room. Nora and Charlie would come get her afterward. The baby in Nora's arms. A clean slate. A new story.

When the moment came, Theresa felt that she might die.

"It's time," said Sister Josephine. "His parents are here." She held out her hands. She began fussing with the baby, even though Theresa still held him. Sister Josephine took a white plastic comb from her pocket and smoothed Patrick's hair. She pinned something small to his diaper.

"What's that?" Theresa asked.

"The Medal of the Immaculate Conception. We give them to all our babies when they go home."

"The Miraculous Medal," Theresa said.

"That's right. Just one more minute now. Say your good-byes."

The nun left the room.

Theresa looked down at the tiny silver oval. There was a ring of blue around the edge. The familiar Virgin, bathed in light, and the words *O Mary, conceived without sin, pray for us who have recourse to thee.*

She thought for the first time in years about how the medal came to be. How the Virgin appeared to Saint Catherine in a Paris church and commanded her to make these medals, so that they might protect whoever wore them. Theresa's favorite part, always, was the rebellion. She loved when Mary said, *God wishes to charge you with a mission. You will be contradicted, but do not fear; you will have the grace to do what is necessary.*

Theresa felt the power of Mary and all the saints with her now.

When Sister Josephine returned and said, "All right, darling. Give him to me," Theresa said, "No."

She said it softly. Even so, she surprised herself. Saying no to a nun!

The sound grew louder. "No, no, no, no. No."

"Sister Bernadette!" Sister Josephine said, panic in her voice. She went quickly from the room.

Theresa looked out the window at where Mary had been, and then down at the medal. Saint Catherine. And here, all these weeks, they had called her Kate. She understood.

The nuns flew in, their black robes swooping like witches' cloaks. Sister Bernadette didn't say anything, just came to her and tried to take Patrick from her arms. Theresa held tight to the child and screamed.

She heard the noises and felt shocked by them, as if they weren't coming from her own mouth.

Patrick started to cry.

"See what you've done to him?" Sister Bernadette said.

"He's mine!" Theresa yelled. "They can't take him!"

Sister Bernadette said sharply, "You signed the paper. This child shouldn't suffer for your sins. Give him to me before I call the police. You're an unwed, unfit harlot." She turned to Sister Josephine. "I warned you this would happen."

Sister Josephine looked distressed. "If you love him, let him have a real home," she said. "A mother and a father. Someday you'll have a child of your own. For now, you'll make a lovely auntie."

When Theresa glared at her, Sister Josephine said, "I'll get the sister."

Nora walked in a few minutes later, Charlie behind her. They were dressed in their Sunday best, as if they were off to Easter Mass.

"Don't make me, Nora!" Theresa begged.

"Everyone's excited to see you," Charlie said. "Mrs. Quinlan keeps saying the house isn't the same without you. We're supposed to go over there for dinner tomorrow. She's making a strawberry pie."

Theresa regarded Nora and Charlie, husband and wife. They expected her to go home and eat pie and invent stories about the summer, as if her son had never been born. After they had forced her to come here.

Her sister was forever trying to tame her, clean her up for the world. Nora had married a silly man she didn't love. How could the fact of his existence make her more of a mother than Theresa was to her own child?

She could tell from their faces that they were just as terrified as she was.

Theresa was growing tired. She needed Nora to understand.

"I had a sign," she said, bitter tears pricking at her eyes. "He's meant to be mine. I'll take him away from here tonight."

"Where would you go?" Nora said.

"Please help me," Theresa said. "Please. If you don't, I'll find a way to keep him just the same. I'll tell everyone what you've done to me. I'll scream it in the streets. I'll run off with him and you'll never find us."

"Theresa!" Nora said.

Her sister came up close. She made her voice soft and low, the way she did when Theresa was a child and needed soothing.

"You're going to be a teacher," Nora said. "You're going to meet a wonderful man. Remember the ones your friend on the ship told you about? Rich and handsome. You'll find one just like that. And Patrick will always be near you. This is the only way."

"Stop this chatter now," said Sister Bernadette. "There will be no more discussion."

She took the baby from Theresa's arms and handed him to Nora.

Part Three

2009

6

THE NUNS AT THE Abbey of the Immaculate Conception chanted seven times daily at the ringing of the bells. The two a.m. call to Matins was the most difficult, and so, Mother Cecilia believed, most important. She had long since trained herself to wake up for it, to dress and get to the chapel, alert and attentive to the prayers at hand.

On Monday morning at one-thirty she rose in darkness, and noticed the silence. After seven straight days, the rain had stopped. Over the course of the previous week, every corner of the abbey's four hundred acres had gotten so thoroughly drenched that the flat rubber soles of the nuns' shoes sank into the grass and seemed to want to stay there, stuck in the mud, forcing the grudging earth up with each step.

All over the property, the branches of two-hundred-year-old pine trees sagged, threatening to snap. In the raised vegetable beds, the last of the winter broccoli stalks grew heavy with water. The beanstalks that climbed the lattice fence shook in the wind. The goats and cows and llama had to be coaxed from the barns with ripe pears. Even the dogs— four yellow Labradors who had spent so many happy afternoons getting filthy in the river—wanted to stay indoors, darting out only a few feet from the porch and right back in again each morning. The river itself had overflowed, swamping its banks.

Inside, moisture clung to every surface. Someone was assigned to wipe down the valves of the chapel organ at regular intervals for fear that they might rust. Wooden doors throughout the dormitory had swollen from the humidity and refused to shut. A damp cold filled the long stone corridors. Everyone was in a wretched mood. Old tensions resumed, and new ones sprang up like mushrooms, taking them all by surprise.

In her cell, rain dripped through cracks in the ceiling into three saucepans at the foot of the bed. Every night, she listened to the rhythmic tapping of each drop as it landed and wondered how they would afford a new roof.

But now, at last, it was over. After Matins, she fell back to sleep in an instant. When the bells rang again at dawn, she dressed, feeling content. She went about her morning plans—Mass and paperwork and baking bread—with a cheerful sense of order restored. She praised the beautiful day to the postman and the youngsters staying in the guesthouse. They all complained that the air had turned cold, but that was to be expected in Vermont, in January. It was the unseasonable warmth that had brought them rain in the first place. She preferred the winter weather. Even at her age, she still got excited by the sight of the abbey in snow.

Breakfast was served promptly at eight. She slipped into the refectory a minute before the hour and took her seat. There were at present thirty-seven of them. They ate their meals in silence at two long, thin wooden tables, side by side, no one facing anyone else. She and the mother abbess sat together at a small head table. Today, as usual, the others bowed before them as they filed in. Because Mother Cecilia recalled with perfect clarity when they were a pair of young postulants, this always took her by surprise.

While they ate their eggs, their bread and jam, she noticed Sister Alma looking at her from across the room. Mother Cecilia nodded, and the girl nodded back with a sad smile. She supposed Sister Alma would come to her afterward seeking counsel, as she often had recently. In four days' time, she would make her final vows. They had all been anticipating it, making preparations in the kitchen and the guest quarters. On Thursday, Sister Alma would become Mother Alma, a permanent member of their community.

You weren't supposed to be more or less fond of one girl or another. But Mother Cecilia couldn't help privately favoring some. Sister Alma had arrived seven years ago, with a master's in fine arts from the Rhode Island School of Design. She was a painter in New York who had begun to show her work in galleries, to make a name for herself. But then she felt called to something greater. She came to the abbey wearing platform sandals with black leather straps that wrapped around her calves and a dress that was longer in the back than it was in front.

Like many of them, Sister Alma started as an intern. She lived in the women's guesthouse for four months and helped with the harvest. She mopped the church floor and scrubbed the pails the nuns used to churn butter. At the end of her term, she asked for a meeting with Mother Cecilia. Of all her jobs, the role of novice mistress was the most essential. Mother Cecilia was the one who helped them decide whether or not they belonged here.

In that first meeting, Sister Alma spoke of how with thirty had come the realization that many of her friends were only playing at poverty. Once some milestone was reached—a birthday or a marriage or a birth—they moved into million-dollar brownstones. They invited people over for brunch in the garden, and everyone commented approvingly on their beautiful furniture, their elegant sense of style. No one asked where the money came from, perhaps because they knew—rich parents or a fortuitous marriage, or a fortuitous marriage to someone with rich parents. Suddenly, after a decade devoted only to ideas and emotions, *things* had become paramount.

She spoke too of the burdens of technology. There was not a young one through the door these recent years who failed to mention how pleased she would be to give up her email account, her cell phone. The word they all used was *noise*. They could barely stand the noise. Life had become too full of it. There were some in the abbey's hierarchy who questioned this motive. A few thought it showed a lack of devotion, but Mother Cecilia disagreed. Every generation had arrived at the abbey burdened by its own trials. Each nun was a product of her time, like anyone. Over half a century, she watched them come in waves. In the seventies, they came seeking peace, community, social justice. Now they wanted life to have meaning. They wanted quiet around them and within. Anything might have led them here. What kept them here was faith.

Some convents had girls as young as sixteen, seventeen years old streaming in, though she doubted many stayed for long. Immaculate Conception did not accept women who hadn't had some life experience, a talent or a profession.

One of them had been a Broadway actress, another a Wall Street banker, another still a state senator in Wisconsin. They had a sculptor, whom the abbey sent to Rome to learn marble carving, and a former chemist who made perfumes. Their gifts from those past lives enriched the present.

Sister Alma said a professor of hers had told his students that the artist's life was unthinkably hard, that if they could envision themselves doing anything else, then they ought to. It applied just as well to being a nun, she said. Mother Cecilia agreed, and yet she thought it could apply to anything—a mother's life was that absolute and could never be undone. Still, most women chose it.

But the artist parallel was a good one. Perhaps an artist felt more deeply than most people, and yet the trade-off was the doubt. She had once read that it took Gilot hours every morning to get Picasso out of bed and to work. A daily ritual of despair to hope.

Faith was not a constant. Faith took reviving. A nun did not become a nun all at once, but bit by bit. This was what she planned to remind Sister Alma of after breakfast. But when Sister Alma knocked on her office door, she bowed before her and said, "There was a call for you on the hotline this morning, Mother."

Mother Cecilia gestured for her to come in.

They had added the hotline for those who couldn't get to the abbey to have their prayers heard. They prayed for whatever they were asked. For personal tragedies and world disasters. For soldiers in Iraq and cancer patients at the hospital up the road. It was not unheard of for a caller to have some personal connection to one of the nuns, but Mother Cecilia had never before been the reason for a call.

"The woman's name was Nora Rafferty," Sister Alma said, glancing at a slip of paper in her hand. "She wanted me to tell you that her son died last night. He was in a car accident. It must have been weather related. She said there was no one else involved."

She felt like the air had been squeezed from her lungs.

She tried to keep her voice even. "Did she say which son?"

"She said his name was Patrick."

In the last picture she ever saw, he was sixteen years old. It was how she imagined him now, though he had turned fifty in August.

"Did you know them well, Mother?" Sister Alma said.

"A long time ago, yes."

The girl looked surprised. As far as anyone but Mother Placid knew, Mother Cecilia had no people of her own in this country.

"I'm so sorry," Sister Alma said. "I'll pray for them. And shall I add him to this evening's prayers?"

"No," she said. But then she changed her mind. "Yes, I mean. That would be nice. Thank you."

Sister Alma left the room and closed the door behind her.

Mother Cecilia began to cry. A car accident. No one else involved. She had made peace with her decision long ago. To leave him with Nora was to leave him to Nora. But Nora hadn't done enough. She hadn't listened. Now this.

She took a breath.

At Immaculate Conception, they believed that dealing with their struggles in the service of God could have a positive effect on the rest of the world. When you took your final vows, you became a religious and then every act you did became an act of religion. She was meant to wrestle with what was difficult in life, especially in her own family.

Compassion then. For Nora, for herself. For choices made in another lifetime, when they knew nothing of the world, nothing of their history. Nothing even of their own bodies and what they were capable of. The silence was a form of violence. She had tried to get Nora to see it, but Nora refused.

She pictured her now. Distraught. But surrounded by her children. Her husband. Charlie's enormous family, all those characters she had lived with once upon a time. Nora's children were grown. She had often imagined them married with children of their own. Settled, content. Nora and Charlie, the proud grandparents of an ever-growing brood. She wondered now if Patrick had left behind a wife. Daughters and sons who loved him.

Mother Cecilia got up from her chair. She walked outside, feeling light-headed.

She found Mother Placid doing the composting.

Mother Placid wore her heavy denim habit with a sweatshirt over the top. Work boots with yellow laces; the edges of the soles caked in mud.

Her dear old friend, keeper of all her secrets. So long since the two of them came through the abbey gates together, since they called each other by their given names. Decades had passed since the last time she thought of herself as Theresa.

Seeing her expression, Mother Placid gave her a worried smile. "What is it?"

Mother Cecilia took hold of the other woman's arm to steady herself. "Patrick is dead."

"My God. What happened?"

"A car accident. My sister called."

"Really."

She had not spoken to Nora in more than thirty years. The letters Mother Cecilia had written were returned, unopened. Dozens of them, still in a box beneath her bed.

"You should go to Boston for the funeral."

"I can't."

"Yes you can. This is just what we voted on."

She said it as if it were that simple.

The trips home had been controversial with some of the oldest nuns. They ran counter to what the cloister had been built on for centuries— you came, and if you were devout, you never left. But in recent years, some abbeys had begun to soften the rules. If someone died or was dying, if your family needed you, you could go away for a short time. The abbey had decided to allow the visits in extreme cases, but until now they had only been theoretical.

Mother Cecilia had argued that these visits were crucial. Motive and intention were everything. Half the postulants would leave for good, either by their own decision or at the vote of the other nuns. The ones who stayed were called to it and could not be pulled away by circumstance.

She had never dreamed that she'd be the first to go. That Patrick would be the reason.

"I can't leave you now," she said. "Not with Bishop Dolan set to arrive any day. Bearing bad news, I would assume."

"You go when you're needed. Isn't that what we decided? I for one am not at all afraid of Dicky Dolan."

"Please don't call him that. You make me nervous."

"It seems to me that it's right," Mother Placid said. "Nora wants you there. Think about it. Pray on it."

"I will."

7

JOHN RAFFERTY SIPPED HIS COFFEE, regarding his wife as she screwed the back onto a pearl earring, her head cocked to one side.

"What time do you think you'll be home?" Julia said. "Because. You know. The thing."

She nodded toward their daughter at the table.

Maeve sat staring at her phone, earbuds jammed in, oblivious.

John's flight to Chicago was at ten. He'd return on the four o'clock. It was not a good day for a teenage mini-drama, but then, it never was.

"I'll definitely be back by eight. Eight-thirty at the latest," he said.

He almost set his mug down on the kitchen island, but at the last second, he remembered the new countertop. Julia had had the white marble installed a month ago. The previous marble—only a year old—was black, which, she said, washed out the rest of the kitchen. John thought he could see what she meant. He preferred not to think about the cost. If they could get a few years' use out of the white, it might not seem so extravagant. He just wouldn't put anything on it until he was fifty.

"You okay?" Julia said.

If she knew what he was thinking, she would say they both worked hard, they could afford it. She would tell him to relax. John sometimes wondered if anyone, upon being told to relax in such a manner, had ever actually succeeded at relaxing.

"I'm fine," he said.

"We're leaving for school in five minutes," Julia said.

Maeve didn't look up.

"Hello!" Julia called. "I need to be in the office by eight-thirty. Big client coming in at nine. Chop-chop."

She sighed. "She's ignoring me."

"She can't hear you," he said, lying for Julia's benefit.

John walked over and tapped Maeve on the shoulder.

She pulled out a single bud.

"Your mother's talking to you. Go get ready for school. You're leaving in five."

She half glared at him, but she got up, shuffled off.

"And we're having a family meeting tonight!" Julia shouted after her. "Get pumped for that!"

"Does she seem off this morning?" Julia whispered once Maeve was upstairs. "Do you think she knows that we know or is she just—being herself?"

"The latter," he said.

Julia could always come up with a reason why Maeve was being a shit. She was underslept from going to a slumber party. She was in a fight with a friend. Her upcoming math test had her on edge.

The truth was that the day she turned thirteen, their daughter had begun to torture them like it was her job. Julia especially. Maeve spoke to her in ways John would never have dared speak to any adult, especially his mother. When he even thought of it, he swore he could taste the soap Nora had used to wash his mouth out thirty years earlier.

Julia was raised the only child of academics in Palo Alto, parents whose cultural preferences were as important to her upbringing as the lessons of how to tie her shoes or stop at the crosswalk. They liked Simon and Garfunkel, and Joan Didion, and Ethiopian food. She was expected to like these things too. More than that, she did like them. Half the albums she now owned had been pinched from her father's collection.

John thought it best to take his parenting cues from her.

When Maeve was small, he played Barbies with her and Calico Critters and beauty parlor. (*I can't picture this,* his sister, Bridget, said when Julia mentioned it once.) Had his own parents ever gotten down on the floor and played with them? He was positive they had not. But after a day spent fighting with overblown, self-satisfied politicians and their hangers-on, there was nothing John enjoyed more than giving voice to a tiny plastic rabbit, or a Ken doll with painted-on sideburns. It took so little to delight his daughter then.

Even when Maeve was a toddler, Julia felt it was important for them to speak to her with respect. If Maeve begged for one cookie too many, Julia tried to explain precisely why it was a bad idea instead of just saying no. John's mother would have said something like, *The doctor called and told me that if you eat another bite of sugar, your stomach will explode and you'll die.*

It amazed him how mild Julia was, how patient. She didn't yell or even have a look that communicated the threat.

You'll spoil her rotten, Nora warned. *Children crave discipline.*

But Maeve was a miracle. The thing they had tried for and wished for, and finally gotten. They were more terrified of scaring her than they were of spoiling her. Every interaction felt important, as if she would be talking about it in therapy twenty years on if they didn't play their cards right. When he was a child, John's mother might slap him with one hand and, a minute later, give him a Popsicle with the other, the whole thing forgotten, forgiven.

There's no justification for physical abuse, Julia said. *Why would I want my own child to fear me?*

He thought the word *abuse* was going too far, but he didn't know how he could ever hit Maeve and then look her in the eye. Had John feared his mother? Yes, of course, without question.

Throughout Maeve's childhood, their only form of discipline was time out. It wasn't exactly a torture chamber. Maeve was made to sit on the bottom step of the staircase with a book for five minutes. He had noted an expression on her face during those sessions. John thought about it a lot these days. It seemed to say, *This is a joke and we both know it. This will accomplish nothing.*

Maybe his mother had been right.

Now Maeve lived inside her cell phone, constantly laughing or gasping at something she saw there. When Julia asked, "What is it?" Maeve would say without fail, "Nothing."

They had once been close, but now Julia said the only time she learned anything about their daughter's life was when she was driving Maeve and her friends to soccer practice or the mall. In the backseat, they'd dissect in great detail who they were mad at, who was mad at them, who had kissed a boy. The girls called kissing "scooping," so she wouldn't know what they were talking about. Julia longed to know more. But, she said, her only parental superpower was invisibility. If she asked a question, she would break the spell.

Maeve's adoption had taken on new importance to her. Here too, she found them lacking. There had been one horrible fight when he could almost see the words taking shape in her mouth. Just as John began to wonder how he might stop them, they were out.

You can't tell me what to do. You're not really my mother.

A few months ago, Julia had started checking the browser history on Maeve's laptop to make sure she wasn't developing an eating disorder or chatting with forty-year-old men. John was against it. He said she was bound to discover something awful if she looked hard enough.

Lo and behold, last night while Maeve was sleeping, Julia found the browser open to a page called the Finding Place. It was an online group offering to reunite girls with their birth mothers. There were discussion topics like Not Fully Belonging in Either World and Was It Legal Adoption or Trafficking?

Julia brought the computer to him, held it out as if it were evidence from a crime scene. They had talked about it for three hours, time he was planning to use to prepare for today's meeting. They hadn't revealed to Maeve yet that they knew. They would tell her tonight, once he got back.

John could tell Julia was on edge about it. He wanted to console her. But the timing was bad. He needed to focus. He needed the money this trip could potentially bring in. Otherwise, something would have to give.

His cell phone buzzed on the counter.

Julia was closer.

"Is it the car service?" he said.

She looked down. "It's your mother."

It was as if he had conjured her with those words, *car service.* As if Nora knew somehow that he was not driving himself to the airport—the only fiscally sensible choice, since he was returning in just a few hours—

but that instead, John was taking a hundred-dollar car ride so that he could stare at the *New York Times* on his BlackBerry in traffic.

"I'll call her back," he said.

Julia's phone started to ring. She took it from her pocket and frowned. "Nora again."

"It's about the article," John said. "Let it go to voice mail."

He had expected her to call yesterday, to congratulate him on the great piece in the *Globe*. The headline made the cover of the Sunday Metro section: "State Senator–Elect Rory McClain Vows to Fight Opiate Abuse, Recalls Childhood Friend's Long Battle."

It had taken weeks of finagling on John's end. He thought it was a brilliant way of silencing all the naysayers from the old neighborhood, who claimed Rory was out of touch with his roots. Try saying that once you knew that one of his best buddies from high school, blinded as a teenager, had ended up a dropout, living among the junkies on the streets of Portland, Maine, for years and years. Until Rory got involved and brought him home to Dorchester, set him up with an apartment and a job washing dishes in his cousin's coffee shop in Adams Village.

The paper had put a photo of Rory and his family on the front page of the section. Inside, on page eight, was a small black-and-white picture of the two friends, Rory and Peter O'Shea, as children. The pair of them in their swimming trunks at Carson Beach, arms around each other's shoulders.

John was quoted in the third paragraph. All day yesterday, people had called him to mention it. But Nora stayed silent.

She had something out for Rory, for no reason John could comprehend. Maybe, like a lot of people, she didn't trust an Irish Republican. Or maybe she thought Rory was full of himself. But that couldn't be further from the truth. He hadn't even wanted the article. John had heard him tell the Pete O'Shea story at a small fund-raiser. When he suggested they run with it in the press, Rory said he wouldn't feel right about it—that he hadn't done anything to help the guy that anybody else wouldn't have done. That was Rory McClain. Humble to a fault.

Rory was a few years older than John, his brother Patrick's age. Patrick couldn't stand the guy either. *He was a bad seed in high school,* Pat said when John first asked if they knew each other. John thought it was more about him stepping into Patrick's territory, or some macho nonsense like that, than it was about Rory himself. It all came to a head on the day of Maeve's confirmation eight months ago, Patrick making a drunken scene. They hadn't spoken since.

At the confirmation, Pat got all bent out of shape when he saw Rory and his wife at the church.

"What's that shithead doing here?" he said.

"Shut up," John whispered. "You know I'm working with him now. Whatever it is, Patrick, keep it to yourself."

During the lunch at John's country club after, Pat got wasted. An old client of John's somehow mistook him for a coworker of Julia's.

"So you're a lawyer too?" the guy said.

Patrick laughed, an obnoxious drunken snort.

"He runs a bar," John said, and if there was a hint of condescension to his tone, then good. Pat deserved it.

His brother looked him in the eye. "We can't all be professional sellouts."

John's client smiled awkwardly and got up to refresh his drink.

"Fuck you," John said under his breath.

Lunch passed in normal order. Soup then salad, then salmon or chicken, whatever a person chose. The waitresses were just pouring the coffee when there was a commotion in the lobby. John made a gesture that everyone should sit tight, and then he left and found Patrick and Rory stumbling out of the men's room.

Chip, the manager of the club, got between them.

"He actually tried to hit him," an old man in a sweater vest said, astonished. He was pointing at Patrick.

Chip set his eyes on Pat. "Sir, that's not the sort of behavior we allow here," he said in a stern voice. "I know you're a guest of Mr. Rafferty, but—"

John saw the red and blue lights flashing through the front windows. Someone had called the police. His cousin Conor was behind him a minute later, walking across the lobby, pushing through the front door. John knew Conor would meet the officers out front, explain that he was a Boston cop himself, that it was just a family thing.

"There's really no need for this," Rory said to Chip. "It was a misunderstanding."

Nora came from the dining room then, with such a crumpled look on her face.

Pat walked out, with Nora on his heels.

"I am so sorry," John said to Rory. "Are you okay? I don't know what to say. I'm mortified."

"Don't worry about it," Rory said, clapping him on the back. "I've got drinkers in my family too. He was just having a bad day. Come on, let's go have some cake."

He never mentioned it to John again, even as the memory made John burn with shame. He had known for a long time that Patrick couldn't stand him. But who did a thing like that? What had he ever done to Patrick to make him want to humiliate his own brother?

Patrick sent Julia roses from Stapleton Floral the next day, and Maeve a crisp hundred-dollar bill tucked into a greeting card. But that had been it for John.

Nora refused to take sides, which John saw as her taking Patrick's side, since he was clearly in the wrong. She said it was unthinkable for brothers to go on this way over something so small. She told John that the McClains were bad people. That he shouldn't have gotten involved with anyone from that family. But Nora had nothing to back it up, just a gut feeling. She had moved away thirty years ago—any petty grudge she held would be ancient history.

Maybe, like Patrick, Rory was a little wild in his day. But like John, he had made something of himself. They had a lot in common. Rory's dad had been a bigwig at the Edison. He died the same year Charlie did. Rory wasn't John's biggest client by a long shot, but his win in November had been an important one, unlikely as it was. Even then, Nora didn't offer congratulations. John thought Patrick might finally apologize: to him, to Rory. But Patrick didn't say a word.

There were plenty of times over the years when the two of them stopped speaking for weeks or months at a stretch. John had once taken the girls to Castle Island for lunch during one of these periods. They parked their car in the lot outside Sullivan's and looked out over Pleasure Bay. Patrick happened to pull in right beside them, a cheap-looking blonde in the passenger seat. Julia didn't even notice him there. John and Patrick sat, eating their hot dogs side by side, never once acknowledging each other's presence.

———

After Julia left to take Maeve to school, Nora called again.

John stood in the driveway in his suit and overcoat, his briefcase on the ground behind him, waiting for the car to arrive. The air was so cold that it almost hurt to breathe. He threw some salt down, careful to avoid his good shoes. He didn't stop to answer the phone. It would be more efficient to call his mother back from the airport, when there was time to kill. While he had these few moments alone, he needed to think about strategy for this afternoon. He wanted to impress upon the client that, while he might be the most expensive option, you got what you paid for. Would they go for that?

He looked down the block, at all the other houses just like his. The first few months they lived here, he had pulled up in front of the wrong one at least once a week.

The development was eight years old. New houses made to look old on streets that hadn't been there a decade ago, with names like Oaken Bucket Road and White Dove Lane. Theirs was called Hidden Valley Drive.

Your street is named after a salad dressing, his sister, Bridget, had said. *You need to own that.*

She was obsessed with the size of the house. *Whatsa matter, John Boy? You couldn't find a bigger one?*

What could he say? Somewhere along the line, a six-bedroom brick colonial had come to seem normal. One time in ten, he might arrive home from work and marvel like a kid. *A mansion,* he would have called it when he was young. His mother still called it that. Two times in ten, the house came into view and his chest clenched, thinking of what would happen if things took one bad turn and he lost it all. His family thought he was rich now, but he and Julia had nothing compared to most of the people in their circle.

Part of him still felt as if he had tricked Julia into thinking he was one thing when in fact he was another. You could make yourself look like anything at college, away from your family. He and Julia were so young then. She was the most incredible woman he'd ever met. He was willing to say anything to have her. Now the fear that spiraled through his head late at night was that one day she would look over and realize he was an imposter.

The fear kept him going. That, and the thought of his parents, who had done so much to give their kids a better life. None of them had done anything to equal the sacrifices Nora and Charlie had made. His mother didn't even have a high school education. His father, just that. Yet somehow they had supported a family of six in a country that wasn't their own. Through means no one had ever understood, they had left Dorchester and moved their children into the biggest, nicest house in Hull when John was eleven years old. Hull wasn't an expensive town, like the one he lived in now. But even so.

For forty years, Charlie held court at Doyle's Hardware Store in Quincy Center. He worked his ass off, painting houses inside and out. In the winter months he hung wallpaper and did odd jobs. But when he wasn't working, he was at Doyle's. People came to ask him which colors they should go with, how to fix a leaky kitchen faucet. Charlie loved being the expert. The guys at Doyle's sent him all their customers. If you bought a can of paint from Mike Doyle, Charlie Rafferty would be the one to put it on your walls, guaranteed. When a Home Depot opened in Quincy, Doyle's was forced to close. Charlie kept working, but without his spot at the shop, he was diminished. He went to Home Depot on a Saturday morning and eavesdropped on the salesmen, then gave the customers his own unsolicited opinion.

For a time, he had wanted John to come into the business with him. Charlie seemed almost disappointed when John got into Georgetown on a scholarship, even as he bragged about it to everyone he met.

John had wanted to work in politics since he was five years old. After he graduated, he got low-level campaign jobs—working for a guy running for Cambridge city councilor, and then the first female treasurer of Rhode Island. He got a rush from helping them win. The late nights, all hands on deck. He believed in the things they said. It meant something, just to be near a person like that, to fetch him a glass of water or call her a car. His father was so damn proud. He'd show up at a speech in a high school gym, fifty miles from home, just to see John in action.

At twenty-eight, he went to work for a Democratic consultant, a guy known for running all of Boston's big races. His boss never let him do much more than go to campaign events out in the boonies. So many events, he barely ever saw his wife.

John wanted so badly to stand out. He worked like a dog. He applied for better jobs. But guys like him were a dime a dozen. It was impossible to compete. He tried to play up the Irish thing, but even a story of two parents off the boat wasn't worth much. The kid in the office next to his at the State House had a mother from Donegal who had lived in Hyde Park for forty years and still spoke only Irish.

When John asked his boss and other older guys in the party why he wasn't rising as fast as he thought he ought to, they clapped him on the back and told him to be patient. *You're one of the most talented young operatives we've got,* they'd say, before passing him over for yet another promotion.

After she finished law school at BU, Julia suggested they start fresh somewhere else. The thought terrified him. In Boston, John ran into someone he knew everywhere he went. He liked that. He knew every shortcut in the city, every detour. He knew the best bars and restaurants, half the cops, and all the politicians. He was stuck here, and he loved it here. He wouldn't know where to begin in some other place.

Julia got hired on at a good firm. She outearned him year after year. She said that was a ridiculous thing for him to be bothered by, but John sensed that she was getting impatient. He wasn't living up to the promise she'd seen in him once. So he started his own shop, a one-man operation with exactly one client—the underdog in a city council race. It was a risk he regretted immediately. But six months after he opened his doors, the day before his thirty-eighth birthday, John was approached by a Republican, a wealthy Mormon businessman, who wanted to be governor of Massachusetts. He said he needed an insider heading up his campaign, someone the establishment would recognize as one of their own so that his differences wouldn't scare them as much.

John asked for two days to think it over. He felt sick about it. A Republican. A Mormon. He didn't believe in half the guy's positions. And what if his big break—the right one—was just around the corner? When he asked his parents what they thought, Charlie was horrified. Nora, when pressed, said, "What does it matter? They're all crooked anyhow."

But the money could not be beat. And life was disappointing sometimes. You moved on, you took a different course. Or else you could end up like his brothers, rehashing the same old stories, wasting your life on what-ifs. John said yes. He tried not to think about how many other guys had turned down the offer first.

His risk paid off. His man won, against the odds. Soon enough, he was working for a governor. The organization had strong business ties, tons of money, deep loyalty. Based on one glowing magazine profile, written by a friend of a friend of Julia's and denounced by half his peers, John got a reputation for making GOP miracles happen in blue states. He was approached by Republicans from around the country who wanted help with House and Senate runs. By thirty-nine, he was one of the highest-paid consultants in the business. It wasn't Wall Street money, but it was more than he had ever made before.

It only got better when the governor decided to run for president, putting them both on a national stage. Once, John had had to sell the guy to Massachusetts as a Republican who leaned left on social issues. Now, he was the Irish Catholic who traveled the country putting religious right-wingers at ease, about the Mormonism, the liberal positions on gay marriage and abortion. John's presence, his very name, seemed to say that he wouldn't stand behind someone who wasn't just as conservative as they were.

John changed their minds. He got five former ambassadors to the Vatican to back his guy publicly over two Catholic rivals ahead of the New Hampshire primary. It felt good to be useful. In the end, the governor was the party's runner-up for the highest office in the nation. They were already laying the groundwork for a 2012 run.

John had a staff of fifteen people. Gorgeous, massive offices in Government Center. Most of his revenue came from lobbying now, and a growing list of corporate clients. He knew there were those who said it was all one big conflict of interest, but he didn't let it bother him. His only regret was that his father hadn't lived long enough to see him reach the top.

If he ever felt a twinge of doubt, he'd write a big check to Bridget's dog shelter, or to the Home for Little Wanderers. John couldn't stop now, even if he wanted to. Julia had grown up with money. When they were young and had none, she swore it didn't matter. But the better they both did, the more extravagant her tastes became. Her handbag from some no-name boutique was no longer good enough. She needed Chanel. They got upgraded to first class on one flight, and afterward coach seemed like an unfathomable nightmare.

They sent Maeve to private school and horseback riding lessons. She'd been getting hundred-dollar haircuts on Newbury Street since she was nine. They had a beach house now. Both houses had to be decorated with antiques, where once mass-produced Crate and Barrel stuff had sufficed. Meanwhile, his mother thought even Crate and Barrel was a hideous rip-off. "I have lots of nice pieces in the cellar, you should take a look," she said to Julia whenever Julia told her they had gotten something new. Which was often. She had a habit of changing her mind about furniture, casting off perfectly good things to his sister or a neighbor down the block.

To Julia's credit, she had come to understand that his mother didn't appreciate aesthetics, only a bargain. When Nora asked where they'd gotten a ten-thousand-dollar Georgian campaign desk, Julia said without blinking that she'd bought it at Pottery Barn.

He sometimes thought that if his mother saw his credit card bills, his mortgage, she might lose the power of speech. John was spending every penny he earned, saving next to nothing. It was the opposite of what he'd been raised to do.

He named his company Miltown Strategies after his parents' hometown, an homage to the American immigrant story. His mother was not impressed. *People won't know how to spell it, John. Nobody's ever heard of that place. You should call it something catchier.*

Nothing he could do was ever good enough for Nora. Sometimes it seemed like she had barely registered John's existence, even if—as his wife liked to remind him—his entire life had been shaped by the quest for her approval. His stock had only gone up when he gave her a grandchild.

She was far more proud of Patrick's bar than of anything John had done.

It had always been Pat's big dream to open a place of his own on Dorchester Avenue. Because one more dive bar was just what Dorchester needed. He talked about it all the time back when he was working on the loading dock at the Conley Terminal in Southie, loading and unloading shipping containers—they were filled with seafood one day, beer the next, scrap metal after that. It seemed like the bar idea would never go any further than fantasy until Patrick caught what he referred to as his big break.

While he was working, a line snapped. A crate fell to the ground, severing two of his toes. Had Patrick been a couple of inches farther to the left, it might have taken off his whole foot. A few inches farther than that and he would have been a dead man. But, painful though it was, he could live without a couple of toes, especially when he was awarded two hundred grand for his troubles. Pat used the money to open the bar.

Nora acted like it was some great accomplishment, when Pat had only gotten his wish because of a stupid lawsuit. He wasn't paying attention. He was probably drunk on the job. Now he had his best friend and his little brother running the bar. Fergie and Brian. The Dream Team.

The black town car pulled up right on time.

John saw the driver make a move to get out and open the door for him. He gestured for the guy to stay where he was.

"I've got it," he said.

He slid into the warm backseat. "How's it going, buddy?"

The driver just nodded in reply.

John saw himself through this guy's eyes and felt the need to say something. Whenever he hired anyone to do some menial job, he had a pathological desire to let that person know that the two of them weren't so different, that John was well aware of it. *My uncle Lawrence used to drive a bus,* he thought of saying. *Then later, he became a chauffeur. Did he ever have crazy stories. I bet you've had some colorful characters sitting back here, am I right?*

There were two small bottles of water tucked into the seat-back pocket. He took hold of one instead of speaking, unscrewed the cap.

His phone rang again.

"My mother," he said to the driver.

John picked up, prepared for her to say that she had seen his name in the paper, prepared to downplay his own pride now that he had hers.

"Where have you been?" Nora said. She sounded frazzled. "I've been trying and trying, you and Bridget both. And Julia. It just rings. There's been an accident, John."

"Oh God. Are you okay?"

"Not me," she said. "Patrick."

He stiffened. "Is he okay?"

"John. He's dead."

"Go back," John said to the driver before he replied. "Turn the car around."

8

BRIDGET DIDN'T NOTICE THAT her mother had called that morning because she was in bed with Natalie, and then walking the dog with Natalie, stopping for coffee along the way. She brushed her teeth at the sink while Natalie showered and lingered in the bathroom as it filled with steam, carrying on a conversation about Natalie's boss, taking in the clean soapy scent of her shampoo, pulling back the curtain for a kiss. They ate Greek yogurt and strawberries in the kitchen. In the background, a BBC reporter's silvery accent told of atrocities in faraway places they might or might not be able to locate on a map.

Bridget was dressed for the day in jeans, sneakers, a navy blue crew-neck sweater. The same uniform she'd been wearing since the second grade. Natalie wore black high-heeled boots that ended just below the knee, a fitted grey dress, and a long black coat open over the top. Red lipstick, a gauzy silk scarf. Her red hair hung to her shoulders.

They looked always like characters in two different plays. When they went out on a Saturday night, Bridget spent ten, fifteen minutes max ironing a shirt, running a comb through her short brown hair. She would be dressed and on the couch with enough time to watch four innings of baseball before Natalie was ready to go.

They said their good-byes at the door now.

"Love you."

"See you tonight."

After Natalie was gone, Bridget drank one more cup of coffee alone. Sunlight flooded the windows and the hardwood floors, giving the illusion that it wasn't bone cold outside. The apartment had been Natalie's first. She went with the place. Bridget saw her in the careful details. Framed abstract watercolors on the walls, purchased from a friend with a gallery in Williamsburg. Different ceramic bowls in the cupboards for pasta, yogurt, cereal. A larger bowl at the center of the kitchen table with nothing in it, strictly decorative. A pair of antique brass bookends shaped like hound dogs sat on the mantel, a gift from Natalie to Bridget on the occasion of the shelter's tenth anniversary.

Until she moved in three years ago, Bridget had lived like a bachelor. Her brothers joked that she had taken a vow of poverty. She didn't care much about things. She had nicer-than-expected mismatched furniture, passed along whenever her sister-in-law redecorated. But her prized possessions were an old Trek bicycle, two milk crates full of records, and every Celtics game of the 1986 season recorded on VHS.

Her life then had consisted of a date here and there, a short-lived love affair once in a while. Visits to her mother in Boston at the holidays. Work, mostly. At home, it was just Bridget and Rocco, an aging pit bull, together in a dim apartment. Content to be a couple of old grumps forever, until Natalie came along and let in the light.

She tried now to picture a high chair at the end of the table, a baby's toys strewn across the rug. A time when leisurely mornings like this one would be a thing of the past.

In advance of her thirty-fifth birthday, Natalie had announced that the gift she wanted most was not jewelry or tickets to a Broadway show, but a baby.

Bridget had never thought of herself as particularly maternal. She couldn't muster much enthusiasm for baby pictures, or for the fact that one more human being had learned to correctly identify the letter *D*. When she thought about motherhood, she thought of her own mother and her aunts, who, when she was young, liked to sit around on someone's front porch on summer nights, playing cards, smoking, and drinking Canadian Club. They had always seemed a bit bored, dissatisfied by their children, yet later, all they spoke about was the desire for grandkids. They had sacrificed everything. The least their daughters could do to pay them back was to suffer in a similar fashion.

Bridget still wasn't entirely convinced. But she believed that Natalie deserved to be a mother, if that's what she wanted. And, to her surprise, at forty-four, she found that the idea of having a baby with Natalie excited her at least as much as it terrified her.

A year had passed since Natalie first raised the issue. It sometimes felt like since then, they had spoken of nothing else.

Bridget thought they might consider adopting, like her brother John had. But Natalie had given it far more thought. She explained to Bridget that gay couples were banned from adopting from most foreign countries and several states. And anyway, she wanted a child who shared her blood. She wanted to give birth, for reasons Bridget could not fathom.

Natalie knew which baby names she liked, and she had found a top-rated clinic where she would be inseminated. They had chosen a donor, though they had yet to actually purchase his sperm. They called him by his official profile name: International Archeologist. He was five foot eleven, 175 pounds, with blond hair and blue eyes.

Hobbies: The Brazilian martial art of capoeira, running twenty-two miles per week

Ancestry: Swedish

Donor look-alike: Paul Bettany, Paul Newman ("But those two look nothing alike," Bridget said.)

Personality: His positive outlook is contagious!

Bridget wondered what was to stop the sperm bank from telling them all this when in fact the guy was a short, depressive high school dropout who worked at Burger King. She kept the thought to herself.

It had taken them months to decide. Night after night they lay in bed, scrolling through profiles. You could go by any attribute. Eye color, blood type, even the sound of a man's voice, recorded in short audio clips, or the age of his oldest living relative. They grew drunk with choosiness.

"He has to have gotten at least a fourteen-eighty on the SATs," Natalie said once.

"You realize if you'd used that criterion to find a partner, I'd be out," Bridget said. "By a lot."

"Good golfer!" Natalie declared at some point. And at another: "Disqualified! His favorite animal is the cat."

Bridget refused to short-list anyone with a sleazy profile name. There was a So Smooth. A Dr. Feelgood. One was called I'll Just Have Water ("Translation: alcoholic," she said).

She wondered what compelled a young man to take this particular route to making extra cash. How many of them would think about it differently in ten or fifteen years? One night, she lay awake thinking about her youngest brother, Brian. All the debt he'd racked up in his twenties, following a dream that didn't pan out, living on the road for so much of every year, and now living at home with their mother because, she assumed, he was broke. She texted him: *If you ever need a few extra bucks, ask me, okay? Don't do anything stupid.*

Brian just replied: *?*

When they finally settled on a donor, Natalie's credit card in her hand, fingers poised over the keyboard to make the purchase, Bridget panicked. Though it should have been obvious much sooner, that was the first time she realized she would have to tell her mother.

Her brain tried to find a way around it. She pictured herself arriving home at Christmas with an infant in a carrier.

Whose baby is that, Bridget?

Who? Him? Oh, never mind.

"Before we buy the sperm, I feel like I should warn my mother that this is coming," she said.

Natalie, whose parents had known for ages, blinked. "Oh. Okay."

Three months had gone by, and still Bridget had not done it. A few weeks ago, when they were home for Christmas, she tried. Natalie and Julia planned a lunch at the Four Seasons, making the whole thing seem like Bridget's idea. But it was their kind of place, not hers.

When Bridget invited her mother, Nora seemed skeptical. "Just the two of us? Why on earth would we go there?"

"I want to do something nice for you, that's all."

Neither of them was comfortable. Bridget wore an old pair of black dress pants and a black silk blouse. She looked like an aging cocktail waitress. She could barely breathe. The food was too precious, the room too stuffy. When the waiter brought out a bottle of champagne after the plates had been cleared, Nora looked around as if the place were bugged.

"What in God's name?" she said.

The first time Bridget brought Natalie home, her mother said, "Natalie, you have such style. You should take our Bridget shopping."

It occurred to her then that Natalie was the daughter her mother was praying for all those nights when they were kids, the whole family kneeling in front of the sofa, saying the rosary as they listened to Cardinal Cushing on the radio.

Nora was forever trying to improve upon Bridget, her criticisms most often wrapped up in what she considered compliments.

You've such a nice face. Why won't you do anything with it?

To leave those cheekbones bare is a sin against God.

Do you know how pretty you'd look if—

If you'd just tweeze your eyebrows. Grow out your hair. Put on some lipstick, Bridget, it won't kill you.

At the party she threw every year on Christmas Eve, Nora introduced Natalie to cousins and neighbors as "Bridget's friend from New York" or else, on a few unfortunate occasions, "Bridget's roommate."

"Your mother cannot possibly think that at your age, you just decided to get a roommate for the hell of it," Natalie had said on one of those nights, tucked into Bridget's childhood bed beside her, an air mattress made up and untouched on the floor.

"I think that's what she wants to believe," Bridget said.

"So she doesn't know you're gay."

"Maybe it has nothing to do with gay. Maybe she just thinks you're way out of my league and can't imagine why you'd live with me other than to go halfsies on the rent."

She pulled Natalie into her arms, hoping the joke would smooth over the pain in it. Sometimes Bridget thought Nora knew and chose to ignore it. Her mother had a knack for blocking out what she didn't want to be true. Other times, she thought Nora truly didn't know, even though Bridget had told her.

Her sophomore year at UMass, she had sex with a woman for the first time. It happened the night before she went home for Thanksgiving, and it was all Bridget could think about—reliving those moments as she passed the cranberry sauce and watched the Macy's parade on TV and talked about football with her father.

She had determined to come out to her mother on that trip. After dinner, while everyone else was napping, and Nora scooped the leftover vegetables into a giant serving tray so that they looked like the Irish flag—a thick stripe of green beans, then mashed potatoes, then squash—

Bridget said, "Mom, I have to tell you something. I don't want you to be upset." Nora looked up at her, a spoonful of potatoes suspended midair.

"I'm mostly seeing women these days. I think that's where I'm headed."

Bridget bit the inside of her cheek as she waited for her mother to react, but Nora's expression was unreadable.

"Do you understand?" Bridget asked after a long silence.

"Yes," her mother said.

"You do?"

"Yes."

Nora didn't add *I love you*, but she never said that.

Bridget couldn't believe it had been so easy. She felt a huge weight lifted from her shoulders until Christmas a month later, when Nora said, "Bridget, Tommy Delaney's home! You should go down the hill and see him. Eileen says he still has a thing for you."

When she was a freshman in high school, she had tried to date one guy, the only guy who asked. A kid from the neighborhood. The son of her mother's friend. They went out for maybe a month. Nora had never let it go.

Bridget looked at her mother with wide eyes.

"What?" Nora said. "I'm not saying you should marry him. Just—a winter romance might be nice."

The morning rushed by, like every morning at the shelter, a haze of routine and surprise. Bridget let in the three kids who were scheduled to volunteer, hosing down crates, filling water bowls, walking dogs. She only ever hired boys who were scrappy and strong, but sweet. Boys who reminded her of her brothers when they were young.

She and her assistant director, Michelle, traded off early mornings. Michelle had already been here at six and was off now to meet with a prospective donor, the kind of thing Bridget hated to do. They made an ideal pair—Michelle was good at talking to people who loved animals. Bridget was good at talking to the animals themselves.

A cacophonous chorus of barks and cries swelled when she opened the door into the back. She greeted all eighteen dogs, nine cats, two lizards by name. This afternoon, she would take three Cane Corsos to the vet to be fixed. She regarded them now, feeling sorry for them, for what they didn't know about their own fate. She made a mental note to buy them some sliced turkey from the bodega at the corner, a small consolation.

At nine-thirty, she got a call from a buddy at the police department. A hoarding situation in the Bronx, thirty-nine guinea pigs. Would she take them? Yes, she would take them. She had never turned an animal away if she had the room. He knew this, they all did. That's why they called her first.

It wasn't until she was alone in her office, just before ten, that Bridget dug her cell phone out of her coat pocket and saw that her mother had called seven times. John had texted too: *Call me ASAP.*

"Oh," she said. "Shit."

Bridget held her breath as she dialed. She knew how this went. She had nineteen first cousins. Ten aunts and uncles. There were so many of them in the family that when tragedy occurred, instead of being shocked by it, the bigger shock was that somehow all of them managed to make it through so many days and years unscathed. Then you got a phone call, and the world took on a different shape.

She braced herself to hear Nora say that some elderly relative had died in her sleep, though she held out hope that this was one of those calls from her mother that had the whiff of somber urgency but was in fact just a heads-up that Macy's was having a white sale.

From Nora's hello, the weariness in it, Bridget could tell the news was bad.

"Is it Aunt Kitty?" she said, wanting her mother to spit it out, whatever it was.

"It's Patrick," Nora said.

Patrick. Bridget's chest felt like it would burst.

Never in a million years.

Nora was speaking, but to Bridget, the words came through in a blur. *He swerved into a wall. He died on impact. He didn't suffer.*

Already, the consolations.

Her legs shook. She leaned against a chair to steady herself, then decided just to let her body slip to the floor.

Even as her mother said that the wake would be tomorrow afternoon, with the funeral to follow on Wednesday morning, Bridget's mind grasped for a loophole. It had to be a mistake, a joke. It couldn't be true that there was nothing they could do to save him.

Her teeth chattered. Her body was in revolt.

"I'll be there in a few hours," she said.

"Why don't you come in the morning?" Nora said. "It's not a good idea to drive so far after you've had a shock to the system like this."

Her voice was cool, calm, as if she weren't part of the tragedy, just a helpful travel advisor.

"Are you sure you want to do the wake so soon?" Bridget said. "You could wait a day or two. Give yourself a chance to—"

"I need to get it behind me," Nora said.

"I understand. How can I help? What do you need?"

"I need to hang up now. I have to go to Patrick's and find his suit."

"By yourself?"

"Of course."

Bridget hesitated, wanting to ask if that was a good idea.

"It's nothing," Nora said, before she could get the words out.

She always acted like an emotion expressed was the most dangerous thing in the world. When Bridget fell down as a child, her mother would pull her to her feet and tell her she was fine. Willing it to be so. Ignoring whatever pain she might be in, as if not mentioning it would make it just dissolve. In adulthood, the same impulse took on different forms.

Her father's death too had come out of nowhere. A fast-moving cancer, the reality of which had yet to sink in for any of them by the time Charlie died. Bridget remembered Nora, calmly walking arm in arm with Brian and Patrick into the funeral home, instructing them all not to cry.

At home, Bridget tried to pack. But she couldn't seem to remember how. She found herself pulling one item of clothing after another from the drawers, an indiscriminate pile forming on the bed. She wanted to call John, and yet somehow she knew that once she heard his voice, this would be real. So she went and sat on the sofa and stared at the wall instead, the dog lying at her feet. After a while, she got up and made tea because it was what her people did at times like this. At the last second, she added bourbon instead of milk.

Bridget called Natalie twice but couldn't get through. She didn't leave a message. It wasn't the sort of thing you could say on someone's voice mail. And if she was being honest, she wanted to be alone. She would hate for Natalie to come in now and hug her, say that everything would be all right. She was her mother's daughter, she supposed. Prickly when she was most in need of love.

She pictured Patrick's body on a gurney somewhere. She could not get the image from her mind.

Her brother had been a drinker. But then, so were half the people they knew. They were supposed to accept that what he did when he was drinking didn't count. It wasn't real behavior. When he was young, Pat made stupid mistakes all the time. He got into fights. He drove like a maniac. But, for the most part, she had thought all that was behind him.

Bridget petted Rocco's neck. His white fur was gone in patches, his eyes clouded over with a milky glaze, close to blind. Once, he was so strong he could pull her to the ground if she wasn't careful. Now sometimes Bridget had to carry him up the three flights to the apartment.

When John and Julia's daughter, Maeve, was six, she was terrified of him. Bridget brought the dog home to Boston one weekend. During a cookout in her parents' backyard, she held Maeve's tiny hand and had her stroke Rocco's back. "People sometimes do bad things to dogs like him, but he's sweet, see? It's not his fault."

Maeve nodded earnestly. Nora stood by, with a wide-eyed expression that said perhaps this was true, but every so often you read about one of these dogs eating a child's face off, and if it happened to her only grand-daughter, she would have Bridget killed.

Patrick was there, a beer in hand. He laughed. "Calm down, Ma," he said.

No one else would dare talk to Nora like that. But Patrick could do no wrong in her eyes.

The four Rafferty children had their roles. Patrick, the wild one, their mother's favorite. John, the overachiever, their father's favorite. Bridget, the girl (a girl being its own thing, no additional personality traits needed or noticed, except that she was never quite girly enough). Brian, the baby.

When he was born, Bridget was ten. Everyone assumed she'd want nothing more than to push Brian around in a stroller all day, pretending he was hers. But Bridget would rather be off, playing at the beach, riding her bike. She was forever bringing wounded animals home—pregnant cats and garter snakes and birds with broken wings.

It was Patrick, at sixteen, who loved Brian most.

Bridget imagined herself, John, and Brian in the front pew at Saint Ann's in two days' time. Heads bowed as a priest sprinkled holy water on a wooden box. Patrick inside, when he should be there beside them.

Patrick hated priests. When they were younger and went to Mass as a family, Charlie gave them each a dollar for the collection plate. Pat pretended to drop his in the basket while actually crumpling it into his palm and up his sleeve. He said the priests didn't deserve the money.

"They spend it all on booze," he said. "And their beach house. Father Riordan drives a Cadillac. Vow of poverty, my ass. That's what Fergie says."

Years later, Patrick told Bridget more. About what a priest had done to his friend when he was a kid. They were at Patrick's bar, commiserating about the church, the two of them the family's only defectors. Pat gestured to his buddy pouring a beer from the tap.

"Fergie went through hell," he said. "His mother didn't do a thing about it. The kid can do no wrong after that as far as I'm concerned."

Pat wouldn't say which priest it was. Fergie had sworn him to secrecy. But Bridget thought she knew. Her brother was kicked out of Saint Ignatius Prep at the end of his freshman year for spitting in the face of the principal, Father McDonald. An episode so astonishing that they were forbidden from ever mentioning it at home.

He never went back to church as an adult. But now that he was gone, it was all in Nora's hands. And so a priest would be the one to usher Patrick from this world.

John called just after two.

"Jesus fucking Christ," he said, instead of hello.

"I can't understand it," Bridget said. "I just cannot comprehend. He drove into a wall and that's it, he's gone? What happened? Is it possible there was something wrong with the car? Has anyone looked into that?"

"Bridget. He was drinking. He died doing what he loved."

"That's not funny," she said.

"I'm serious. That asshole never cared what he put Mom through. Or any of us for that matter. Now we get to pick up the pieces."

"You can't call a dead person an asshole."

She knew he didn't mean it. This was just how he got. Mad first, and then sad. He would only say it to her. Not to Julia. Never to Nora.

"How are we supposed to explain this to Maeve?" he said. "We're having a family meeting tonight. Well, we were going to have one anyway but not on this topic. I'm supposed to be in Chicago right now, and instead I'm dealing with the fact that Mom wants me to give a eulogy for a guy I couldn't stand."

He would do it. John was the one who did things like give eulogies, because Bridget was too awkward and Brian, much as he worshipped Patrick, would sooner jump in the coffin with him than address a crowd.

Bridget and John were born a year apart. They had always gone together, even though they were as different as two people could be. As kids, their conversations could turn from light and meaningless into something charged in an instant. Before anyone noticed what had happened, they'd be down on the kitchen floor wrestling, rolling around, kicking each other until they cried or laughed or Nora started hitting them with a broom, as if she could sweep away the whole ugly mess.

Bridget knew John in a way no one else did. He was rich as Croesus now, with a new McMansion in Weston and a new personality to match. But she could still call him out the same as ever.

When they were kids and any of the local politicians shook hands at a parade, John wasn't at all afraid to say, "I want to be like you one day, sir." The eyes on Billy Bulger or Joe Moakley, even the mayor, Kevin White, would just light up. "Is that right?" they'd say.

In this manner, he'd gotten himself tours of the State House, hundreds of buttons and personal letters, visits to his third grade class. He grew addicted to the attention.

Bridget wondered what all those good Irish Democrats thought when John made a fortune helping the other side.

She was shocked when he told her over dinner seven years back that after a decade and a half spent toiling for Democrats, he had taken a great job, a killer job, working for a Republican.

"Honestly, they're all the same," John said. "The older I get, the more I see that. I want to work for the guy who respects me, who will put my talents to use."

Bridget didn't say anything. She was thinking that she had read somewhere once that when a person began a sentence with the word *honestly*, it usually meant he was lying.

"It doesn't mean I'm a Republican," John went on. "If you work at a shoe store, does it mean you're a shoe?"

Bridget nearly choked on her beer. "You did not just make that comparison."

His business was booming now, conservative clients full of optimism, overpaying him, as if the recent election had never occurred. She wondered if, seeing history made, her brother regretted his choice. She wondered what it was about John that allowed him to make it in the first place.

"What am I supposed to say about Patrick?" John said now. "We haven't even spoken in eight months."

Sometimes Bridget forgot. Her two older brothers were often at war, but they were oddly fine in each other's company. You didn't notice that they never addressed each other directly unless you looked closely. At family gatherings, everyone was speaking so fast, talking over one another, finishing stories someone else had started, contradicting the endings every time: *"That wasn't it! What he said was—"* They all laughed before the teller could finish, knowing what was to come. In a good-natured way, almost as terms of endearment, they called each other *moron, idiot, simpleton, homo.* Words were nothing to them.

"How's Brian handling all this?" she said. "I need to call him."

"Don't know. He went AWOL after Mom told him. Just ran straight out of the house, apparently."

"Jesus. He must have been with Patrick last night, right? They were probably both working at the bar."

"And Brian's probably back there now," John said. "I wouldn't worry. Though Mom is freaking out about it, of course."

"Have you seen her?"

"Yeah, we're at her house now. Julia and I brought Maeve over. We brought her some lunch. Just subs from Victoria's. She doesn't want to eat."

Bridget pictured Nora, despondent at her kitchen table.

"Talk about when we were young," she said. Nora would like that best.

"What?"

"The eulogy. Tell the old stories. Tell the one about the lobsters."

During the Blizzard of '78, when all the stores were shut and the power was out, Patrick had walked in out of the snow with an armful of lobsters that had washed up on the beach, his boots dripping water onto the kitchen floor. His handsome face, his black hair, that smile. The whole family applauded. They had a feast that night and the next, keeping the lobsters cold out in a snowdrift by the porch.

When Natalie finally called her back, she sounded distracted, busy. "Sorry, sweetie, I've been in meetings and I had that lunch with my boss. What's up?"

It was like she was calling from some other realm. Meetings and lunches still meant something. Ordinary time hadn't stopped. Part of Bridget wanted to protect her, let her stay there.

When she told her what had happened, Natalie said, "I'm coming straight home."

As soon as she walked in the door, she pulled Bridget to her, the smell of the cold still in her hair. Bridget collapsed in her arms, wishing now that she had gotten Natalie there sooner.

Natalie rushed into the bedroom without taking off her coat, then popped her head out.

"It will take me five minutes to pack a bag. Just give me five minutes and we'll go."

Bridget followed her.

"My mother said to drive up in the morning."

"But shouldn't we be doing something? Doesn't she need help?"

"You know my mother."

Nora never trusted anyone but herself to do anything domestic, as if it would dim her power somehow. If she died tomorrow, none of them would have the slightest idea how to cook a roast or where she kept the vacuum.

At Christmas a few weeks earlier, Bridget sat at the kitchen table drinking a mimosa as Nora made the gravy. She had thought to herself, *Pay attention. You might need to know how to do this someday.* But she hadn't watched. Instead, she wandered into the living room, where her brothers were watching football. She sank down into the quicksand of the couch cushions and ate cheese and crackers and onion dip until she felt too full to go near the actual meal and had to be pulled up by Brian and Patrick when Nora called, "Dinner!"

Bridget realized now that that was the last time she would ever see Patrick alive.

Natalie packed for them both. She ordered Thai food from Bridget's favorite spot, but neither of them ate.

They put the TV on, just for background noise, and huddled together on the couch. Over and over again, Bridget had the feeling of forgetting for a moment and then the terrible recollection of what had happened, where they were.

While they sat there, noodles growing cold on the coffee table, her eye kept landing on their bags in the corner. A thought crept in.

"I know I promised I'd tell my mother about the baby thing the next time I saw her, but you know I can't tell her now, right?" Bridget said. "Now isn't the time to break the news."

"Sure," Natalie said. But then she added, "It's not cancer, you know. It's good news, a baby. It might actually make your mother happy once she has time to get used to the idea. She must want you to be happy. I'm sure when all is said and done, she'd rather you just be honest."

Happiness was not a state to which Nora had ever aspired. She had always tried to impress upon her children that she and her cohort had never worried about anything so trivial as whether or not they were happy.

And honesty. Bridget wanted to say that this was Nora they were talking about. Nora, who, when the conversation arose about how to talk to Maeve about her adoption, had said to John and Julia, "Why do you have to tell her at all? I had a friend from church with two adopted sons and they never had an inkling."

"Well, Maeve is from China, Mom, so I think she'll have an inkling," John had said.

Natalie looked prepared to dig in further now, but then she said, "I get it. I understand."

"You do?"

"Yes. Take all the time you need. Although—we could just order the sperm so we know we have it."

"No," Bridget said. "I should tell her first."

Natalie tried to hide her annoyance. "Why?"

"I don't know. I just feel like I should."

"And you're sure this isn't your way of giving yourself an escape hatch?"

"Of course not!" Bridget said, when in fact she wasn't sure of it at all.

Natalie was her family now, the person she most needed to protect. But Nora. Bridget worried about her too. She was seventy-three, which wasn't that old anymore. But Nora seemed old. Bridget had friends whose parents went on bicycle tours of Europe and posted their photos online. Nora refused even to email. She said she was past the point where any of that would make sense to her. A foreign language. What would she make of a baby shared by two women, the father a stranger whose face they had only ever seen in an old childhood photograph posted online?

This wasn't a reality Bridget had imagined for herself. She hadn't prepared her mother for it.

Natalie didn't understand that Nora's love came with strings. That her faith told her someone like Bridget, like Natalie, was less than, just by virtue of who she was. Their child? What would Nora say about that? In the eyes of the Catholic Church, birth could be a miracle or a sin, depending.

Bridget and Natalie were almost a decade apart. It made a difference. Natalie was born into an age of acceptance. She hadn't quite processed that when it came to being gay, Bridget's memories were not those of a gentle sexual awakening at an indulgent women's college, fuzzy heart-to-hearts with one's understanding parents. Repression was the order of the day in her house growing up. Nora and Charlie slept in separate beds. Privately, Bridget and John referred to them as Bert and Ernie. She believed it was entirely possible that they had only had sex four times, each encounter resulting in a child.

Every year on her mother's birthday, her father gave her a drugstore greeting card with two words written on it—her name at the top and his at the bottom. They had never been the type to argue, but Bridget's parents existed in separate worlds. She was certain they had never gazed into each other's eyes discussing their fears and dreams. *Nora*—Happy Birthday!—*Charlie*.

Bridget remembered how, for a few years while she was in grade school, there were two women living together in a house at the end of Sydney Street. They kept the lawn up beautifully, planted peonies, and sat on the porch on summer nights like everyone else in the neighborhood. Her parents were friendly with them, said hello. But once, passing by in the car, Charlie said under his breath, "Lesbians." Bridget hadn't heard the word before. She could tell it was something shameful, disgusting.

"I thought they were sisters," Nora said, and Charlie threw his head back and laughed.

Bridget was seven at the time, and in love with her best friend, Molly Quinn, though she didn't think of it as romantic love, particularly. She was just infatuated with Molly—the long brown hair that she let Bridget brush after school, the smell of Ivory soap on her skin. When Bridget said once that she was going to marry Molly, Nora looked at her, stricken, and then turned away, pretending it hadn't happened.

Two decades later, on Saint Patrick's Day 1992, Bridget was visiting Boston for the parade and the annual party thrown by her aunt Babs and uncle Lawrence, as she did every year. She was twenty-eight years old. That year, a group of out gay people wanted to march. It had caused an uproar, gone all the way to the state supreme court. The group was granted access in the end. When they went by, people hurled beer cans and smoke bombs. A huge guy in a white Irish knit sweater held a child, wearing a smaller version. Minutes earlier, the guy had been tearing up as he sang "The Unicorn" to his son. Now he screamed, "Quarantine the queers!" Others joined in. An old lady with a green carnation corsage pinned to her coat held a sign that read AIDS CURES GAYS.

Bridget's relatives weren't the people shouting or throwing rocks. They were the ones standing across the street from them, doing nothing about it.

As a child, Bridget loved the Catholic Church. She was jealous that John got to be an altar boy. That he sometimes got to skip school to work a funeral. Funerals were better than weddings, he said. You got the best tips. Bridget idolized the priests and imagined that she herself might become one someday, though she couldn't say how. But in time, this had changed.

When a priest on the news that night said that to allow gays to march was to condone immorality, she couldn't shake her bitterness—that this institution that had ruled their lives, these men with all their perversions stood in judgment of her. That after so many years in their presence, she stood in judgment of herself.

Her mother was nodding at the TV.

There and then, Bridget vowed that she would never force the issue with her. She wasn't a rebel. Deep down she wanted to please Nora. She wanted to be known by her too, but that mattered less.

Now Bridget's life was different, and soon this would have to change. She couldn't lose Natalie. That was a fear she wouldn't even entertain. But with Patrick gone, her mother shattered, how would she find the words?

Patrick had been the first in the family to meet Natalie. They liked each other from the start. They were an unlikely pair—her brother, still clinging to the Boston tough guy thing, a guy who ran a bar and had never been to college. And Natalie, who graduated from Barnard, who did Pilates three times a week, who spoke in the calmest tone, the voice of someone who actually meditated rather than just thinking about it from time to time. But they got along, bonded over the Red Sox and a shared love of Frank Sinatra.

Bridget hadn't introduced them on purpose. On a Friday night in October 2004, when the Red Sox had just won the World Series, she and Natalie got drunk on margaritas at a Mexican restaurant in Midtown. They had only been dating a few months, but already it felt serious. Sometime around nine, Natalie joked that they were so close to Port Authority they should probably jump on a bus up to Boston for the victory parade. By two a.m. the joke had turned into a plan.

As they sped up 95, the bus full of happy, drunken idiots like them, Bridget thought of how she had never been to Boston without telling her family. There was something liberating about it.

They took a long walk at dawn, then went for breakfast. An hour later, coming out of a diner by South Station, they ran smack into Patrick and Brian and their cousins Matty and Sean. She remembered how the back of her hand was touching the back of Natalie's. The look on Natalie's face when she pulled away.

They chatted with the guys, who, it turned out, had the same plan in mind. All five of them went to a bar by Government Center for early morning beers.

When Natalie was in the bathroom, Pat said, "Awesome girl. Cute too. Ma know about her?"

"No."

"Have you ever thought of telling her?"

"Patrick, I've thought about it my whole life."

"Tell her, then. Believe me, Bridget. She has secrets of her own worse than that."

9

YEARS AGO, Pat hung a clock over the bar. An illuminated glass dome the size of a beach ball. On the hour, the Budweiser Clydesdales marched in a circle around the edge.

They mocked him for it at the time.

"What?" Pat said. "The guy gave me a great deal." And Fergie said, "The only deal that makes sense is if he paid you to take that thing off his hands."

Brian watched now as the Clydesdales made their move and the clock struck one in the morning. He and Fergie had decided to stay open, to honor his brother. The bar filled up early, people standing shoulder to shoulder, wanting to pay their respects. Out front, someone left a tall candle flickering at the curb. There were several bunches of flowers too. Drugstore roses, the petals tinged brown. Tulips in clear plastic sleeves.

It was closing time, but Brian and Fergie didn't tell anyone to go. The bar was boiling hot, even with the door cracked, even in January. Men's long sleeves were rolled to the elbow, and women's hair pulled up off their necks. Sweat pooled at their temples. Brian tried to float on top of the voices. Whenever someone offered to buy him a shot, he threw it back like it was the antidote that would save his life. Still, he couldn't keep the thoughts from rushing in.

He came out from behind the bar now and made his way toward Patrick's office, pushing through the crowd. He'd been working up the courage to go back there all night. As soon as he was in, Brian closed the door. He switched on the light, looked around. He was looking for a note, even as he hoped there wouldn't be one. A note would settle it. There was an old slip of paper taped to the desk. Printed with the last lines of the Act of Contrition: *I firmly resolve, with the help of Thy grace, to sin no more and to avoid the near occasions of sin.*

It was a joke. That was what Fergie called Patrick sometimes: the Near Occasion of Sin.

There was a bottle of whiskey with only a thin coating of brown liquid left at the bottom. Brian picked it up, turned it over in his hands.

Yesterday had seemed like nothing special. But now the memory of it would be more important than any other day. Patrick still here. Nora not yet transformed into whatever her grief would make of her. Brian should have insisted on driving his brother home or forced him into a cab. He would regret it for the rest of his life. That was why he'd run off when his mother told him the news. He couldn't face her.

How could a drive Pat had made a million times before end like that? How could someone so entirely alive just disappear? Brian's mind hadn't yet accepted it as fact.

He closed his eyes, determined to focus. He would go over every second of Patrick's last day, find the signs, as if he might change the outcome if he got it right.

"Start at the beginning," he said out loud.

Fergie opened up on Sundays. Brian wasn't due at the bar until six.

He woke with vague plans to do a few chores for his mother—she had been after him to dust the ceiling fans and put the boxes of Christmas decorations back in the attic. He assumed the smell of bacon floating up from downstairs was an incentive to make sure he followed through.

He got out of bed at nine, showered, put on a polo shirt and jeans. Then, as he did every morning, he went to the kitchen, ready to be fed. Nora stood at the stove, her back to him. Brian kissed her on the cheek, sat at the table, and picked up the newspaper. He pulled out the sports section.

She set a plate in front of him.

"Are you coming with me to the ten o'clock?" she said. "It'll be Father Callahan, I think."

"Not today," he said. "I've got too much to do."

He had been avoiding church for weeks. Whenever he went, he saw his old high school coach. O'Leary would give Brian the eye, tap his watch. A reference to a conversation they'd had after Mass a few months ago. *When do you plan to retire?* Nora had asked. *As soon as your son agrees to take over for me,* Coach O'Leary said. He followed up the next day by phone to say that he had been serious. Brian had no interest, but Nora never stopped bringing it up. She had even gotten Patrick on her side.

She gave Brian a disapproving look now, but she didn't push it.

While she was gone, he masturbated. He watched the Celtics game he'd taped the night before. He took a nap. In the afternoon, he played *Grand Theft Auto* in his bedroom for three hours, until his mother called up, "Four!"

Brian hit pause.

He was the only one of them who had ever lived alone with Nora, her fourth and youngest child. The number four was written into all the tags on his clothes when he was a kid, and even now when she wanted him, it was, *Four! Time for dinner! Four, can you change the lightbulb in the hall?*

"Yeah?" he called back.

"Did you do the boxes?"

"Yup!"

He got up and did the boxes. The ceiling fans as well.

Before he left for work, they shared a dinner of leftover chicken.

"You're closing tonight?" she asked.

He nodded. His mouth was full.

"What time?"

"One," he said. "It's always one. You know that."

"But I don't like it."

"So you're hoping the answer will change if you ask me enough times?"

"I suppose so."

They smiled at each other.

She took a bite of her chicken, chewing it slowly, then taking a long sip of water.

"I was over to see your aunt Kitty after church," she said. "Brought her her groceries. She said your cousin Conor was there for a visit yesterday, with Marie and the kids. Isn't that nice? He belongs to the Hoosic Club in Milton. They were on their way there for lunch. Did you know he's going to retire this year? At fifty! And with a good pension. That's what Kitty said. It seems like a nice way of life, being a policeman."

He gave her a look. "Ma."

"What?" she said. "I'm only making conversation."

A few minutes later, he was in the driver's seat of his car, waiting for it to warm up. Her car was parked in front of his in the driveway. For the first time in a while, Brian noticed the shadow of a bumper sticker, long ago scraped off, but for the letters *nd In*.

He looked away, then backed up into the street.

When he reached the bar, there were only a few of them there.

Joe, by himself today. He was usually with George and Wally and Dick and Ed, a crew of white-haired guys with booming laughs who had lived their whole lives in this neighborhood. They came when it was Dan O's and they came when it was Colony, and they came when it was Rafferty's. No allegiance to any particular name on a sign, only to one another. Two seats down from Joe was another old-timer Brian didn't recognize, a guy with a bald head and a white T-shirt, a combination that put him in mind of Mr. Clean. A young couple sat in a booth. The girl craned her neck to apply lipstick in front of the mirrored wall.

The bathroom door swung open and a guy in a Tom Brady jersey stepped out.

"Hey QB, big game tonight?" Fergie said.

"Screw you, Ferguson," the guy said.

They laughed.

Brian had come to relieve Fergie, but Fergie didn't go home. He never did. Instead, he poured himself a beer from the tap. He had the *Herald* folded in his back pocket. He opened it up, took a seat, and spread the pages out in front of him on the bar.

He had been Patrick's closest friend since kindergarten. They made a funny pair. Fergie was short and bulky, with shaggy blond hair that he could never seem to figure out what to do with. Next to Patrick—tall and handsome, all thick black hair and broad shoulders—Fergie looked like a disheveled kid. Patrick had a mustache now, a strangely unflattering choice.

On his forty-eighth birthday, he'd partied too hard, gotten wasted, fell face forward into a bar stool. He ended up with a cut above his upper lip, and then a tiny scar. The facial hair was meant to hide it, but Brian thought the scar would have been the better option. Fergie loved to give Pat shit about that mustache, as if it had put them on an even playing field, lookswise, for the first time in their lives.

A girl came in. She looked about twelve, but she was wearing a UMass hoodie. Twenty-one, twenty-two max, Brian thought. He was all ready to ask her for ID when she said to him, "Can I hang a flyer for the Brendan Moynahan 5K?"

"Of course you can, sweetheart," Fergie said, pointing to the door she'd just come through without looking up from his paper.

The back of the door was plastered in flyers. *The Eddie Farrell Memorial Golf Outing. The Terry Sweeney Foundation Auction. The Sons of Éireann Firemen's Funeral Fund Barbecue.*

They watched as the girl added hers to the mix.

"That's a lot of dead Irishmen when you think about it," Fergie said.

At six-thirty, Patrick arrived. The energy changed, as it did whenever he entered a room. It was like a famous person had just walked in.

Pat came behind the bar and filled a pint glass with water. His rule was that they could, and did, drink their faces off anywhere else. But not here. Even when they were off the clock, though Pat rarely mentioned that to Fergie.

"You see the new place finally opened across the street?" Fergie said. "Dottie's Wine Bar." He held a hand straight up and then tipped his fingers forward.

"I saw," Patrick said.

"Dottie's," Fergie said. "On Dot Ave. Aren't they clever. Won't last six months, mark my words."

Patrick shrugged. "Ehh. Good luck to 'em. Maybe it'll keep the yuppies out."

His bar was an old-school dive, five blocks from the house where the family lived before Brian was born. The front windows were small. The room was as dark at lunchtime as it was at midnight. Pat had it set up exactly the way he wanted it. A long wooden bar, red leather banquettes, a concrete floor. A pool table and a dartboard in the back. A jar of pickled eggs on the bar, which nobody ever ate. Cash only. Pat loathed the thought of anything trendy. His motto: "No frills, no food." They would not serve pressed sandwiches or have karaoke on Tuesdays. They would stick to the basics.

It had taken Brian three months to persuade him to stock a beer besides Bud, Bud Light, and Guinness. He suggested Blue Moon. "Girls like it," Brian said. "Trust me." Pat only acquiesced after an arm wrestling best-of-three that left Brian's shoulder aching for a week.

That Patrick had gotten the place was something of a miracle. He never forgot how lucky he'd been.

When their father was still alive, he came to watch the Patriots games on Sunday afternoons. Sometimes Nora came with him and ordered a cup of tea.

"Does it feel like a pub back in Ireland, Ma?" Patrick asked her.

"I wouldn't know," she said.

But Brian could tell she was proud.

The bar was usually full of Pat's old friends. They knew him from high school, from Little League, from Florian Hall, through a cousin's friend's cousin who had dated him in 1989.

"Bri," Pat said now. "Look alive."

Joe had lifted his empty glass. He was the only one who ever ordered red wine, but Pat kept a bottle of cabernet under the counter just for him. He had a soft spot for the guy. Joe had two grown sons who wouldn't give him the time of day. When his gallbladder ruptured, Pat was the only one who went to visit him in the hospital.

Brian found the bottle, refilled Joe's glass to the top, as he knew his brother would.

"Sorry for the wait," he said.

"What do you make of this, Raf?" Joe responded, pointing to the TV over the bar.

Brian hated when they called him Raf. A name from another life.

He looked up. A blond ESPN anchor in a short skirt was interviewing a Red Sox pitcher, recovering from Tommy John surgery.

"He's done. He'll be out for the season," Brian said.

Mr. Clean two seats over looked at them, wanting into the conversation.

"I wouldn't be so sure," he said. "It's January. The kid's young, he'll bounce back."

"Careful there, buddy," Pat said. "That's a former pro ballplayer you're talking to. My brother used to play for the Cleveland Indians."

He still sounded proud after all these years.

The guy looked impressed. "Is that right?"

"Not exactly," Brian said.

"Double-A," Pat said.

Even that was a stretch. Brian was only there for two seasons before they moved him down to Single-A, where he stayed for the rest of his career.

"What position did you play?"

"Second base."

"A five-tool player, this kid," Pat said. "All muscle. What did you have, eight percent body fat?"

"Wouldn't know it to look at me now," Brian said, to get out ahead of what he assumed they were thinking.

He had gained sixty pounds since he was in peak shape. He never worked out anymore. He let his body get a little flabby, embraced the slight beer gut as an occupational hazard. He thought once that baseball was his whole life before him, but it was just a moment, that was all. He would have preferred never to talk about it again, but the guys at the bar were obsessed. Most days, he let them have their way. When you had lived the dream of everyone else, you weren't supposed to tell them the truth. If they thought you had gotten the best and still couldn't be happy with your lot in life, what shot in hell did they have?

Brian was drafted straight out of USC. That first year, every bit of it was a joy. Ten hours a day outside, forty degrees in Akron in April, and he was thrilled. He made less than minimum wage. He only got one day off a month. Traveled by bus. Lived in a motel room with no fridge, no stove. He ate mostly fast food and peanut butter sandwiches; they all did. Hope kept them going. They were in purgatory, but at any minute they might be released up to heaven.

Double-A was full of guys on their way to the big leagues, or else guys who'd come down from the majors for a while to recover from injury. There were a few who moved down further from there, but Brian barely took note of them. He assumed he would only go in one direction. Then he tore his Achilles in the second game of his third season. They moved him down. "Just for now," they said.

Five years in Peoria, Illinois. Five years of sleeping on a sofa in a one-bedroom apartment shared by seven guys. Five years of being told that his body was a machine that required the highest grade fuel, when he could barely afford a Big Mac. Everything extra went on a credit card. He would think about it when the season was over.

Brian still loved to play, but there was no dignity in it anymore. Single-A was all about stunts to fill the seats. Once a season, the team brought a live camel into the park. Every night, between the third and fourth innings, four guys dressed as a hot dog, relish, ketchup, and a French fry ran clunky laps around the field, racing to the finish. The crowd screamed out for their favorites, louder than they ever screamed for any player. They didn't get too used to anyone, since they knew a guy might be called up anytime.

When kids were waiting for him outside the park, wanting his auto-graph, or standing over the dugout, gloves in the air, their faces say-ing that if he'd just toss them a ball, it was all they'd ever need to be happy, then Brian felt like he had made it. He'd arrived. But the gimmicks brought him back to earth. They weren't there for him. They were there because it was SpongeBob SquarePants night.

When he was home in Boston, everyone wanted the details. They asked what the guys in the clubhouse called him, and when he said Raf, that's what they all started calling him too. His father and his uncles and every guy at Patrick's bar had suggestions.

"Tell the coach he needs to move you up in the order."

"Keep your chin up. You're meant for the majors. You'll get there."

They had no idea what it took to get there, how enormous the line was between really good and great.

His fourth and fifth years, Brian got injured again and again. Pulled a hamstring, hurt his back. For a while there, he liked his Oxy a little too much. When Pat caught him popping pills far outside of the season, he said, "What are you doing that shit for? Knock it off." And Brian did. His brother's disapproval was more powerful than any twelve-step program.

By the time the team released him, seven years in, he was done. His only shame was in thinking about Patrick and Nora. The two people who had been to every Little League game he ever played, every game at Hull High. He worried he was letting them down.

In the off-season, Brian lived at home with his parents, helping Charlie out with painting jobs to make extra money. When his baseball career ended, he moved back in. It was supposed to be temporary, while he paid off the credit card debt. But he got lazy or comfortable, or both. Then his father got sick. After Charlie died, Brian couldn't leave Nora alone in the house. He had been there ever since.

Pat gave Brian a job at the bar, full-time.

"Until you catch your breath," he said.

Somehow, seven years had gone by.

Everyone at the bar still associated Brian with baseball. They thought of him as their in-house expert. What he wished he could say to Joe now, but didn't, was that every mention of an active player filled him with jealousy, reminded him that in the end he hadn't been good enough. So many ugly thoughts but not a single one uttered out loud. The worst part was that he'd loved baseball more than anything since he was a kid, but now he could hardly stand the thought of it.

"Mulcahey!" Pat yelled at a guy taking a seat at the bar.

Pat made a big show of going around, hugging him.

Brian had no idea who he was, but that wasn't uncommon. The bar was Patrick's domain.

"You're back," Pat said.

"Just for a few days to see my mother. She had to have her hip replaced."

"Jesus," Pat said. "Sorry to hear it. Give her my best. Tell her to call me if she needs anything after you're gone."

"Thanks, pal. She's doing her physical therapy now. I'm stealing an hour away. There is only so much *Judge Judy* one man can take."

Patrick turned to Brian. "Mulcahey grew up on Crescent Ave. with us. Moved out to Atlanta when he got married. Did you two even meet last time he was in? How long's it been, Mulcahey? Five years? Six? You were here for your sister's kid's graduation."

"That's right. Good memory."

The guy had a Boston accent, like Patrick, like most of them in this place. Their parents had Irish accents, and Patrick had a Boston accent, and Brian had no accent at all. The family moved to Hull the summer before he was born. As a kid, he used to stand in front of the mirror talking to himself, pretending to sound like the rest of them.

"How's your sister doing?" Mulcahey said. "My sister was asking for her."

"She's good. She's still in New York, running the animal shelter."

"God love her."

"She specializes in rehabbing pit bulls. You know, after they come out of the dog fighting ring or whatever."

"Jesus."

After college, Bridget followed a few friends to New York for the summer. She never returned. In the early years, she was going out with a group of retired cops every night, a band of tattooed vigilantes who called themselves the Angels. They got animals out of all kinds of hideous situations. Brian once had to leave the room as she told John about somebody's cocker spaniel, left tied up outside the grocery store while the owner went in for milk and later found by the Angels, dead, with its mouth duct-taped shut. "Used as bait in a dog fight," Bridget said. "Sick fuckers."

Sometimes a crackhead stole a five-pound designer dog from a parked car, then sold it on the street. The Angels tracked the dog down. If someone left a dog out in the cold, they'd build it a doghouse. When the Angels rescued an animal, they brought it to a shelter. They never knew what became of it after that. Bridget said some of the shelters were great, but it was easier to get a cute puppy adopted than an older dog that had been through something. She wanted to open her own place, where the neediest cases would get the attention they deserved. She saved until she was able to do it. Nora seemed vaguely embarrassed by Bridget's work, but Pat bragged about her. He did a fund-raiser for the shelter every year at the bar.

"And how's John?" Mulcahey said. "Does he ever bring the governor in here for a few rounds?"

Brian knew Pat wouldn't mention that the two of them hadn't spoken in a while. Every guy who came into the bar thought Patrick was his best friend. But he hardly shared anything about himself. He didn't trust people.

"My brother John's too good for the likes of us," Patrick said. "My brother John belongs over there at Dottie's Wine Bar."

Mulcahey laughed. He ordered a Guinness. Pat poured it himself.

"You know John's name was in the *Globe* today, right?" the guy said, taking a sip from the glass when Patrick handed it over.

Pat shook his head.

"You didn't see it?"

Fergie raised up the *Herald*. "We don't read that rag around here."

"It was an article about that kid—what's his name? McClain?" Mulcahey said. "The one who just won for state senate. This whole story about how his best friend got robbed in high school and ended up blind. Do you guys remember that? Oh man, it was awful. He was just walking down the street in broad daylight, and boom—these pieces of shit came out of nowhere. I think they stabbed him in the eye. Or did they shoot him?"

"Did they ever catch them?" Brian said.

"It was a bunch of black kids from Mattapan," Fergie said.

"I thought it was Whitey Bulger and those lowlifes," Mulcahey said. "The kid's father owed them. Wasn't that it, Pat?"

Patrick shrugged. "I don't remember it, to tell you the truth. I think maybe we had moved away by then."

"Right," Mulcahey said. "I forgot. You left in seventy-five."

"Yeah. How'd you remember that off the top of your head?"

He shrugged. "Half the neighborhood moved that year."

The family had left soon after some judge decided to desegregate the Boston public schools by busing poor black kids from Roxbury into Southie and poor white kids from Southie into Roxbury. Neither side wanted it. Most of the kids who lived on Crescent Ave. in Dorchester went to Southie High. Patrick was one of them. He got bused for a year, and then the family went to Hull.

From what Brian had heard, everything was bedlam that first year. Riots in the streets, people dragged from their cars and beaten to death. It was shameful to admit now that this was the reason they had gone away, that they had abandoned the old neighborhood. The family never talked about it.

"So what does this blind kid have to do with Rory McClain?" Pat said.

"I guess he was homeless. Hard for the poor bastard to find work after what happened. Heroin got him. But Rory's been trying to help him get back on his feet. And he's making the whole opiate thing a big part of his plan once he's in office. Good guy, I think. My mother's crazy about him. Even if he is a Republican. Her sister owned a triple-decker on the same block as Rory's parents for years."

"Leave it to Rory to save the day," Pat said.

He had a strange look on his face.

For as much as Patrick was the life of the party, he had an angry streak.

He loved to fight. Once, at a crowded bar in Faneuil Hall, the girl he was with said she was pretty sure some guy had touched her ass. *Which one?* Patrick asked. She pointed, and he threw a punch, just like that. Afterward, the girl said maybe it hadn't been that guy, she wasn't sure.

Rory McClain had brought this out in him on the day of Maeve's confirmation. Pat got all worked up for reasons Brian couldn't understand. He assumed it had more to do with Pat's feelings toward John than it had to do with Rory. And Pat had been drinking all day.

"Well. If you'll excuse me, I've gotta go in and pay some bills," Patrick said. "Customers prefer it when you keep the lights on. Great to see you, Mulcahey. Come back in before you skip town."

"I will."

They embraced and then Patrick walked toward the office, shut the door hard behind him.

A few minutes later, the guy finished his drink and left.

Fergie stared at the closed door of Patrick's office. Finally, he went over and knocked, but Pat didn't answer, and Fergie knew better than to barge in. Sometimes Patrick went dark. He went somewhere they couldn't reach him. In those moments, it was best just to let him go.

When Patrick resurfaced, it was almost eight. The bar had filled in. A group of guys in their twenties, dressed in soccer uniforms, had just ordered a round of Blue Moons.

Fergie smirked as Brian poured them.

"Ahh, the Brian Special," he said.

Pat came behind the bar. One of the soccer players held out his beer, still foaming at the top. "Excuse me. Sir?" he said. "You wouldn't happen to have an orange slice?"

Patrick looked around like he had the wrong guy.

"No," he said finally. "I don't have a fucking orange slice. Get the fuck out of here."

Brian raised his eyebrows as the kid skulked back to his table. Fergie doubled over laughing.

"Christ," Patrick said. "Great. Now I can't remember what I came out here for."

He went back into the office.

"Is he shit-faced?" Brian said.

"What? No. I think he's just fired up."

An hour later, at nine on the dot, Brian called the house to check on his mother, as he did every night. He worried about her when she was home alone. He pictured her up in the den, reading one of her mystery novels, oblivious to the madman trying to break in downstairs.

"Did you lock the doors?" he said when she answered.

"Of course I did."

"What are you doing?"

"Reading," Nora said. "Or trying to. There's something funny going on with the boiler. Will you have a look in the morning?"

"Sure. Why are you talking so softly?"

"I have a tiny headache, but I'm fine."

Patrick came out of the office again, shouting Brian's name.

"He's on the phone with his girlfriend," Fergie said.

Brian gave him the finger as he answered his mother. "Why don't you take an Advil?"

He didn't know why he bothered to say it. He knew she would act like he had just advised her to smoke crystal meth.

"You know I don't like to take that stuff," Nora said. "I don't want to get dependent."

"Tell her I'm gonna send my ironing home with you tomorrow," Pat said.

"Christ, you two have got to be the oldest mama's boys on the planet," Fergie said. "We should call the Guinness World Records people."

"The woman does a crease like none other," Pat said.

It seemed like whatever was bothering him before had subsided. He sat at the bar beside Fergie, looked up at the TV.

As Brian said good night to Nora, he noticed that Patrick's eyes were half open, as if he was dozing off.

"Did you have a couple before you got here, buddy?" Fergie said.

Patrick didn't answer.

Fergie raised his voice. "Hey, Tom Selleck. I'm talking to you."

Brian didn't hear his brother's response because at that moment, Ashley Conroy walked in. She came straight over, leaned across the bar, and kissed him. Fergie and Patrick and even old Joe whooped and ooohed like a bunch of girls in the sixth grade.

Brian could feel himself blushing. He poured her a rum and Coke.

Ashley was a cute blonde, a slightly trampy dresser, several years younger than him. They met four months ago at the bar, while she was out on a pub crawl for a friend's bachelorette. That first night, he watched her move through the room, every part of her bouncy yet firm, the perkiness of youth. While her friends did a round of tequila shots, she collected five business cards in rapid succession, got a guy to take a condom out of his wallet and give it to her, and drew an anchor tattoo on yet another guy's arm with a Sharpie. After each interaction, she crossed something off a piece of paper in her hand. She noticed Brian looking and came straight toward him. He looked away, pretended to be wiping down the bar with a rag.

"Give me your underwear," were her first words to him.

"Excuse me?"

"Or let me take a shot off your stomach? It's for this scavenger hunt we're doing. I was late joining my girlfriends at the last place so they've given me a ten-minute head start here. Just trying to make it count. Your name's not Jordan by chance, is it?"

He laughed, befuddled. "No."

"Well, can I at least have your phone number? That's an easy one. It requires nothing of you but it's worth seven points."

"Why not," he said.

He ended up going home with her that night.

Brian didn't think she was all that smart. But then, no one had ever mistaken him for one of the great minds of our time. He had never figured out how to match the words he said with what he was thinking. People at the bar joked that he was quiet because Patrick talked enough for the both of them.

Maybe Ashley had as much going on in her head as he had in his, even though she only ever talked about celebrities he'd never heard of and the secrets of friends he'd never met. She wanted a commitment. Twice now she had asked him for a "state of the union." Both times, Brian succeeded in ignoring the request.

He wasn't half as good-looking as Patrick, but Brian didn't have much trouble meeting girls. The fact that he lived at home with his mother ruled out most women his own age. But the baseball thing helped. That, and the way he was so often silent. A girl with enough imagination could project anything she wanted onto him.

Women were crazy about his brother. As soon as one was hooked, Pat was on to the next. Brian supposed he had taken this approach as a model without meaning to, though for him it felt temporary. When he was playing ball, he never lived anywhere long enough to make a commitment. Eventually, he would settle down. He was still young. Thirty-three to Pat and Fergie's fifty. As much as he aged, so did they, so that by comparison, Brian felt like a kid.

Things were slow for the rest of the night. At some point, he noticed that Patrick was no longer there. He thought maybe his brother had left without saying good-bye, or gone to the corner to get a slice of pizza.

At a quarter to eleven, Ashley said, "Is he okay?"

He turned to see Patrick stumbling out of the office in his coat, car keys in hand.

Pat looked back at the floor behind him with disdain, as if it had tripped him on purpose.

"Christ, Fergie! Clean that up."

"Clean what up?"

"There's some shit on the floor. I almost broke my neck."

"I'm off the clock," Fergie said.

"Well, clean it the fuck up anyway."

Fergie looked at Brian. He made a face that Patrick couldn't see.

"I'm heading out too," Fergie said. "I'll drive you."

"No. I'm gonna drive myself. I have my car here."

"Pat," Brian said. "Let him take you. I'll put the car in front of your place later. Here, give me your keys."

"I need my keys to start my car," Patrick said, the words coming out extra slow, a revelation.

He dropped the keys on the floor.

"Okay, man," Brian said. "No way in hell you're driving."

"What the fuck are you guys talking about? I haven't had a drop."

Patrick was so indignant that Brian almost wondered if it was true.

Before anyone could reply, Pat scooped up the keys and was out the door.

Fergie followed behind.

"See you tomorrow," he called to Brian.

A minute later, he was back.

"That asshole pushed me down," Fergie said, with a mix of amusement and disbelief. "Your brother is stubborn as a mule, I swear to God. Well. Good thing he doesn't have far to go."

They laughed. The night went on.

When Brian was cleaning up before close, he noticed a glow emanating from below the office door. He went in there to turn off the lights. There was an empty whiskey bottle on the desk, but he didn't think much of it.

By then, Patrick was gone.

The space between two days could be a lifetime.

Twenty-four hours later, Brian stood alone in the office, whiskey bottle in hand, trying to block out the noise from the crowd of mourners outside.

He wouldn't go back to his mother's tonight. After they closed, he'd go to Ashley's apartment, which would only be slightly more bearable. Ashley and her roommates would moon over him, asking again and again if he felt like talking.

The one thing that might make him feel better would be fucking Ashley in the dark, the smell of her lotion like candy, forgetting for a few minutes. After, he would have to lie there listening to her tiny snores, remembering again, but still it was better than going home. He knew it might cost him later, that she would make it mean something. But Brian was willing to deal with that when the time came.

Part Four

1958-1967

10

IN THE MONTHS BEFORE her wedding day, Nora wished she could confess to Oona all that had happened since they arrived in Boston. They had promised to write every day, and they did, at first. But after a while, they both slowed down. Things got busy. A letter took an age to arrive. By the time you sent one and got one in return, everything you'd written had ceased to matter.

There were things she didn't dare put in writing. If they were together, Nora would tell Oona about that kiss on the boat. She would tell her how she was careful around men after that, and about the last dance she went to on Dudley Street. How a sailor pulled her up from her chair, not listening when she said that she didn't feel like dancing. When they moved together, he sent currents through her, a sensation she had never felt with Charlie. She knew it was wrong. She went to confession. She stopped going to the dances.

Nora scolded herself—she was shy and dull and ought to feel grateful that someone wanted to marry her. But when Charlie came upon her alone in the hall at Mrs. Quinlan's and kissed her neck in rapid motion, like a woodpecker tapping on a tree, her body tightened up in refusal.

She had once thought a husband was secondary to so much else in life, but when she saw the way Lawrence and Babs looked at each other, laughed with each other, Nora understood that she had been wrong. All around her, young people seemed to have love like that, a kind of love she hadn't known existed outside of a movie screen. She was furious with her father for making her come. Furious with herself. She never should have agreed to it. Her reason for being with Charlie was gone, and her distaste for him mounted with every bad joke, every booming laugh. Nora's stomach cramped whenever he mentioned a wedding. Mrs. Quinlan said she couldn't understand why they were dragging their feet. She didn't feel right having an unmarried couple living under her roof, even if they were on separate floors. Still, Nora delayed and delayed, claiming homesickness, and later nerves about everyone looking at her.

She knew that she would leave him. She could even convince herself that it was the kindest thing. There was nothing wrong with Charlie. He could find another girl, a better girl. He claimed he wanted Nora. But she didn't believe he thought there was anything so special about her. It was just that a plan had been put in place and he would look foolish if it didn't come to pass.

Nora knew she couldn't leave yet. But she fantasized that one day, after Theresa was settled, teaching, she might just slip off after work and disappear. She was twenty-two. She could have a different life.

She reminded herself to try to be grateful in the meantime. Her sister was doing well in school and would soon be a teacher. Theresa had only gotten the chance because of Charlie. They lived with his people, worked for his people.

When Kitty told them about the mess Theresa had gotten herself into, everything changed at once. Nora saw her sister in the bedroom that night, looking the same as ever, and wanted to slap her. Her rage frightened her. She was afraid to speak. All that she had done, she had done for Theresa. How could this be the result?

Nora's anger was a shield, staving off the guilt that threatened to consume her. Theresa was in this country because of her. She had wanted Nora to go to the dances, and Nora had refused for her own selfish reasons. A sailor. Imagine it. If she had gone along, none of it ever would have happened.

For a short time, she convinced herself they could go on, with nothing but a slight delay in their plans. But the day she brought Theresa to Saint Mary's, as they sat in that too-hot office, looking up at the nun who would be Theresa's warden, Nora was struck. It was the way the nun spoke of the good Catholic family who would take the baby. Until then, she had only been thinking of her sister, herself. Now she saw that there was a child coming.

She was ashamed to have brought Theresa to such a place. If their mother was looking down on them, what would she think of Nora now? The nun's words seemed to have no effect on Theresa. She only cared about Walter, about putting all this behind her and returning to him.

Nora wished she could be as selfish, as irresponsible as her sister. Just let the baby go. Let them both go. She had given enough of her life over to caring for other people's children. But she sobbed in the car on the way home. Hysterical in a way Charlie had never seen her.

"I never should have come here," she said. "I hate this city, I hate everything about it. I hate all the people."

She stopped just short of saying she hated him.

Charlie gave her a sad smile. "Isn't there anything you like about Boston?"

Nora thought it over. "Brigham's vanilla ice cream," she said. "That's it."

Charlie said he would find Walter, convince him to do the honorable thing. And so they learned that Walter McClain was married, that he had a child of his own.

Nora couldn't sleep for thinking about her mother, about her guilt. About the regret Theresa would feel later if she let this happen.

She wept over it, but she knew what she had to do. There was only one way.

She approached Charlie before breakfast.

"I'll marry you now," Nora said. "Under one condition."

To her astonishment, he agreed.

The nuns didn't like the idea. They said it was unorthodox, that a family had already been selected.

"There's the issue of the fee we would collect from them," Sister Bernadette said.

"We'll pay it, whatever it is," Nora said.

They were married at the church the next morning, with only the custodian for a witness. Later, they told everyone that Nora's shyness wouldn't have allowed for anything more extravagant. Standing at the altar in a simple blue Sunday dress, she could only look at the priest, not at Charlie. She thought of Lawrence and Babs, inseparable on their wedding day. Babs shrieking with delight at the sound of champagne being uncorked for a toast.

Nora and Charlie moved to the top floor of a three-decker on Crescent Avenue. The rent was a hundred dollars a month. Mrs. Quinlan collected hand-me-down furniture for them. Each object carried the odor of someone else's home. The worn sofa smelled of pipe tobacco. The threadbare carpet was like an old dog.

The families below were Charlie's cousins. Mr. Fallon on the bottom floor owned the house. The Sheehans lived in the middle. The wife, Christine, was Mr. Fallon's daughter. She had only been married five years and already she had four children. They kept the doors to their apartments open at all times. Whenever Nora went up or down the central staircase, she had to greet them again, smile at their jokes and their invitations to come for tea.

The bathroom off her kitchen had been converted from a pantry. Nora shook from the cold when she stepped out of the tub. Their bedroom was off the kitchen too. There was a second bedroom down a long narrow hallway by the front door, across from the living room. They were to keep this open for family coming over from Ireland. And there was a small dining room, with pocket doors. "You can change it to a bedroom after the first baby comes," Mr. Fallon said with a wink.

Nora was careful not to look at her husband.

From the first night, Charlie wanted to make love, but she refused. This marriage was for a purpose. The outcome of what he was asking was too uncertain. It might lead them into even more of a mess.

"It's what married people do," Charlie said.

"I know, but I can't."

"We could have the lights on."

"Oh Jesus, Mary, and Joseph."

"Or we could have them off!"

"Tomorrow," she said.

But the next day came and then the day after that, and she was no closer to being ready. Weeks passed. The longer they waited, the more tortured she felt.

They slept in separate beds on either side of a nightstand. She lay there many nights, thinking of home, wishing she could go back. Not just to the house, or to her family, but to her girlhood.

As soon as they were married, Nora began wearing the loose-fitting sack dresses Babs had worn throughout her pregnancy. At work, she complained to Mrs. Byrne of nausea. She placed a hand on her stomach, feigning absentmindedness, when she knew they were all looking. Nora sent Charlie alone to family parties, told him to make sure to say that she was tired lately and not feeling well.

"Aunt Nellie asked if you're expecting," he reported one night, and she saw that her plan would work.

She ran into Mrs. Quinlan at the chemist's, and Mrs. Quinlan said, "Mrs. Byrne tells me you haven't been well."

"I'm in bed every night by six," Nora said. "I've been sick to my stomach ever since we were married."

"You need to see the doctor," Mrs. Quinlan said with a knowing smile.

Thou shalt not lie, she had been taught since childhood, and since then Nora had obeyed. But she had never known how easy it was. How one lie could lead to the next and the next and the next.

Every time she visited Theresa and eyed her sister's growing belly, Nora felt sick. She knew she had to tell her the truth—that Walter was married, that they would take the child. But it was so hard to say. Finally, they took Theresa to Hull, a town on the beach, to break the news. It was such a lovely night and Theresa was in such good spirits that Nora couldn't do it there. She waited until the last minute, just before Theresa was due back at Saint Mary's. The car ride was agony, knowing what she would have to say when they stopped. Charlie was nervous, talking under his breath to Bobby Quinlan, who wasn't there, but whose car they had borrowed for the evening.

"Your tires are balder than your head, Bob," he muttered.

Nora told Theresa by herself. Up at the top of the stairs, beneath the porch light, before the sweeter of the nuns opened the door and said it was time for bed.

Every night, Charlie flattered her. He begged, he made jokes, he stamped his feet.

"It's natural," he said. "Everyone does it. Please. For the love of God."

Nora wanted to die when he raised the subject. She wanted to fall through the floor and land on Mr. Fallon's fireplace and just disappear. She wanted to tell Charlie that she had never once heard a good thing about sex. Oona said it hurt terribly, and the nuns at the convent school said it ruined a woman. And just look at Theresa.

Nora had never spent so much time alone with Charlie. His jokes grated on her, his need to talk all night when she might have liked some peace and quiet. She was embarrassed by his presence when she was wearing her nightgown, or brushing her hair, acts that had been private, before.

Once or twice a day, he came close to giving her a heart attack with his screaming. He'd shout, and she'd run to his side, afraid that something horrible had happened. From the sound of him, she'd think he had chopped off a finger, when in fact he had stubbed his toe or read in a letter from home that his football team was out of the running for the season.

If she could sit with Oona for a minute, Nora would ask her what marriage was supposed to feel like. If Oona felt the way she did. There was nobody here she could ask. Nora wondered if another man would please her more, or if she was just being picky. Maybe it was always this way when you got up as close to someone as she was to Charlie. She imagined a soft-spoken husband who brought her thoughtful gifts, who wanted only to be with her on a Friday night, not sweating in a room full of cousins, everyone laughing and drinking and talking too much as if they hadn't seen one another the day before.

The face she pictured belonged to Cillian, the boy who kissed her on the ship. He was shy like she was, or so he said. She knew that she didn't know anything about him, really. But sometimes Nora wondered what he was doing, if he had found a girl to love, if he had stopped feeling homesick by now.

While Theresa was away, Nora often imagined her homecoming. Her sister, flush with gratitude for all they had done. But Theresa seemed angry most of the time. She didn't seem to understand what any of it meant. She didn't believe that it was settled, that the baby was Nora and Charlie's now. Theresa said something that first afternoon home about how she and Patrick would board a bus and go away. As if they had anywhere to go. Nora rebuked her and then felt sorry for it. She said, "We will raise him together."

Charlie gave her a look that said she had made a mistake, saying a thing like that.

Theresa thought his birth was a miracle. She talked nonsense about a vision of the Virgin Mary, how the Miraculous Medal the nurses had pinned to the baby's diaper was a sign.

Even for Nora, there was a sense of movement to it all at first, like it wasn't quite settled yet. Like maybe they could fix it. They still hadn't realized there was no way the arrangement could work.

They put Patrick in the bedroom down the hall. They turned the dining room into Theresa's room.

"For now," Nora said.

Mrs. Quinlan insisted on hosting the christening party. Aunt Nellie said Nora would have to be churched ahead of it.

"What's churched?" Theresa asked.

"A ceremony where a new mother is cleansed. The priest says a blessing that she made it through the birth. It's private, but you should come to support your sister."

On a stifling hot Saturday morning, Aunt Nellie and Mrs. Quinlan met Nora and Theresa at the church. All four of them covered their heads with silk scarves.

Theresa's stomach still bulged out slightly beneath the light fabric of her dress. Her breasts were fuller than before. Nora wondered if the others noticed. She hadn't known how of the body it all would be. She herself still wore the baggy dresses she'd been in for months. She was as slim as ever, and this people did comment on, praising her for the good fortune of having a figure that barely showed the strain of pregnancy, of birth.

Nora sweated now. Her skirt clung to the backs of her legs. Kitty was watching the baby for an hour. It was the first time in three weeks that Nora had been apart from him. She felt as if she had escaped.

They went up the church steps and into the vestibule. The lights were low. It was much cooler there than it was outside. Aunt Nellie opened the door that led into the church. Mrs. Quinlan and Theresa went through, but when Nora tried to follow, Aunt Nellie held out her hand.

"No," she said. "You wait here. That's the point. You can't come in until he's purified you."

Aunt Nellie followed the others, the door closing behind her with a boom. A moment later, she returned.

"Take this," she said.

She handed Nora a lighted candle and left again.

Nora stood there, holding it, waiting.

Finally, the priest came in. Nora had smiled at him many times after a Sunday Mass, in this very room, Charlie shaking his hand. But now he bore a solemn expression. She knew somehow that she was not to say a word.

He wore all white and held a golden chalice. He dipped his finger into it and made a cross on her forehead, the cool holy water dripping down her nose.

"The earth is the Lord's and the fullness thereof," he said. "Enter thou into the temple of God, adore the Son of the Blessed Virgin Mary who has given thee fruitfulness of offspring."

It was too intimate a moment, the smell of his breath in her face. Nora thought this might be her only chance to say that they had lied. It was one thing to lie to the family, quite another to lie to God Himself. But she couldn't say it.

He offered her the edge of his robe, and she took hold of it. The priest led her into the church, cold and dark and empty but for the three heads in the first pew, the flickering votives at the back of the room. In silence, he led Nora to the altar, and then he instructed her to kneel. As he prayed over her, she looked out and saw her sister's eyes glowing in the candlelight.

Nora had to leave her job to stay home with the baby. There were days when she spoke to no one but the coal man and others when Charlie's cousins from Ireland overtook the rooms of her apartment. They were teenagers, mostly. Their first time away from home. They expected her to cook for them, to clean up their messes. When their boisterous conversations made Nora feel like the odd man out in her own kitchen, she journeyed to Hull in her mind. That night with Theresa, the last time she had seen her sister happy. The beach and the cinema and the roller coaster, the houses crowded on the hills like teeth, the people inside them deciding for themselves how to pass the time.

She could cry for hours, letting her resentments unspool. During the day, she thought of how her sister's life hadn't changed at all. Nora was the one making the sacrifices. She was the one to suffer for Theresa's sins.

Her life in the house was a world away from what people knew of her in the street.

"Nora, he's beautiful," they said when she pushed the baby in his pram. "That dark hair! Those eyes!"

She smiled and thanked them, knowing just who the child resembled.

Women talked about good babies and fussy ones. Nora couldn't tell the difference. Patrick cried all day. She wasn't any good at soothing him. The baby, if not her baby, was her family. She ought to love him more. But she couldn't help thinking of him as a child she was minding, waiting for the moment when he was no longer her concern.

In the evenings, Theresa cared for him. Nora knew far better what to do with an infant, but Theresa knew her own baby best, or anyway, he wanted her most.

Every night, several times, Nora was awakened by his cries. Right away, she would hear Theresa's footsteps padding down the hall. She heard her sister singing to him, talking to him. She felt the deepest sadness then, for all of them. For herself and for Charlie, that this had been thrust upon them. For Patrick, who might only ever know a mother who didn't love him. Most of all for her sister, who loved the child so much, who was only a child herself.

One morning in early November, the toaster went up in flames. Nora screamed and dumped a sack of flour on it to put out the fire. White dust wafted through the kitchen like snow, landing on every surface—the floor and the table and the baby's eyelashes. It took her half an hour to clean it up, Patrick wailing all the while. They had a new washing machine in the cellar but no dryer. Earlier, Nora had hung all their clothes out as she usually did. She went back to fetch them in the afternoon, while the baby slept, and found that they had frozen solid on the line. She gathered them up anyway, stormed up the stairs in a state.

When she reached the door to her apartment, Mrs. Quinlan stood there, her cheeks wet with tears. For a moment, Nora thought their secret had been discovered. But then Mrs. Quinlan blinked and said, voice trembling, "My mother's died."

She held a small rectangular box.

"Her prayer cards," Mrs. Quinlan said. "I think she would have liked for Theresa to have them. She was the only one who ever showed an interest. My mother is so fond of you girls. *Was* so fond."

Nora took the box. She had often seen Aunt Nellie spreading the cards out on the dining room table in the evenings. It seemed impossible that she could be gone.

"I'll give them to her," Nora said. "I'm so sorry. Do you want to come in? I can help with anything you need."

The next day, she stood in awe of the scene at Murphy's Funeral Home, the whole place teeming with flowers. Aunt Nellie wore a fine suit in her casket. Nora had never seen anything like it. In Ireland, there would have been just a wreath or two to adorn the grave. The wake would have happened at home.

She was seven years old when her mother died. Old ladies from the church came to dress her in a robe and fresh slippers, to lay her out on her bed, like she was only going off for a nap. Afterward, they sat in the kitchen drinking tea with Nora's gran, who kept saying, "It isn't right, losing a child," as if she might convince God of His mistake and have her daughter back. The door to the house was left open. All day, people came in and walked straight to the bedroom to see her. Nora felt like a ghost. She wondered if she too had died. Hardly anyone took note of her except to frown and say, "Poor girl," or "You mind your father now. Look after your brother and sister."

Men came in the evening. They had real drinks and joined her father to sit up all night with the body. They spoke in whispers. In the morning, she was bold enough to approach the bed. Her father did not try to stop her. Nora went up close. She touched her mother's cheek.

Aunt Nellie's funeral was a Solemn High Mass. As the priest spoke in Latin, his back to the congregation, Nora remembered how Aunt Nellie told her that before she came to Boston, her family had given her an American wake.

"I was as good as dead to them," Aunt Nellie said. "It'll be easier for a girl like you to get back there eventually."

Nora wondered at the time why Aunt Nellie couldn't travel home to Ireland now, as easily as she herself could. In the church pew, the answer came—Aunt Nellie no longer had anyone to go back to.

She had liked to tease the young people in the family about how easy it was nowadays. Aunt Nellie hadn't gone through New York but straight from Cobh to Massachusetts. She told Nora that when she and her family arrived at the port in New Bedford, a woman wasn't allowed to leave without a male relative. Aunt Nellie was fifteen. Her older brother was asked, "How much is two and two? How much is three and five?" Aunt Nellie was asked, "Do you wash a staircase from top to bottom or bottom to top?"

One brother, twelve years old, got sick with an eye infection on the boat ride over and was denied entry, sent back to Ireland alone. The family never saw him again.

Nora said she didn't know how they could bear it, or how Aunt Nellie managed to remain so devout.

Aunt Nellie just shrugged and said, "Live long enough, and life teaches you that God is not your lucky rabbit foot."

Nora thought of this as she sat in the church, bouncing her sister's child on her lap. The baby began to shriek during the eulogy. People turned, and Nora felt her face and neck go red. She tried to quiet him. She looked over at Theresa, who stared straight ahead.

They went back to Mrs. Quinlan's house after.

Mrs. Quinlan put her head down to cry as she filled a red Coleman cooler with cans of Narragansett. Nora told her to sit down, and she took over—lining up several bottles of Seagram's Seven on the table, setting out the cake and salad, the roast chicken and potatoes that Mrs. Quinlan had made.

"The love's gone out of her cooking," Charlie whispered, but everyone ate just the same.

The gathering lasted all afternoon and well into the night. There was music in the parlor; instruments Nora hadn't seen since she left home were pulled out from under beds and from high shelves in closets, taken from their cases and played to perfection. Afterward, the women congregated in the kitchen as usual.

Mrs. Quinlan asked to hold Patrick.

"He's a beautiful boy, Nora," she said.

Everyone nodded and clucked in agreement. Nora met Theresa's eye and smiled. Her sister looked down at the floor.

Babs leaned against the cabinets, several whiskies in. She bounced her own fat baby on her hip. Conor had weighed eleven pounds when he was born.

"Such a big boy!" someone said, tickling his chin. "The birth must have been excruciating."

"No," Babs said. "I had the twilight sleep. I woke up and my hair was done and I was holding a baby in my arms. It was after that I felt it all."

Nora stared at her, wondering what twilight sleep was. Babs caught her looking.

"Nora had a much easier time of it," she said. "Her Patrick was a prince from the start, as we all know."

Nora tried to smile. Her husband had made up a story about the birth. When Lawrence asked how long it lasted, Charlie said, "Fifteen minutes."

She supposed he had no clue how long these things actually took.

"That's all?" Lawrence had said.

"Yes!" Charlie said. "My boy couldn't wait to greet the world."

Babs seemed to resent Nora, and Nora in turn felt guilty, for the ease of the birth that had never actually occurred.

Babs said now, "But Nora, you have a secret, don't you?"

Nora knew her blushing had once again betrayed her. She met Theresa's eye.

"Babs, leave it alone," Mrs. Quinlan said.

"I'm just saying. You were married in April. And Patrick was born in August. Is that why you didn't wear white on your wedding day?"

The other women laughed in a way that let Nora know they'd been discussing it. She was seven months married and still a virgin, and now they would accuse her of this. She wasn't sure whether to laugh or cry.

Nora ran upstairs to the room that had once belonged to her and to her sister. Kitty lived there alone now, for the time being.

She could hear Babs calling, "I was only teasing! Come back!"

Then footsteps on the stairs.

A moment later, Kitty entered the room.

"Don't worry about her. She's a twit and everyone knows it."

"Is it what they're all thinking?" Nora asked.

"It doesn't matter what they're thinking. You've got to learn to stand up for yourself, Nora. This family has a way of forgetting what it doesn't want to know. A year from now, no one will recall that there was ever anything funny about it."

Nora thought of something that hadn't occurred to her before, though it should have. Kitty knew everything. She suddenly felt afraid of her.

And envious too—Kitty had walked away from her marriage, and yes, those women in the kitchen whispered about it all the time. But what did Kitty care? She was free.

Babs walked in. "Don't be mad at me," she cooed. "It was a joke. I'm just jealous. Sometimes I wonder how you and I went through the same thing. I'm still lugging around all these extra pounds. You had such an easy time of it. I said to Lawrence the other night when we saw you, 'Did Nora even have that baby, or was he left on her doorstep by a stork?' You didn't put on an ounce."

Nora felt exhausted. She wondered how much longer she could keep up the lie, even as she understood that she had committed herself to it for life. She had wanted to take shame off of her sister and she had wanted Theresa to know her son. She hadn't considered herself. The shame this would bring upon her. The fact that they would all know there was something funny about it.

"You never saw Nora at the beach," Kitty said. "She was as big as a house when she got those baggy dresses off. The size of her ankles. My God. Sorry, Nora."

Nora looked at Kitty, grateful.

"It's all right," she said. "You're only telling the truth."

Her sister was quiet on the walk home. She refused to look Nora in the eye.

Charlie went to bed as soon as they got in, so it was just the two of them, Nora and Theresa, standing in the kitchen. Nora handed Patrick to her sister. The weight of him stayed in her arms. She shook them out at her sides. Her back ached. Her head felt like it was about to split open.

"You love that they all think you're such a fine mother," Theresa said. "You love when they tell you how beautiful he is."

"Keep your voice down."

"Why? You're afraid someone will hear?"

"You ungrateful thing," Nora said. "Do you know what they all think of me because of you? I never wanted any of this."

"Say it. You never wanted him."

"Of course I don't want him."

She went into her room and slammed the door. Charlie was awake. He looked at her. Nora wanted to tell him what Babs had said, but she couldn't. She got straight into bed and closed her eyes.

Around midnight, she heard the baby shriek.

Patrick's cries went on and on. Nora flipped from one side to the other. She put a pillow over her head. The baby kept crying. She wondered how long he could go on like that before he would suffocate.

Charlie stirred.

Nora sighed. She threw back the covers and stormed down the hall to Patrick's room. He lay in his crib, eyes open wide, tears on his cheeks, arms outstretched to her.

Nora picked him up, kissed him.

"All right," she said. "You're all right now. Where's your fool mother? Let's wake her, shall we?"

She went toward Theresa's room, taking in the smell of the baby, giving herself over to the strange hour. Nora didn't bother to knock. She just opened the door and started speaking. "The baby needs—"

The room was empty. Nora thought of Walter, of those dances on Dudley Street. Would her sister be stupid enough to return there?

Then she saw the piece of paper on the still-made bed. She went closer. Nora looked down and read what her sister had written.

Please make sure he knows how loved he is, until I come back.

She ran downstairs, calling out to the neighbors, not caring if she woke them, no longer herself. Someone must know something.

But no one in the house had seen Theresa go.

In the months that followed, Charlie stayed out late at the pub most nights, and that was fine with her. She didn't thrill to the idea of his return from work. There was such tension in the apartment when they were together. His humor dimmed. Without her income, they had only enough money to cover food and the rent, and some weeks not even that much. She could tell he blamed her for it.

Nora wondered where her sister had gone. She didn't know what to tell her father. Theresa didn't know anyone in this country, other than them. *Until I come back,* she had written. When would that be? In the beginning, Nora looked for her everywhere. She spent hours bouncing Patrick in front of the living room window, expecting to see her sister come up the road at any moment.

She began to tell herself a story. When Theresa returned, she could have the baby. Nora would go away, leave this all behind. Do what she ought to have done in the first place, if she had been brave enough.

The baby had colic, and ear infections and croup. She was forever calling the doctor. One morning when she had been up all night with him, she sat down and cried at the table after Charlie left for work. Her sister had trapped her here, and there was nothing she could do.

What was she so afraid of? Why didn't she ever say boo to anyone? She should have let the baby go. By trying to save things, she had made a mess of it all.

She went to the medicine cabinet in the bathroom for an aspirin. Her sister's pink lipstick lay abandoned on the bottom shelf. Theresa had made her try it once, before their first Dudley Street dance.

Nora took the tube in hand now and lifted the lid. She ran the color over her lips as she looked in the mirror.

"Let's get your coat," she said to the baby.

She pushed the pram faster than she ever had, all the way to the Edison plant. When they arrived at the building—massive, boxy, windowless, the color of fog—Nora pushed open the heavy front door and guided the pram inside.

"I need to talk to Walter McClain," she said to the secretary in the main office.

The secretary blinked. "I don't know who that is, ma'am."

"He works here. Go find him or I'll scream."

The woman looked alarmed. She scrambled to her feet.

Walter appeared several minutes later.

"Hello," he said. "You wanted to see me?"

"I'm Theresa Flynn's sister."

"Is that right?" he said, trying to sound jovial, as if they were two old friends. He eyed the secretary. "Let's go outside, shall we?"

They stood on the steps of the building.

"Theresa is gone," she said. "No one has seen her."

"I haven't seen her," he said, defensive. "Since."

"Oh, I know that."

Walter pointed at the carriage, peering inside. "Is this the baby? Her baby?"

The baby was so clearly his, if anyone's, but he wouldn't dare say it.

"He's my husband Charlie's boy," she said. "And mine."

Nora hadn't blushed. Her sister wasn't here to say the words for her. She would say them for herself.

"You owe me something," she said. "What Patrick deserves. That's his name. Patrick."

"What is it you want?" he said.

"I don't know yet. But someday I'll know, and you'll give it. You can't unsee what happened. I won't let you. I just wanted to tell you that."

Dear Oona,

After all your years living in town, I wonder how you find the farm. I suppose it's the opposite way for me here. When I first arrived, the strangest part of this new place was the light. It was so bright, even at midnight. I shut the curtains, shut my eyes, and still it never seemed to get dark. I thought of how at home the nights were black, with nothing to illuminate objects, near or far. You closed your eyes, and you opened them, and there was no difference in what you saw. The streets are so busy here. There are too many strangers in the house. Yet I am mostly alone. One thing no one prepares you for with a child is how alone you'll be. How overwhelmed and yet how bored! But I try to keep busy and happy. I miss home, and you.

Yours,
Nora

Dear Nora,

The big news from here is that Malbay Manufacturing is sending me and a few other married girls to Shannon to get trained as overlockers. They'll set me up with a special machine to use at home once I'm back, so I can do all the hardest hems and seams right from my own kitchen table. It was difficult being out here in the country at first, and as you know, that was the least of my difficulties. I'll confess to you that I was properly miserable in the beginning. But after you left, my mother said I must make my happiness here. Bloom where you're planted, she told me. I have tried my very best. I hope I will see you before long, somehow, PG.

With love,
Oona

Nora ran her fingers over the *PG. Please God.*

She prayed for the same.

Theresa had left Aunt Nellie's prayer cards behind on the kitchen windowsill. Whenever she had a spare moment, Nora used them and tried to speak to God the way Aunt Nellie did. Some days she swore it was working. Others, her prayers only felt like wishes, sent off into nothing.

As he got older, Patrick cried less. She could reason with him, make him laugh. She began to take pleasure in the way he showed such simple wonder at all things—a car, a bird, a yellow dandelion growing out of a crack in the sidewalk. Somehow it felt like magic when, for the first time, he did what every other child did. Took a step, grew a tooth.

I'm your mother now, she said. Trying to convince him, and herself. Nora longed for her own mother in a way she hadn't since she was a child. She recalled her mother's sternness, her competence, and attempted to imitate it. All the time she had spent looking after her brother and sister had been no preparation for this. She thought of poor Theresa, who had never had any mother but her.

Nora missed her sister's sparkle. All the color in her life came from Patrick now.

"Mama," he called her, and her heart swelled. His first word, said over and over again like a prayer.

One Saturday morning, she awoke on her own, the sun already bright outside the window. Nora was amazed. The baby had outslept her!

She stepped into the kitchen.

Charlie was feeding Patrick a bottle, telling him a story about a difficult customer as if he were a sympathetic pal.

"And I told her peach is no color for a house, ma'am," he said. "I told her pale yellow, now that is what you'll wish you'd gotten if you don't do it now. She went with the peach."

He looked up and saw Nora there, smiling.

"You got up with him?" she said.

"We thought we'd let you sleep in today and have a morning chat, man to man."

She pointed at the bottle. "How do you even know how to do that?"

"What? Warm a bit of milk up on the stove a minute? I did it for my younger brother all the time. Jack only got as fat as he did because of me and my way with the bottle."

Nora was flooded with warmth for him. It surprised her to find that there were parts of Charlie she did not know.

This became their Saturday morning routine. When Nora came out of the bedroom and saw the two of them at the table each week, she felt something like love.

Whenever Charlie got a paycheck, he left her a quart of Brigham's vanilla ice cream in the icebox, and when she emptied it, he left another in its place. She noticed that his easy laughter was returning as he told silly stories to their son. He started telling his bad jokes again, and Nora tried to laugh.

They came to a peaceful acceptance. They had made a decision that would fuse them for the rest of their lives. They could choose to be content with it, or not.

Two years after they were married, Nora stood at the sink washing dishes.

Charlie came home from the pub. She could hear him taking his coat off in the hall, then walking quietly toward her so as not to wake Patrick. She was about to say that his dinner was on the counter as he entered the kitchen. But before she could speak, Charlie smiled at her strangely, walked right over, and kissed her, holding on to her longer than usual.

Nora took his hand, led him into the bedroom. If she didn't do it now, she might never. She didn't turn on the light. When they made love, he touched her as if afraid she would break, or possibly change her mind.

Afterward, he petted her cheek.

"Nora Flynn," he said, addressing her by her old name, which she still thought of as her real name. "The only girl I ever loved."

"Oh, go on," she said.

"It's the truth. I loved you from the first time I saw you."

Her sister would laugh at her. For all the times she had wondered why Charlie had married her, made the sacrifices he did, Nora had never once considered that this might be the reason. She wondered if it was true. He didn't show love like a man in a movie might. Still, he had done something extraordinary for her.

From then on, they kept to their separate beds, but every so often one of them or the other would creep across in the dark.

Bloom where you're planted, she told herself, every day. Bit by bit, it worked.

From the time Patrick was a month old, people asked when she was going to have another.

For so long, it didn't happen, and Nora assumed it never would. She had worried about becoming pregnant too fast, but in the end she felt silly for ever having been afraid.

When Patrick was four and she found out she was going to have a baby, her first thought surprised her: she worried that she could never love another child as much as she loved him.

When she saw John in the hospital, red faced and wrapped in a white blanket, the delight in Charlie's eyes frightened her. She knew what he was thinking.

"He's the spitting image of me as a baby," he said, beaming.

She thought of Patrick—he didn't look like her husband at all.

As she was putting him to bed her first night home from the hospital, Nora said, "Do you know why I named you Patrick? Because that's the middle name of my only brother, Martin. And when I first saw you, I thought of how much you looked like him. You could be twins! Of course, he's a lot bigger than you are. He's twenty-five years old!"

"Twenty-five!" Patrick said, in awe at the thought of a number so vast.

He asked her for a picture. She told him she would find one and hoped he would forget. So the seed was planted and every now and then she tended to it, reminding him of this fact that was not a fact but seemed like one the more she said it.

At some point, Nora stopped worrying that her sister would never come back and instead began to fear that someday she would.

II

A WEEK BEFORE SHE LEFT BOSTON, Theresa rounded the corner after work and ran straight into Walter McClain, out walking with his wife and child.

She had just noticed, pulling on her coat, that she had spilled something down the right side of her blouse. She wiped away the liquid, leaving a shadowy stain. When she looked up, there he was, laughing at something his wife had said. She was a tall and slender brunette, holding a baby with black hair, just like Patrick's. Walter didn't see Theresa, or anyway he didn't acknowledge her. He just kept strolling along as if no one had passed.

In that moment of recognition, such an unfolding of emotions— *I know him. It's him. Oh God, him. Will he? No.*

Relief that turned quickly to despair.

She realized then that she hadn't spilled anything. It was her milk, seeping through her shirt from inside.

Already, she had felt that she was coming undone. She never slept anymore. She was up all night, waiting for Patrick's cries to pierce the silence, her heart racing. There were visions that refused to leave her. Lying on the table, left for dead. The nurses pretending she wasn't there as she screamed in pain. Everyone pretending.

She found small tumbleweeds of hair on her pillow when she woke in the morning. When she looked in the mirror she could see the white shock of her scalp in places. After she gave birth, she bled for six weeks. She had no idea if this was normal, and there was no one she could ask. She wanted to tell Nora, but her sister was so angry that Theresa didn't dare.

She wondered if she might die. Part of her hoped she would. That they might come in one morning and find her pale and bloodless in her bed.

That last morning at Saint Margaret's was like a half-forgotten dream she could not piece together no matter how she tried. If she could only manage to do this, she thought, then maybe she could make sense of what happened.

"I'll leave now," she had said, even after they'd gotten home from the hospital. "I'll take Patrick and I'll go."

But she felt weary, light-headed. Her plan seemed deranged. Where would she go? How would she manage?

So she cared for the baby at night, at home, when no one could see. In the beginning, that was enough. She only wanted to keep him close. Again and again, she reminded herself of this fact. When she was strong enough, she would take him away. But when she saw Walter, Theresa doubted she would ever be strong again.

Days later, Aunt Nellie died. Sitting in the church as she was eulogized, something broke in Theresa. Patrick cried and she felt her milk come. She wanted to snatch him from her sister's arms. But everyone was watching. She stared straight ahead to keep from crying. The tears spilled out of her anyway, the tears and the milk, her body turned to liquid, washing away the last bit of herself she could remember.

It was torture, listening to Charlie tell the story of Nora giving birth. Fifteen minutes! She knew Nora hated it too. Nora hated all of it. She hated Patrick.

Her sister's last words to her would stick in Theresa's mind.

Of course I don't want him.

It occurred to her then that she would have to leave without the baby. They would all be better off. If her sister was ever going to love Patrick, they couldn't continue on this way. She knew where she would go. She took the envelope from a drawer, the return address scrawled in the upper left-hand corner. It was not a home, but a school. *Saint Hugo of the Hills.*

Theresa gathered the clothing Babs had given her and all the money she had saved, which wasn't much. She left a note for Nora. Then she crept into Patrick's room, her bag weighing on her shoulder. For years to come, she would remember the sight of the baby sleeping in his crib, an angel. She longed to take him with her, though she knew she couldn't manage it yet.

She took his Miraculous Medal from the top dresser drawer instead, something to remember him by. She slipped it into her coat pocket.

Theresa hoped he knew somehow that she would be back to get him. She debated whether or not to kiss his cheeks, knowing that she might wake him. She did it anyway, feeling his soft, soft skin against her lips, hearing his cries begin just as she shut the front door and ran.

She rode the train to South Station and sat on the steps amidst the bums and the drunks, and the occasional crowd of late-night travelers coming off a bus. She didn't much care what anyone did to her, but no one did a thing. Occasionally she saw a figure coming toward her and thought it must be Nora, come to take her home. But then the woman would come closer and she would see that it was a stranger.

Theresa pulled the envelope from her pocket, read the letter. It was nearly a year old now. *Please look me up if ever you find yourself in Queens.*

As morning broke, she went to the ticket counter and asked for a one-way fare to New York. She rode with her bag on the empty seat beside her to discourage company. They had made this journey in reverse two years ago, Nora and Charlie in the front seat and her in the back, looking out the window, taking it all in. Now she faced straight ahead, eyes squeezed shut.

Theresa stood waiting on the steps of Saint Hugo of the Hills when school let out. She watched the door for close to an hour, wondering if her friend even worked here anymore. Finally, Abigail came out, blond curls bobbing, tortoiseshell glasses on her nose, just as she had been on the ship when they met. Theresa recalled the hours they'd spent gossiping on the deck, the boys they mooned over in the ballroom.

"Abigail!" she said loudly, grabbing her arm when she got close.

Abigail seemed frightened, pulling away.

She didn't recognize her.

Theresa had another memory now, of the day the letter arrived. Her sister scolding her. *She's only being polite, she's not inviting you.*

"It's Theresa," she said. "From the boat to New York."

Abigail cocked her head. Finally, she smiled.

"What in the world?" she said. "What are you doing here?"

She hugged Theresa, invited her to come to her apartment for a cup of tea. As they walked along, past a row of shops, Theresa caught their reflection in a glass storefront. Abigail was more or less unchanged, but Theresa looked like a different person.

"My sister died," she said, concocting a story on the spot. "I'm on my own now. That's why I've come to you. I didn't know where else to go."

Abigail looked stricken. "That poor girl. I remember—she wasn't well."

She said she was engaged at last and would be leaving the city soon. They had already bought a house in New Jersey, not far from her in-laws.

"It isn't fair how some people end up with so much," she said. "While others— I want to help you. You're a good girl, Theresa. You don't deserve this."

The timing was the first stroke of good fortune she had had in ages. Abigail arranged it so that Theresa took over her job when she left, teaching ninth grade. She moved into Abigail's studio apartment. The building was tall and beige and uninspiring. The cramped apartment was on the fourteenth floor. Her view was of a billboard advertising Swanson TV dinners. An illustration of a woman, twenty feet tall and yet somehow still dainty, wearing a pink dress, smiling at a box of frozen chicken and potatoes as if it were a puppy. Behind her, a dopey husband with his golf clubs signaled to a pal in the doorway that he could stay. *Extra Guest for Dinner? You're Ready for Him!*

Abigail left behind the bed and the dresser and the kettle, as well as a list of all the places Theresa could go to meet people from home. There were Irish pubs and clubs all over this part of New York, but she didn't wish to visit them. She wanted nothing to do with the Irish now, or with anyone.

Theresa rarely saw the people who lived in the apartments around her. But she could smell their strange cooking through the walls, could hear the booming voices, words spoken in languages she couldn't comprehend. It gave her a start when a voice was raised or an object dropped on the floor up above her head. Everyone was a stranger to her now. The world seemed menacing in a way it hadn't before.

The school looked like a prison or a factory. She thought of the country schoolhouses back home, of the pupils a teacher might know not just for a year but from the time they were babies until the age of ten or eleven. There, a teacher had a hand in shaping them, but here they were so rambunctious, so old, already formed. They didn't mind her, no matter how she tried.

Some mornings she dreamed of finding a way to board a ship back to Ireland. She imagined tucking into a plate of her grandmother's barmbrack, studded with raisins. She could almost taste it. Theresa missed the sound of her voice, how she muttered in Irish when she didn't want the children to know what she was saying.

But she didn't write home to tell them where she'd gone. She wondered what Nora had told them. By now they must know she had run away. Theresa would speak to them all when she was ready, when the time came for her to take Patrick back. Then they would tell everyone the truth.

She missed the bustle around Mrs. Quinlan's dinner table. She missed Nora most of all. The safety of her, the one thing Theresa could be sure of in this world.

Her entire life consisted of her pupils and her apartment. She didn't think she deserved any more than that. In the teachers' lounge, when girls talked about the men they were seeing and when they might propose, she sometimes wished to break into their conversations. But then she thought better of herself. What could she possibly say?

Theresa ate lunch alone at school, and dinner alone at home, forcing the food in. She ate oatmeal for dinner. She hardly knew how to prepare anything. Someone else had always done the cooking for her—her sister or Mrs. Quinlan or her gran. Nothing tasted like anything. Sometimes she forgot to eat. She looked in the mirror and was surprised to see how gaunt she had become. Her breasts and stomach sagged like deflated balloons, but the rest of her was all sharp angles, bones pressing through skin.

She went to church every few nights and prayed with a dozen old ladies. She said the Hail Mary until the words ceased to make any sense.

Her sorrow was her one companion, ever present, making her arms and legs sore, as if she'd just climbed a mountain. Some mornings it was a struggle to stand and get dressed. She slept and slept and slept. On the weekends, she slept all day, and then was awake at night, her heart pounding in her chest as she remembered it all, as she wondered what Nora and Patrick were doing at that minute.

On more than one occasion, she had visions of cutting her wrists, or going up to the roof and jumping off. But this was a sin so grave that she tried to banish the thought as soon as it came. She saw before her the image of her younger self on her confirmation day. The bishop asking what happens if you die in a state of mortal sin. And Theresa, cheerfully reciting the answer. *You go to hell,* she said then with a smile, fully believing that no circumstance could ever befall her to make her enter into such a state.

She carried Patrick's medal wherever she went, worrying it between her fingers, praying for him.

Another Saint Hugo's teacher lived in her building. For months, they rode the elevator together most mornings by chance and walked to school a few staggered feet apart. The woman might smile at her, and Theresa would look down at the floor.

One morning, the woman said, "This is silly. I'm Cathy Tursi. I teach eleventh grade."

"Theresa Flynn," she said softly. "Ninth."

They began to travel to and from work together on purpose after that. If the elevator doors didn't open on fourteen, Cathy waited for Theresa in the lobby. Their short walks were a highlight of her day, though she let Cathy do most of the talking. She was a few years older than Theresa. Cathy asked where she was from, whether she was dating anyone. Theresa was naturally inclined to tell all her stories to a new friend, but now she evaded even the most basic questions.

"You're a mystery, aren't you?" Cathy said, undeterred. "That's all right. I'll figure you out eventually."

Theresa wanted to be figured out, yet when, on a Tuesday night, Cathy invited her for dinner, she said no. For weeks, she declined Cathy's invitations, even though the old part of her wished she could go, wanted a friend.

Then Cathy came to her door and said, "This time it's serious. I've been stood up by my boyfriend. I've got a pot roast for two in the oven and I'm not in the mood to argue. You're coming over and that's that."

It was the first meal Theresa had shared with another person in seven months.

Cathy's apartment had the same layout as her own. She had warmed it up. Hung pictures, dropped rugs, painted her walls a pale blue. The shelves were full of books. She had a sweet old cat that liked to curl up on the windowsill, basking in the sun. Theresa's place was empty, a faded square and a nail where each of Abigail's pictures once hung, the cold bare floor against her feet each morning a kind of penance. Now she wanted to lie down on Cathy's carpet and never leave.

Cathy reminded Theresa of a more grown-up version of the woman she herself had once been. Everyone liked her. And for some reason, she liked Theresa. Having one friend made all the difference. She could feel herself returning when Cathy was there. It was in her nature to laugh, to flirt, to gossip, to be curious. Theresa grew afraid to be alone with her thoughts.

Cathy's boyfriend, Arthur, was a truck driver who was gone five days a week, including weekends. Theresa and Cathy went to the ten o'clock Mass at Saint Hugo's together every Sunday and afterward to the diner on Grand Street for coffee and eggs.

After Theresa had been in New York a year and a half, Arthur introduced her to a friend of his, Roger, a handsome American who worked as a policeman in the city. The four of them went dancing or to a movie in the early evening. Theresa let Roger kiss her but not all the other things he wanted to do. Her took her for an innocent, a virgin.

Theresa never mentioned Nora or Patrick, or even that she had once lived in Boston, to anyone. The memory didn't leave her, but it faded some, enough so that she could breathe, so that her heart stopped racing at every moment of the day. She still prayed for them. She still thought she might go back and get Patrick, bring him to New York.

One December morning as they walked to school, Cathy said, "Arthur says Roger just adores you. He's had a lot of fun these past few months. Could you see a future with him?"

"No," Theresa said. "Not with him or anyone."

"Oh." Cathy looked surprised. Theresa herself was surprised.

"Are you all right?" Cathy said.

A question so simple, she couldn't help but answer. "No."

Theresa started to cry.

"Do you want to talk about it?"

She shook her head.

Cathy put an arm around her. She looked so concerned.

"I'm just in a funk lately," Theresa said, trying to make it seem like less than it was.

They were silent for a long while, and then Cathy said, "Do you remember I told you how my mother and I go on retreat to a convent in Vermont every couple of years?"

"Sure."

"We were supposed to go for a weekend this winter, but with my sister having the new baby, my mother can't get away. I was looking forward to it, and we booked the room and all. It's just occurred to me. Maybe the two of us should go. A change of scenery might do you good. It's a beautiful place."

"I'd love to, but I can't," Theresa said. "I'm busy then."

Cathy laughed. "I didn't say which weekend it was."

Theresa swallowed. Her throat felt tight.

A vision of herself screaming in Sister Bernadette's face, clinging to her child. A story she could never tell.

"I have a thing about nuns."

"These are easygoing nuns, kind nuns, I swear. It's the quietest place I've ever been. When you get there, this sense of absolute tranquility comes over you."

"No. I can't."

"You'll love it," Cathy said. "I promise. It's not at all what you think."

Theresa looked at her friend and smiled. Cathy had a way of making her do things she never thought she would.

"All right," she said at last. "Just for a night or two."

They drove up on a Saturday morning. Theresa was anxious, but she tried to focus on the surroundings and the conversation. Vermont was beautiful—curtains of tall trees in every direction. They turned off the highway and drove through a quaint town square, then followed a winding road through the countryside, past farms and fields, until Cathy said, "Here it is."

The first thing Theresa noticed was the emblem of the Miraculous Medal emblazoned on the gates.

"What is that doing there?" she asked.

"It's their symbol, I guess you could say. You see it all around here."

Inside the gates, Cathy stopped the car in front of a massive stone building.

"It's converted from an old brass factory," she said. "Isn't it amazing?"

Attached to the building at either end were high wooden fences, ten or twelve feet tall. They made Theresa wonder what was on the other side.

An entryway with walls made of stained glass jutted out at the front of the building. They went in. The room was a conservatory. There was a small fountain flanked by birds of paradise, peonies, alliums, cactus plants in all shapes and sizes. At the back wall, a short flight of stairs led to an open door, a small, dark vestibule. Inside the space was another door, the top half of which was a wooden grate. A nun stood behind it. She looked trapped in there, a prisoner, but she smiled warmly. It was impossible to say how old she was.

She greeted them in Latin. Theresa didn't know how to reply, but Cathy said something brief and formal, also in Latin.

And then the formality was over. The nun squeezed Cathy's hand through the grate.

"We're so happy you're back."

"Sister Ava, this is my friend Theresa Flynn. Theresa moved to New York from Ireland."

"Ahh," the nun said. "With your family? Your husband?"

"Just me," Theresa said.

"How brave," the nun said.

No one had ever said that to her. Theresa and Nora came alone, just as millions of other girls had before. No one she knew seemed to think of it as brave. It was simply what one did.

Sister Ava told them lunch would be served in the women's refectory in an hour. Afterward, if they liked, the nuns would put them to work.

"We'd love to, Sister," Cathy said. "Thank you."

When they were back outside, she said, "When you work with them, you get to go into the enclosure."

The other side of the high fence.

Saint Gregory's guesthouse was a creaky old cottage with wide wood plank floors. The house was empty when they arrived. Theresa stepped from the front hall into a cozy living room with two floral couches and two armchairs, one blue and one white. The room was lit by lamps. Books were everywhere—on the coffee table, the dining table, the end tables, on the built-in bookshelves that flanked the stone fireplace. A mix of religious and not, left by guests, she supposed. Green potted plants sat on the shelves and climbed the lace-curtained windows. Dark wood beams lined the white ceiling. Paintings of the Madonna and Child hung on every wall.

The pink afternoon light as it shone into this room gave Theresa a sense of peace she hadn't felt in ages.

Cathy showed her the dining room with its plain wooden table and chairs. No two chairs were the same. In the kitchen, the plates too were all decorated in different patterns, most of them chipped here or there. The refrigerator was full of homemade jam and bread and raw milk from the dairy.

Every bedroom was named for a saint. A chalkboard listed their room assignments. They'd be sharing Saint Lawrence on the second floor. A woman named Maura would be in Saint Agatha on the first. There were four more rooms besides. In their bedroom, the mattresses were so old and soft and thin, you could feel every spring. Threadbare towels and sheets sat folded at the foot of each bed.

Lunch was fried fish and French fries with tartar sauce. Mushy peas. Raw milk. Tea and cake. It was served in the same stone building Theresa saw when they arrived, which she now knew was the enclosure where the nuns lived. She and Cathy entered from the public side, a door that led to a tiny dining room but with nothing to connect it to the rest of the building except a window with a wooden grille crisscrossing it.

The nuns who had prepared the food handed it through the grille. The brief glimpses of them, standing there in full habit with a steaming bowl or glass jug of milk in their hands, did something to Theresa. She felt desperate to pass through that wall and sit down to eat with them in their private quarters, though she couldn't say why. Maybe it was just the old curiosity that Nora was always trying to tamp down in her, the sense of not knowing, and as a result wanting more than anything to know. The nuns were friendly, they smiled. They seemed tranquil, satisfied, in no rush. But they said almost nothing, leaving her to wonder how they ever came to live in a place like this.

Her job that afternoon was to work with Mother Lucy Joseph in one of the gardens.

The nun was probably in her late seventies. She said she'd had a recent injury and couldn't do much. "You'll be doing most of the work, I'm afraid."

She instructed Theresa where to cut back the plants, big and small. Some were just weeds, but others were actual tree branches. Theresa got the enormous shears around a particularly thick branch and pulled the handles together as hard as she could. The sharp blades nicked the branch, exposing the green flesh beneath. But she couldn't get the blades any tighter than that.

"Let me try," Mother Lucy Joseph said kindly. She took the shears, and with a quick snap, the branch fell to the ground.

"Well then," Theresa said.

The nun winked. "I've had a lot of practice."

"May I ask you a question, Mother?"

"Of course."

"How old were you when you came here?"

The nun stood up straight. "Much younger than I am now. Older than you, though. I was an opera singer in a past life."

Theresa thought she was joking, but the woman went on. "I sang at Carnegie Hall. I had the biggest record contract of any American opera singer in history up until then. But. At a point, it all began to feel flimsy. So. Now I sing the Divine Office louder than most would probably like me to, and that suits me fine."

An orange cat sat watching them. "That's Chester," the nun said.

Theresa saw another nun, a young one, toss a tennis ball to a collie as she hauled out the trash.

She had the feeling that the immediate, the task at hand, was everything here. She thought about the women in the teachers' lounge at school, who seemed to be waiting for something better, some man who might set life in motion.

At five-thirty, the nuns sang Vespers in the chapel, separated from the pews by a black metal gate.

In the half hour between Vespers and dinner, Theresa and Cathy escaped to the Gulf station in town, a ten-minute drive away. It was the closest marker of civilization, the only one near enough for them to get there and back in time. All the shops were closed, but the Gulf sign glowed.

"My mother and I made this our tradition. We always came to the station and got a bottle of Coke from the machine. Good to know that there is still a world out here and that we will soon be back in it," Cathy said. Theresa agreed, even though she had felt elated during Vespers, a sense of lightness coursing through her.

They got back two minutes before the start of dinner. The only other person at the refectory table was Maura, whose name they had seen on the blackboard. She was a nervous-seeming woman, the mother of a young postulant. She had a short silver bob, poufed up and flipped at the ends. She wore a black dress, belted at the waist. Theresa wanted to ask her so many questions, but she held back.

The nuns sang Compline at seven-thirty, after which all work was complete. The women were expected to be in the guesthouse for the night.

Theresa and Cathy got into their beds with cups of peppermint tea and talked about the day, about the nuns themselves. Theresa was reminded of something. Remembering it for the first time in so long, she laughed. "I wanted to be a nun when I was small," she said.

"So did I," Cathy said with a smile. "I think all Catholic girls go through that phase, don't they?"

The bed was uncomfortable, springy. Theresa was sure she wouldn't sleep. But as soon as her head touched the pillow, out she went. She couldn't remember ever sleeping so well, not since leaving home. Not since leaving Patrick.

The next morning, the bells woke her at six o'clock.

"They have to pray again already?" she whispered.

"Yes. They prayed at two a.m. too! You must have slept through the bells."

"Could we have gone?"

"No. That one is done in the enclosure."

Once again, the forbidden nature of the thing intrigued her. She felt as if she would do anything just to be there, to hear the voices rising into one in the darkened chapel.

The nuns couldn't technically talk to them outside of private parlors or while they were working together, but they found their ways. After eight o'clock Mass, a nun approached and handed them each a slip of paper. Theresa's said that Mother Monica would pick her up at ten to go clean out a house on the far edge of the property.

At five after, the nun pulled up in an old Ford station wagon.

"Who are you?" she asked with a frown through the open window.

"I'm Theresa Flynn, Mother."

"Where's Maura?" she asked.

"I'm not sure."

The door to the house opened behind her, and out she came.

"Maura!" the nun exclaimed joyfully, as if they were the best of friends. "Such a delight to meet you!"

She reached across and opened the passenger door from inside. Maura got in front, so Theresa sat in back.

On the drive, Mother Monica explained that a nun had made her final vows a few days ago. Her family had stayed in Saint Gertrude's guesthouse, and it was now their job to tidy up after them.

They passed fields of grass, dried to a wheat-tinged gold. There were massive pine trees clustered around them, and maples that she thought must be glorious in autumn. Theresa felt sad that she wouldn't be here to see them. Two old boxcars stood in a field—the nun said one was used as a pottery studio, the other for stained glass. A shed behind them was the blacksmith's workshop.

She explained that whatever the abbey had was donated. Hence the denim habits that they wore to work outdoors—someone had provided reams and reams of the stuff, and the nuns had found a clever use for it, as they did for all things.

Saint Gertrude's was a white farmhouse with a wide front porch. They entered through the kitchen. Mother Monica pulled sheets and towels from the clothes dryer, placing them in a wicker basket.

"Theresa, was it?" she said.

"Yes, Mother."

"Why don't you go upstairs and vacuum the bedrooms and clean the bathroom? Maura, you stay here with me and fold all this laundry."

There wasn't much laundry to fold. Certainly not enough for both of them. Silently, Theresa questioned the logic of giving up her weekend to come clean a bathroom that had been dirtied by strangers. But she wasn't about to argue with the nun. She walked upstairs, found the vacuum in a narrow broom closet in the hall.

The guesthouses were lovely, but when she looked closely, she saw the humble nature of it all. In the bedrooms, ceilings were lined with cracks.

Below drafty windowsills, paint peeled off the wall and fell in flakes to the floor. Electrical outlets were dead or hanging loose. Nothing matched.

Every so often, Theresa would go to the top of the stairs and listen.

"Sister Jane is a beautiful fit here," she heard the nun say. "The mother abbess says she's never seen a girl take so naturally to the abbey."

Theresa understood that Sister Jane was Maura's daughter.

In the afternoon, Theresa and Cathy worked with Sister Antonia on a patch of grass outside the Monastic Art Shop. A young Japanese maple stood there. Sister Antonia explained that the tree was diseased, and the salt brought in each winter on the snowplows was making it worse. They were to build a fence out of wooden stakes she had sharpened earlier that week, joined together by a long sheet of thin metal and a roll of burlap. The aluminum she had had for years, the burlap she didn't know what she'd do with until the idea came to her that morning. Nothing wasted.

"Didn't cost a penny!" the nun said.

Theresa wondered how old she was, how long she had been here. She mentioned in passing that she had studied philosophy for twelve years. She had wrinkles all over her face. Her designation, sister, meant she had not yet taken final vows.

They worked for hours in the cold, using heavy mallets to drive the stakes into the ground. Theresa could see her breath. She was reminded of the farm back home in a way, yet this was entirely different. Not a man in sight.

When they were half finished, Sister Antonia went into the enclosure kitchen to make them a pot of tea so they could warm up. She returned with a metal teapot and three paper cups. She filled the cups to the top, handed one to each of them. Cathy and Theresa began to drink. The door to the art shop opened, and out came the big-haired blonde who volunteered at the register. Theresa had overheard her earlier, gossiping away with a customer.

Sister Antonia raised the remaining cup of tea, the one that she had intended for herself, and said, "Judy, tea?"

"Sister! Thank you!" the woman said. "It is chilly out here, isn't it?"

She had only been outside for thirty seconds, Theresa thought. She was about to climb right into a warm car and, no doubt, drive home to a big warm house.

"We're so grateful to you for the five hundred dollars," Sister Antonia said. "We've designated it for the chapel roof. It will be a godsend."

"Good, good," Judy said. "And what have we here?"

"A fence that we pray will stay standing for at least a few more weeks," Sister Antonia said. "It's ugly, but it'll be enough to protect the tree."

"What you need there is a low stone wall," Judy said.

The nun laughed, as if it were a fantasy beyond all reckoning, which Theresa assumed it probably was.

"I'll talk to my husband," Judy said. "I'm sure we can cover it."

After she drove off, Sister Antonia said, "We are so fortunate to have her. She's marvelous."

Did she actually think so? Walking the property that morning, Theresa had noticed bands of loudmouthed women who came to see the crèche and go to Vespers and the shop. Her own uncharitable reaction to them made her think that she could never be a nun.

Some of the nuns seemed to be without motive. Others had a clear agenda, a more businesslike approach. Mother Lucy Joseph was articulate and kind and warm. Mother Helena was stern, but with a soft heart. This one, Sister Antonia, was a salesman. They needed all of these things in balance. They needed to sell themselves. They thanked their benefactors during Prayers of the Faithful. They required money and recruits, and yet they couldn't be so bold as to actually ask for either one. Theresa thought of the greeting the portress had given her, inquiring whether she had come to America with a husband.

As they were packing the tools into Sister Antonia's pickup truck, she said to Cathy, "We're all so happy to see you here again. The mother abbess hopes you might join us one day. She thinks you have a calling."

"Not me, Mother, I'll be engaged soon," Cathy said.

Theresa wasn't sure why this surprised her. And she couldn't say why it hurt her feelings to be excluded from the abbess's remarks, even as she felt relieved that the comment hadn't been directed at her. She reminded herself that she had not yet met the abbess.

Late that night, from the bathroom at the top of the guesthouse, Theresa found that she could look across the road right into the nuns' dormitory. She felt a sense of longing mixed with revulsion. She was so grateful that she still had the option to leave when she liked.

Before they went home the next morning, Cathy said they should each have a parlor. Theresa's was with Mother Lucy Joseph, the nun she had worked with in the garden. They sat in separate rooms, connected through a grate like the one in the dining room. Theresa tried to see all that was on the other side. She could make out a wooden cross on the wall, a stack of books on a shelf in the corner.

"You've been a very good helper," Mother Lucy Joseph said. "How did you find your time here?"

"Oh, I enjoyed it very much. I don't want to go back to New York." Theresa laughed as she said it, meaning for her words to sound light, but Mother Lucy Joseph didn't reply. She let the comment sit there between them.

"I've never had a parlor before," Theresa said. "I'm not sure what I'm supposed to talk about. God?"

Mother Lucy Joseph laughed. "You can talk about whatever you like. Tell me what's in your heart."

Theresa found herself saying that teaching was often exhausting, that she wondered if the job, which she had always felt drawn to, really mattered at all.

"My students don't seem to get much from the lessons," she said. "But maybe that's my fault."

"Why would it be your fault?"

"Maybe I'm too distracted."

"By what?"

She had a choice. To keep the conversation at the surface, or go deeper. She had never confided in a nun before. But Mother Lucy Joseph struck her as wise, unflappable.

"There are things I regret deeply, Mother," she said. "I've hurt people I love. But I try to get on with it. I try to keep my feelings at bay."

"Why?" Mother Lucy Joseph said.

"What do you mean?"

"I mean let yourself feel something. Don't be afraid."

In the car on the way home, Theresa told Cathy everything. About Walter and the dances and the nuns at Saint Mary's. About Nora and

Charlie. About Patrick. Theresa felt afterward as if someone had filled her body with air where it had once been made of lead. She felt as if she might float out the window and up up up into the sky.

Theresa and Cathy returned to the abbey for a weekend every other month or so, keeping to their routine. They always slept in Saint Lawrence, always took their nightly drive to the gas station to get a bottle of Coca-Cola, to remind themselves that they were free.

It was on Theresa's fifth visit that she finally asked Mother Lucy Joseph what she had been wondering. The nuns created such peace for their guests, but did they feel it themselves? Was such a thing even possible?

They were washing gardening tools in a metal basin filled with warm, soapy water. Wiping rakes and hoes and shovels down with motor oil. In the barn behind them, a John Deere tractor sat surrounded by wheelbarrows, tarps, milk crates.

"The orientation of all we do is to remember that it's in the direction of something bigger," the nun said. "On the outside, you feel taken up by this peaceful energy. Once inside, you realize you have to create it. If you're frustrated, you can't just go off. I'm interested to know, my dear, why do you ask?"

Theresa said she was only curious.

The nuns invited Theresa and Cathy to come and stay for the month of July, when school would be over for the year.

12

CATHY AND ARTHUR were engaged in early June. He gave her a ring with a tiny diamond in it, and she wore it everywhere, tilting her hand this way and that, admiring how the stone sparkled in the sun. Theresa worried that Cathy wouldn't want to go to the abbey now. But on the first of July, off they went.

As soon as they reached the gates, Cathy took her ring off and placed it in the glove box.

"For safekeeping," she said.

Sister Ava greeted them in Latin and then immediately squealed, "Congratulations! Have you chosen your wedding dress yet?"

Two weeks passed in blissful occupation, the two of them caught up in the nuns' daily rituals. Then, as planned, Roger and Arthur came for a visit. For the first time since leaving New York, the girls curled their hair and powdered their faces. Cathy put her ring back on.

The nuns gave them the weekend off. The four of them spent the days swimming in the nearby lake, browsing in antique shops they could never afford. Theresa enjoyed herself, but she didn't feel well. Her head ached, her stomach was a jumble.

On Sunday night, the couples split off. She and Roger had dinner and drove until they found a quiet road beside a stream. The evening light was fading to darkness as they walked, hand in hand. He kissed her, ran his palm along her back, and lower, to her bottom, leaving it there, a question mark. She had the strongest urge to ask him to make love to her, though she didn't say so. She couldn't explain why to herself, but she kept thinking it would be her last chance.

She cried as they said good-bye at the gates. He wiped a tear from her cheek and kissed her, saying, "Silly girl, we'll see each other soon."

She looked past him, to the image of the Miraculous Medal, forged in iron. It was then that she understood. She had assumed the Virgin Mother was guiding her to Patrick. But now she saw that the medal had been drawing her here.

Theresa was quieter than usual over the next few days. She worried that Cathy might find her behavior strange, but her friend was distant too. She didn't seem to notice. One night, Theresa couldn't sleep. At three in the morning, she got out of bed and went to the bathroom window, looking over at the building where the nuns lay sleeping. A single light was on on the third floor. She saw a flash of black pass through it. Here, in this place, through these women, Theresa had felt the pure presence of God in a way she hadn't since she was a child. She wondered if her devotion was real, something she could sustain for the rest of her life. Or if one day the spell would be broken and she would see that she had only been seeking an escape.

Deliberating from here, from the outside, seemed pointless now. She knew that there was only one way to know. She felt elated. She couldn't sleep for thinking of how excited she was to tell them what she had decided.

A few hours later, she and Cathy dashed through fat raindrops to get to breakfast, the collars of their jackets pulled up over their heads to protect their hair.

Theresa said, "I want to join. I want to stay for good."

She held her breath, waiting for Cathy's reply. She thought her friend might try to talk her out of it. She almost hoped she would.

But Cathy stopped, stood still, as if she no longer noticed the weather. She took both of Theresa's hands in her own.

"So do I," she said. "I've been thinking about nothing else since the start of summer. Longer, maybe. Oh, Theresa. How will I ever explain it to him?"

Finally then, Theresa wrote to her grandmother. She begged forgiveness for not writing sooner. She told her she had been teaching in New York, visiting the nuns with some frequency, and that she was living with them now.

Her grandmother wrote back, *Your father and I don't understand. What on earth are you doing there?*

As postulants, they wore a plain black dress, a white veil. They learned to speak Latin and chant the psalms. They were to read *The Rule of Saint Benedict* every day, until they had committed all one hundred pages to memory. This part, Theresa enjoyed. It felt like going back to school.

They were to relinquish all worldly possessions. This too was easy enough for her. She had already left everything she knew behind, not once, but twice. She thought of Cathy's home. Her books and her small black-and-white television. Her darling cat, who had gone to live with her parents. The man she had planned to marry. If Cathy could do it, then so could she.

They learned quickly how vast the distance was between being a visitor to the convent and becoming nuns themselves. There was no longer any escape, no more drives to the gas station to catch their breath.

Their lives were constructed entirely of rules. There had been times in her life when Theresa felt as if she was under someone else's control—Nora's, mostly—but she had a knack for finding ways around that. Now the entire goal was for her own desires to be expunged. Her free will relinquished.

Postulants were not to share their worries with one another, to chat, to idle. Speaking to outsiders without permission was forbidden, as was unnecessary laughter. (*Was laughter ever strictly necessary?* she wondered.) Her letters had to be given to a superior, unsealed, before they could be mailed.

Ora et labora. Prayer and work. That was all that her life would be here.

Theresa discovered that the nuns walked slowly, hands tucked, eyes lowered, not because they chose to, but because it was mandated. They weren't to rush or to run. This made her want to dash around the property with arms outstretched.

Every infraction was punished severely. If you were a second late, you were made to kneel and kiss the floor. She thought of the factory back in Ireland, where her pay was docked if she came in more than three minutes past the hour. She had found the policy overly strict at the time. Now Theresa saw that those three minutes were a gift. They accounted for being human.

She no longer even had Cathy anymore, not in the way she once did. They could exchange only the rare whispered conversation in passing.

When Cathy came down with the flu and had to stay in bed for a week, Theresa thought to bring her a hot lemonade. A few hours later, she was called to the abbess's office.

"Is it true that you entered another nun's cell?"

"Excuse me, Mother?"

"One of your fellow postulants saw you and reported you. You know particular friendships are forbidden."

"Particular friendships, Mother?"

"You will have to be punished."

She was embarrassed by how quickly the tears came when she was rebuked for some mistake or another, which she was, nearly every day. The only person who had ever spoken harshly to her before was Nora, and then there was love in it, an almost amused resignation. Not so here.

Inside the dormitory, the small bedrooms were drafty and bare. The building was silent but for the occasional muffled cry of a girl in the night. The sound made her think of Saint Mary's, of the time when Patrick was only hers, though she hadn't wanted him then. She chastised herself for this now. It seemed a person never had the information she needed at the moment it would help her most. She prayed for him first thing each morning and last thing every night before bed. Somehow being here, the intensity of the quiet, put him at the forefront of her thoughts as he hadn't been since the night she left him.

Cathy told Theresa in a stolen moment that her family was devastated. They longed to have her back. They were allowed to visit twice. Her father cried at both parlors. Arthur wrote and wrote. Her mother reported that he came to them and said the nuns had brainwashed her and they ought to call in the police, the president, the FBI. Cathy was surprised by how hurt her parents were. She had three aunts and one great-aunt, all of them nuns. But that was different. None of them were cloistered.

Theresa's own father wrote to say she was making the wrong decision. It hurt her deeply until she realized that he knew the cloister meant she would never return home.

After a year, Theresa and Cathy both joined the novitiate. They were given their habits and their names in a joint ceremony on a sunny afternoon. The mother abbess cut off their hair, placing the long strands in a golden bowl. A party in the Jubilee Barn followed. The one festive day of the year. Cake and ice cream and wildflowers on all the tables. Cathy was to be called Sister Placid, and Theresa, Sister Cecilia. The elders warned them that a year was nothing. That one or both of them would most likely leave in time.

The canonical year came next, a period of no contact with the outside world. When it ended, Arthur was truly gone. He had married someone else. When Sister Placid's parents came for the first time after such a long absence, she said, her mother acted as if nothing had changed. She insisted on calling her Cathy and wanted to catch her daughter up on all the news—her sister was pregnant again, seven months along. Mrs. Kennedy had given a tour of the White House and the whole thing was shown on television and her taste was impeccable. Outside, it was 1962. But here, nothing was any different than it was a year or a decade before.

Sister Placid said her father was no longer crying. Now perhaps, he was angry.

"All he could talk about was the paint everywhere, how it's peeling, how it doesn't look good," she said.

A week later, walking to the chapel, Sister Placid saw her father on a ladder painting the barn. The abbess said, "He volunteered to do the whole place for free. Anything to be near you, I suppose."

Her own family was so far away that it was impossible to say whether they approved of what she'd done. But her father's and Gran's letters were kind from then on, accepting her decision. She didn't write to Nora. Every letter her grandmother sent mentioned this fact. Her gran insisted that they must talk to each other, and Sister Cecilia realized that Nora hadn't told the family the truth. Gran thought they had merely had a disagreement.

Two years at the abbey behind her, and still she often cried for half the day. Mother Lucy Joseph told her this was as it should be, that any girl sailing through with a smile was lying to herself, to them all.

The outward tranquility did not reflect their inner turmoil. She thought that if they could somehow hear what was inside them all at once, the sound would be thunderous. Her own doubts were a constant stream of voices in her head, all of which boiled down to a single question: Was she in hiding, or was she home?

Sometimes she thought she must be insane to stay here, when she could be in New York City, looking at a dress in a shop window, riding the subway to the Metropolitan Museum of Art. She thought every night of simply walking out. Down the hall of the dormitory, down the three flights of stairs that led to the front door. They weren't locked in. She could do as she pleased. Could slip out and hitch a ride to the one bar in town and get drunk and kiss a stranger and be back in bed by dawn. She could even go to the bus station and catch the Greyhound to Boston, where she might pretend the whole thing had been just a whim.

But she never left. Never even slipped through the abbey gates and walked alone down the darkened road at midnight, as a few of the other novices admitted to doing. She stayed enclosed, even when it felt like drowning in molasses, even when she could not breathe. Beneath the raging doubts was a low, steady voice that said to keep on. She made long lists of things she could not live without—lipstick, gossip, the smell of the ocean. But then she found that she could live without them after all.

One of Sister Cecilia's many jobs was to answer letters requesting prayers, and those that had been sent in gratitude for prayers the nuns had already said. This task let her know that it mattered, that they were doing something good here, even when it couldn't be seen.

She harkened back to her childhood saints for courage. She had once found such romance in their struggles. She recited from the Rule, the same line again and again. *Do not be daunted immediately by fear and run away from the road that leads to salvation. It is bound to be narrow at the outset.*

The weather that third winter was bitter, bleak. A week before Christmas, a package arrived. It was addressed to Theresa Flynn, the name scratched out and *Sister Cecilia Flynn* written in below. She tore back the brown paper and saw the wool in a pale shade of violet. Her grandmother had sent a gorgeous sweater she'd spent the whole fall knitting. The postage alone would have cost more than she could afford.

She lifted the sweater to her face and swore she could smell the kitchen fire back home. It brought to mind a vision of her gran sitting at the table in the firelight, stitching away, humming under her breath. She felt the strongest desire to return to her. That night, she slept with the sweater pressed against her cheek.

The next morning, the novice mistress took the sweater away.

"It will go to a more senior nun," she said. "Saint Benedict regarded private ownership as a vice. He instructed his followers to depend on the monastery for everything. It's too soon for you to have such a gift."

When spring came, the abbey was suddenly beautiful, every tree and flower in bloom. The change in the air made her think of what springtime had meant to her all her life, until now. The possibility of new love. The smell of a handsome stranger's skin at a dance. Pretty dresses, flirtatious smiles in the street. None of it to be hers ever again.

Things she might never have noticed before could bring her to joyful tears. A red-throated robin in a tree, a row of purple rhododendron bushes, ten feet tall. But with this joy came fresh doubts. Sometimes she worried that her love for God wasn't as strong as her love of this place and that eventually that unfortunate truth would force her to go.

She confessed her feelings to Mother Lucy Joseph when they were working in the garden one morning.

"I don't think of God every second of every day," she said.

"And what do you think God is?" Mother Lucy Joseph replied. "You're not spending your days thinking of a man in flowing white robes, is that it? Well, that's not God anyhow."

She was surprised when Mother Lucy Joseph took her hand. "God is here, in the calluses on your fingers from all the work you've put in planting so that we can eat."

"Did you know from the beginning that I would join?" she asked.

"I had an inkling on the day we met."

"But you didn't say anything."

Mother Lucy Joseph pulled the brim of her gardening hat close to her forehead. "In my opinion, it's not for anyone else to tell you what's inside yourself."

She wanted to share her whole story then. To tell Mother Lucy Joseph about Patrick, about Nora. She knew that if she stayed, she would have to confess it eventually. But it had been so long since she felt such warmth. She didn't want to lose the other woman's affection.

Everything she and Nora knew about each other, they learned through relatives in another world. News had to travel from one of them across an ocean, and then back to the other. Their gran kept them informed in vivid detail, hoping for a reconciliation. Gran wrote to her about Patrick, Nora's beloved boy. And then about the births of another son and a daughter in turn.

One day, feeding calves with Sister Placid, it struck her that she had stopped thinking of them by their given names. For so long, she wanted to call her friend Cathy, had to stop herself every time. Her own name, Sister Cecilia, felt like something she was wearing and could take off at any moment. But without noticing, this had changed. She was here, she was in it.

The rules softened some as she proved her dedication. The low, steady voice beneath got louder and louder as her doubts shrank down to a whisper. She knew from what the other nuns said that they might never go away completely. But it was something.

Still, she did not know if she would stay for good. Some women left after years. Sister Ann had lived at the abbey since she was twenty-seven. She walked out weeping one morning when she was forty. What life would she have now? She seemed so disappointed, and yet she knew somehow that she had to go.

"How?" Sister Cecilia asked Mother Lucy Joseph.

"In time, you just know."

When someone who had been there far longer than she had went away, all the doubts returned. Longevity was no mark of anything. Things could come apart so fast.

"But that's true for everyone," Mother Lucy Joseph said. "Think of a marriage, husband and wife. The piece of paper, the white wedding dress, they don't promise anything. A person has to stay there, fight for it, every day."

Her last hesitation when she thought about taking final vows was Patrick. She had been picturing him as a baby all this time, even as she knew he was getting older. She lit a candle in the chapel each year on his birthday, watching the flame, thinking of him as he turned four, then five, then six, then seven. What did a seven-year-old boy look like?

She would have to give him up once and for all if she stayed. She knew that she already had. He was only a memory now. A medal in her pocket. Still, she thought of him, and of Nora, all the time. She herself might have once imagined women running off to convents to hide from some unwanted truth. But her experience proved just the opposite. To sit alone with your thoughts in silence for so long, you had no choice but to confront them. The calm came not from slipping a habit over one's head but from facing down all that plagued you and coming out on the other side.

After much prayer, and with Sister Placid's encouragement, she wrote to Nora at last. Nora wrote back with news of her children. They corresponded once every few months after that. Their notes at first were cordial, formal. Nothing like their relationship had been. But they grew warmer in time.

In their sixth year at the abbey, Sister Placid took her final vows, becoming Mother Placid. Sister Cecilia still wasn't sure she would stay. She thought of Patrick more and more. She had believed she was past it, but the yearning for him returned. She dreamt of him. Finally, she told Mother Lucy Joseph what she was wrestling with.

She had always feared that were it ever made known, she'd be penalized or forced to leave for keeping such a secret. But there were nuns here, widows mostly, who had grown children. Mother Lucy Joseph, in her calm way, said that if the child was safe and happy, if she had asked God's forgiveness for any wrongdoing on her own part, then she ought to feel forgiven.

"I've always had this belief that I would go back for him one day," she said. "Maybe it was a fantasy to begin with, but if I stay here, that possibility dies."

"Perhaps you need to see him once more to be certain," Mother Lucy Joseph said.

And so she wrote to Nora. *If you ever want to visit the abbey, you could bring your children on our annual fair day next month. I wouldn't be able to spend much time, but we could at least say hello.*

She put it that way, *your children,* so as not to scare her sister.

Nora took two weeks to reply. She wrote that she had never told them that she had a sister. She was sorry, but that was the truth of it. Sister Cecilia wrote back right away. *They don't have to know who I am. I'd just love to lay eyes on them.*

On him.

Finally, Nora said they would come.

Sister Cecilia watched the gates all morning, waiting for them to drive in. On this one day a year, the abbey was open to the public, a fund-raiser where people could see how the farm worked. But the nuns were meant to observe their usual silence. She knew she would only have a minute.

When she saw them emerge from the parking lot, she walked toward them, meeting them on the dirt path that ran alongside the sheepfold. Nora wore a smart skirt suit and heels, pink lipstick, like the kind she herself had once worn. She looked entirely like a woman now, all the girlishness gone from her.

The children too were neatly dressed, the boys in jackets and pressed pants, the girl only two years old, wearing a yellow party dress and Mary Janes, a white straw hat, a pair of white socks trimmed with lace.

"Good morning," Sister Cecilia said, meeting Nora's eye.

Nora didn't recognize her. "Good morning, Sister."

Slowly, she saw the fact of it sinking in on Nora's face. She let out a laugh.

"Theresa?"

Nora looked like she might crumble for a moment, but then she stood erect.

"This is my friend, Sister Cecilia," she said. "Say hello, children."

"Hello," they replied in unison.

It surprised her that Nora and Charlie's children spoke with American accents. It seemed impossible that the two of them could create something so entirely of this place.

John and Bridget looked alike. They looked like Charlie. Patrick was tall and beautiful. He put her in mind of a man she had not even thought of in years. Theresa couldn't take her eyes off the child. She wanted to ruffle his shiny black hair. To kiss him all over his face.

"It's a beautiful place," Nora said. "I hope you're happy here."

"I am," she said. "How's Charlie?"

"He's fine. He's taking the boys on a camping trip next week."

They held each other's gaze a moment longer, until a commotion pulled them apart. Patrick and John were wrestling in the dirt, laughing.

"Brothers," Nora said with a shake of her head, just as the little girl jumped on top of the pile.

"Bridget!" Nora shouted, her voice stern. "Your dress!"

She shook her head. "That one gives me no peace. She reminds me of you."

They both smiled.

Then, "Up! All of you!" Nora commanded.

This was not the shy and stammering older sister she had once known. Nora was a proper mother now. The children fell in line.

She looked at her boy. Patrick had a family. A brother and a sister, a mother and father. Things she never could have given him. Right now, at this moment, she believed that they had both ended up where they belonged.

"I'd better be off," she said. "So much work to do. I hope you enjoy the day. There'll be sack races and demonstrations with the cows and horses later. If you hurry to the dairy, you can learn how cheese is made."

"Let's say good-bye now," Nora instructed the children.

They stood in a row, and Sister Cecilia hugged each of them. A small embrace for Bridget and for John, and a longer, tighter one for Patrick. She bent to smell his hair, allowed herself this one indulgence.

She hugged Nora. She had intended to apologize, but instead she whispered, "Thank you."

One month later, she took her final vows.

Part Five

❧

2009

13

Nora always planned the wakes. Made the phone calls and summoned the priest, arranged with the undertaker what the deceased would wear and whose lilies should sit closest to the casket. She decided who would be invited early, to pray over the body before the crowd came. She put someone in charge of the guest book and someone else in charge of placing framed photographs around the room, on mantelpieces and end tables, though later she would rearrange them when that person wasn't looking.

Nora had everyone back to the house after, nothing fancy, just cold cuts and lasagna, highballs and beer. They'd stay as late as they stayed. Somehow, by the time the funeral ended next morning, she would have managed to make a feast. Honey-glazed ham, au gratin potatoes, Parker House rolls, and green beans. Cookies and hermits and pies. In recent years, some had begun to suspect that the desserts were store-bought, though Nora denied it. A SWAT team with dogs couldn't find a bakery box in her kitchen trash can, or in the barrels behind her garage.

Her own funeral was planned and paid for. Matching coffins had been selected one sunny Saturday twenty years back, when she and Charlie were in their early fifties. They purchased a burial plot so prematurely that the man they bought it from ran off with the money and they had to pay a second time. Nora had made clear—not in writing, but by stating it on numerous occasions since her children were young—that the flowers should be all white, that her funeral Mass should begin with "Ave Maria" and end with a stirring rendition of "On Eagle's Wings."

When Charlie died, she made the arrangements herself, though everyone offered assistance, told her to take it easy. The routine was a comfort. She did not know how to be a widow, but she knew how to make a dip for the potato chips out of sour cream and powdered onion soup mix. She knew exactly how many glasses they would dirty. She knew that if someone spilled red wine on the sofa, a robust sprinkling of salt would pull up the stain.

Patrick's death was something else entirely. And still, she did not take to her bed or beg for a pill that would make her fall asleep and forget. She just got on with it.

It was noon and the wake was at four o'clock. She had fifteen pounds of potatoes peeled, two lasagnas in the oven, and three dozen stuffed mushrooms prepared in the fridge. She had been up at five to scrub the floors, to wash the vegetables, to bake the hermits, to get the ice buckets from the cellar, to roll fifty plastic forks and knives into purple paper napkins, each of which she tied with a thin white ribbon.

All morning, neighbors had come by, dropping off coffee cakes and casseroles. Eileen Delaney made a point of being first at the door, blue morning light in the window, a stack of baking dishes in her outstretched arms. A black puffy coat swallowed her from chin to ankle, like she was walking around inside a sleeping bag.

When they first met, Nora thought Eileen was a busybody, a pest, not to be trusted. But thirty-five years had passed. Now Eileen was probably her closest friend. They had both lost their husbands, a circumstance that evoked either pity or fear. To say you were a widow was to remind everyone else that one day they too would be alone, and if not alone, then dead. Terrible to think this was the outcome of even a good marriage. It wasn't a topic to bring up at book club, but Nora and Eileen talked about it some, and that helped.

Eileen was doing online dating. She thought Nora ought to try it too, but Nora couldn't imagine what she would say to a new man at this point in her life. Never mind what she would make of some stranger's body, or he of hers. Eileen had always been a flirt, lingering longer than she should have when she took Charlie's coat at a party, telling him how handsome he looked. Old age had distilled her down to her essence, as, Nora supposed, it had done to them all.

Eileen wanted to come in, keep her company, but today, Nora didn't want a soul in her kitchen. She told her to go.

"My boys send their love. They'll both be there this afternoon," Eileen said, lingering on the stoop. "Tommy's divorce was finalized yesterday, by the way. Just between us. Don't tell him I said anything."

"Of course I won't," Nora said.

She was appalled at herself for being capable of brightening, but she brightened, the tiniest bit.

Tommy was the only boyfriend of Bridget's she had ever known about, and only then because Eileen had come upon the two of them kissing in her basement rec room when she went down to put a load of clothes in the wash. Around the same time, Babs had discovered her daughter Peggy was taking the Pill. Nora was seized by the fear that Bridget might become pregnant. She searched her drawers while she was at school but found nothing. Even so, she forbade Bridget from bringing boys into the house. Later, Nora feared that she had driven the point home too hard. To this day, Bridget had never once brought a man home.

The romance between Tommy and Bridget was ages ago. High school. But Nora held on to it. Tommy Delaney gave her solace when a certain unnameable fear buzzed at the back of her skull.

As she set the potatoes to boil, Nora imagined the undertaker down at O'Dell's, getting Patrick ready.

She was in and out of his apartment yesterday, feeling guilty, as if her presence were an intrusion. Which was absurd. The dead had no privacy. She would have to clean the whole place out in a week. Even so, she went straight for the closet, kept her head down. She found the good suit he wore to weddings and wakes, a shirt, clean underwear, shoes and socks, and then she left the bedroom at once.

Her grandmother always said a dead man's spirit didn't leave his home until his body was in the ground. A silly country woman's superstition. And yet Nora could swear the rooms were still warm with Patrick's presence, as if at any second he might jump out from behind a door, that mischievous smile on his face—*Surprise! I was only joking, Ma.*

On her way out, she took in the sight of his small, tidy living room, the remote controls lined up on the coffee table. In the kitchen, there wasn't a dish in the sink. Nora had only been there when Patrick was expecting her. She felt proud, seeing how neat he kept the apartment for his own sake. It said something about a person.

She wished she could ask him what had happened. Already, she understood that the not knowing would compound the pain for as long as she was alive. She wondered what Brian thought, but he hadn't come home last night. He wasn't answering his phone.

When Nora got the call from the hospital, Brian was still at work. He had come home in the meantime, assuming her car was in the garage and she was asleep. He had gone to bed, unaware that anything had changed. What a thing to wake up to.

She had last seen him yesterday morning. He sat at the table, a paper napkin tucked into his shirt, a sausage link between two fingers, raised to his lips. Had it been another day, Nora would have told him to use a fork. As it was, she said, "There's something I have to tell you. I wish I didn't have to, but I do." Brian held the sausage midair while she spoke, expressionless, frozen in place. When she was finished, he dropped it on the plate and walked out. He hadn't been back.

She knew he didn't always sleep at home, but until last night he had at least had the good manners to give the illusion of having done so. Sometime after dawn, Nora might be awakened by the reassuring sound of Brian opening the front door, creeping up the stairs. Last night, she was wide awake until morning, waiting for it. She wondered who he was with, how he was getting through.

She had been greedy, keeping him home with her. She often voiced concerns about his job, his aimlessness. When his old high school baseball coach mentioned at church that Brian would make a good replacement for him, Nora called the man the next day and asked if he was serious. When he said that he was, come to think of it, she told him to try again, that sometimes Brian needed a little push.

But Nora had never suggested that he move out. In her mind, his presence was the one thing stopping her from being old. She still had someone to look after. Brian was quiet. It was easy to dismiss him, as Bridget and John did. But he was very sensitive. An observer. Nora talked and talked to Brian. He never said much in response, but she knew he was listening, which was more than she could say for the others.

John had come to see her yesterday, with Julia and Maeve. They brought sandwiches and talked about everything but Patrick—the cold snap and the school play and the food. Nora wanted them to acknowledge the loss. She wanted them to say his name.

It made her sick to think of John and Patrick, estranged for no good reason. She had pleaded with John to put things right. He was the one who needed to do it, since he was the one who had initiated the silence. If only he would say hello to his brother. How hard was hello? She could barely look at John now.

But Nora had been happy to see her granddaughter. They took Maeve out of school early, which she herself never would have done. Whether or not it was a good idea, she was grateful. Maeve was getting older. Nora wanted to hold tight to her childhood. Little ones made everything better—there was no point in Christmas presents without believers, no reason to take pictures of a bunch of slightly overweight, pasty adults. Brian was her last hope for more grandchildren, and Brian was in no rush.

When Maeve went to the bathroom, Julia whispered, "I'm worried about how tomorrow will be for her."

Nora had told them a hundred times to take Maeve to a stranger's wake for practice, but Julia thought it might be scarring. That was the word she used.

Over the years, Nora and Eileen had made a sport of critiquing their daughters-in-law. She regretted now some of the things she had said. Early on, she didn't know what to make of John's wife. They didn't get married in the church. Julia said she wasn't sure she wanted children. Nora asked John, if they weren't doing it for God or for children, then who was their marriage for? "It's for us," he said, as if it should be clear.

Mostly, in the beginning, Julia and Nora communicated through Bridget's dog at family gatherings. They passed entire holidays this way. Julia would say, "What are you looking at, Rocco?" And Nora might add, "Rocco, do you see a squirrel? Tell Grandma. Do you?"

In time, after Maeve, it had gotten easier. But there were still reminders that John had married someone not quite like them. Of course, John himself wasn't quite like them anymore.

Julia had suggested that Nora hire a caterer. *Let yourself off the hook. Give yourself a break.* She didn't understand that seeing off your dead wasn't a responsibility that you foisted onto strangers.

Years ago, Nora's sisters-in-law would have helped her on a day like today. Babs would be bragging about her children, and Nora would be annoyed, jealous that Babs's brood never seemed to give her a moment's worry. Kitty would be pouring herself some gin as she trimmed the string beans, making Nora nervous. She missed their company now. Babs, five years gone. Kitty living out her days in a retirement community, doing watercolors, playing bingo, flirting with the few surviving men.

When the phone rang, Nora felt a small burst of relief.

"Brian?" she said, sure it was him.

A young woman's voice she didn't recognize said, "Mrs. Rafferty?"

Nora almost hung up. A telemarketer at a time like this.

Then the woman said, "This is Sister Alma at the Abbey of the Immaculate Conception. We spoke yesterday."

"Oh," Nora said. "Yes."

She had regretted making the call as soon as it was over. It hadn't been kind of her. A strange impulse, to lash out at Theresa after all this time.

"I'm sorry to bother you. I'm sure you must be busy. But Mother Cecilia asked me to call ahead and tell you that she'll be arriving at three o'clock."

"Arriving?"

"She's coming down to Boston to be with your family for the wake and funeral."

"Can I speak to her?" Nora said. Blood pumped like mad in her ears.

"I'm afraid she's already on her way. It was very last-minute. That was why she wanted me to tell you. If you could give me the name of the funeral home, I'll pass it along to her when she calls in."

Nora told her the exact location of O'Dell's as if her sister were a welcome friend. She said thank you and hung up, and then she sat down to catch her breath. She wondered if she might have a heart attack and die. That might not be so bad. Better than facing things, maybe.

She looked around the room, imagined it full of people, tried to picture Theresa among them. For a second, Nora wondered what she would think of the house. Suddenly, the kitchen disgusted her. Old and worn as it was. Yellow Formica counters and maple cabinets were the style when they moved in. She had never replaced them. Every time John and Julia came over, they remarked on how easy it would be to give the room a face-lift. And it was true, wasn't it? Why had she never done it?

She thought of Patrick's Miraculous Medal. She had given it to him years ago, made him promise to wear it for protection. He did still wear it, sometimes, out of respect for her. But it hadn't been with him when he died. Theresa had been the one to send the medal in the first place, the summer he was seventeen. Now Nora felt the need for Theresa to see it on him, as if to say that its absence hadn't been the cause of what happened.

She picked up the phone and tried Brian again, and when he didn't answer, she called John.

You've reached John Rafferty, founder of Miltown Strategies. I'm unavailable at the moment, but your call is very important to me. Please leave a message and I'll be back to you just as soon as I can.

Communication was supposed to be the thing now. In theory, you could reach anyone anytime. When Nora saw her children, they always had their phones in hand. When she called her children, they rarely picked up.

"John," she said. "I need you to go to Patrick's on the way here before the wake and bring me the medal he wore. He needs to be wearing his medal. It's silver with blue around the edges. On a long silver chain. It will probably be in the box on his dresser. Or I suppose it could be in a drawer. Or—oh, I don't know. Just look around. There's a key under the mat. Call me so I know you got this, please."

Right now, the medal seemed like the most important thing in the world.

Nora stood up. She took a head of iceberg lettuce from the colander beside the sink and placed it on a cutting board. She chose a knife from the block, much sharper than the job required. A knife that could cut through bone.

As far as she knew, Theresa wasn't allowed to leave the abbey for the rest of her life. Nora had called her as a form of punishment, she supposed, just as the silence had been up until now. It hadn't occurred to her that Theresa might actually come.

Once the children were grown, there had been times when she had thought to tell them the truth. Or part of it anyway. She would tell them she had a sister. But the elements of the story were impossible to separate. If she had a sister, why had she never said so? Why didn't they ever go to see her? If Nora said that she had taken them to the abbey once, that she and Theresa wrote letters for years, then they would want to know why they had stopped. And she couldn't tell them that. She had never even told Charlie.

She cut the iceberg in two, the halves landing with a satisfying plop. The thing before her looked like a child's severed head.

It was so like Theresa to just decide, to have a stranger call and announce her arrival. Never mind what it might do to Nora. She could still recall every bit of her anger over what her sister had done.

She chopped and chopped and chopped, as beads of water leapt from the greens and landed on the countertop.

From time to time, she had considered Theresa's point of view, allowed herself to wonder if her sister's way of thinking would have made the situation any better. Mostly, Nora forgot about the things that might catch up with her. A person did it to herself just by being alive. Planted little bombs without realizing that they had the potential to go off so many years later.

Try as she might, her sister was never far from her thoughts. Nora thought of her whenever it was absolutely necessary to drive through Dorchester or down Dudley Street. She saw her in Bridget, who was every bit as pretty as Theresa, though Bridget mostly squandered her good fortune. She wore her brown hair cropped short, so that from behind, Nora sometimes mistook her for one of the boys. She refused to wear makeup, or a skirt. The past four years, Nora had given up commenting on Bridget's appearance for Lent. But sometimes it hurt to look at her daughter. Nora knew what she could do with that face if she tried.

Bridget preferred dogs to people. She would forgive a dog anything. She was as devoted to poor, pathetic animals as Saint Francis himself. It was admirable, in its way. But she wasn't a grown-up. She wasn't lady-like. She went up on rooftops to pull trapped squirrels out of gutters. She battled men who ran dogfights and old women who tried to poison feral cats. She lived in an apartment with a roommate and a pit bull in what Nora considered a bad part of Brooklyn, though Bridget said there were no bad parts anymore. She was forty-four and saw nothing wrong with this arrangement.

Nora saw Theresa most of all in Patrick. At his best and at his worst, he was like her. Charming, a flirt. Loving and loved. He had Theresa's rebelliousness, her impulsivity, her willful streak. Nora didn't like to think it, but there was some of Walter in him too. Patrick could be sneaky. He could make a mess of things and then just walk away. Nothing at all like Nora or Charlie, duty bound until the end.

And Patrick looked just like Walter.

There was no one Nora's children had grown up with who couldn't pass for the sibling of anyone else. With the exception of the odd redhead or bottle blonde, most everyone they knew in Dorchester had dark hair and blue eyes—Nora and Charlie and the pharmacist at the corner and old Mr. Fallon in the apartment downstairs. And Nora's children. If you paid attention, you would see that Patrick's hair was not brown and wavy like the others', but black and curly. His eyelashes were thicker, the color of his cheeks less ruddy. He was tall like them, but his limbs were long and lean.

Before they moved to Hull, on the rare occasion when they passed Walter McClain in the street with his wife and children, Nora held her breath, waiting for someone to connect the dots. But nobody ever had. No one looked that closely at a boy.

When the lettuce had been chopped as fine as it could be, she placed the pieces in a glass salad bowl. She began slicing a red onion, the smell filling her nostrils.

She thought of Maeve, who had attended an expensive private school since she was five.

"It's a Quaker school, actually," Julia liked to say, but no Quaker Nora ever heard of would charge twenty thousand dollars for kindergarten.

Her own children had attended Catholic school. They had discipline, obedience, and the fear of God drilled into them, day after day. At Maeve's school, they learned to be creative. To be good friends. To Drop Everything and Read.

From the time Maeve was five, Nora picked her up on Tuesdays and Thursdays and kept her until John or Julia finished work. She tried to supplement Maeve's education by teaching her manners. She took her to afternoon Mass once in a while, since she knew John and Julia never did. She gave her boxes of monogrammed stationery, wrapped in pink paper, to entice her to write thank-you notes. Julia wouldn't know the importance of a thing like that, but it mattered.

Nora remembered Maeve, six or seven, sitting on the sofa in the den upstairs, repeating something her teacher had said that day: *Secrets secrets are no fun, unless they're shared by everyone.*

"But if it's shared by everyone, then it's not a secret," Nora said with a frown.

"Nana," Maeve replied, exasperated. "That's the point."

When Nora was young, no elder told a child—even a grown one—anything at all. It wasn't a secret. They just weren't entitled to know. Conviction in this belief had been handed down through the generations like a cherished heirloom. She sensed that this was changing, that the world was awakening to all sorts of ideas that seemed perfectly frightening to her. But maybe Maeve was right. The secrets had done no one any good. They had rotted Patrick, twisted everything, led them here.

For all her careful orchestrations, he still had his suspicions.

The night after Charlie died, Patrick said, "Who is my real father? I know it wasn't Dad."

Nora didn't know how to answer.

"Not now," she said. "Please."

Later, she felt ashamed. She had acted like it cost a person nothing to ask a question like that. But she didn't undo it. She told herself that if he asked again, she would put it right. But Patrick never did.

Nora was covering the finished salad in plastic wrap when she heard the front door swing open. She ran to the hall, and there stood Brian, wearing the clothes he'd left in yesterday.

He smelled like he'd rolled around on the floor of the bar. She wondered if he'd slept there. Seeing his face, she felt more relieved than the situation warranted, as if Patrick himself had walked in.

"Brian Rafferty! Thank God. You scared me half to death. I tried to reach you."

"I didn't have my phone."

She was going to tell him. Of them all, he would judge her the least. He was her baby boy. Nothing she did could ever be wrong in his eyes.

But the words wouldn't come. She needed more time.

"Go and get cleaned up," she said. "I ironed you a shirt. It's on the bed."

He walked toward the staircase, then looked back over his shoulder. "I'm sorry I worried you, Ma."

He sounded so sincere, like Patrick when he was a teenager. Nora never doubted their contrition.

If she opened her mouth and spoke, she might cry for a year.

Nora tipped her chin toward the upstairs. She gave Brian a smile.

14

JOHN, JULIA, AND MAEVE left the house ten minutes behind schedule.

The whole family would gather at Nora's and then drive on to the wake as a group. They would all sleep at her place tonight and travel together to the funeral tomorrow. John couldn't say why they did it this way, only that they always had.

In the passenger seat, Julia held two enormous platters on her lap.

He had told her not to order anything, tried to get her to see that Nora wouldn't appreciate the stuff. She would see the store-bought symmetry as a flaw, not a virtue.

But this morning, a teenage delivery boy stood at John's front door balancing two trays covered in plastic. *Brie platter and stuffed dates, and the crab cakes with shrimp shumai?* he said, reading from the slip. The kid was wearing a white T-shirt in thirty-degree weather. His car was still running in the driveway, exhaust pouring from the tailpipe. John just sighed and felt around in his pocket for a tip.

He wished Julia would understand it without his having to explain. His wife had gone to Georgetown and BU Law. These things his mother toiled over, Julia would handle with one phone call. He already knew that when he died, trim young men in black uniforms would pass around trays of canapés and chicken on skewers. What was so wrong with it? It was what he would do in the same situation. But to John, it felt like something would be lost.

"Why does a dead man who hardly ever set foot in a church have a

sudden need for religious jewelry?" Julia said now. "Is your mother trying to trick God into thinking Patrick was devout?"

The word *God* slipped out of her mouth as if surrounded by finger
quotes.

I need you to go to Patrick's on the way here, Nora had said on his voice
mail, like it was nothing out of the ordinary. *He needs to be wearing his
medal.*

His brother's place in Dorchester wasn't on the way and she knew
it. The detour would add forty minutes to the drive to her house, out
in Hull, at the end of the earth. And John had no desire to go looking
through Patrick's things. It was a job for Brian. For anyone but him.

Julia reached out and turned up the heat. A moment later, the car felt
like an oven. She was always cold. John glanced over at her. She wore
small diamond earrings, a simple fitted black dress that landed just above
the knee. Conservative, but sexy in its way. He knew that beneath her
black pumps, her toenails were painted the same shade of red she had
selected at her weekly pedicure for as long as he'd known her. A color
called Russian Roulette.

Among the crowd they would see today, she would stand out. Some
of the women he grew up with could be considered pretty if you begged
forgiveness. If your definition of pretty included big white arms, thick
calves, freckles. He had married a girl of a different order. Toned and
tanned with shiny, shampoo commercial hair. Perfect from any angle.

Julia tilted her head toward the backseat.

"I'm worried about her." She whispered, even though there was no
need.

Maeve had her headphones turned up to top volume. He could hear
muffled traces of her music over the car radio, probably damaging her
eardrums for life.

"I think all this has her more worked up than she's letting on. The open
casket." Julia shivered. "She's never seen a dead body. Hell, I hadn't seen
one until I married you."

Julia thought everything to do with wakes was barbaric, odd. Her family would have Patrick cremated by now, his ashes scattered to the wind
while a woman in flowing robes played Joni Mitchell on a harp.

Fifteen years after they got married, she was still ill at ease with the formalities, the rituals of the Raffertys. Whenever she was with them as a group, he could tell she wished she were home in California with her own parents. There, they would be drinking wine barefoot by the fire pit, arguing about some new novel or movie. Not sitting around a table covered in white linen, everyone's head bowed as Nora led them in saying grace.

Julia's family had an ease about them. When they stayed with her parents, her mother wasn't in the kitchen in the morning, hovering over the stove. She might have left some fruit on the table, or muffins from a bakery in town, along with a note. *Gone to yoga! Back by noon!*

As a kid, Julia said, she liked to imagine herself as one in a raucous brood of siblings, forever fighting over their toys or who got to sit in the front seat. She fantasized about a mother who did not work but instead stayed home and baked brownies. This mother never ran late or said *shit* under her breath in traffic. She kept a well-stocked fridge, which contained things like Jell-O pudding and whole milk and bologna. Not only did she never lose her keys, she knew the exact location of everyone else's keys at all times.

But when Julia actually encountered this mother, in the form of Nora, she was slightly appalled. She questioned her in ways John never had. There was a whole life he wouldn't have known if not for his wife. He had grown up a ten-minute drive from downtown Boston and never set foot in the Wang Center or Symphony Hall. Now they took Maeve to the *Nutcracker* every December. They had a subscription to the A.R.T.

John loved taking vacations with Julia's parents, to the house they rented every summer on Nantucket. Carol and Fred were easy to be with. They all liked the same things. The one time he invited Nora and Charlie, his mother announced the minute she was off the ferry that she had brought sandwiches wrapped in waxed paper to save money on lunch. When they went for cocktails at the White Elephant, his parents had a fit over the cost. They made a thing of just ordering iced tea. Two days later, everyone was lying on the beach, relaxing, when out of nowhere Charlie shouted, *Sixteen dollars for a margarita! I can't get over it.*

His father had died by the time John and Julia bought the Cape house four years ago. Her parents sent champagne. Nora's first response was, *Did you have someone inspect it? Has anyone looked at the roof?*

No, Mom, the whole thing is probably going to collapse on top of us, he said.

But John felt it then, the sensation that he was just like her. Full of dread. Maybe the roof would fall in. Maybe all of it would disappear. He was kidding himself if he thought he could transform into some carefree moneyed type just by signing a purchase and sale.

Instead of the family meeting they had intended to have last night, the three of them sat in the living room and talked about Patrick.

"Is there anything you want to ask us?" Julia said. "Anything at all, sweetie."

"What happened exactly?" Maeve said, in a curious, detached way, as if they were discussing the sudden death of a B-list celebrity they'd seen in a movie once.

"He was drinking and driving," John said. "Your uncle made a lot of bad choices in his life."

Later, Julia said he had been a little harsh.

"I thought we were supposed to be honest with her," he said. "Let her think about that the next time she considers getting into a car with some scumbag who's been drinking."

"Honey, she's thirteen. She doesn't exactly go out joyriding with guys we don't know." Julia paused. "What do you think happened? Why now?"

"I think if you drive drunk enough times, you're bound to drive into a wall eventually," he said.

"Should we have put something in the death announcement in the paper to acknowledge it?" Julia said. "In lieu of flowers, send a donation to Mothers Against Drunk Driving? Something like that?"

"No."

His mother put no premium on the truth. She would never admit, maybe even to herself, how Patrick had died.

John had heard Maeve on the phone after the family meeting. She wasn't broken up.

My uncle died. I don't think I'll have to take the algebra quiz tomorrow. What? I know. My aunt's coming from New York. My mom said we'll probably all go to the funeral together in a limo.

Her words chilled him. Her giddy tone. Maybe every parenting choice they'd ever made had been a colossal mistake, turned her into the monster he saw before him. *A limo.* Christ.

"She barely knew Patrick. They had no relationship," Julia pointed out when he asked if it was weird that Maeve wasn't more upset.

This made him feel worse, though it was a simple fact. He and Patrick had never gotten along, not since John was a kid. Patrick and Maeve only saw each other a few times a year, at the holidays, when each of them had other people around whose company they preferred. Patrick might ask her how school was going, what she had planned for summer vacation. The generic questions you asked a child you didn't know very well.

When Bridget and Nora talked to John about what had happened, he sensed that beneath their words was an accusation: *Of course you're not sad. You didn't even like him.*

It was true that he didn't feel sad. Instead, anger radiated through him. Shock. John's first thought had been for his mother. His second was about his big meeting in Chicago. He would have to cancel. *My brother passed away,* he said into the phone.

Oh my God, I'm so sorry.

He felt as if the sympathy was unearned, as if he should explain further. Only later did he think of Patrick himself.

Around three a.m., John gave up on trying to sleep. He decided to catch up on work emails, but when he opened his laptop, blue screen glowing like a beacon in the darkened bedroom, his fingers wandered to Facebook instead. Patrick wasn't on it, but the bar had a public page. A few dozen people, most of whom John didn't know, had commented already.

Brian and Fergie, I am so sorry for your loss. Hang in there.

Sorry for your loss!!! RIP Pat.

Last night's rager proved that you are gone but not forgotten. We will never forget. xoxoxoxox

Buddy, I will see you on the other side. I'll bet you're up there right now, doing shots of Jameson with Hendrix and Sinatra. Save me a seat. [Forty-two people like this.]

John closed the laptop.

After that, he walked the halls of the house. When his toe caught on the cord of a lamp that sat on a desk in the hall, he felt rage. He punched the lamp, the base landing on its side, a chunk of porcelain breaking off, falling to the floor. He didn't pick it up.

He would prefer to be sad in a straightforward way, like he had been when his father died. But for most of his life, John had hated Patrick. He was forty-five years old and there were events from childhood that he was still not over and probably never would be.

The oldest set the tone. Patrick had caused their mother heartache, so John decided early on to be the good boy, the perfect one. It wasn't easy. He was so often seen in relation to his older brother. In school, they expected him to be bad. Even in adulthood, whatever idiotic thing Patrick did left its traces on him.

Nora asked him to give the eulogy, because he always did it. John said yes. There was no one else. He was the only responsible one of them all. He'd like to be shit-faced, hanging out in some bar, like Brian. Or several states away, coming up in the morning, like Bridget. But instead he was in his mother's kitchen two hours after hearing the news, watching her pick at a turkey sub he'd brought over. He was there to support her, even as her face reflected pure heartbreak back at him, never the son she wanted most.

Maeve hadn't wanted to go to her grandmother's after they took her out of school. She acted pissy the whole ride over. When Nora opened the door to them, she extended her arms wide, and John's pathetic heart leapt to get in there. But Nora was reaching for Maeve, not him. His daughter jumped into his mother's arms and smiled, transformed into an angel, making him crazed and relieved in equal parts.

As he navigated through the traffic on 93 South, John looked back at Maeve in the rearview mirror. He thought about the meeting they had intended to have last night. He would just as soon pretend Julia had never seen that stupid website. So Maeve was looking. It didn't mean she actually thought they had kidnapped her. They had always known that one day, most likely, she would want to seek out her birth mother.

Julia was excited about the idea, at least in theory. She said they would go back to China when the time came. They owed Maeve that, and they owed it to the birth mother, to show her how well Maeve had turned out. But that was when they believed it would be difficult, if not impossible, to find her. Before the Internet came along and made the world a smaller place.

He knew they would discuss it once the dust settled. A death did that. Made the most important things you had to do in a day feel inconsequential. It turned out almost everything could wait.

He wondered if Julia would mention the website to his mother and figured she probably wouldn't.

Back in the beginning, they hadn't told either set of parents that they couldn't get pregnant, that they had tried everything. Bridget was the only one in the family who knew the extent of it. When they announced that they had decided to adopt from China, the reactions were predictable. Julia's parents sent a gorgeous coffee table book with black-and-white pictures of Tibet, and dozens of peonies, apparently China's national flower. His mother acted out.

Julia described the situation to Nora over dinner—the one-child policy, mothers forced to leave their babies in parks, or on the side of the road, girls abandoned in droves. Nora seemed to be listening with compassion, but then she said, "A child belongs with his real family. No one can ever love him as much."

Julia's voice faded. "I'm sure the mothers there love them as much as they can. But it's systemic. These women are under so much pressure. They'll have their homes destroyed if they don't comply."

"Then these babies are being taken from them," Nora said. "You'd be stealing someone's child. When I was young, they did it to the Catholic girls. They were teenagers. They had no idea what they were agreeing to."

Julia wept and John felt like strangling his mother for being so closed off, so insular, so stupid. She hadn't understood that they were telling her, not asking. No doubt, part of her reluctance had to do with them bringing home a child who didn't look like the family. He thought it was maddening, and yet that same night he told Julia that he'd like for the baby to have an Irish name.

When they arrived home from Beijing, Nora had the whole family waiting to greet them at Logan Airport. She had asked Bridget to drive up from New York and convinced Brian and Patrick to wear collared shirts for the photos.

Julia approached Nora first, the baby in her arms.

"Meet your granddaughter, Maeve," she said.

"She's enormous," Nora said. "There's no way she's only one year old."

But that was her final protest. Then she took hold of the child and was in love.

Weeks later, underslept, Julia became distraught, crying over her inability to soothe Maeve. Nora came to their house to help and Julia said, "You were right. She can sense that I have no idea what I'm doing. I didn't give birth to her and she knows it."

Nora took Julia's chin in her hand, held it firm. She said, "Giving birth has nothing to do with it."

John knew that had meant more to Julia than all the flowers her own mother could ever send.

He pulled into the CVS parking lot without signaling. He wanted to buy cigarettes, but Julia had made him quit years ago, before Maeve, theorizing that his smoking might be why she couldn't get pregnant. (For the same reason, they had sworn off booze for a year, they had stopped taking hot showers. She had made him change from briefs to boxers, one size too big.)

"I'm gonna get some mints," he said. "I'll be out in a minute."

Julia pointed at Maeve. "She needs maxi pads."

"Now?"

"You need them when you need them, John. Do you want me to do it?"

He shook his head, walked inside.

Every CVS on the planet smelled the same. There was something reassuring in that. He went straight to aisle three. Not his first rodeo. Maeve preferred the Always brand, ultrathin, with wings. John put a hand on the dark green package, then made his way toward the register.

His father never would have been in this position in a million years. Whenever Charlie called to order a pizza, he'd offer the delivery guy five bucks to pick him up a six-pack and whatever else he wanted from the store. John once opened the door to a kid holding two large pepperonis, a toothbrush, and a bottle of Tums.

Once, his mother had gone to the supermarket and his father had her paged because he'd forgotten to tell her to get potato chips. Nora, who might have been fifty at the time, didn't hear the page, but she saw a girl who worked there approach a ninety-year-old woman, saying, "Excuse me, ma'am. Are you Nora Rafferty?" So she said, "I'm Nora Rafferty. What's going on?" and the girl said, "Your husband said to look for a little old Irish lady."

Maxi pads. His father would have flipped out just hearing the words.

Julia hadn't been raised to cater to men. John had to fall in line. They took turns emptying the dishwasher. They paid someone to clean the bathrooms and vacuum the floors because she didn't want to do it. The one and only time he'd made the mistake of telling his mother he was babysitting for Maeve on a Saturday night while Julia went out with friends, he got a lecture in four parts about how it was impossible to baby-sit one's own child.

John took his place in line behind a woman whose toddler was trying to convince her to buy him a candy bar. Ahead of them was a teenage couple, probably skipping school, buying God knows what. Just another afternoon. He wanted to shout, *My brother is dead!* But instead he paid the cashier and gave her a smile.

"You have a good day now," she said.

John nodded. "You too."

Back in the car, Maeve said, "I'm texting with Aunt Bridget, Daddy. She said to tell you she and Natalie and Rocco will be at Nana's in an hour."

More words than she had said to him in a week. *Daddy.* Pathetic how much it meant to him. Like he was a nerd and Maeve was the most popular girl in school.

"That's good," he said. "Wait, Rocco is with them? She's bringing a pit bull to a wake and funeral. Seems appropriate."

"Dad. He's her *child.*"

"I doubt she'll bring him *to* the wake," Julia said.

His daughter had her own thing with Nora, and with Bridget, separate and apart from him. John got a kick out of this. He liked that Maeve loved Natalie too. He was happy for his sister. Before, he and Julia had worried that Bridget was lonely. "Bridget's married to her job," Nora liked to say. He wondered if she actually believed it.

Natalie was the first girlfriend she'd ever introduced them to. John had imagined the girls Bridget dated would look like she did, but Natalie was a knockout. The kind of girl he would bring home. She seemed completely smitten by Bridget, the two of them so blatantly in love. Though Bridget shut it off when their mother was present. In Nora's company, you might have thought they were just friends. For this reason, he didn't think Nora could necessarily be blamed for referring to them that way, though Julia thought it was appalling.

Last summer, down the Cape, John and Maeve sat on the front lawn waiting for the two of them to arrive for the weekend. He thought that maybe he ought to explain. Bridget and Natalie lived together. And Maeve was old enough.

Aunt Bridget and Natalie are more than friends, he said, picking at the grass. *Special friends, I guess you would call them.*

You mean they're a couple, she said.

Yeah. That's it. Sometimes women love other women, men love other men. It's sort of about the person, if that makes sense. You fall in love with a person. I know it probably sounds weird to you, but it's not weird. It's a good thing. Do you want to ask me anything about it?

She looked at him like he was nuts. *No.*

It's okay if you do. I know it's kind of weird.

Dad, there are three lesbians in my class.

Really. In the seventh grade.

Well, one of them's bi if I had to guess.

When they reached the Dorchester exit, Maeve leaned forward and said, "Take us by your old house, where you had to share the room."

The way she said it made sharing a room sound like a fate so cruel it might only befall an orphan out of Dickens. This annoyed him slightly, but then he had made her into the girl she was. A house teeming with people was exotic to her. They had four bedrooms they didn't even use. Maeve liked knowing that some summers it was John and Patrick and six cousins from Ireland, all crowded into the front bedroom. Her favorite thing was when John said he had never been alone, outside of the bathroom, until the fifth grade.

He didn't much feel like driving his brand-new SUV into the old neighborhood, even as he loathed himself for thinking it. There was the car itself. Three weeks old, and not a scratch on it. And then there was the bumper sticker he'd gotten, which he liked at first but now felt embarrassed about. Just three letters in an oval: *OFD*.

Originally from Dorchester.

When one of his clients saw the sticker, he said, *My parents grew up there too. Everyone loves being from Dorchester as long as they don't actually have to live there anymore, am I right?*

That had stuck in his craw, although it was true. John didn't want to live there. He had scrubbed every bit of Dorchester from the way he spoke. He cringed now when he heard anyone—his brothers, his cousins—pronounce potatoes *bah-day-das* or say *irregardless* or *so don't I,* when they meant *regardless, so do I.*

He could turn the language on and off. In some circles, the dropped *R*'s of his childhood were a plus. But this was not the case, for the most part, in the company he kept now. He considered the sound of every syllable before it left his mouth.

John had a gift for modulating his personality to suit whomever he was talking to. It seemed to him that Patrick was the same guy no matter where he went. Himself, always. He envied that. John was a shapeshifter, a pathetic pleaser, though it suited him to be this way sometimes. He owed his career to it.

He turned right onto Crescent Avenue.

"There it is," he said, slowing down.

They had painted the outside, changed it from blue to white.

John looked up at the corner window. He could almost see his brother beside him there, the two of them shoulder to shoulder as boys, watching a lightning storm, before things went wrong between them. A few years later, Patrick crawling out that window, tapping on it just before dawn, John sleepily crossing the room to let him in, so happy to be in on the secret.

He felt wistful as they drove off. Maybe Julia could sense it. She reached over, took his hand.

"Look!" Maeve said.

John and Julia turned to see a RORY MCCLAIN FOR STATE SENATE sign secured to someone's front porch, left over from the election two months ago.

"That's your guy, right?" Maeve said.

"Yup. That's my guy."

"Cool."

Maeve nodded approvingly, and then retreated back into her music. John allowed himself a moment of pride with the comment. It might be months before he got such an enthusiastic response from her over anything again.

Two minutes later, they were flying down Morrissey Boulevard. When the sign for Saint Ignatius Prep came into view, Julia met his eye and he nodded. He had told her the story so many times.

John was eight years old when Patrick got in. From then on, it was his dream to attend. Maybe it was petty that he still cared so much. What happened hadn't altered the shape of his life. But it was one of those memories that stung every time, even all these years later.

As a freshman, Patrick got kicked out of Saint Ignatius.

The next day, they sat around the breakfast table in silence until Nora said, "We didn't cross the Atlantic for this."

It was a line their parents had uttered so many times, meant to shame the Rafferty children into good behavior. They who in their unremarkable lives had gone no farther than New Hampshire, and then only to stay in a motel for their second cousin's wedding.

"In fact," Charlie said, "maybe it's time for us all to go back to Ireland for good."

John could never tell whether his father was joking when he said such things.

"We're not going to Ireland," Nora said. "Honestly. It's that Michael Ferguson. He's a bad influence. I've said it from the start. I don't want you hanging around him anymore."

Patrick rolled his eyes. "Fergie wasn't even there, Ma."

"He didn't have to be."

Patrick was enrolled in public school after that. Southie High. And though John might have expected him to get involved in the fray that came along with busing, Patrick seemed to behave himself. Until the end of his sophomore year, when there were two policemen at the door one morning. There must have been a family party that day. John remembered he was wearing a suit. His mother sent him and Bridget outside.

Soon after, Nora announced that they were moving. Not to a familiar suburb—Quincy or Weymouth—but to Hull, where people they knew might go to rent a house for a week in August, but not to live. John knew the move must have something to do with Patrick, with those policemen, though he wasn't sure what.

Everyone they knew lived in Dorchester. Their relatives were packed into three-deckers, piled one on top of another. They got together every weekend for parties and ran into one another on the sidewalk while out buying a quart of milk. John didn't know a single person in Hull. His older brother had ruined his life.

Nora said they would adapt, they would get used to it. And they did, more or less. Soon enough.

John's parents seemed surprised when eighth grade came around and he reminded them that he'd be applying to Saint Ignatius Prep for the fall. Whenever he'd mention the school, Patrick would make fun of him—*Why the hell would you want to go there?* So John just stopped talking about it.

His application was ready to go three months before the deadline. John was determined to deliver it by hand. But his mother kept putting off driving him to Dorchester. Finally, she agreed to take him, the day before it was due. He had chosen the clothes he would wear and everything. Shined his shoes. But at the last minute, he got a stomach bug. Pat was going into town anyway. Nora said he could drop the application off to the secretary in the front office.

When John protested, she raised a finger and said, "Straight to the secretary, and right back out, Patrick. Don't go any further. You've had enough trouble there."

John was nervous all day.

"What did the secretary say?" he asked when his brother came home that night.

"Best application she's ever seen."

"Really?"

"No. She didn't say anything."

He waited and waited for a letter, a call. Months passed. Finally, his father called to see what the status was. That was when they learned that the school had never gotten his application.

Charlie roared at Patrick about it. Patrick said he couldn't remember whether he'd brought the application in or not.

There was no doubt in John's mind that he had done it on purpose. Pat showed no remorse. He couldn't graduate from Saint Ignatius, so John wouldn't either. And maybe Nora felt this way too. She said that either way, it was no great loss.

"The bus ride from Hull would be endless," she said. "Can you imagine it, John?"

A week passed and all she could say to him was, "Go tell your father you're not too upset, so he'll lay off your brother."

After that, John understood that his brother had never liked him. He hardened his heart to Patrick. Still, as they got older, in times of trouble, Patrick had no problem turning to him. He never asked Bridget or Brian for money. He knew they had none to give. John had cosigned leases, lent Pat thousands of dollars he knew he'd never see again. The summer John got married, Pat didn't have a car. John let him borrow his for the entire month of July, while he and Julia were away on their honeymoon. Patrick got God knows how many parking tickets, which John only learned about in September, when he came out of a dinner with clients to find a boot on his Mercedes.

He found a way to laugh about it. The story became a punch line.

When Patrick had his windfall, he spent most of the money on the bar, but some of it he blew on stupid gestures—a fur coat for Nora, which she would never wear. A riding mower for Charlie, even though the lawn was not that big. When the Powerball went to an unprecedented four hundred million, Patrick spent a grand on tickets, tossing them like confetti on Christmas Eve, wanting everyone to get in on the action. He never offered to pay John back what he owed him.

Even then, John managed to stay cordial. He thought he deserved some credit for that. When Charlie got sick, John took the whole family on a trip to Ireland. He paid for them all, including Patrick, without complaint.

Their most recent fight, eight months ago, had been one of the worst. They hadn't spoken since. Of course he felt bad about that now. He wasn't expecting Patrick to drive into a wall and die. Had he known, maybe things would have ended differently. But John would be damned if he let himself feel guilty. It had all been Patrick's fault.

You should have compassion for him, John, Nora said. *Things haven't come so easily to him, the way they have to you.*

Like he had done nothing to earn his success.

He's your brother, *John.*

As if brotherhood were sacrosanct. As if no matter what a brother did to you, there was no choice but to forgive and forgive and forgive.

In the past year, outside of family parties, they had run into each other three times. Once at a wake. Once at a fund-raiser. And then at a Red Sox game, both of them sitting right behind the dugout. John was there with clients. He had paid through the nose for the tickets. Patrick was with Fergie, many beers into the night. He had probably charmed or bribed his way to the front.

What annoyed John most was that Pat always seemed to be having a hell of a lot more fun than he was. He supposed that's what your life could look like if you had no responsibilities. People John knew from Dorchester spoke of his brother with reverence. *Great kid,* they'd say, even now that Patrick was fifty years old.

John had never been to Patrick's apartment. He double-parked in front of the address his mother had provided. A small, shabby-looking brick building.

Julia offered to go in for him, but he was afraid of what she might find.

"Just make sure no one taps my bumper."

"I'll fight them to the death," she said.

As he shut the car door, his phone started to vibrate in his pocket. He assumed it would be Nora, but when he pulled out the phone, he saw Rory McClain's home number.

"Rory," he said, picking up. "Your ears must be burning. I'm in Dorchester. Just saw one of your signs."

"Is that right?" Rory's tone was hesitant. "Listen, John, I don't want to keep you. I just wanted to say that I heard about your brother. I wanted to send my condolences."

"That's kind of you. Thanks."

John noticed a woman about Pat's age smoking on the stoop. She wore a winter coat over bare legs, fluffy white slippers. She had foam curlers in her hair and sunglasses on.

"I'm not going to be able to make the wake," Rory said.

"Oh. Sure. I understand."

"There's something I want to tell you," Rory said. "This is hard to say. How do I put this? I should have mentioned it sooner. When we started working together maybe, or, I don't know. I guess I'd be lying if I said it never crossed my mind that it could come up. But you're the best at what you do, John. I wanted the best."

"What are you talking about?" John said.

Julia was watching him from the car, confused. She gestured for him to get inside and out of the cold, like he might have forgotten why they had come.

"Patrick and I had kind of a history together," Rory said. "That thing at your country club, it wasn't totally out of nowhere. This is why I didn't want the *Globe* to run that story about me and Pete O'Shea. About what happened to him. The thing is, Patrick was the one who did it. Who blinded him. It wasn't a robbery, John. It was a fight. I was there too. It was right before your family moved away."

He thought of the police officers at the door. He thought of his mother, suddenly hell-bent on Hull.

"Jesus," John said.

"I never blamed him," Rory said. "No one ever pressed any charges. We made up that story about a robbery to protect ourselves. We were all as guilty as sin."

"Guilty of what?"

"It was a bad situation that got out of control. Just stupid kid stuff. But I can't stop thinking about the article yesterday, wondering if he saw it. I pray it had nothing to do with—" He stopped talking.

"I should go," John said. "But thanks for telling me. I'm glad you did."

He wasn't glad, but what the hell else could he say?

John squeezed past the woman smoking on the stoop, feeling like a visitor from some other planet.

"Pardon me," he said.

Inside, it smelled like cooking. Like Pam and grease and burnt toast. He followed the grubby hallway to the end, as Nora had instructed. The apartment was on the ground floor. *Last door on the right,* she'd said.

Patrick had a brown doormat with the word WELCOME printed on it. John wasn't sure why this should surprise him, the deep uncoolness of it.

He took the key from under the mat and opened the door. He was expecting pizza boxes and beer bottles on every surface, signs of a party. But the apartment was orderly, spare. Had his mother already cleaned? On the living room wall, there was a poster of Fenway Park in a cheap plastic frame. John kept moving, down the hall, into the kitchen. A sad little space with fluorescent lights, painted a cheery yellow, which somehow made it seem even sadder. He opened the fridge and found it empty but for a half-drunk bottle of blue Gatorade. The freezer contained only vodka and three Lean Cuisines.

He had a flash of his own house, the impressive brick façade and clean white columns. The massive lilac bushes that bloomed white in springtime.

The notion that no one was to blame for Patrick's death but Patrick himself was something John had been positive of until this moment. But was he, on some level, responsible? For pushing the article, for teaming up with Rory in the first place?

Nora had told John to stay away.

Patrick had blinded someone. John couldn't imagine his mother knowing such a thing, keeping silent all these years. She could only have known in some vague maternal sense that Pat was in trouble, that they needed to go away.

He had to tell somebody. Bridget. Nora.

Things haven't come so easily to him, the way they have to you.

It was true. Things had come easily.

John followed the dim hallway until he reached the bedroom.

He was the oldest now.

He went to the window, pulled back the shitty blinds, and took in the sight of his girls, his world, waiting for him on the other side.

15

THE STORY OF THE DAY Patrick was born was a hallmark of the family mythology, repeated again and again by their father. Like all Charlie's stories, it got bigger, funnier, more impressive over time. Patrick came into the world fifteen minutes after they reached the hospital, the fastest birth on record at Saint Margaret's. They had rushed there, Nora shouting Hail Marys all the way, Charlie running every red light. He didn't have time to buy cigars, but one of the richest men in Boston happened to be in the waiting room—depending on the day, Charlie might claim it was the mayor or a millionaire lawyer or a judge. The man gave him a box of the finest Cubans. So happy was Charlie to have a son that he insisted everyone smoke them, even the nurses.

Bridget's father had told this story every year on Patrick's birthday, until he was gone. Five years had passed since she last heard it.

She thought of this now, as they followed Nantasket Avenue all the way out to Hull, waiting for the moment when the town would appear at the tip of the peninsula, a sight she had loved since the family moved here the summer she was ten. She thought then that she had been given the greatest gift. Each day, she swam until her fingers pruned, the water bitter cold. She bought a Bomb Pop from the ice cream truck and adored how it dripped red, white, and blue down her chin. She forgot September would come again.

The extended family in Dorchester whispered about where her parents had gotten the money for the house. Bridget overheard her uncle Jack say that Charlie won it gambling. The neighbors downstairs, who were distant cousins, believed they had been cheated out of some phantom inheritance.

Charlie said they had simply saved well. But Bridget and John suspected Aunt Kitty had been the one to help their parents. In the early seventies, her long-estranged husband died of a sudden heart attack while out jogging. They had never divorced. Kitty inherited all his money. Bridget was told that the man had died before she had ever been told he existed.

Maybe it explained why it felt as if Kitty was their responsibility. Nora acted indebted to her, taking her advice, or at least pretending to. Charlie did everything for his sister that a husband ought to do, usually before he did it at his own house—the raking and the shoveling and the repairs. Nora never complained. In recent years, she had cared for Kitty, bringing her groceries and oversize bottles of wine, shuttling her to appointments at the hospital and the hair salon.

Hull was a summer town. Most of the cottages on the bay weren't even insulated. Nine months a year, only every third house was occupied. On a grey winter day, it could feel bleak, depressing. Today this seemed right, given the occasion. They had buried her father on a glorious sunny morning, a backdrop that felt almost vulgar at the time.

Bridget tensed as Natalie swerved a hair over the yellow line and ever so slightly into the oncoming lane before correcting herself. She wasn't used to driving the van. Wasn't used to driving at all. Usually Bridget did it, but today Natalie had insisted.

You were up all night, sweetie. You need to rest.

Never mind that she had been up too.

When Charlie died, Bridget came alone, her hands shaking the whole way. She had to pull over four or five times. It was such a comfort, having Natalie beside her.

They passed Ahearn's Bakery, and Bridget noted the rainbow flag flying out front. It had been there a few years now.

Marie Ahearn's parents owned the bakery. She was the first girl Bridget ever kissed. Bridget knew from Facebook that Marie came out to her enormous Catholic family years ago and it went like a dream. The Ahearns had adapted. After college, Marie moved in with a woman she met working at State Street Bank. They got married. Marie's mother made them a three-tiered wedding cake with two marzipan brides on top. Now they had a house in Newburyport and a twenty-foot blowup of Pat Patriot, which they inflated and displayed on their front lawn on game days.

If anyone had told Bridget when she was young that Massachusetts would be the first state in the nation to legalize same sex marriage, she never would have believed it. The world had opened up in ways she hadn't seen coming. But her family had not. They all knew Bridget was gay, with the possible exception of Nora. It was something her brothers accepted, but they didn't celebrate it. Or even talk about it much. Sometimes she wished this age of openness hadn't come when she herself was still locked in some fundamental way. Maybe it would have been better, easier, if people just agreed to keep their sexuality to themselves.

Natalie would think Bridget was deranged if she said it out loud. They were about to bring a child into the world. The child (a boy, she was already sure of it) would see them, as they could see their own parents, from so close up. It made her desperate to find a way to be better, now. Before he arrived.

She realized they had missed the turnoff.

"Bang a u-ey," Bridget said.

Natalie gave her a surprised grin. "Excuse me?"

"Turn around."

"I like when your Boston comes out."

Bridget smiled. As a kid, she never would have believed that she'd leave. Even after she did, New York wasn't supposed to be forever. There was a constant pull toward home. Every time she heard the church bells ring in her neighborhood in Brooklyn, she thought of Nora. On a nice afternoon in spring, she might think of the crowds at Fenway Park, how the opening notes of "Dirty Water" put a lump in her throat. But Bridget had accepted that she could never move back here for good, even if she wanted to. She had put it from her mind.

A minute into town, Natalie slowed to a stop at a red light. Nantasket Beach was on their right. Once, Paragon Park had stood on the other side of the road, running parallel to the water, the horizon eclipsed by a white roller coaster. From its highest peak, you could see the city skyline in the distance. Now the park was gone, condos put up in its place. Only the carousel and the penny arcade remained, as if to assure you that you hadn't dreamed it all. Amazing how the people and places that once mattered most would vanish, and still you carried on.

When they first decided to use a sperm donor, Natalie asked if Bridget thought one of her brothers might want to do it.

"Then the baby would be related to us both," she said.

"Dear God, no," Bridget said.

The thought of having such a conversation with any of her brothers was unfathomable.

But now, part of her wished they had asked Patrick. He was the handsomest of all the boys. For the rest of her life, she might have gotten to see his face smiling back at her, instead of the face of International Archeologist/Number 4592.

They reached Peachtree Street and Natalie accelerated up the hill, making them both jolt backward.

"Sorry," she said.

"Take it easy there, lead foot."

When they got to the house, she parked the van behind Nora's car in the driveway.

"Let me just call the shelter and check in," Bridget said, reaching for her cell phone in the cup holder.

Natalie put a hand on her hand.

"I'm sure Michelle's got it under control," she said. "Bridget. Just be here."

She nodded. They got out.

A brand-new SUV Bridget didn't recognize sat at the curb. On the back of the SUV, a BMW, was an oval-shaped bumper sticker that contained the letters *OFD*.

Originally from Dorchester.

"Oh Jesus, John," she said.

She supposed he had to be seen in Boston, had to defend the idea that he loved Dorchester so damn much but chose to live in Weston, chose to send his daughter to some pretentious prep school. Still. Bridget would have to give him shit for it. It was all that he deserved.

She unloaded the bags from the back as Natalie led the dog up the front steps.

Bridget followed, thinking of how she would walk right into Natalie's parents' house, a member of the family. But here, Natalie—her friendly, outgoing Natalie—waited to be let in.

When Bridget opened the door, Rocco raced toward the kitchen, leash trailing behind.

They could hear low voices down the hall.

"Are you ready?" Natalie said.

"No," Bridget said. "Let's go home."

From a stand in the corner, the Infant of Prague stared at them. The statue wore a red satin robe, a sky blue crown. It had been decapitated countless times over the years, by hockey sticks and flying elbows. Nora always dutifully glued the head back on.

Bridget dropped the bags in front of Julia and John's enormous wedding portrait. A friend of their cousin's, a crime scene photographer with the Boston Police Department, had taken all the pictures that day. He gave them a terrific deal but he had no idea how to take a photo of a living human being. The shots were stiff and posed, or else he only managed to capture a shoe, an elbow.

She hung their coats and then they followed the dog into the kitchen.

Brian was leaning against the counter in his suit, staring off into space, his eyes glassy. Wasted or crying, she couldn't tell. There were three empty beer bottles lined up behind him and a fresh one in his hand. Whenever Bridget pictured him, he was still in peak shape, all muscle, the body of an athlete. It took her by surprise to be reminded that he had let himself get kind of fat. The sight of that double chin, the paunch beneath his shirt, depressed her.

John and Maeve sat at the table, each looking at a cell phone screen. Julia was bent in front of the fridge, trying to jam a large platter into it. She sighed and tried the freezer, exposing several quarts of Brigham's vanilla ice cream, Nora's only vice.

"Hey," Brian said, bending to rub Rocco's cheek.

"Hi," Bridget said.

She wanted to ask if he was all right. He and Patrick were so close. But Brian never said much and Bridget didn't know where to start. Not with everyone standing around.

"How was the drive?" Julia said. "We just got here ourselves."

She came over and hugged Natalie, and then Bridget. Bridget stood limp in her arms. As a rule, the Raffertys were not huggers.

Her sister-in-law looked perfect, as usual. She wore heels over black stockings. Her dress seemed like just a plain black dress to Bridget, but later Natalie would tell her who had made it, what it cost.

Bridget had always thought of Julia as low-key, thrifty. She was forever bragging to Nora about deals she had scored while shopping. But when Natalie first met them, at a casual backyard barbecue, she took one look at Julia and whispered, "I can't believe she's playing volleyball in those sandals." "Why not?" Bridget said. "They cost twelve hundred dollars." The information was like a firecracker in her pocket that she might choose to light up at any moment, making her mother's head explode.

Maeve came and hugged them now too.

"Dad, come on," she said. "Give Aunt Bridget a hug."

John made a grudging show of getting up, ambling toward her. They pretended to recoil from each other.

"God, you people," Maeve said.

Bridget smiled.

She felt something crack open in her when she and John embraced. She started to cry. Her stupid brother, the big idiot, her companion through this life. She had always felt safest with him.

John looked so sad when they pulled apart. She couldn't stand the look on his face.

"New car?" Bridget said.

"Yeah. Nice, huh?"

"Oh yeah. Cool bumper sticker too. Though wouldn't it be more efficient just to tape a sign to the window that says *I'm a douche. Please slash my tires?*"

Brian snorted, beer bubbling out of his nose.

"Fuck off," John said with a smile.

"Dad!" Maeve said. "Pay up."

She charged them five dollars for the F word, as she called it, and a dollar for everything else. She cleaned up at Rafferty family functions. She had once told Bridget that she'd never made a cent off Julia's side.

"Put it on my tab," John said.

Maeve looked like she might protest, but instead she returned to her phone.

John had given Maeve a claddagh ring to match his own when she was ten. She had worn it ever since. But Bridget noticed now that the ring was no longer on her finger.

Recently, Maeve had texted Bridget: *I feel like my parents don't want me to be Chinese. Not really.*

Bridget texted right back, wanting to pick up the phone and call but knowing it was unlikely that Maeve would answer. Maeve conducted all serious conversations over text. Bridget said she didn't think it was true. She reminded Maeve how John and Julia had kept in touch with some of the families who adopted at the same time they did. They got the girls together every year. She told her niece that if she were their biological child, there would have been other issues. No girl felt like she belonged in her family at thirteen.

Talk to them about it, she said.

Privately, she thought there were things John and Julia might have done differently. Natalie agreed. They themselves would have handled the situation with more sensitivity.

It was so nice to be on the cusp of parenthood, to be able to judge other people's choices with confidence, not yet having made any mistakes of their own.

When Charlie was still alive, he and John were always talking to Maeve about Irish pride. They told her she was Chirish—Chinese and Irish. But no one ever said two words about China. She was the only child of her generation in the family. Nora and Charlie had expected a dozen grandkids, but instead they just had Maeve to carry on the legacy. Even her name had been chosen for this reason. Julia resisted at first. She thought it was a ridiculous name to saddle her with. Maeve Rafferty. For the rest of her life, every job interview she ever went to, they'd be expecting a freckle-faced redhead to walk through the door.

Bridget remembered Maeve, in second grade, assigned to write about her ancestry for school. The family had gathered at her mother's house for dinner. Charlie was already sick then, with only a few months left. Still, he was as exuberant as ever, looking over the family tree of Raffertys and Flynns Maeve had created on a green poster board.

It seemed odd to Bridget then that Maeve knew nothing about the family she was born to, not even the woman who gave birth to her. But she could rattle off the names of her great-great-grandparents on both Charlie's and Nora's sides. She wondered if Maeve ever thought about it.

Maeve had prepared a list of questions for them about life in Ireland.

Nora never spoke about the past. So they all turned to Charlie, even when Maeve said, "What did girls wear to school where you grew up?"

"They wore a uniform," Charlie said, looking to Nora to complete the thought.

Nora sighed, as if it were a great effort to tell them. "A jumper and a skirt, navy blue. We never wore navy after that."

"What did you do on your birthday and at Christmas, to celebrate?"

"Birthdays just came and they went," Nora said. "At Christmas, we might get a doll, or a holy picture, which was a real novelty then. We were reared very plainly. Our parents were strict but we never knew the difference. Not at all."

It came out as one word when she said it. *Notatall.*

Even this amount of candor from her mother surprised Bridget. Perhaps she was willing to talk about Ireland now because it was for school. Or because she was sweeter with Maeve than she was with the rest of them. Or maybe spending her days tending to a dying husband made reminiscing seem a more appealing distraction than it otherwise might.

"There was no such thing as anything going to happen to us," Nora continued. "At six or eight, I'd take my brother to the sea alone. But it was a hard life. None of the pampering and the presents you're used to. Children were put to work."

"Did you get an allowance at least?" Maeve asked.

"Heavens no. An allowance!"

Nora said it as if an allowance were a baby giraffe or a Lamborghini.

"In the town we came from, they didn't get electricity until the early sixties," she said. "Even then there was just one plug, in the kitchen. It took another ten years before you had them in every room. And no one had telephones until 1984. My best friend, Oona Donnelly, was the first to have one. People lined up on a Sunday at her front door to make a call. Of course, two years after that, the knitwear factory in town closed. A shock to everyone. Poor Oona lost her job. Lots of people had to move away. They went off to Shannon or Limerick or London."

"Jesus," John said. "Isn't there anything positive you can tell her?"

Charlie cleared his throat. "Maeve, we come from the west of Ireland.

Cromwell drove us there. *To hell or to Connacht,* he said. The ones who survived were made from the toughest stuff. Those were our people. Your people."

They had all heard it a million times.

"He makes it sound very grand," Nora said. "But we were both raised on filthy farms, for heaven's sake."

Impossible to picture it, knowing Nora as they did. As a woman with a four-bedroom house, wall-to-wall carpeting. A woman who hated dust and dirt and counted frozen vegetables among man's greatest inventions.

"You can put this in your report," Charlie said. "Your grandmother was so courageous that she came to America all by herself, at twenty-one. Alone completely."

Bridget's mother was giving Charlie the deep frown she made in response to half the things he said.

Bridget hadn't ever thought of it before, but it was remarkable.

"What was it like, Nana?" Maeve said.

Nora forced a smile. "I met other girls. We danced and sang the whole way here. We had a grand time. There was even a swimming pool on the ship!"

Bridget saw her father light up, the face he made when it was time to turn from serious to joking. "It wasn't so easy for my lot!" he said. "We were in steerage, beneath all the rich people. There were rats and dead bodies in the hold. One day the boat took on water. We knew we were going down. I peeked into a doorway and there was this little old Irish couple hugging in their bed, waiting for death to take them home to Jesus."

"Dad, shut up, you're reciting the plot of *Titanic,*" John said.

"Was I?" Charlie said. He gave Maeve a wink.

"Maeve and I have a little announcement," John said. "Do you want to tell them?"

Maeve nodded vigorously.

"We got a brick at Ellis Island!" she said.

"A brick?" Bridget said.

"If you donate a certain amount, they put a brick in the walkway with your family name on it, to commemorate relatives who came through there," John said. "As of next week, the Raffertys will get their very own brick. We'll put a picture of it in Maeve's report."

Nora and Charlie were silent.

"What?" John said.

"It's very nice," Nora said to Maeve.

"But no one in our family went to Ellis Island," Charlie said.

"What?" John said. "You said you came through New York."

"We did, but Ellis Island was closed by the time we got there."

"All right, but what about all your relatives who came over at the turn of the century?"

"They came straight to Massachusetts," Charlie said. "New Bedford. And a few through Gloucester."

John's face sank. "Gloucester," he said. "That's not very exciting."

Charlie pretended to hear a voice from inside the wall. "Your ancestors say they're sorry to disappoint you."

When Nora walked into the kitchen, her view of Natalie was temporarily blocked by the open refrigerator door. Natalie had joined forces with Julia, the two of them trying to fit two large platters into an overstuffed fridge.

"Julia, what on earth are you doing?" Nora said. "Bridget, you're not dressed."

"Hi, Mom," Bridget said.

"John, did you get it?" Nora said.

He reached into his pocket and pulled out something tiny. "Is this the right one?"

Nora squinted and went up close. "Yes!" she said. "Oh, thank God. Before we go, I need to talk to you all."

Natalie stood to her full height now. Nora regarded her as if she were a stranger selling encyclopedias door-to-door.

"Oh," she said. "Hello."

"Hi, Nora," Natalie said. "I'm so, so sorry. How are you?"

Bridget's mother looked about a thousand years old in her black skirt suit. She wasn't wearing her usual pink lipstick. Without it, you could see how terribly thin her lips had gotten, or maybe they were always that way underneath.

"I brought some appetizers for later," Julia said. "I'm just trying to make room."

"I wish you hadn't done that," Nora said. "Careful you don't let all the cold air out. The neighbors keep dropping things off. They think we're going to starve. Eileen brought enough for an army. Oh! Bridget, Tommy will be there tonight. His divorce is final now, but don't say anything."

There was a shift in the room's energy. Julia gave Natalie a sympathetic shake of the head.

"Mom," John said. "Who cares about Tommy Delaney?"

He looked flabbergasted. Bridget loved him for that look.

She felt a sudden urge to escape.

"I should iron my shirt," she said. She looked at Natalie. "I'll just be a minute."

Bridget felt bad leaving her there, but her stomach tightened and didn't unclench until she had the shirt in hand and was descending the basement stairs, toward the ironing board beside the washing machine.

Nora had a yard sale after someone in the family died and donated what she could to the Morgan Memorial. Whatever was left ended up down here, as if maybe—even though she literally could not give it away—somebody might want it someday. The Ping-Pong table was heaped with relics. It had buckled in the center, around the net, where enormous Tupperware bins were stacked, all filled. A stranger's smiling face in an old photograph was pressed against the side of one bin, like the poor woman was trying to escape. You could tell she was at a party, her head thrown back in laughter.

Nora's own relatives back in Ireland were long dead. The family in America was Charlie's, but she took care of them all. Visiting them in the hospital in their old age, and later handling the details of their deaths. If someone hadn't saved for a proper funeral, Nora and Charlie paid. One long-lost great-uncle in Seattle to whom nobody had spoken since 1967 was flown back to Boston and laid to rest for all eternity with the very Rafferty clan he had gone to great lengths to escape in life. "That'll show you, Seamus," Charlie said at the burial.

As she waited for the iron to heat up, Bridget poked through the odd container. A box that once held ice skates now overflowed with black-and-white pictures, curling in at the edges. The lid on a lobster pot could be lifted to expose a naked doll, a red Magic Marker wound slashed along one arm, and a bright blue ball glove, the tag still on. Her father had gotten the glove on sale at Caldor. John pointed out that it was for a lefty—none of them could use it. But Charlie's enthusiasm was undiminished. *It was marked down seventy percent!*

Bridget replaced the lid now. She told herself not to look any further and went to do the ironing. Snooping around down here once when she was twelve or so, she had found what seemed to be a love letter at the bottom of a shoe box, addressed to her mother.

No one can know about what we've done, it said. *My wife couldn't bear it. Nor your husband, I would imagine.*

Bridget showed the note to John but they never discussed it again. It was the kind of thing that disturbed you so thoroughly, you had no choice but to put it out of your head and go on. She only thought of it every now and then, a quick, unpleasant zap of recognition.

Why did people save what they didn't want found? Maybe because you never dreamed you'd actually die. There was always time to get rid of your ghosts.

When Bridget returned to the kitchen, everyone had retreated to his or her separate corner, but for Brian, who sat alone drinking a beer, lost in thought.

She walked on and found John coming down the stairs.

"Hey," he whispered. "I have to tell you something. Don't say anything to Mom."

He paused, and it was as if they were ten again, him waiting for her to swear on a stack of Bibles.

Bridget nodded. "What?"

"Rory McClain called me a little while ago, and—"

The look of concern on his face morphed into a huge smile. Bridget turned to see Maeve standing behind her.

"Hey, kiddo," she said.

Maeve gave her a salute.

"Bookmark that for later," John said.

"Bookmark what?" Maeve said.

"Just something about—" John said, and Bridget could see the wheels turning. "The stock market."

Maeve sighed. "Sure."

"Later then," Bridget said and carried on to her bedroom, where Natalie stood, hanging their clothes.

"Hi," Bridget said. She could tell from Natalie's expression that she wasn't happy. "I'm sorry for leaving you alone with the crazies."

There was a long silence, and then Natalie said, "Look, I know it's a hard time. But I feel like we're so close to doing the whole parent thing, really doing it. And then I get a reception like that from your mother and then you just flee. You have a sudden need to iron? It makes me feel like I'm kidding myself."

Bridget regarded Natalie, the one person who had accepted her in all her oddness, all her sorrow. Something fell away.

"Okay. I'm going to tell her about the baby right now."

Natalie widened her eyes. "Now?"

"Yes. Right now."

Bridget kissed her and then turned on her heel, the freshly ironed shirt still slung over her shoulder.

She found Nora sitting alone in the living room, waiting for the rest of them to be ready.

"Mom," she said. "Can we talk a minute?"

"Yes," Nora said. "I want to talk to you too. Come and sit. There's something we should discuss. I wanted to tell all of you at once, but you're never together."

They had all been together fifteen minutes ago. Bridget thought of her mother's performance in the kitchen and wondered if Natalie's presence had stopped her from saying whatever it was she wanted to say.

Bridget sat on the sofa beside her.

She was overtaken by a fear that her mother somehow knew already. She would try to talk Bridget out of the baby, poison her mind against the whole idea. Of course it would seem terribly odd to her. Just as it had when John and Julia announced they were adopting. Nora wouldn't get to have any uncomplicated grandchildren. It had all been so easy for her generation. There was nothing to think about then. They got married, they had babies the old-fashioned way, the end.

"There might be a nun at the wake," Nora said.

"That's what you wanted to tell me?"

Her mother nodded.

Bridget rolled her shoulders back. Nora bringing up the idea of a baby, she realized, was not her fear but her fantasy. That her mother might see her as she was.

"Anyway," Bridget said. She searched for a way in. How could it be so hard to say this? "I was thinking about you and when you first became a mother. It must have been difficult for you."

She thought Nora looked almost suspicious. "What do you mean by that?"

"Well, just that you were in a new country, you didn't have your own mother to help you. If a woman has her mother on her side, then—"

"My mother died when I was a child," Nora said, as if Bridget might not know.

"Right." She was making a mess of this. "I just meant you must have missed her then. You never talked about her much."

"I never had a lot of time to think about it," Nora said. "I suppose that was a good thing."

"Maybe. I've been thinking a lot about mothers and daughters. Well, mothers and babies, I guess. Because . . ."

Nora looked annoyed now. "I was trying to tell you something."

"Oh. Okay. Go ahead."

"Well." Nora tapped the tips of her fingers against her thumbs. "What was it? Oh yes. Do you remember my sister?"

"What?"

"My sister. Theresa. She goes by some other name now."

She said it all as if Bridget had merely forgotten.

Bridget tensed. "What are you talking about? You don't have a sister."

"Yes I do."

Her mother was having a breakdown. Or maybe this was the beginning of dementia, triggered by grief.

Bridget spoke slowly. "No, Mom, you only had a brother. Martin, in Ireland. He died. Remember?"

"I haven't lost my mind, Bridget," Nora said. "I'm trying to tell you something. I had a sister. Or, I still do have one."

"Back in Ireland?"

"No. She's here. We came over from Ireland together. She's a nun. She lives in a convent in Vermont."

Bridget looked toward the doorway. It was too strange an admission. She didn't know what to think. She wanted to get up and leave, or shout for John or Natalie to come in and tell her how she ought to feel.

Instead, she asked, "Why have I never heard of this person?"

"I took you to see her once, when you were kids."

"No you didn't."

"I did."

Nora frowned. "We had a falling-out years ago. But I called her yesterday and it seems she may be coming here today. I just wanted you to be prepared."

Bridget sat back in her seat.

She had long known that in this family, the truth got revealed belatedly, accidentally, drunkenly, or not at all. But still, she felt hurt. She remembered now, the image her father had put in her head, a strange sort of untruth that had been more real to her than the flesh and blood mother standing across the room. A young Nora on a boat to America. *So courageous. Alone completely.*

But Nora hadn't been alone.

Bridget thought of what Patrick had once said about their mother. *She has secrets of her own worse than that.* She hadn't asked him what he meant by it. Maybe she didn't want to know. She wished he were here now to tell her. That letter she had found in the basement as a kid resurfaced, as if it were folded in her lap.

"A sister," she said.

Nora seemed relieved to be understood.

"Yes."

Bridget felt protective of her mother. Why would this sister want to show up now, at Nora's lowest moment? The fact of her coming didn't seem to be a comfort. And yet Nora said she had called her. Bridget wanted to ask what happened between them. But from her mother's tone, she could tell that there would be no more discussion. *Nora giveth, and Nora taketh away.*

Conversations with her children had never been a way of explaining the complexities of life or instilling vital wisdom, but rather the shortest possible means of shutting them up. When they were kids, if they had a problem, be it a splinter or a broken arm, she'd tell them to offer it up. If

Bridget complained that one of her brothers, or someone at school, had wronged her, her mother would say only, "God is not your lucky rabbit foot."

Once, John asked why they hadn't seen their uncle Matthew and aunt Joanne in months. Nora laughed, as if it should be obvious. "They live all the way in Saint William's and we're in Saint Margaret's." No one said out loud that the parishes were both in Dorchester, a mile apart.

Sex was the greatest mystery of all. It never got mentioned in any way.

When Nora was pregnant with Brian, Bridget asked where babies came from.

Her mother didn't even glance up. "You buy them at the store."

Bridget thought this explained a lot about the Rafferty children. Why Brian had never introduced any of them to a girl, not even his prom date, whom he insisted on picking up alone without allowing Nora to take a single photograph. Patrick always had a different woman by his side but never the same one twice. And he never brought them home. Only John did that—a long line of acceptably preppy Catholic girls, ending with Julia, the child of two agnostics, something Bridget knew must plague her mother, though Nora never said so.

Just one more thing she didn't say.

It was why Bridget couldn't say what she needed to now. Maybe she shouldn't need the approval of someone who refused to see her or to let her in. It was easier to forge ahead with your mother's blessing but insane to delay your life waiting for it, if the chances were good that it was never going to come. Loving and knowing weren't the same.

"What did you want to tell me?" Nora said after a while.

"Nothing. We'll talk about it later."

Part Six

Part Six

1975-1976

16

O N TUESDAY MORNINGS while the children were at school, Nora attended the Legion of Mary until eleven-thirty. But on the first Tuesday in May she decided to skip it just this once to get an early start on her shopping.

She was to host a christening party the following Sunday and there was lots to do. The babies, twins—a boy and a girl—belonged to Charlie's cousin Fergal and his wife. Fergal had lived with Nora and Charlie when he first came to America at eighteen. He and Nora had gotten into it a time or two, when he stumbled in drunk on a Saturday night, riling up the boys, telling them ghost stories, daring them to sneak a slice of cake from the kitchen.

But now Fergal was twenty-five. All grown. He had found himself a lovely girl.

Everyone said Nora would be well within her rights to sit this party out, since she herself was seven months along. She wondered if that was all of it, or if they were thinking too that she had her hands full enough with Patrick.

She insisted, of course. She had once been so shy, a stranger in her husband's family. But in time, she had found her place. When Mrs. Quinlan got too tired for the job, Nora took over as the hostess, the one who always had her refrigerator stocked and her front door open. In the early days, something usually went wrong—she overcooked the turkey, or the freezer gave out and the ice cubes melted. But now she could throw a party with her eyes shut. During Lent, she ran the fish fry at the church on Friday nights. She planned the Easter egg hunt for all the children in the parish. Nora hosted birthdays and Christmas Eve. So many evenings, when she had planned to get the children bathed and into bed early, dissolved into hours of singing and drinking in the kitchen, Charlie's people filling every corner.

There were moments when she longed for quiet. Nora dreamed of a house far from here. Every Sunday, she looked at the real estate offerings in Hull. Months ago, she tore a listing from the newspaper and taped it to the bedroom mirror. A black-and-white picture of a black-and-white colonial, a sprawling front porch. Four bedrooms, three baths. A sliver of an ocean view from the window at the top of the attic stairs. The house on Peachtree Street was like something from a movie. It spoke to her of a certain promise of American perfection, of Donna Reed and apple pie. She checked every weekend that it was still for sale. As she got ready each morning, Nora thought, *Maybe someday.* It was only a daydream. They could never afford it.

Since they were married, they had lived as frugally as they could manage. They never went out to dinner or took a vacation. Her children brought a tuna-fish sandwich to school each day, even though they begged her for fifty cents to buy the hot lunch. They only had the one car. When Charlie finished work, he would phone home, let it ring three times, and then hang up to save the price of the call. Having received the signal, Nora would retrieve him.

Now there would be another child and all the costs that went along with that.

Nora was embarrassed when she found out she was pregnant again. She was almost forty. She had no business having another baby. She had been positive Bridget was their last. She gave away the crib, the mobile, the pram. It had been ten years since she'd washed baby clothes, since she'd smelled the bitter loveliness released by a bowl of Pablum as she stirred warm milk into the papery flakes.

The doctor who delivered John and Bridget had retired. Nora went to see his replacement. When the man walked into the room, she assumed he must be someone's teenage son. Once he introduced himself as the doctor, she considered running away.

"Before we take a look, I'll ask you just a few questions," he said. "When was your first pregnancy?"

Nineteen sixty-three, she thought.

"Nineteen fifty-eight."

"Seventeen years ago!" he said. "A lot has changed since then. And you have three children altogether, is that right?"

"Yes."

"All born here at Beth Israel?"

"My first was at Saint Margaret's."

Everyone in Dorchester had her babies there. But Nora could never set foot in Saint Margaret's after Patrick. Charlie's family teased her for acting high and mighty, too good for the local hospital.

The unwed mothers' home where Theresa had spent all those months still stood on Cushing Avenue. Whenever she passed by, Nora held her breath the way she had when she passed a graveyard as a child.

"Have you given any thought to Lamaze?" the doctor asked. "Most of our patients find it very relaxing."

"I don't know what that is," she said.

"And your husband. He was with you for the delivery last time?"

"My God, no."

"But this time he will be," the doctor said, as if leading her to the conclusion.

The thought of Charlie in the delivery room. He'd faint. He'd end up being admitted to the hospital himself.

"I don't think that's a very good idea," she said.

"Give it some thought. It's what we recommend these days."

She laughed about it later with Kitty and Babs. But when she mentioned it to Charlie, he surprised her. He said he'd like to be there. Nora was still thinking it over. While she labored with Bridget, Charlie had been at the Eire Pub with his brothers. It seemed a better place for him.

Just as she was headed out the door to the market, the telephone rang. Nora realized she'd made a mistake picking up when she heard Babs's voice on the line. Babs never stopped talking once she got started.

Today she was on a tear about the busing.

She and Lawrence had moved to South Boston years ago. They bragged about how wonderful a place it was, as if it were a foreign country, not just another section of the city, five minutes from where Nora and Charlie lived. They were so close together that Patrick was zoned for South Boston High School and went there now, with Babs's oldest, Conor.

"The school year is practically over, and they're still out there, protesting," Babs said. "Everyone needs to calm down. Those policemen, letting their horses just do their business right in the street, never bothering to pick it up. It's unseemly."

Nora stifled a laugh. Boston caught up in a race riot, and Babs was worried about manure on her shoe.

Though she knew it wasn't funny. In the past year, she had seen this city at its worst. She had come to know it in a different way. Nora went and had lunch with Babs at her place on the first day of school and when she walked out, an angry mob had filled the streets. They were burning Judge Garrity and Mayor White in effigy, dummies made to look like them strung up on lampposts.

Boys as young as her John was were out there throwing rocks at state troopers and buses full of children. Nora worried about Patrick. She prayed he would not get caught up in the fervor like so many others had, unaware what they were even fighting for.

Babs wouldn't have to worry about her Conor. Nora never told her about her fears. The only person she told was her sister.

When she first learned that Theresa had gone to the abbey, Nora saw it as a pose, something she was hiding behind. When, after years of silence, Theresa asked her to bring the children there, Nora half assumed her sister had only invited her because she wanted to be talked out of staying, and that she would be leaving with Theresa in the passenger seat. The prospect had terrified her.

But when she saw her in her habit, Nora was struck by it. That, and the way Theresa spoke. She seemed so mature. She seemed serene. The anger Nora had felt, the speeches she had given in her mind, were irrelevant. She wasn't angry anymore. Selfishly, she felt relief. Her sister was no threat to her now.

In the years since her visit to the abbey, they had written frequent letters. They talked in something close to the familiar way they once had. Nora looked forward to the envelope in her mailbox—the abbey's signature image, the same one printed on the Miraculous Medal, stamped on the back in purple ink, a phrase in Latin looping around it.

When Patrick was eleven, she made the mistake of telling Theresa that she was fed up with him. How the discipline that left Bridget and John quaking had no effect whatsoever on him.

In her letter, she told Theresa how she was walking home with the shopping one evening when she heard laughter overhead. She looked up to see Patrick and Michael Ferguson running from one rooftop to the next, jumping the narrow distance between them. Her chest locked. She wanted to scream up at Patrick to stop, but she feared that her voice would startle him and he would lose his footing. Nora was trapped there on the sidewalk in a state of terror. As soon as he was on the ground, she dragged Patrick home and sent him to his room, where he was to remain for a week.

She had shared it as just a story, the exasperation of motherhood. When she got a letter back, her hands shook as she read it.

Dear Nora,

Try not to be hard on him if you can manage. I know we have both sacrificed so much for Patrick, and that your love for him is enormous. Please know that I pray for him every day.

Nora hadn't realized until then that Theresa must still see Patrick as her own.

She prayed for him. How nice.

Nora wanted to write back that she prayed too. In addition, she had spent years changing diapers, tying shoes, stepping on the sharp edges of tiny toys, telling small people, and then not so small ones, what they could and could not do with their time. Motherhood brought with it so much repetition. She marveled at the sandwiches alone. She had made thousands by now. Tens of thousands.

Her children were there in the dark half-moons beneath her eyes, a product of sleeplessness brought on by colic, by strep throat, by a teenage boy who'd snuck out of his room again. Her back ached from carrying infants and toddlers all over creation. On her right hand was a spot that looked like crinkled Saran Wrap, the remains of a burn from when Bridget knocked a scalding cup of tea over at breakfast. Motherhood was a physical act as much as an emotional one. It took every part of you.

After that letter, she was less forthcoming with Theresa for a while. Nora sent her sister Patrick's school picture each fall, along with pictures of the other children. But she did not share the details of his life, besides the generic—she did not say that she made her sons wear jackets and ties for school picture day, even when they begged and cried and said no one else dressed up like that anymore. She said Patrick liked hockey and baseball; that his best subject was math; that she had baked him a birthday cake with a B in the middle and black and gold icing, a Bruins theme.

They went on like this for years, Nora keeping the darker parts to herself.

But when Patrick got thrown out of Saint Ignatius last year, she was so stunned that she ceased with the pleasantries and wrote to Theresa to say how worried she was. The priest in charge, Father McDonald, said he had never known a child so obstinate.

Nora had walked in on them, seen the scuffle herself, or else she never would have believed it. She only drove to pick Patrick up that day because of the rain. He was getting over a cold. She didn't want him walking in bad weather. She wasn't planning to get out of the car. She had her foam rollers in, beneath a silk scarf.

At three, she watched as the flood of emerging children turned to a trickle. No Patrick. Fifteen minutes later, drumming her fingers on the steering wheel, Nora decided to go look for him.

She climbed the steps, opened the school's front door. She followed the long linoleum corridor toward the office, hoping she could ask the secretary to have him paged. There was no one at the desk, but there was a bowl of butterscotch candy. Nora was just reaching for one when, through a door that opened into an office, she saw the principal, Father McDonald, grabbing her son by the throat with both hands, holding him up so that his feet dangled off the floor.

The priest's face was covered in sweat.

Nora ran in, and he released Patrick at once.

"I'm sorry to have to tell you what your son has done," he said, wiping his hands on his slacks.

Father McDonald said he had given Patrick detention and, in response, Patrick spat right in his face.

"He's lying!" Patrick yelled, and she was mortified. It was the first and only time since he was an infant that Nora thought, *This boy is not my creation.*

Patrick was expelled on the spot.

She didn't dare tell Theresa that he spat in a priest's face. Nora couldn't bring herself to write the words. But she told her all the rest.

Theresa called her on the telephone in response, for the first and only time. She was supportive and kind. She had become a good listener. She had grown up, Nora thought. Theresa said to remember that Patrick was a good boy; that she was talking to God on his behalf and all would be well in the end.

Nora now told her sister things for her own sake, but she did it for Theresa's as well. Theresa could never experience the simple pleasures of life. She had banished herself from the world as a sort of punishment. Sometimes Nora thought the right thing to do would have been to help her find a way to leave the convent. But Nora was too afraid. She couldn't undo what had happened. She couldn't give Patrick back. So instead, she tried to remind Theresa that all lives had their challenges.

She admitted to her sister that she often found Charlie irritating. He was a good father, but he got carried away. Years and years ago, she wrote to Theresa and told her how he brought home baby chicks at Easter without asking her first. The children, being children, were elated. Nora calmly explained to him that they lived in an apartment, and adorable chicks would one day grow into chickens.

For a few weeks, she let the baby birds live on the cramped back porch.

One morning, when the children were at school, she looked out the kitchen window and couldn't see the birds in their box. She opened the door, stepped out. The box was empty. Nora somehow knew what had happened before she knew it. She looked over the railing to see the squashed yellow splotches on the pavement three stories down. She braced herself for the inevitable long conversation with Mr. Fallon downstairs. When she told him what had happened, he kept her there, talking about his bad tooth and the rain they sorely needed, before opening the back door and saying, "I'll leave you to it then."

Nora wore blue rubber gloves printed with daisies. She tried to focus on the pattern as she lifted the limp little bodies and placed them in a garbage bag.

She told the children she had given the chicks to a farmer. They'd be so much happier on the farm, eating grass and roaming in the sunshine.

"What was the farmer's name?" Bridget asked.

"Farmer Jones."

"Can we go visit the chicks sometime?"

"Of course."

Her daughter seemed satisfied with that, but then, every few months for the next three years, Bridget would ask over dinner, "When are we going to visit the chicks?" Nora would look at her husband, give him a tight smile.

Theresa thought the story was gruesome. *Oh, you poor thing,* she wrote. And Nora felt that she had done her job.

There were things she did not tell her sister about marriage. How the only place she and Charlie connected, always, was in the bedroom. That it was lovely. Early on, they were bashful. They had only ever made love to one another. But in time, they grew to understand each other's bodies as they might never understand each other's minds, each other's natures.

She didn't tell Theresa that despite all that was bad in him, Nora could never forget what Charlie had done for her. When she was young and thought of marriage in the abstract, she believed it was about two individuals, each living a mostly independent existence. Now she saw that marriage was like being in a three-legged race with the same person for the rest of your life. Your hopes, your happiness, your luck, your moods, all yoked to his.

Babs was still talking at a quarter to ten.

Nora was half listening, pulling her shopping list from her coat pocket, adding a couple of things she had forgotten—*butter (3), brown sugar.*

At this rate, she could have gone to the Legion after all.

"Conor was up studying all night for the big test," Babs said. "Patrick too, I'll bet."

"Mmmhmm," Nora said, though of course he hadn't mentioned it.

She thought she heard someone enter the apartment.

She held her breath a second. But then she told herself not to be silly. It was probably just the wind. When she heard footsteps, Nora decided it must be Mr. Fallon. She put on a smile, though it annoyed her that he thought he could walk right in. She stretched the phone cord as far as it would go across the kitchen, just able to stick her head out into the hall.

Patrick stood there, covered in blood.

"Babs," she said. "I have to go."

She hung up the phone.

"I didn't think you'd be home," he said.

Patrick looked at the doorway he had just come through as if considering whether he ought to run right out again. It wasn't even the blood that scared her. It was the expression on his face.

"What happened?" she asked, rushing toward him.

When Nora got closer, she saw that he wasn't hurt. The blood wasn't his.

"Oh God, what happened?"

He confessed it all at once. He had skipped school, gone to meet Michael Ferguson at his apartment. A group of boys were in the process of beating Michael when Patrick arrived.

"I didn't know what to do," he said. "I panicked. I grabbed the first thing I could find. A broomstick, with one of those metal points at the end. I hurt someone, Ma. There was so much blood. I got them off Fergie, but they chased me."

Nora felt unsteady. She walked into the living room, sat on the arm of the sofa, and bent her head down.

He followed behind.

"They'll kill me," he kept saying. "They'll come for me, and they'll kill me."

"I'm calling the police," Nora said.

"No! Please. That will only make them more angry. It'll make things more dangerous for me."

"I don't believe it," she said.

His voice turned to a near whisper. "I hurt him bad. He could be dead for all I know."

"Patrick!" she said. "How could you do this?"

He cried in her arms. "I was trying to be good. I didn't mean for it to happen. But there was nothing else I could do. Was I supposed to stand there and let them kill my best friend? After everything Fergie's done for me?"

Nora hated the sound of his name. Michael Ferguson had seemed like trouble to her since the day she first saw him, when the boys were all of six years old. He was dirty, his skin tinged brown, his hair greasy. His mother was a bad drunk. Nora knew she ought to have compassion for him. But instead she just felt fear. She wished she could go back and forbid the childhood version of her son from spending time with him. Now it was too late.

"What has that boy ever done for you?" she said.

"You don't want to know."

"Tell me."

And so Patrick told her that since grade school, the same group of boys had taunted him, teased him, saying Charlie wasn't his father. Only Fergie had ever stood up in his defense.

"And just who do they say your father is?" Nora asked, trying not to let him see that she was shaking.

"They don't," he said. "They just say—never mind."

"No," she said. "Tell me."

His face went red. "They say you were pregnant when you married Dad. And that I don't look like the others. I don't look like him."

"Nonsense," Nora said. "I've told you. You look like my side. My brother. Those boys only wanted to get a rise out of you."

This stupid place. The way a story moved through it because no one had anything better to do. The petty gossip, the vicious things people said just to entertain themselves. It was no less provincial than the village where she was raised. This hadn't started with children.

She made him say who the boys were.

"Pete O'Shea was the one who got hurt."

"And the others?"

"Matty McGinness. Owen Breen. Tom Cleary. Rory McClain."

Walter McClain's son.

Whether the boy knew the truth about his father, or just sensed something in some strange, sideways manner, she couldn't say.

"There's one more thing," he said. "But I know you won't believe it."

"What?"

"When Father McDonald said I spat in his face."

"Yes."

"I didn't."

She shook her head. "I don't want to hear it. Not now."

"He got wind of what the boys were saying about me, and he started saying it too, when we were alone. He'd find me in the bathroom, or at my locker, and he'd say, 'You're a little bastard.' He did way worse to Fergie."

"Oh, Patrick."

"I swear. He's a weirdo. He tries to be pals with the kids. It's pathetic."

Nora didn't know whether to believe him.

Sometimes she thought that all her son's problems could be traced back to the fact that she hadn't loved him right away. *Of course I don't want him,* she had said. He was right there in the room, in her sister's arms.

"Just promise me you won't send John to Saint Ignatius," Patrick said. "He's already obsessed with going there and he's only eleven. Don't let him go, Ma. I'm telling you. He's just the type that priest would—"

"Patrick," she said. "Don't try to change the subject."

She knew that she should go to the police, that Charlie would demand it if he knew. But she could feel the remorse in him. She told Patrick to take a shower, to go into his room and close the door. Not to tell anyone else what he had told her, even his father. She washed the blood from his clothes, folded them, and left them in a neat pile on top of his dresser.

She went to the market and bought every last item on her list.

The police arrived the morning of the christening, as Nora was trying to get the family out the door to church.

She didn't hear them knocking at first. She was yelling at Bridget to hurry up. It had always been a battle to get that child into a dress. Nora bought her barrettes and ballet slippers, luxuries she would have adored when she was that age. Bridget left them all in the packaging. She preferred jeans and her dirty old tennis shoes.

Some part of this was Nora's fault. She had let her only daughter play like a boy, with the boys, until she had no femininity about her. She shouldn't have allowed Bridget to go out with Charlie, helping to paint houses with the rest of them in summertime. She should have put her foot down about Bridget taking in all those strays. She was obsessed with rabbits and dogs and lizards and worms. She showed no sign of growing out of it, even though she had reached an age where she ought to.

Each of Nora's children had arrived on this earth as him- or herself. The more she knew them, the more she felt it to be true. They were so different from one another, and from her.

Charlie was shouting something. She tilted her head to hear him.

"What?"

"I'll get it," he said.

She walked out into the hall and saw him leading two officers in uniform toward the kitchen.

At least they hadn't come a few hours later, when the apartment would be full of people.

One of them was tall and handsome, with a dimple in his cheek. The other, short and stocky. She watched them take note of her in her dress and hat, her white gloves. They looked at the table, piled high with cakes and muffins, fruit salad, five pounds of bacon layered between sheets of paper towel.

"Can I get you fellas a cup of coffee?" Charlie said, his voice calm, though she thought she sensed concern in it.

"No thank you. Looks like you've got company coming. We'll be quick. We're looking for your son Patrick."

"He's not here," Nora said lightly, as if her heart weren't thumping hard in her chest. "He went out early to do some errands for me."

"Are you aware that he didn't show up to school on Tuesday?"

"No," Charlie said.

Nora looked at John and Bridget in the doorway, the pair of them pretending not to listen.

"You two, wait for us outside."

They did as she said.

The officer waited until they were gone before he continued. "A boy was badly injured in a robbery that day. They think he could be blind for the rest of his life."

"Jesus," Charlie said.

"We just want to talk to everyone who was involved."

"You think Patrick was involved?" Charlie said.

The officer shrugged. "The boy who was hurt isn't giving up any names. We're working backward to try to sort out who was there, starting with the truants."

"Patrick was home with me all day on Tuesday," Nora said. "He had the flu."

The policemen looked surprised. "Oh. All right, then. Sorry to waste your time."

Nora let them out.

Back in the kitchen, Charlie said, "Patrick had the flu?"

"Yes. A twenty-four-hour thing, you know."

"You didn't mention it. Is there anything you want to tell me, Nora?"

He had been good to Patrick, but even Charlie must have his limits. She didn't want him to stop loving the boy.

"Bad enough for them to accuse him. Not you too," she said.

"I wasn't accusing anyone," Charlie said. "Accusing him of what?"

In church an hour later, she realized that the policeman had said the boy, Pete O'Shea, might have ended up blind. He hadn't died. Her son was no murderer. For that, in spite of everything, Nora thanked God.

She watched as the priest sprinkled holy water onto the twins, brand-new to this world. She considered what Patrick had told her about Father McDonald. For the first time in years, she thought of the priest in Ireland, sliding his hand down the front of her sister's dress, and her best friend Oona's, and who knew how many other girls. She never would have dared tell her father. The priest would have been sure of that.

This, then, was the hardest part of being a parent. Your children had their private worlds, where you could never protect them. They were yours and yet not yours.

The morning after the christening, Nora woke Patrick early.

"We're going for a drive," she said. "Come on."

He protested, but not for as long as he usually might.

The city streets were quiet. They got onto the expressway, then took the exit for Route 1, where all the stores and buildings eventually gave way to nothing but towering pine trees, the sameness of it all almost hypnotizing her as she drove along. When they reached the second hour in the car, he asked where she was taking him.

"You'll see," she said.

"Vermont?" he said, reading a road sign a while later. "What the hell is going on?"

"Language, Patrick," she said.

She left him in the small town square. It was a sweet, old-fashioned place, a town young lovers might run off to for a long weekend in the fall. Nora pointed at a five and dime. A neon sign in the window advertised a soda fountain. She gave Patrick some money, told him to go get a milkshake. She would meet him in an hour.

Then she turned down a long country road and followed it for miles.

At the abbey gates, Nora slowed to let two young nuns cross the path. With them were a pair of teenage girls in short skirts, their long hair hanging to their waists.

Nora parked by the main building and entered a room made of stained glass. The sun shone through the panels—bright red and green and yellow. The space was full of flowers.

A nun answered the door inside and said something in Latin.

"I'm here to see Mother Cecilia," Nora said.

"Have you booked a parlor with her?"

"No."

"Then I'm afraid she can't see you."

"Tell her Nora Rafferty is here, please."

"She'll be with other guests for at least an hour, I'm afraid."

"I'll wait."

"There is no guarantee she can see you today, ma'am. She's busier than ever since she was elected prioress."

Nora made her tone stronger. "I will wait."

She sat in the vestibule in silence for forty-five minutes, until she heard a conversation on the other side of the door. She couldn't make out the words, but she swore she could hear Theresa's voice. She expected her sister to appear, but instead the other nun returned.

"Mother Cecilia says she can see you for a parlor now. Just go back out the way you came and enter the third door on the left. It will say *Saint Barnabas*. She will meet you inside."

When she thought of the word *parlor,* Nora pictured a dusty living room crowded full of Victorian furniture. But the room was more like a large confessional, the size of a kitchen pantry. Just enough space for two wooden chairs. There was a counter, with a wooden grate on the top that stretched to the ceiling. On the other side, a larger room, a single chair.

Nora sat for some time.

Finally, Theresa entered the room on the other side.

"Nora," she said. "My goodness. What a surprise. I'm so happy to see you."

She smiled at Nora's belly. "Look at you! How are you feeling?"

"Oh, all right. A little tired, but fine."

So odd to see her in person for the first time in this many years, and to have to do it through a fence. No touching, no hug hello. When they were children, Nora had cleaned the dirt from beneath her sister's fingernails, had coaxed the soft, honeyed wax from her ears.

She got right to it, thinking of the time. Patrick would be waiting.

Nora said he was in trouble, she told her sister everything. She said she remembered Theresa telling her in a letter that the abbey invited young people to stay for the summer, helping on the farm.

"I thought you could keep him here for a few months until I can figure out what to do next."

"Now?"

"Yes. Right away. I have a bag packed in the trunk. It's not safe for him at home."

"Right now there's no room in the men's guesthouse. Not until the end of summer."

Her sister was silent for a long time. Finally, she said, "I'm happy you came. I am. I've been trying to find a way to tell you something. I've been praying hard over what to do about Patrick. Nora, I think it's time we told him the truth. Your coming here like this makes me think it all the more. I will take him. I'll find the space. But let me tell him while he's here, all that you did for us."

"Us?"

"Me and him. Or we can tell him together if you want."

"That's not for you to decide."

"It's for both of us to decide."

Nora stood up. Anger coursed through her.

"This was a mistake."

"Nora, please."

"You think you can hide away here and feel superior to us? Make your grand proclamations from the safety of that ridiculous costume. I see right through you, Theresa." She used her sister's given name on purpose. "You will never see my son."

Theresa kept her voice calm. "I've learned that it's best to be honest. With yourself, with others. With God."

"How easy for you to say when you've run away from every mess you've ever made."

She looked taken aback. Her skin was thin. No one ever said an unkind thing to a nun.

"You don't know how much I think of you, Nora. I worry for you. It's not necessarily good to just take things on. To allow yourself to be burdened. Or to feel burdened."

"What are you saying?"

"I want to help you."

"I don't need your help."

"You've had to live with so many lies. You married a man you never loved. You have a right to feel angry about it."

Nora turned for the door. Then she looked back at her sister.

"I will never know how you sleep at night. Here, of all places. This is where you choose to hide?"

"I'm not hiding. This is a special place, Nora. So much good is happening here. Let me tell you about it."

Nora opened the door and walked out. Her sister called after her, but Nora knew she could not follow. If nothing else, she took solace in that.

What Theresa had said about Charlie stung the most. Poor Charlie might have given up more than either one of them. One Christmas Eve, after far too much brandy, his sister Kitty said to Nora, out of the clear blue, "You don't love my brother, but you like him, that's enough. Maybe someday, after he dies, after a nice long life, you'll find real romance if you want it."

Nora burned with shame that anyone should know this about her now, after she had lived half a life with this man.

Maybe it was true that Nora had married him without loving him, but then maybe he had only wanted her in the beginning for the land he thought she'd bring. Land they hadn't laid eyes on in twenty years and would likely never see again. He was no older then, when such a thought occurred to him, than Patrick was now. Charlie claimed that it had always been about love. A nice idea, that. One she believed in on some days and not on others.

Their marriage was never built on romance. It was built on a sense of duty. It could weather disappointment. They had had hard times and good ones, mostly determined by what the children were doing at a given moment. She thought a marriage that was only about the two of them, or any two people for that matter, would have been too much pressure. Your children, your family gave you a reason to keep on. Theresa wouldn't understand a thing like that.

When Nora got home that evening, she started supper, then went to her bedroom to change. She stood before the mirror, staring at the newspaper clipping for the house in Hull.

A thought came to her. She left the apartment and went up Sydney Street. Walter McClain was an executive at the Edison now, with four or five children. She knew just where he lived. After fifteen minutes, Nora reached the top of Savin Hill Avenue and saw the enormous yellow Victorian, covered in ivy.

She found him watering the plants in his front yard.

He recognized her right away, though it had been years since the last time they spoke.

"Is everything all right?" he said. He looked over his shoulder.

"No it isn't. My son Patrick has gotten into some trouble. We're going to leave here, you'll be happy to know. We're moving away."

"Is that right?"

"Yes. And I need money for a house. You're going to give it to me."

"Excuse me?"

Nora kept her voice calm. "I told you the time would come when I'd need something and that you would give it. Now is the time. Don't be mad at me. Your own son is to blame."

"He's not my son," he said, and Nora hated him with fresh intensity.

He had lived all this time, she thought, really believing this. She didn't think he ever wondered or worried about her boy. He was a contemptible man, and yet he probably appeared normal, even upstanding, to the people who thought they knew him. To his own wife. The two people responsible for Patrick's creation were so unfit to love him. How could God account for such a thing?

"I was talking about your Rory," Nora said. "You two are the reason my children have to leave their home. So I suggest you help me, or I will ruin your life."

He scoffed. "I've been living with the threat of that for sixteen years, haven't I?"

"You'll never hear from me again after this," she said. "You'll be free."

A girl about twelve or so came to the screen door then. Nora smiled at her, as if she was only a chatty neighbor making small talk. She walked on.

The next morning, after Charlie had gone to work, someone rang her doorbell. She went down the three flights, heart pounding. Walter stood there, handed her an envelope, and walked away. Nora took it up to her bedroom and ripped it open. He had written her a note.

No one can know about what we've done. My wife couldn't bear it. Nor your husband, I would imagine.

It was written on a plain white sheet of paper, wrapped around a check. She put the check in her pocket. She could hear someone coming toward her. Nora shoved the note into a shoe box on the floor, kicked it under the bed. John entered the room then, said they would be late for school if they didn't hurry.

Charlie made all the money, but Nora was in charge of the accounts. She paid the bills. When she told him she'd been saving all these years, socking money away, that they had enough for a down payment, he kissed her and said, "Clever girl." He never questioned how for a minute.

They moved just after the last day of school.

A neighbor showed up at the door of the new house not half an hour after the moving men were gone.

"Eileen Delaney," she said. "I was out pulling weeds when I saw the trucks go by and I thought I ought to come over and introduce myself."

But it couldn't have been as spontaneous as that. She had brought them a spider plant, an almond cake.

Nora wore a shapeless green maternity dress, no shoes. She was exhausted, but she smiled and insisted that Eileen come in.

Eileen told her that the garbage got collected on Tuesdays and Saturdays, that the mailman's name was Mort, and he liked you to remember it and call him by it, or else a bill here, a postcard there was likely to go missing.

Nora stood surrounded by boxes, while Charlie sat in the living room, in a folding chair in front of the television. John and Bridget were running up and down the stairs like hooligans.

"Two, and a third on the way," Eileen said. "You've got your hands full."

"Actually, a fourth on the way. We have one more up moping in his room. Patrick. He's sixteen."

"Ahh," Eileen said. "Mine are eight and ten. I'm planning to run away when they reach that teenage stage."

They laughed, as if it was the funniest thing in the world.

"He's mad at us for making him leave a cramped apartment in Dorchester for this," Nora said. "His own bedroom and a big backyard. Can you imagine?"

She played back the words in her head, wondering if they sounded forced.

"Dorchester," Eileen said. "My husband's cousin is a teacher there. Did your oldest go to Dorchester High School?"

"No. He went to South Boston High. We lived closer to it, so that's where the city sent him."

"Oh. South Boston? I understand. Such a pity, all that's happened."

Eileen thought they were here because of the busing. Everyone seemed to think it.

Nora had been fine with Patrick getting sent to another school. She told him to get on that bus to Roxbury and never mind the rest. But it was an easier explanation than the truth. She could tell already that Eileen was the type of woman who would repeat and repeat the story to the neighbors. She herself would never have to explain. They could start over here.

A few days later, Nora was back in the Dorchester apartment to sweep out for the new tenants. In the mailbox, she saw the familiar envelope— a letter from the abbey—and felt a hint of warmth toward her sister, despite what had happened. It surprised Nora that Theresa had found it in herself to apologize so quickly for the terrible things she had said.

But then she saw that the letter was addressed to Patrick.

Nora ripped it open.

Patrick, You won't remember me, but I know you are in pain, and that so much in your life feels confusing. If you ever have questions, I might be able to help answer them. Don't hesitate to contact me at the address above. Yours, Mother Cecilia Flynn

P.S. I include a medal, given to you when you were born. I hope you'll wear it for protection. I believe in its powers. I should never have taken it in the first place. I'll tell you the story if and when we speak.

Nora's chest tightened. She crumpled the letter in one hand. In the other, she held the medal.

She had had no confidence, no voice as a girl. She was timid. Perhaps Theresa thought she hadn't changed. But Nora's children had made her tough. On their behalf, she was able to do whatever needed doing.

She spread out the page and read the note over again and thought, *You will never be allowed to know my family now. Theresa, what have you done?*

17

Nora was on her back, bare legs stretched out before her, propped up on her elbows so she could see John and Bridget at the ocean's edge. Beside her on the blanket, the baby lay on his stomach in just a diaper. Brian was threatening to walk soon. When that day came, she knew, she'd never rest.

It was the Fourth of July. Charlie had the day off. After breakfast, before it got too hot, they had taken the children to Paragon Park.

Patrick refused to join them. But John and Bridget were gleeful, whooping around in dizzying circles on the Tilt-A-Whirl, rushing down the high peaks of the flume ride, their T-shirts and shorts getting soaked. They let them each spend five dollars in the arcade. John used all his money on Skee-Ball trying to beat Bridget's high score, which he eventually did. He always had to be the best, a quality Nora disliked in him.

Charlie thought the boy would be president one day. He said John was the smartest of their children, and though Nora didn't disagree, she thought there was such a thing as too much praise. She didn't want him to get a big head. She told Charlie it wasn't right to favor one child over the others and he just laughed.

What? Nora said.

You with your Saint Patrick, he said.

After the arcade, they came to the beach. Nora had bought Bridget a new bathing suit for the season, blue with sparkling gold stars. Bridget wore it now, beneath one of Charlie's old undershirts, the white cotton draping off her like a sail. She insisted on wearing the shirt, even in the water.

Nora sighed.

She picked up her book to read and then a shadow appeared, blocking the sun. Charlie. He wore khaki pants and a button-down shirt over his swim trunks. On his feet, a pair of sandals and thick black socks. Set against everyone else on the beach, in all their revealing glory, he looked like a man from another century.

Charlie held out a cup of frozen custard. "For you," he said.

Nora took it, smiled up at him. "Sit."

"I thought I might go back to the house and mow the lawn."

They both knew he was going to check up on Patrick.

"Come on," she said. "Sit for a while."

Charlie plopped down beside her and tickled the baby's cheek.

They were exhausted in the beginning. But so far, they were having more fun than they'd ever had with the others. They felt at ease, they knew how to do it all; they'd done it three times before. They wouldn't get to do it again, so why fret about anything?

Brian was the first baby she brought home from the hospital to a real house. It made such a difference, not having to carry the child up three flights just to get to your own front door.

Back in Dorchester, when it snowed, Charlie had to shovel out a parking space in the street and fill it with garbage cans or a lawn chair when they drove off. On the coldest days, people would slash your tires if you dared to steal a spot. Now they had a garage and a driveway and a backyard of their own, with no one looking down at them from above. She could sit out there in her nightgown if she liked and drink a cup of tea with the baby on her shoulder.

In Hull, Charlie's relatives couldn't stop by at all hours, on their way to church or coming home in the evening. They had fewer houseguests, since not so many cousins wanted to stay so far from the city. Nora could read a book after dinner. There was a tiny room on the second floor that she claimed for herself. She had initially thought to put the baby in there. They had four real bedrooms besides. But as soon as they got to Hull, Patrick said he wanted to sleep in the attic. Knowing all that he had been through and how little he wanted to be there, she thought she might as well let him have his way.

So what was meant to be Patrick's room became the nursery, and the nursery—which wasn't big enough for a child, anyway—became her sitting room. Each time Nora went in there and closed the door, she got a rush. Without her needing to say so, Charlie somehow knew not to bother her there. He'd stay downstairs watching television after the children went to bed.

They still saw the family often, driving up to Boston almost every week for a wedding or a birthday party or a First Communion. Nora had thirty-five Raffertys at her house for Christmas Eve. When she came down in her bathrobe the next morning, half of them were still there. Piled on the kitchen table was a stack of hostess gifts as tall as she was; more bottles of Baileys and boxes of chocolate than they could ever hope to consume. She had seventy people for a luncheon after Charlie's uncle died in the spring. The relatives marveled over how much space she had in the cupboards, over the big backyard and the size of the bedroom closets.

When Nora and Charlie told them they were moving, some had acted offended, ever on alert for family members who thought they were better than the rest.

"How can you swing a whole house on what you make?" Charlie's brother Lawrence asked, as if it were any of his business.

"Who would want to live all the way out there?" Babs said.

John and Bridget hadn't wanted to leave their cousins and friends behind, but they had adjusted well to Hull. Patrick, less so. He hadn't made any friends at school. Nora accepted his somber disposition as something they would have to bear for now.

She herself was happy here. She thought this could be the happiest time of her life, if not for Patrick's struggles. But as far as she had seen, life rarely let you be purely joyful. There was always something there to torture you if you let it.

She hadn't spoken to her sister in more than a year. Nora knew it was up to her to fix things. Theresa didn't have any way to reach her. Nora hadn't told her about the move. Sometimes she thought she was ready, but then the memory of what happened filled her with such anger. Give it one more week, she told herself. One more month.

At noon, Nora looked up from her paperback to see John running toward them.

Two young things in bikinis laid down towels a few feet away and then began to cover their lithe bodies in oil. Nora wore the yellow bathing suit with a ruffle at the belly that she had been wearing for the past several years. It had stretched, but so had she with Brian, so it still fit her fine.

John reached them, out of breath, just as she was getting to the good part in her book. Nora pretended not to see him.

"Are we going to drive into Boston for the fireworks tonight?" he asked for the hundredth time.

"If you're good," she said without looking up.

John had been excited about the Bicentennial ever since President Ford came to Boston in the spring, to light a lantern at the Old North Church. A week ago, John insisted they hang red, white, and blue bunting on the front porch.

"How do they make fireworks, Ma?" he said now.

Nora sighed. "They do them off the side of a ship so no one gets hurt," she said. "You should never go near fireworks unless you're a professional. Boys get their fingers blown off."

"But how do they get the fireworks in the air?"

"Gunpowder."

In truth, Nora had no idea. She thought gunpowder had something to do with it, but she couldn't remember what.

"Someone shoots a gun?" John said, wide-eyed.

"Yes."

He nodded, then ran back to join Bridget in the water.

Charlie gave her a look. "Is that how it's done, then?"

She swatted him with her book. "Well, you weren't any help."

By late afternoon, the crowd thinned, people going home for the day.

The older kids needed to shower before they ate dinner and went into the city. The baby needed a nap.

Bridget and John approached the blanket.

"We're bored," John said.

"How can you be bored with all this around you?" Charlie said. "My God."

"We're bored," John repeated.

"We should be getting home anyway," Nora said.

"No!" the children shouted.

"Come play in the water with us, Ma," Bridget said.

"It's too cold for me."

"It's not cold once you get used to it. Please?"

"Bridget, God gave you brothers so that I'd never have to go in the ocean if I didn't feel like it."

"Dad?" Bridget said. "Will you come in?"

"Ahh, second fiddle. That feels nice," Charlie said. But he was already unbuttoning his shirt to expose the whitest chest in America.

"Just a dip," he said. "I've got my togs on underneath."

"Togs!" John exclaimed, embarrassed. "Dad!"

"What am I supposed to call them?"

"Shorts? Swim trunks?"

Her husband pretended to consider this. "I prefer togs, thank you."

"And those sandals," Bridget said. "You can't wear them with socks. No other father I know would do that."

"You two are very opinionated today," Charlie said as he got to his feet, peeling off the black socks.

The three of them ran toward the waves. The sounds of the amusement park were carried toward them on the wind—the tinkling music of the rides, the gleeful screams from the roller coaster.

She watched as Charlie splashed the children, the two of them screaming, laughing.

Togs.

Nora's children took for granted what was once nearly unbelievable to her. They were being raised as Americans, but not by Americans.

She had accepted that this was home. Charlie never had. Ever since he arrived in Boston, he talked about how he would one day return to Ireland. He told tall tales about the good old days. To listen to him, you'd never know how they struggled.

Charlie refused to cultivate an interest in baseball, even though John and Bridget were obsessed. At Little League games, other fathers would be shouting at their sons from the bleachers, frenzied, red faced. Charlie would be asleep. Nora cooked spaghetti and tuna noodle casserole and American chop suey from recipes she clipped out of *Good Housekeeping*. Her husband wouldn't eat them. He went to ceilidhs twice a month, dancing to the old Irish tunes with long lines of elderly ladies. He came home humming "The Stack of Barley." "The Siege of Ennis." He insisted that Bridget do Irish step dance when she was young, though she barely lasted a year.

Their new neighbors, Eileen Delaney and Betty Joyce and Dot McGuire, whose families had been in America for two or three generations, talked about being Irish more than anyone she had ever met. They collected Belleek china painted with shamrocks. They wore claddagh rings. They played the Clancy Brothers at parties. As actual Irish people, Nora and Charlie were like celebrities to them. Charlie reveled in this, but it embarrassed Nora.

When she left Ireland, she hadn't thought it would be forever. It hurt so much to recall all that was lost. Her father and grandmother had died without her ever seeing them again. They had only ever gotten to know her as a timid girl. Nora had lied to them to protect Theresa and, she supposed, herself. Without meaning to, she built a wall between the family she had made and the one from which she came.

Her brother was still home on the farm. He never married. Martin was nineteen when she left. Now he was almost forty. It seemed impossible. He sent her a photograph and Nora cried to see that he was bald. She sent him one back, of the whole family on Easter morning. When her brother replied, he said he couldn't wait to see them all. Nora stared at the words, doubting he ever would.

She sometimes yearned for Miltown Malbay, for the smell of the air, the views from the cliffs off Spanish Point. They had so much space in the country. She could go days without seeing anyone besides her family. Now, there were people crammed in everywhere she looked.

Certain cousins, having made as much money as they wanted or needed in America, had moved back for good. Others they knew had been to Ireland for visits. After Kitty came into her money, she went, and kept going. Babs said Kitty only went home to brag. She wore a mink coat when her brother met her at the airport in Shannon and refused to take it off the entire trip.

Oona Donnelly wrote to Nora about it.

I saw a woman dressed to the nines in the square last night. I said to the children, would you look at that. Then I realized it was Kitty Rafferty, your sister-in-law. Didn't she look just like a film star!

Charlie said he would like to go, and Nora replied that it was too expensive. They couldn't leave the children. She could come up with a hundred reasons why now wasn't the time, why home was not a place one went for a visit.

They left the beach at four o'clock, the children pink cheeked, freckles spreading across their faces. She had learned to keep a basin of water on the back porch, where they each took a turn dipping sandy feet. Nora opened the back door that led into the kitchen. There was Patrick, drinking a beer at the table.

"What do you think you're doing?" she said.

"Toasting the Fourth of July," he replied. He tipped the chair backward onto two legs. Nora had never known a child like him. A boy with no fear.

"You're seventeen," she said.

Unbelievable that when she came to this country, she was only a few years older than he was now. Theresa was his age exactly. Patrick wanted so badly to be a man, but he was a child in every sense.

"Let him have one," Charlie said. He raised a finger at Patrick. "Hear me? One."

Charlie went upstairs to take a shower. Brian reached out for Patrick and Patrick took him from Nora's arms.

He loved the baby and so she knew that he was good.

"We'll grill dinner outside tonight," Nora said now. "And then we're going into Boston for the fireworks. Will you come with us?"

Patrick shook his head. "Ma. I have plans."

"Boys from school?"

She held her breath while she waited for his response.

"Nah, I'm going to Castle Island. Fergie and some other guys are gonna hang out and watch the fireworks from there. I'll ride in town with you. Get the Ashmont line to Fields Corner."

"I want you home right after."

"We were going to go to Lucky Strike."

"Bowling?"

"Yeah."

He could lie like that, right to her face. But what could she say? If she forbade him, Patrick would only go ahead and do it anyway.

"I don't want to hear about any trouble," Nora said. "I want you to be careful."

Brian had fallen asleep on Patrick's shoulder. She took the baby from him and went upstairs to put him in his crib.

She needed a miracle for that boy. She thought of her sister's silly medal.

I believe in its powers, Theresa had written in the letter she sent him.

Nora didn't quite, yet she had never been able to throw it away.

She went into her room, opened her jewelry box. She found the medal where she had left it a year ago, hidden in a small satin bag, stuffed with cotton. She found an old chain and threaded it through the loop at the top.

Nora returned to the kitchen, where Patrick sat alone.

"I don't ask you for much, do I?" she said.

He smiled, uneasy. "No."

"I need you to do something for me. If you think it's silly, that doesn't matter. You'll be a good boy and humor your mother."

"All right," he said, just before she draped the chain around his neck.

"You have to promise me that you will wear this always."

He laughed.

"Patrick, promise," she said in her sternest voice, which still had never been enough to reach him.

But now he looked up at her. He looked her in the eye.

"I promise," he said.

18

MOTHER CECILIA SET a bud vase on the end table. The head of a fat white peony lolled at the top. She adjusted the stem right, then left, then straight up and down. When she pulled her hand away, the flower fell back to its original position.

She cocked her head, regarded it. Then she heard the door to the guesthouse open and the sound of several pairs of feet in the front hall.

The Sisters of Saint Joseph came on retreat for one weekend each summer. It had always been her job to make sure their rooms were tidy, their beds made up, the windows thrown open to the sweet smell of the grass outside. She had placed a tray of just-baked muffins on the table for them, and a pitcher of iced tea in the refrigerator. She made sure the kitchen was stocked with the abbey's finest offerings—raw milk and cheese, jam and several loaves of fresh bread.

She had been prioress for more than a year now, second in command after the abbess. She knew she ought to pass this task along to one of the postulants, but she enjoyed it too much. Their friends in active orders got worn down by the world. Their communities were shrinking, they had elderly sisters to care for. All of it weighed on their minds. They came here to refuel, to breathe the fresh country air, to reflect on what a year had brought. She saw it as her duty to revive them.

She went to the door to greet them, hugging and kissing them all. They didn't wear habits anymore. They wore plain skirts and jackets now, or dungarees with a smart silk blouse. It was eighty degrees outside. Mother Cecilia swore she would try not to envy them as she sweated away in her robes.

Sister Evangeline, the most outspoken of them all, held forth a tiny American flag.

"For the prioress," she said.

As she took it, Mother Cecilia must have made a face that conveyed her confusion.

Sister Evangeline laughed. "It's the Fourth of July."

"Is it?"

The noontime bells rang.

"I'm off," Mother Cecilia said. "Get yourselves settled. I'm so happy to see you all again."

"We'll see you over there," Sister Evangeline said.

Mother Cecilia went to join the others in the chapel, still holding the flag in her hand. She had no time to set it down. She hid it inside her sleeve and took her position.

They chanted gloriously for their fellow sisters. She looked out and smiled at the visiting nuns, lined up in the first pew on the other side of the gate.

The nuns from the abbey ate lunch in the enclosure. They had prepared a beautiful meal for the Sisters of Saint Joseph to have in the refectory. The usual two hours of silence followed, but later that afternoon, Mother Placid invited the sisters to have tea with the two of them in her private living room. Just before they arrived, she and Mother Cecilia set out cookies, milk, sugar cubes.

The last abbess, in office for forty-two years, had kept the room dark, with heavy drapes and velvet furniture, enormous couches and chairs that swallowed a person when she sat. Mother Placid lightened it up. She pulled down the drapes. The sun shone in now, onto oatmeal-colored sofas and a pair of bright blue wingback chairs. She had gotten throw pillows, a floral rug. The first time Mother Cecilia saw it, she thought of Mother Placid's old apartment in Queens. Even there in that cold, blank building, she had created warmth, home.

"Just a reminder," Mother Cecilia said. "We have to be aware of what we say to them. Our positions now demand it."

"We, huh?" Mother Placid said.

"All right. You, Mother Abbess."

The Sisters of Saint Joseph spoke more frankly to them than most people would. Mother Placid had a tendency to get swept up in it, to say things she might later regret.

Her friend smiled as the others knocked at the door.

"Come in, come in," they said.

They talked about the year gone by. About world affairs and family matters. About the fund-raising efforts they had started for their retirement. They were heroic nurses who served the poor in Philadelphia. In the spring, they had lost the building their order had lived in for a century. Now the nuns lived in apartments, spread all over the city.

"It's different," Sister Emily said, sipping her tea.

"It's awful," Sister Evangeline said. "It's not what we signed up for at all. We've lost our community. At the hospital, it's a new battle every day. The bishops make it impossible for us to do our work."

The others looked down, quiet for a minute.

"Should we open a bottle of wine?" Mother Placid said, and they all cheered.

Mother Cecilia shook her head.

Two winters back, when Mother Placid had just been named abbess, there was a blizzard, power out to half the state. A homeless shelter in Manchester asked if the abbey might be able to take in three or four children for a week. Bishop Dolan, speaking on behalf of the pope, said it was impossible, not what the abbey was there for. He said to tell the shelter that they would pray for the children.

"The bishop says we cannot take three or four," Mother Placid said into the telephone, as Mother Cecilia looked on. "He was very clear that we must not do that. So! We will take ten or twelve."

"Tell us," Mother Placid said now, to the nuns.

Sister Evangeline looked at the others.

"Go ahead," said Sister Rebecca. "We all know you have plenty to say."

"We're in trouble. A few of us specifically, myself included. They're after us for telling some female patients that they should be using birth control. Telling them that it's not a sin, and though they can't get it from us, we can tell them where to get it."

"Oh, this again," Mother Placid said. She was on her feet, pulling glasses from the hutch in the corner, handing them around.

Mother Cecilia tensed up.

"You can't imagine coming face-to-face with a woman who can't feed the children she already has and having to tell her that God insists she have more," Sister Evangeline said. "The bishops have never been in that room."

"But we have to do what the church dictates," Sister Emily said.

"Our gift to the church is to be with the people on the margins, people who are suffering. We can't afford to see things in black and white," Sister Evangeline said. "It's 1976. Abortion is not the only ill. War and hunger are also right-to-life issues."

"We know how it is," Mother Placid said. "We understand." She filled Sister Evangeline's glass.

"For this, they call us radicals. Heretics."

"What nonsense," Mother Placid said. "But! We need look no further than our history books for reassurance. Nuns have triumphed over a delinquent leadership before. It's a common enough mistake to believe that one's own time is the most progressive, the most advanced. That human nature only improves upon itself. But in fact, things move in cycles—good to bad and back again."

Mother Cecilia gave her a pleading look. The bishop had said they could not be seen as supporting nuns like these in their efforts, even though they did support them. It was one thing to listen, and even that was a danger. But Mother Placid had no business getting into a conversation.

Even in this company—maybe especially so—they had to be mindful of whom they served. They could speak freely only to one another.

Fourteen years ago now, Pope John XXIII had told the clergy to open the windows of the church, but there had been little more guidance than that. Members were meant to revisit their founders' intentions, to revise their constitutions, to modernize. Nuns on the outside went back to their given names, they stopped wearing the habit. Inside the cloister, they were supposed to be more obedient, more conservative than ever.

"I envy you," Sister Evangeline said. "You don't have to deal with any of this. The politics of it all."

"There are people who think we're not doing much up here, just praying all day," Mother Placid said, a hint of defensiveness in her tone. "We don't have a hospital or a school, but we have our doors open and we greet the world there."

"I know," Sister Evangeline said. "I didn't mean—"

"You've had all these young people running around here for the last few years," one of the others said. "Surely it comes up when they talk to you. Maybe by being so traditional, by escaping notice, this is the only place where anything truly radical can happen."

Mother Cecilia smiled, betraying nothing.

"Whatever it is, it's worked," Sister Emily said. "You've brought in so many young recruits. It's a real success story, and all thanks to you two. You must be the youngest prioress and abbess in the country."

They were thirty-six and forty-two, respectively. Sometimes Mother Cecilia thought a thirty-six-year-old had no place being in a role of such importance. She nearly said so, but then Sister Evangeline said, "You deserved to be elected. You saved this place."

In the early seventies, they had nearly lost the abbey. After the deaths of several senior nuns, their numbers were shrinking. Their cash reserves were low. The roof leaked. One of the barns was ready to collapse. They didn't have the funds to repair it. They kept the heat and the lights in the church turned off, even during Mass. In winter, they wore coats over their habits. They could see their breath as they sang. Their meals, which had once been ample, became simple, sparse. They had to sell whatever they could get out of the dairy. They lived off of clear soups and vegetables and bread. Everyone lost weight. Without the gardens, they might have starved.

But then they were visited by an intervention of the Spirit.

They had four hundred acres. From time to time, outsiders staked their claim on far-off corners of the property. The nuns mostly let them alone. But when groups of young people started camping on the land, pitching tents, staying for weeks, they debated whether to tell them to leave.

In the dormitory at midnight, they could hear guitars, laughter from across the fields. On a cool autumn evening, the nuns might smell a campfire as they walked to the chapel for Vespers. The young people seemed to think they were hiding. When a nun caught sight of them— the girls in their skimpy skirts, their flowing dresses, the boys loud and long-haired—they would freeze a moment, like deer, and then run off. Finally, Mother Placid approached them and said they could stay, but they had to work, and they had to talk. That's how it began.

They were mostly college students or recent graduates. Intrigued by Daniel Berrigan and the notion of priests burning draft files. Repulsed by the assassinations of Martin Luther King and Bobby Kennedy, and later, by Kent State. They were weary. The abbey provided a refuge.

They were the youngest people the nuns had seen in years. Their spirits enlivened the place. Soon they came by the dozens, men and women alike. They hungered for peace and community; they wanted to give more to the land than they took. They wanted to learn about communal living, and who better to teach them?

The boys painted the buildings, repaired the roof. It was an odd sight—handsome young men in blue jeans and T-shirts where there were usually no men at all. Some of the nuns prayed for the strength to resist temptation. The girls worked alongside the nuns, in the dairy and the gardens. Mother Placid had a gift with them. Most weren't much older than the children they had taught back in Queens. They were not particularly interested in God at the start. None of them came intending to stay. But several of them did. They represented a new generation at the abbey, a repopulation.

As with every major change, there was fierce debate at first. The oldest nuns feared that to embrace such girls was madness, desperation. But Mother Placid saw that the world was changing. They needed to change along with it or they would perish.

"There are as many paths to God as there are souls on earth," she said in a meeting with the abbey's hierarchy. This seemed to move them.

Afterward, Mother Cecilia said, "That was beautiful, the way you put it."

"I agree," Mother Placid said. "But don't be too impressed. That's not me, it's Rumi."

Mother Placid convinced them, of that and more.

The young people all came for parlors. When Mother Cecilia met with them in private, she was amazed at how open they were. They wanted someone to listen. The women, eighteen, nineteen, twenty years old, reminded her of herself when she first visited the abbey. She remembered how it worked. The first time you spoke with a nun, all you saw was her habit. But if the connection was strong enough, by the second or third conversation, you stopped noticing. You might talk for an hour, say your good-byes, and later wonder if she had even had her head covered, though you knew she must have.

They were surprised that the nuns did not proselytize or try to get them to see the light. They just listened. Some only came once or twice. But the ones who returned again and again began to realize on their own that the conversations were about God, even if He was never mentioned. God through the lens of their own lives.

Perhaps their early experience with the church, if they'd had any, was something different. How easily she could recall the fear of arriving late to Saint Joseph's in Miltown Malbay, where Father Donohue would single a person out in front of the congregation if she came in a minute past the hour.

A handful of angry parents asked what exactly the nuns were teaching their daughters. What had their faith meant to them before? A white dress for Communion, a cake with a crucifix piped in buttercream. Simply what they were born to. But now they saw more. The girls who wanted to stay begged to join immediately, but the nuns told them it was too soon. Better to experience something first, just to fill out their humanity, to become whole people, but also to let them have something for the community when they returned. They went off and got degrees, they worked in activism or teaching or the arts. They traveled the world. They kept in touch. She knew they would return when the time was right. If some of them never came back, that too would be the right decision.

Her own early confidante, Mother Lucy Joseph, had died in her sleep in the spring of 1967. It was April, and they were preparing to bless the gardens on the Feast of Saint Mark. They buried her with the others, behind the chapel, under the blooming magnolia trees.

Mother Cecilia swore she felt her spirit each time she set foot in the abbey's vegetable garden, or when she went to the grave and placed flowers in springtime. And especially when, in the presence of some lost soul, she attempted to give her solace.

As many paths to God as people on earth.

There was a girl named Angela, with long straight hair to her waist.

"I love it here," she said in a parlor, their third together. "It's so nice to get a chance just to spend time with my girlfriends in the guesthouse, to get away from the stresses of life. Our guy friends are here too, in the men's guesthouse. We can walk around together, work together without all the pressures of immediately figuring out if we want to go to bed with a person, which is increasingly part of the deal. I'm sorry. I don't mean to be shocking. My mother says I live for the shock value, but it's not true, I swear. I just say what I'm thinking."

Mother Cecilia could laugh, stepping out of her skin, wanting to tell them that she had been a girl once herself. She was not so old that she couldn't remember.

"I think I know what you mean," she said.

When they asked about sex, she was supposed to tell them not to have it. But that felt like a lie. She didn't offer an opinion unless they asked her straight out if it was wrong. Then she told them that it was and that they shouldn't stand in the way of God's plans. Every time she said it, a catch in her throat. A memory of a hospital room in Boston, of the consequences of the thing she had done, which had felt like nothing consequential at the time.

"My parents asked me what I'm doing here," Angela went on. "I told them, 'I talk to Mother Cecilia. She's teaching me how to be happy.' You must have had hundreds of bedraggled hippies tell you their stories by now. You know all the secrets. Who's brokenhearted or falling in love or dropping out of school. You could write a book."

She had begun to see patterns in what the young women worried about. It so often came down to sex. They regretted it. Not the act itself, but what came after.

Though the young ones were responsible for shifting her mind, rattling her preconceptions, it was an older woman, older than her, who truly changed her way of looking at it. Until then, when they asked about birth control, Mother Cecilia toed the party line.

But one day, she was out in the driveway, pulling groceries from the trunk of Mother Annabelle's car, when a woman drove past, slowly, looking at her.

She turned the car around at the entrance to the gift shop. Mother Cecilia supposed she had made a wrong turn.

But the woman was still looking. Mother Cecilia waved.

She pulled to a stop when she reached her, rolled down her window.

"I got lost," she said.

"Can I give you directions back to the highway?"

"No. I'm not a Catholic. Not anymore, I mean. I was, once."

"Well, that's all right. We give directions to all denominations."

She was trying to make a joke, but the woman didn't seem to hear.

"When I saw the abbey here, I took it as a sign. I guess I'm wondering if I might be able to talk to someone."

"I'm very happy to talk to you."

"Do nuns hear confession?"

"We have parlors. We can't absolve you of anything but we can listen."

A few minutes later, they were sitting in one of the small rooms, on opposite sides of the grille.

"Do you need to say a prayer first?" the woman said. "Should I kneel?"

She laughed. "Heavens, no. Just talk."

Her name was Gloria. As a teenager, she had been sent off to a home for unwed mothers. After she gave birth and the time came to hand over the child, she begged to be allowed to keep her. Her parents told her that to move on, to forget, was the only reasonable plan. But she never could forget. Her life spun apart. She married an abusive man and divorced him. She sank into a depression and found no work for years. Now that baby would be eighteen. Gloria still thought about her. She agonized over where the child had ended up. She had no idea of the circumstances. She swore all the time that she saw her daughter, in the street, at the bank.

"God forgive me for saying it, but I wish I had just found a way not to be pregnant anymore," she said.

Mother Cecilia was met with a memory. Kitty Rafferty. Charlie's sister. Her roommate in Boston all those years ago. Kitty had wanted her to take that path. She understood what it would cost to lose a child you had brought into the world, held in your arms.

"Do you know how many of us there were?" Gloria continued. "Thousands and thousands. Forced to hand our babies over. How do they expect us to go on like it's nothing?"

"I don't know," Mother Cecilia said. "Truly, I don't."

"And what about the children?" Gloria said. "A whole generation of them, growing up never knowing who their mothers were."

She wished she could tell Gloria her own story, that she might pass through the grate and hold her hand. God had placed them together for a reason.

She had always felt guilty, as if what happened had only happened to her. Something she brought on herself. But now she thought of her roommates and all the other girls at Saint Mary's, lined up in the hall when the doctor came.

For the first time, she felt angry. For the choices denied her, the things thrust upon her. And Nora too. They were part of some larger system they knew nothing about at the time. Nora had made the sacrifice for them all. She hoped Patrick would know, someday, how selfless her sister had been.

From then on, when the young ones asked, she told them to protect themselves. Their hearts, first and foremost. But all the rest as well. She knew it was a radical decision, one that could get the abbey excommunicated. It was as serious a thing as that. But she reminded herself that they served a higher power than man. Everything they had done was from love—the love of God, the love of this place, and the love of one another. They would do the right thing, but quietly.

A Benedictine took three vows. Stability, obedience, and *conversatio morum*, a conversion of life. All three bound them to the abbey and to their community. But the *conversatio morum* also asked that a nun be willing to change.

She still believed that what happened with Patrick was a miracle. She knew his life with Nora was what was best for him, even though when Nora told her about his struggles, she got nervous.

She couldn't imagine him in some stranger's home. She knew the Blessed Mother had been in that room, had given her the strength, and that the moment had led her here. God met you where you were. He showed you His face when you needed Him most. She prayed that soon enough He would meet her Patrick.

It was with all her learned knowledge and experience that she had greeted her sister a year ago. A moment Mother Cecilia had prayed for. Letters were lovely, but nothing was a substitute for being together.

She had written to Nora when she was elected prioress, told her how they held a beautiful ceremony in her honor. But Nora didn't even mention it in her reply. She wanted to tell Nora how Mother Placid's big mouth often made her feel the way Nora must have when they were girls, and she was always saying whatever came to mind. She wanted to tell her so many things. But Nora seemed from her letters to be frantic, busy, overwhelmed. Mother Cecilia told her to come for a retreat, and Nora brushed it off as if it was an absurd and frivolous idea. *I couldn't leave the children for that.*

There were things she needed to say, face-to-face. Since Nora started telling her about Patrick's troubles, she had thought that what he needed now was their honesty. She had learned over time that to know anything was bearable. It was secrecy that could not be borne. She wanted to free her sister of that burden, and Patrick too. He was practically a man now. It was time.

She still felt this way. But she shouldn't have said what she did. She could tell from the moment she saw Nora that her sister wouldn't be responsive to it.

She regretted what she had said about Nora's marriage. Once, years earlier, she said to Mother Placid, "Imagine living your whole life out with a man, just because once, when you were both impossibly young, he kissed you on the way home from a dance."

But her own words, as she heard herself say them, didn't sit with her. It occurred to her then that that wasn't why Nora had married Charlie at all. She had married him for her, for Patrick. This was what she wanted to say to Nora, that she understood. But the words got twisted. They came out as an accusation.

The things Nora said stayed with her.

I see right through you, Theresa.

I will never know how you sleep at night.

This is where you choose to hide?

She was inconsolable after Nora left. She went to Mother Placid, told her what had happened. She regretted rushing in without listening, which wasn't her way. Not anymore.

Part of her wished she had just taken Patrick on Nora's terms. She wished she had told Nora how the nuns prayed for him every morning at Mass, during the Prayers of the Faithful. Each day at dawn, she slipped his name into the box of intentions. When the priest said, "For Patrick Rafferty," the entire congregation called back, "Lord hear our prayer." On certain days, Mother Cecilia swore it was loud enough to reach him.

She regretted most of all that letter to Patrick, sent in haste, desperation, after Nora left. She had thought in the moment that the medal might be one way she could help him. She wanted him to know that God had used it to guide them both to the places where they belonged. She thought she knew what was best.

She had written and written to her sister to try to make amends, but her letters were all returned. She got permission to make a phone call, but the line in Dorchester was disconnected. She hoped Patrick wore the medal. She hoped he was doing better now. That it had only been a momentary lapse, a mistake born of youth. She prayed for Nora to come back to her and tell her. Each morning, first of all, she prayed for this.

Mother Cecilia was in bed, long since asleep, when a crashing sound jolted her awake. She looked into the silent hall, then out the window. She thought she could make out figures standing below.

She pulled on her robe and went down.

The Sisters of Saint Joseph stood on the dewy lawn, barefoot in their nightgowns, looking up.

Sister Evangeline pointed skyward.

"Fireworks," she said. "They're pulling out all the stops for the Bicentennial."

"Where are they lighting them?"

"Probably just on one of the local farms," she said.

"Some bored teenage boys," someone said.

With that, she thought of Patrick. Any thought of him, a thought of her sister.

Her life was blessed, joyful. She was utterly content, but for the lack of them.

Sometimes she missed a baby boy who didn't exist, who was almost a man now, with such a sharp yearning that it shocked her. Sometimes she indulged in what-ifs. If Patrick had come into the world now, in an age of greater understanding, she might have kept him. Had she been just a bit older, had she had her life established, maybe she would have fought harder. She knew there was no point in thoughts like these. It had happened when it happened. The moment a woman was born determined so much of who she was allowed to become.

Mother Cecilia regarded the pure black sky, sprinkled with stars. Twin sun blossoms exploded gold, bursting forth from the center, showering down in glorious, glittering slow motion.

Some of her fellow nuns had been drawn to the windows. They gazed out through the screens, and she waved up to them. After so many years, they were the ones she knew best. Her memories were mostly of them— a snowy afternoon when they abandoned their chores and sledded down the giant hill at the back of the property in their habits. The February when every single one of them was down with the flu, and still they sang seven times each day. The sight of the postulants, lined up in the meadow, doing their morning jumping jacks, as the dogs looked on, barking. How, on a chilly Saturday, ten of them might gather out in the barn to put up the hay, sweating in peaceful silence as they went about their work.

They were the ones she laughed and cried with, the ones whose trials she worried over, the ones whose quirks drove her mad and delighted her in equal measure. They were her sisters now. Her family.

Part Seven

2009

19

BRIDGET STOOD OUTSIDE the door to the funeral home in the cold, keeping her aunt Kitty company while she smoked a cigarette. It seemed a bold gesture, as if Kitty were giving the finger to death itself. Nobody smoked anymore. Yet here she stood, smoking, because she was eighty-two, it was what she had always done, and she was too old now to change.

For the past few years, Kitty had lived in a retirement community. A nice one, where everybody had his or her own little condo. Where they did yoga and had Italian cooking demonstrations on Friday nights. She always seemed to be dating someone new. Her eyesight was shot, so she couldn't drive anymore. But she kept her old Cadillac parked out front. *In case of emergency,* she said.

Bridget and Natalie had gone to pick her up. Now Natalie was inside with the others. The only one who had yet to arrive was Brian.

Since he appeared to be half in the wrapper back at the house, Bridget had tried to insist that he go with someone else instead of driving his own car.

"I'm fine to drive," Brian said.

"He's fine," Nora said.

She wondered why her mother would rather risk seeing another son drive into a concrete wall than experience an awkward moment. But Bridget left it alone. The fact was, all of them had been in a car with a driver who had been drinking a million times, thinking nothing of it. She remembered when she was six or seven and in the middle of a family party, her mother sent her and John and their cousins along to the package store with their uncle Matthew. He swerved onto the curb. He whooshed past red lights. "It was pink," he said. They laughed and laughed. A great adventure.

Kitty's scalp was visible beneath tufts of white cotton candy hair.

"You need a hat," Bridget said.

Kitty waved her away. "It would wreck my whole look."

Under her fur coat she wore a black velour pantsuit with rhinestones on the front. A pair of black patent leather flats.

She was once a tall and striking woman, but years of slouching had left her hunched. Bridget straightened her own spine, looking.

From this close up, Kitty's deep wrinkles seemed punishing. Her face looked like the shell of a walnut. Bridget had last seen her at Christmas, but she swore that even in the span of a few weeks, Kitty had gotten smaller. There were so many years in the middle of life when a person didn't change much. But old age was like childhood, when if you went a month without seeing someone, you might find an entirely different person waiting.

Despite it, Kitty was somehow still a beauty. Her high cheekbones, her sparkling eyes remained. She still wore red lipstick every day.

Bridget worshipped her as a kid. Kitty was the opposite of her mother. Carefree, living alone off her dead husband's money, not having to worry about children. Kitty retired early from nursing. She took expensive trips and wore nice clothes. Her home was furnished in such a feminine manner that every time Bridget stepped inside, she felt as if she had entered a gingerbread house. There were ruffles on the curtains. Pink wallpaper, and silk flowers in glass vases. Throw pillows, a mirrored coffee table, a crystal chandelier. In the tiny garden out back stood an honest-to-God birdbath, gurgling water at all times.

Taking in the smell of her aunt's perfume now, Bridget had a recollection of Kitty as a young woman, sitting in her mother's kitchen in a black dress, a highball glass in hand, auburn hair falling past her shoulders. Everyone laughing at the story she told.

It had occurred to Bridget on the drive over that Kitty, having grown up next to her mother in Ireland, must already know. Telling her wouldn't be a betrayal.

"Aunt Kitty, can I ask you something, just between us?"

"Of course," Kitty said.

"My mother told me she has a sister."

Kitty pulled her head back in surprise. "She told you."

"Yes. I assume you knew?"

"I knew Theresa. I shared a room in that house on Edison Green with her and your mother, when they were new in town."

Bridget looked at her. It was all so strange and suspicious. And maybe it was childish to feel this way, but it stung a little that Kitty had kept this from her. Why this, when for all of Bridget's life, Kitty had been the one to fill in the gaps in the family story? She was the one who told Bridget that Uncle Lawrence had once been a wild drunk, that he didn't stop drinking until he fell asleep behind the wheel of a bus. The kids knew him as a teetotaler. They only ever saw him drink tonic, though he was a fiend for the stuff. He could wash a sandwich down with a two-liter bottle of Coke like it was a glass of water.

Something awful must have happened. This woman must have hurt her mother in a way that left no room for forgiveness.

"What was she like?" Bridget asked.

"A real hot ticket," Kitty said. "Beautiful girl. She looked like a film star."

Her Irish aunts said any woman who was halfway pretty looked like a film star, the generous words tumbling out of them, one syllable stretched into two. *Fil-um.*

"What else?" Bridget said. She felt far freer to ask Kitty about it than she did Nora. For a certain kind of girl, with a certain kind of mother, an aunt would always be the preferred confidante. An aunt could see you as you were. A mother could only see you as she wished you were, or once imagined you would be.

"It was quite a scandal when Theresa ran off the way she did," Kitty said.

"Ran off?"

"We were all shocked when we found out she had become a nun, I can tell you that. Your mother included, I'd say, though we never discussed it. Your aunt Theresa certainly wasn't the type. Clearly."

Your aunt Theresa. Another aunt. Bridget hadn't thought of it in those terms. Who knew how they might have connected if given the chance? Probably not very well. She couldn't picture herself as close with a nun as she was with Kitty. But still.

"My mother says we kids met her once."

Kitty frowned. "No. I don't think so."

"I don't either. I'm confused. Why did we never hear about this person until today?"

"I never thought it was right for Nora to keep it a secret. But of course I didn't say anything."

"Why not?"

"Oh, Bridget. You can only control what goes on in your own house and sometimes not even that. But if you ask me, Patrick deserved to know."

"Why Patrick?"

She saw something change in Kitty's expression.

"All of you did, I mean. Well, what did your mother tell you about it?"

"She just said she has a sister, and that she called her and she's coming to the wake."

"No. What's Nora thinking? She can't come. They don't let them leave places like that."

There was a long silence while she waited for Kitty to say more. Usually Kitty was thrilled when a secret got told. Then she could reveal all the other secrets that went along with it. To her, a secret was like a diamond—long buried, kept under pressure, then dug up and made into something so much more valuable than the thing it was to begin with.

But for once, Kitty didn't elaborate.

"I don't understand," Bridget said, finally. "Why did they stop speaking?"

Kitty shook her head, as if she couldn't quite remember. "It was such a long time ago now."

Bridget noticed a blonde walking toward them across the funeral home parking lot. The girl looked about nineteen. She gave them a wave. She wore a black minidress with a plunging neckline and super-high heels. No coat, even though it was freezing.

Bridget was positive she had never seen her before.

At that moment, Brian turned into the lot. When the blonde saw him, she smiled huge. A smile that hurt your jaw just looking at it.

Brian got out of his car and walked toward the three of them, hunched down in his jacket, hands pressed into his pockets.

When he reached them, he said, "So. I see you've met."

"No, actually," Bridget said. "Hi, I'm Bridget. His sister."

"This is Ashley," Brian said.

"His girlfriend," Ashley said.

Kitty tossed her cigarette and they all filed inside. Brian held the door. Bridget was the first one through, providing a chance for her to raise her eyebrows at him.

She made her way toward Natalie.

"I was just talking to Kitty about the nun," she said.

Natalie nodded.

Nora stood whispering with Mr. O'Dell at the center of the enormous viewing room, even though there was no one there to take issue with their volume. John and Julia were with her. Maeve was arranging photographs on a table while also typing away on her phone. Bridget wondered what she thought of all this. She wished desperately, suddenly, that John and Patrick had been closer, so that Maeve might have known Patrick better, the parts of him that were easy to love.

The open casket had been positioned in its usual place against the far wall. There were flowers arranged all around it. Enormous baskets of lilies, roses, tulips, and orchids, all white. A potted white hydrangea, which would eventually be planted at the grave. Her mother needed things to be just so. Everywhere, but especially here. As if she could change the fact of death itself if she exerted enough control over the situation.

Bridget hated this place, the forced hush that covered over all the anguish. The pale pink walls, like the inside of a shell, a color that was probably meant to soothe but had the opposite effect on her. She felt a strong desire to punch a hole through the inspirational psalm scrawled in calligraphy on one wall: *Cast your cares on the Lord and He will sustain you. He will never let the righteous be shaken.*

She thought to herself, not for the first time, that she would never put the rest of them through this. She wouldn't be waked, all of them standing here weighted down by numb sorrow, forced to look at her corpse, or not look. Of course, it might not be up to her. Pat wouldn't have wanted any of this. She would make it clear to Natalie the minute they got home that were she to die, Nora could have nothing to do with it. Natalie was to tell her that Bridget's body had vanished.

Julia came over to the two of them.

"Nora just told us the craziest thing in the car on the way here," she whispered.

"We know. She told me too," Bridget said. "Insane."

Before they could say more, the priest walked in.

"Let's talk about it later?" Julia said.

"Yes. At great length."

They went toward the casket as a group, following the priest across the room as if he were the Pied Piper. The sweetness of the lilies made Bridget want to gag as she got close. She had long associated the smell of lilies with death. She avoided them at the bodega, or on a table in a restaurant. They belonged nowhere but here.

"Is this everyone?" the priest said. He had his back to the casket, while the rest of them were made to face it.

"Yes," Nora said. She paused, as if to count them. "This is the whole family."

"Used to be a lot more of us," Kitty said.

Aunt Kitty's favorite pastime was to tell you over a cup of tea how each of her brothers had died. The next day, she'd run through it all again if you let her. It seemed to hurt her feelings that she had outlived them all, as if God had snubbed her somehow.

Bridget wondered if her mother was expecting her sister to be here by now. She imagined what they would do when they saw each other. Embrace, maybe. Or start weeping. Explain to the rest of them why the hell they hadn't spoken in so long.

She let her eyes land on Patrick's face, felt a jab to the heart, then looked away. Just above his head inside the casket, leaning against the raised silk-covered lid, was a framed picture of him. In it, Pat was sunburned and smiling, sitting on the front porch in shorts and T-shirt, the breeze in his hair. Bridget focused on that.

She didn't face him again until it was time for them each to take a turn with the body. The family members lined up. From the corner of her eye, she saw Natalie go to the back of the room to give them space.

Bridget knelt before him first, crossing herself for her mother's benefit. The tears were automatic.

Patrick held a crystal rosary in his hand. In this way, she knew for certain that he was dead. Bridget half wanted to grab the thing, stuff it in her pocket. It had nothing to do with him.

For some time, Patrick had been wearing a mustache. Nora moaned about it every time Patrick was in her presence. Now the mustache was gone. Bridget assumed Nora had requested this for the viewing. She wondered whose job it was to outfit the dead in so intimate a manner. Would Mr. O'Dell, that moonfaced man, be the last person ever to see Patrick's scarred-up knees, his freakishly long white toes?

The Hail Mary was a muscle memory that came to her in moments like this, even though she hadn't been one to pray in years. She had tried once to attend a Unitarian Universalist church service, but she couldn't locate God there, in that place of rainbows and kindness. She found it all suspect somehow. In times of distress, she returned to the God of her childhood, vengeful yet dependable.

She said every prayer she knew, just to have more time with Patrick. The moments you spent with the dead were like going under water. The sounds of the room went away, and there was nothing but you and the person lying before you.

When she finally stood, Bridget felt disoriented. She looked around at the others. Her family. What remained of her family.

When it was Nora's turn to say good-bye, she knelt before Patrick and though she did not make a sound, Bridget watched from behind as her body heaved up and down, the silent sobs rolling through her. She stayed too long. Eventually, John went to her, rubbed her back, as if drawing her out of a trance.

"It's almost time," he said. "People will start coming in a minute."

Brian went last.

The girlfriend went right along with him. She knelt beside Brian, putting a bare arm around him, rubbing his back, as if the two of them might just go at it right there on the velvet kneeler. John gave Bridget a baffled look.

Here was Brian, putting front and center a girl they would probably never see again after today. Bridget caught Natalie's eye. Off to the side, keeping a respectful distance. The woman who would be the mother of her child. It was no one's fault but Bridget's. She was more like her mother than she cared to admit. Nora was closed off, unable to show herself to them, and this had seeped down to Bridget, cost her enormously.

A few minutes later, when the priest said, "Immediate family members should take their places," Natalie said, "I'll keep Aunt Kitty company."

"No," Bridget said. "Stay with me."

Natalie nodded, and Bridget took her hand, led her to their position. The two of them stood beside John and Julia and Maeve, Nora and Brian on the other side. Bridget didn't look to see her mother's expression.

The seven of them formed an L with the casket, as erect as soldiers or Rockettes. There was a row of tall stools behind them, but none of them sat. Poor Brian's eyes and nose were red with tears that he refused to release. It looked as if they might burst through his pores at any moment.

They accepted condolences from a long line of relatives and friends, strangers and near strangers. Hundreds of people showed up. Bridget's cousins Matty and Sean and Conor were first, plus Conor's wife, Marie, and their kids. They looked like a family from a catalogue. His three sisters, Peggy, Patricia, and Jane, all of them nurses, followed behind— two of them wore scrubs beneath their winter coats, only on an hour's break. Bridget's parents had presumed once that she too would be a nurse someday.

There was a pair of twins, third cousins of Bridget's, a woman and a man, ten years younger than she was. She still remembered their christening party, though she could never remember their names. Each of them had two children of their own now.

Everyone they knew from Dorchester was there, and the neighbors from Hull. Guys who hadn't seen Patrick since high school came, and all the regulars from his bar. If you never had a wedding, your family never got to see the people who loved you in all the different parts of your life, together in one place. There was something beautiful about it. She wished Patrick were here to see. Oh, the women who poured into his wake. She wondered now whether he ever would have settled down with one of them.

Aunt Kitty had taken a seat by the fireplace. Every so often, she gave Bridget a regretful wave.

Nora's eyes were on the door.

An hour passed. The room hummed with low conversation. Dozens

of people stood talking in small groups. Fifty or more waited in line to
pay their respects. Eileen Delaney, queen of the neighborhood busybod-
ies, was there with Betty Joyce, who lived next door to her. When they
reached the coffin, they knelt together, their hips and shoulders touching.

Then they came to Bridget and Natalie, who were first in the receiving
line.

"Honey, how are you?" Eileen said.

Her voice dripped with the sad enthusiasm of a tragedy junkie. Eileen
could go on for hours talking gleefully about someone else's divorce or
heart attack or house fire. She lived for days like this one.

Betty embraced Bridget, the smell of her perfume making Bridget
want to cough. When they kissed, she felt Betty's prickly whiskers on
her cheek.

"Didn't he get a crowd," Eileen said. "The back lot was already full
when I pulled in. There's an actual line of cars just waiting to park."

Natalie looked slightly taken aback by the remark, but Bridget understood. They had all been in this room so many times. You couldn't
help but compare it to wakes past. An untimely death drew the biggest
turnout—the younger, the bigger. Every few years, it seemed, some
teenager in town got in a wreck or broke his neck jumping drunk into
the shallow end of a swimming pool. There'd be a line that stretched
for blocks. Usually, when they were young, there was memorabilia that
hinted at a hobby of some kind—a track jacket draped over the coffin
or an electric guitar propped among the flower arrangements. This told
you how the child would be remembered: *He was the captain of the team,*
they'd say for years to come, even if he spent all his time warming the
bench. *He was going to be the next Clapton.*

Patrick was fifty. Certainly not a child, not even a young man anymore, and yet still too young to die. A few in the room were just beginning to feel the crush of grief that would last for years. But many didn't
even know him. They had come for the spectacle, or because they knew
one of the Rafferty kids from school, or because they wanted something
from John. They were thinking about where they'd go to eat after, they
were establishing themselves as important to the story or not. Bridget
wished she could trade places with any one of them.

"Patrick looks so handsome," Betty said.

"He does," Eileen said. "Very peaceful." She lowered her voice.

"Though Digger O'Dell always makes the hair too big. It's like he thinks the dead might have a gig at the Grand Ole Opry later. Well. We'll see you back at your mother's after."

There wasn't anything more to say, but some old biddy had created a backup in the line, holding John's hand, probably telling him a story he wouldn't remember an hour from now. Eileen smiled at Bridget, holding eye contact for an uncomfortably long moment.

When Brian was born, Nora and Charlie had to go to the hospital in the middle of the night. Eileen came up the hill in her nightgown and slept over so the others wouldn't be alone. She was there when they woke up, to tell them the news. She made pancakes, and afterward, they decorated the porch with blue balloons. It was the summer they moved to Hull, when Patrick was in such a bad way. When Bridget saw Eileen in the kitchen that morning, her first thought was that something horrible had happened to him.

"Oh!" Eileen exclaimed now. She flapped her arms. "There's my Tommy!"

Tommy Delaney shuffled toward them, dragging his feet, flashing apologetic smiles at all the people he was cutting in line. He got to his mother's side and kissed her cheek. He had gotten fat. His gut hung over the top of his pants so that his suit jacket wouldn't close.

"Hi, Ma," he said. "Mrs. Joyce. Bridget, hi. God, I'm so sorry for your loss."

"Thanks, Tommy," she said. "Thanks for coming."

After the three of them had moved along, Natalie whispered, "My competition, I presume?"

"Yup," Bridget said. "I can tell you're shaking in your boots."

Patrick's best friend, Fergie, had arrived, bleary-eyed and drunk. He took his place in line. Bridget kept an eye on him. When he reached her, they made small talk for a while. She didn't want him to move along to the others. She worried how Nora might feel, seeing him like this. Her mother had never liked Fergie. It was always easier to blame someone else for your kid's bad behavior. But finally, Bridget couldn't think of anything more to say. She watched him move through each family member, on the way to Nora at the end of the line.

When Fergie said something that made Brian laugh out loud, the sudden eruption of noise startled Bridget. People turned their heads.

She looked to Julia on the far side of Natalie. They held each other's gaze.

Julia whispered, "Well, that was unexpected." She paused, then added, "What is Brian's date wearing?"

Bridget thought the word *date* was odd, given the context.

Natalie leaned in. "She's auditioning to be a Laker Girl after this."

Throughout the afternoon, they all checked in with Nora to make sure she was holding up. They offered her tissues and cushioned chairs and glasses of water, none of which she wanted.

"I'm fine," she kept saying. "There's no need to make a fuss."

As the hours wore on, the members of the family fell out of line and joined the crowd. Bridget and Natalie drifted from one set of cousins to another, then stood chatting with Maeve and Julia for a while.

"My dad punched a lamp last night," Maeve said.

"Is that right?" Bridget said.

"Yeah. Healthy."

"And who have you been texting all day?" Natalie asked.

Maeve looked bashful. "Nobody."

"It's a boy in her class," Julia said. "Jacob Owens."

"Mom!" Maeve said.

She was truly outraged, and yet Bridget had to smile. She thought her sister-in-law was an amazing mother. Julia knew Maeve, knew all her friends. Unlike Nora, who always gave Bridget something generic for her birthday when she was a kid—a doll or a tea set, something you might give a child you'd never met, simply because she was a girl. When Bridget was young, there was absolutely nothing fun about her mother. Nora was strict, stern, matter-of-fact. She had no interest in knowing anything about Bridget's personal life.

Julia knew which clothing brands and TV shows and bands Maeve liked. She knew which members of the bands were considered the cutest and weighed in with her own opinion. She knew Maeve hated beets, so she simply did not make beets, whereas Nora would have served them up as something close to a punishment.

It seemed unjust that Maeve hated Julia's guts all the same, as if it were written into the code of being thirteen, and no behavior on a mother's part could change that.

Julia was looking at Nora, who stood talking to the priest.

"How do you think she seems?" she said.

"I don't know," Bridget said. "She never lets on, does she. This phantom sister of hers hasn't shown."

"Is it possible she made the whole thing up?" Julia said. "I'm not accusing her of anything, but just maybe, in her grief, she got her wires crossed? Sorry, is that terrible to suggest?"

"No, I was thinking the same thing. But Aunt Kitty remembers her."

"All I ever wanted was a sister," Maeve said. "How could Nana have one and not speak to her? Something bad must have gone down between them, that's all I know."

Julia smiled, shook her head. "I concur," she said.

Half an hour before the wake ended, Bridget slipped into the bathroom. She peed in one of two tiny stalls, then washed her hands in a pink sink, built into a pink countertop. There were flecks of gold glitter in it. The walls were covered in the same pink tile as the floor. On the counter sat a large basket containing breath mints and tissue packets and eye makeup remover. A mourning survival kit. Chipper classical music was piped in through an overhead speaker.

She regarded her reflection in the mirror, touching the creases beneath her eyes. She looked exhausted.

The door creaked open. Her body tightened, preparing for more small talk, readying itself to be trapped with some acquaintance from her past. But when she looked over, it was her mother who had entered the room.

Nora seemed in a daze. In her hand was a stack of Mass cards people had given her, declarations of sympathy, promises that Patrick would be prayed for. She held them forth and Bridget scanned the words.

In Life and Death We Belong to the Lord.
It is in dying that we are born to eternal life.

"I don't want these," Nora said. "I don't want to see them."

Bridget took the pile and shoved them into the trash can.

"There."

"We can't," Nora said. "What if someone sees?"

Bridget balled up a wad of paper towels and tossed it on top.

For a second, Nora smiled.

Bridget wondered if her mother would mention Natalie's presence beside her in the receiving line.

But instead, Nora said, "When your father died, everyone had something to say about it. They asked so many questions. About whether the doctors had done enough, whether they could have tried one more treatment. They talked about their cousins and their friends and total strangers who died of the same thing he did. It made me very uneasy. I don't believe in talking about such things."

"Okay," Bridget said, unsure where this was headed.

"But now, they don't say a thing about what happened to Patrick," Nora said. "Maybe they think I'm to blame. I let him get away with murder all those years. What did I expect?"

"What? No. Mom, he was fifty years old."

She supposed this was how it worked. A mother blamed herself until the end, whatever that meant. Would Bridget feel this way about her own child in fifty years' time? She tried not to think about how old she would be by then.

Nora lifted a soggy prayer card from the counter, where someone had left it behind.

"Oh no, will you look at this."

The card was printed on flimsy paper, a photo of Patrick on one side and a prayer on the other. Nora had had two hundred of them made. Bridget herself always took one at a wake to be polite, but she never knew what to do with it after. She would sometimes find a prayer card at the bottom of her bag or under the seat in her van, a startling reminder of someone she hadn't thought of in ages.

Nora had a place for everything. In her house, every object had at least one other object to contain it. A ring was never left on a table or even naked in a jewelry box, but was instead suspended over the crystal post of a Waterford ring holder, or tucked into the velvet box it had arrived in decades earlier. She kept her lipstick in a magnetized case. When they were kids, a ridiculous doll sat on the toilet lid, with an enormous crocheted skirt like Scarlett O'Hara's. Under the skirt was a single roll of toilet paper.

A fraying blue cardboard box held Nora's prayer cards. It had once had the words *Saints for All Occasions* embossed on the top in gold, but over time, bits of the foil had worn away so that only the shadow of the letters remained. Inside the box, at the bottom of the pile, were the newer cards, the ones she collected at wakes. The rest had been handed down by a long-dead relative Bridget had only ever heard about in stories. The cards were ancient and worn and fragile. Her mother kept them in a precise order and knew if even one was out of place.

When they were young, Nora never let the children touch the cards unless she was sitting with them and they had washed their hands with soap and hot water. It was a clever trick, if that's what it was. It made the cards seem special, magical. They'd beg her to take them out. She had a prayer card for almost anything you could imagine. Bridget's favorite as a child was the Prayer to Mary, Undoer of Knots. At some point in her teens, she realized that this had nothing to do with shoelaces or hair snarls and came to like it even more.

Nora took the limp, wet card now and held it under the hand dryer, shaking the picture of her son vigorously, as if attempting to save Patrick from drowning.

When the dryer finished whirring, Nora said, "She didn't come."

"I know. I'm sorry."

"You don't understand."

"Yes I do," Bridget said, irritated. She was trying to be sympathetic, she was trying not to ask questions, because she knew that's what her mother would want. "You're disappointed. You wanted her here."

"No. I didn't."

"But you invited her."

"I didn't know she could leave. Cloistered nuns aren't ever supposed to leave and you should know that, Bridget."

"Jesus, you're being impossible. You didn't want her here and she's not here. That's a good thing, right?"

Nora didn't say anything.

"So after your sister became a nun, you just never spoke again."

"We did speak. For many years. And then we didn't anymore."

"Why?"

"It's too long a story for me to tell you here. People are probably wondering where we are."

"Why did you call her now?" Bridget said.

But her mother was already at the door, pushing it open, crossing to the other side.

Bridget followed Nora down a dark hallway. When they stepped back into the viewing room, there she was, standing by the fireplace: a nun in full habit—a veil and black robes that covered every bit of her besides her face.

It felt as if they had summoned her out of thin air just by talking about her in the bathroom. Somehow Bridget hadn't fully believed she was a real person until this moment.

The nun was chatting with Aunt Kitty, just as natural as can be.

Natalie, Julia, and Maeve stood several feet away, trying not to gawk.

"Oh God," Nora said, her voice a frantic whisper. "She's here."

She grabbed hold of Bridget's hand, held it too tight. In all her life, her mother had never leaned on her in such a way.

"Let's go say hello," Bridget said, steadying Nora.

"I can't."

"Mom, come on."

The nun didn't see them coming. They reached her just seconds after Kitty waved Bobby Quinlan over. Uncle Bobby they had always called him, though he was not their uncle but a distant cousin of her father's, the son of the woman who put them all up when they first came over from Ireland.

"Look who it is, Bobby," Kitty said. "Theresa Flynn! Do you believe it?"

"My God!" he said. "We haven't seen you in years."

He turned and noticed Nora there.

"Nora!" he said. "I didn't know your sister was coming."

The nun turned her head now and saw them.

"Nora." She smiled warmly, with love. Bridget couldn't help but smile back. The woman's eyes and mouth were so much like Nora's, like her own. Why was it a shock to learn that someone related to you resembled you? Of course she would.

Nora didn't smile. She stared straight into the woman.

Her mother was often appalled by what she saw as lapses in Bridget's manners. Now Bridget felt a need to apologize on Nora's behalf. *Say something,* she thought, attempting to beam the words to her mother's brain.

"I'm Bridget," she said finally, extending a hand. "Nora's daughter. Your niece!"

"Bridget. My goodness, look at you. The last time I saw you, you were just a baby."

Everyone waited for Nora to speak.

When she didn't, Bridget went on. "Did you find the place okay? Where are you staying?"

"At the Ramada in Dorchester."

An absolute shithole, right on the expressway. Bridget looked to her mother, but Nora stayed silent.

The nun looked directly at her. "I just booked the hotel closest to your house," she said. "I didn't realize the wake would be all the way out here."

Nora said coolly, as if it should be obvious, "We don't live there anymore."

Bridget had never seen her mother be so rude to anyone, other than the members of their immediate family.

"If you'll excuse me," Nora said. "I need to say good-bye to Father Callahan."

As she walked off, Bridget saw her mother's hands roll into fists. The nun looked despondent, watching her go.

Bridget tried to imagine these two as children, or young women on the boat to America. Her mother, tough and abrasive and self-assured. The sister, a woman who would go to a convent eventually, probably shy and reserved, scared of Nora. What had happened between them?

Everyone paused, absorbing the awkwardness, then attempting to deflect it.

"So," Bobby Quinlan said. "Your convent is—where, now? Remind me."

"Vermont."

"Did you just come in today?"

"Yes. I took the bus."

"It was good of you to come," Bobby said.

"You don't drive?" Bridget asked, just to have something to say.

"I don't. Unless you count a tractor."

The nun grinned. Not shy, then. She had a brightness to her eyes, a youthfulness almost. She was a sturdy woman. Aunt Kitty seemed brittle, as if her wrist might snap off if she let her arm dangle out the window of a moving car. Nora's body showed its age with a certain sag, as if having completed its work, it would now sink into an armchair and rest until the end. But the nun looked strong. Her face was weathered, tanned like a farmer's.

"Actually, I can drive," she said. "But I've never gone very far. Just short distances."

"You don't go by Theresa anymore," Bobby said.

"No, it's Mother Cecilia now."

"Can I ask you something?" he said.

"Of course."

"Why do nuns change their names anyway?"

"Well, in my case, Mother Teresa was already taken."

They all laughed. Her mother's sister was charming, funny. Totally unlike Nora.

"Where do you live now, Bridget?" she asked.

"I'm in New York."

"Whereabouts?"

"Brooklyn."

"I used to teach in Queens."

Bridget wanted to know when, and whether Nora knew. She had barely gotten her head around the fact of the nun. She hadn't wondered what she did before the convent. Such a strange unfolding, this day.

"I'm just going to go check on my mother," she said. "It's so nice to meet you."

"So good to see you, Bridget. After all this time."

She left the woman talking to Aunt Kitty and Bobby Quinlan.

Always, the story had gone like this: Your father was one of six. Your mother had just the one brother. A whole generation had known and said nothing.

Maybe the secret had nothing to do with her, but it cast certain memories in a different light. She considered her father's inability to tell a story straight. She thought now of their trip to Ireland, a trip Nora never wanted to take. She was melancholy the entire time, even after she went to visit her old friend Oona, the girl she'd been talking about since Bridget was small. *My best friend,* Nora called her, even though they hadn't seen each other in decades. Bridget thought her mother's mood on that trip was down to Charlie being sick. But maybe there was more to it.

Charlie's brother Peter and his two sons still operated the Rafferty farm at that point. Bridget had heard stories about Peter from her father and uncles. They said he was an irresponsible drunk when he was young. They expected him to run the farm into the ground. Instead, it had thrived in his care.

When they visited, they all had lunch together there, laughing with ease as if they had done it a hundred times. At some point, Peter mentioned something about how Charlie was the one who was meant to stay in Miltown Malbay, the only one in the family who truly loved the farm. But her father breezed past the comment with a joke, and Bridget assumed Peter was kidding. Despite the many times Charlie had said he wanted to return for good, she couldn't begin to picture him in this life.

In the early evening, Peter said, "Come on. I'll give you the grand tour."

The whole group walked the land. Green hills in the distance, and beyond them, the sun setting over the ocean. It was such a breathtaking place. Bridget couldn't understand how her parents had stayed away for so long.

"The boys will plant these thirty-five acres soon," Peter said.

"Thirty-five acres?" Charlie said. "But we've only got twenty-three."

Bridget noted that *we.*

"Not anymore," Peter said. "We've expanded."

"How?"

"For a while, the Land Commission was giving abandoned property to adjacent farmers, once a certain amount of time passed. Twenty acres went to me and fifteen to the Cullanans on the other side of it."

Bridget saw her parents comprehend something that she herself didn't yet understand.

"My family's land," Nora said.

"It was just going to waste, Nora."

"What about the house?"

"Nothing's happened to it. It's still there, and in the Flynn name. Go on over and have a look."

Nora's people were all gone. Her only brother died in his forties. Ever since, the house stood empty.

They went inside, the front door ajar, everything coated in a veil of black dirt. There were dishes still in the sink, a calendar on the wall— April 1979. On the kitchen windowsill sat forgotten teacups, a package of cigarettes, an ashtray, and a yellowing photograph of Nora and Charlie and their children. The top half was bleached white from the sun, but Bridget recognized it as having been taken on an Easter Sunday from the shoes she was wearing and the new suede bucks on the boys.

Throughout the house, paint curled off the walls. In the living room, letters and bills were heaped in the fireplace. By a recliner sat a pair of boots with metal horseshoes nailed into their heels.

"To make them last longer," Charlie said.

A picture of the Sacred Heart hung in the entryway, similar to the one their mother had in the kitchen back home.

Down a short hall, in a downstairs room with bright blue walls and twin beds, chunks of the ceiling had fallen to the floor.

Bridget followed her mother in.

"Was this your room?"

Nora nodded. She bit her lower lip.

"Unbelievable," she said. "He took my family's land and he couldn't even be bothered to come over here and look in on our house."

Bridget pulled back the open bedroom door. A woman's hat was suspended on a hook on the rear side, a pink silk flower perched on the brim, perfectly preserved. She loved the thought of her serious mother wearing it once, perhaps not so serious then. Bridget pulled the hat down, held it out to Nora.

Nora took hold of it without a word. She said she wanted to go up to her grandmother's old bedroom, a cubby at the top of a short staircase, to see if her old sewing machine was still there. But Charlie said they'd better not try the stairs.

"Let's go now," he said.

Nora left the hat on a table in the entryway.

As they walked back outside, she cried. Bridget watched as her brother Patrick wrapped an arm around Nora's shoulder. Nora smiled up at him through tears.

Across the way, a herd of cows stared at them as if they knew something. Until then, Bridget had never thought of a cow as a particularly soulful animal, but she couldn't get the sight of their brown, puddley eyes out of her mind.

Her father was able to turn his back and walk off, go to a pub and laugh the night away, point out sights that gave him pleasure. Nora couldn't do the same. She seemed haunted for the rest of that trip. Bridget wondered if they had been wrong to come. She asked her mother if they should do something. Maybe there was a way to restore the house. Even to sell it would be better than to let it collapse.

But Nora said, "It's too far gone. Just leave it, Bridget."

She hadn't mentioned it since.

Bridget found her mother at the table by the door where the guest book sat. Nora acted busy, smoothing out the book's already flat pages, capping the cheap pen that leaned up against it.

"Mom," Bridget said. "Aren't you going to talk to your sister?"

"Of course I will. But I have to talk to everyone. It's rude not to."

"You're not going to let her stay at the Ramada."

"Why not? It's perfectly fine."

"Should I invite her to the house after, to eat?"

"She's a nun. They don't go to things. We'll see her at the funeral."

"Are you sure?"

Nora's eyes had left the conversation. Bridget followed them. Her mother's sister stood alone now, over Patrick's body. They watched as she laid a hand on his forehead, stroking his hair.

"What is she doing?" Bridget said.

Nora shot off in her direction.

One of the neighborhood ladies asked in a stage whisper, "Oh my, who is that?"

"I assume she came with the priest," said Betty Joyce.

"They're not salt and pepper shakers," Eileen Delaney said.

"Well how else do you explain her?"

"I don't think she's anyone important," Eileen said. "Nora would have mentioned a nun."

A moment later, Nora and her sister stood side by side, saying nothing, staring into the coffin. Everyone in the room—for as much or as little as they knew—grew silent at the sight.

20

MOTHER CECILIA SAT at the hotel room window. The second floor was level with the expressway, maybe a hundred feet away. She watched as cars whizzed past.

Mother Placid had worried about her traveling alone. She told her to stay somewhere nice, spend some time, but Mother Cecilia didn't think it was proper. She booked the least expensive place she could find. She would only stay the one night, returning to the abbey after the burial. There were things that needed tending.

When she woke this morning, she was still unsure about whether she should go at all, but Mother Placid insisted, and she knew her better than anyone.

Just before she left, Mother Placid handed her a brown paper bag.

"The girls in the kitchen made you a lunch," she said. "We'll be thinking of you."

As her taxi drove through the abbey gates, Mother Cecilia watched from the back window. They passed the farms that dotted the hills, passed fields of sunflowers and golden corn. Eventually the road spat them out in the center of town. They went by the post office and the antique shops, the old Gulf station and the market. At the traffic light at the corner of Caulder and Bond, the driver slowed to a stop.

Mother Cecilia was used to going straight on from here, to Mercy Hospital, two miles north. In fifty years, she had rarely gone farther. She accompanied Mother Placid to her doctor's appointments at Mercy on the first Tuesday of the month. Otherwise, she only came into town to see the dentist or to vote on Election Day. She was vaguely aware of the sign for 91 South to the left of the stoplight, but it had never had a thing to do with her.

The taxi dropped her at the bus station. She climbed aboard the 7:52 to Boston. For the next several hours, a pair of teenage girls with studs in their faces stared at her. She had almost forgotten the lack of ease that some people, especially young ones, felt around nuns. The average person hardly ever saw a nun in habit anymore. To watch a nun eating a chicken salad sandwich on the bus was an utter sensation.

It was worse now than it had been. A man in the grocery store had approached two postulants just last week and said, "How can you be a part of that hateful church? What are you hoping to accomplish, being held prisoner up there on the hill?"

They had lost one of their loveliest young novices in the recent scandal. Her brother was a priest who had tried to sound the alarm years ago and was dismissed for it.

"How are we supposed to go on, given the church's mistakes?" she asked Mother Cecilia during their final conversation.

"We must remember that the church is not God. The church is just men trying to do their best."

"I'm talking about—"

"I know," Mother Cecilia said. "I don't have a good answer. I wish I did."

Lately, there were some who came to parlors to discuss their own pasts with priests, terrible stories that Mother Cecilia was not technically allowed to condemn, though she did condemn them. The deeper you came into union with God, the more you came to accept people the way they were. And yet, there were some who could never be accepted or forgiven.

She went directly to the hotel from South Station, intending to drop her bag and then take a taxi to the wake so that she could get there right at four. But four o'clock arrived, four-thirty. Five. She was terrified to face them. It was a quarter to six before she could summon the courage.

Now she wondered if she ought to have come at all.

"We'll see you at the house after?" Kitty Rafferty said as they parted ways at the wake.

But Nora hadn't invited her.

She told Kitty she needed to get back. She asked the undertaker to call her a taxi. She stood on the curb in the cold, watching the others bundle into cars in groups of three or four.

You only realized how old you had gotten when in the presence of the people you used to know. When you saw how old they were.

"Where are your brothers?" she had asked.

"Dead," Kitty said. "All of them, dead."

"Not Charlie."

"Yes."

"When?"

"Five years ago. And poor Babs around the same time. She liked you so much. She would have gotten a kick out of seeing you again."

Her memory was pulled to a night in Mrs. Quinlan's crowded kitchen, 1958. The last time she saw any of them. Babs had complained then about Conor's birth, about how much easier it had been for Nora to bring Patrick into the world. But now, here stood Conor, tall and broad shouldered, a married father of three, a policeman. And there was Patrick, a day away from his grave.

No one told her the specifics of what happened. Bobby Quinlan half whispered, "Well, he was a drinker. He liked to have a good time. But you've probably heard as much from Nora."

"No," she said. "Not really. What was he like?"

She took note of Bobby's big white teeth, his shiny bald head. She remembered them.

"He meant well," Bobby said. "Kind of a wild one, though. He kept Nora and Charlie on their toes. He was the life of the party. Millions of girlfriends, so I hear. But he always seemed lonely, somehow. Bit of a black sheep."

She wanted to know why her son's life had been lonely when he was surrounded by all these people. She had thought Patrick would feel a part of their family. But maybe he had known that he was outside of it.

She had never stopped feeling sadness over Patrick, though at some point, she resigned herself to the fact of not seeing him again, of letting her pain be a part of her.

If she hadn't left him, who might he have been? She allowed herself a momentary fantasy, one in which she had not indulged for years. She had taken Patrick with her on that bus to New York, found some way of keeping him. They would have lived together in the small apartment in Queens, his laughter buoying her. A kindly old neighbor would have watched him while she worked each day and when they reunited at day's end, he would jump straight into her arms. There would be an ease between them. Nothing to hide. They would simply be who they were, waiting for the world to catch up. Eventually, they might have gotten a big, fluffy dog, moved to a little house with a front porch in the suburbs, out on Long Island where Mother Placid was raised.

This was always where the fantasy gave way. She never would have known Mother Placid, never would have known the abbey. Nothing had just happened to her. She had made a choice and then she had made another and another after that. Taken together, the small choices anyone made added up to a life. Even coming to America was part of it. If it wasn't for Nora and Charlie, she would most likely have never left Ireland, never known her place in the world. When she saw Patrick before making final vows, she believed this to be true. And believed too that he would be safe in her sister's care.

Looked at another way, she knew that the chance to make that first, most important decision had been taken from her. Nora never asked her if she could have Patrick, she just took him. But when this made her angry, she reminded herself that Nora had only done what she thought was best.

Mother Cecilia regarded Bobby Quinlan. She had wondered if they all knew the truth by now, but he clearly thought she was nothing more to Patrick than a distant aunt.

Perhaps she had known how Nora would be. Still angry, still unable to forgive. Mother Cecilia had asked Sister Alma to call and say she was coming. She didn't want to give Nora the chance to tell her not to. She needed to say good-bye. She had been the only one in the room who loved Patrick when he came into the world. She wanted to be with him now, at the end.

Despite whatever anger she still felt, she had hoped they might rise above it, that she and Nora might console each other. But Nora's face showed that it would not be so. All the terrible things they had said at their last meeting. All the things they had done to each other.

Mother Cecilia was stricken when Nora turned her back and walked away, but still she stood with Kitty and Bobby and Nora's daughter, catching up on the past. She would just get through it.

Left alone, she looked over at the casket and found herself pulled to it. Patrick was alone too for the moment, no one standing by. She went to him.

The last time she saw him, he was still a child. She remembered a fair day at the convent. A blue sky and a gentle wind. A smile on his face.

The man lying in front of her was someone she wouldn't have recognized had she passed him in the street.

All these years, she had imagined a relationship between them. He was still primary to her. But she had only had the thought of him. Now she stood in a crowd of people who had the all of him, and yet maybe they had never loved him enough.

How I failed you, how I failed you.

She saw the medal peeking out from beneath the collar of his shirt. The one she had sent him, the one he was given right after he was born. She had always wondered if it ever made its way to him. She was so surprised to see it now that she reached out and touched it, and then her hand moved up into his hair. The black curls were threaded with grey.

She didn't realize what she was doing until she felt someone's presence at her side and turned to see her sister.

Of all the outcomes she had imagined to the silence between them, she had never considered this: the two of them, standing together, regarding his body. She looked at Nora, who stared straight ahead. One of life's contradictions: how human beings were at once entirely resilient and impossibly fragile. One decision could stay with you forever, and yet you could live through almost anything.

She lived in a place full of women unencumbered by children. An extraordinary thing, even today. But motherhood was often on her mind. Mothers were the ones who asked for most of the prayers. They were sometimes asked to pray for healthy pregnancies, or for a woman who could not bring a baby into this world no matter how she tried. Other times, they were asked to pray for girls who were going to become mothers far sooner than they ever should have.

So much of it—what a body could or could not do—was one of God's confounding mysteries. A child came into the world, always, through a woman. In most cases, this woman would see that child on through life. But not always. Each generation had its version of the story. There would always be girls who had babies they could not keep.

Nora was the only mother she herself had ever known. She had this in common with Patrick, her son.

She tried to take Nora's hand, but Nora pulled away.

Mother Cecilia knew the night would be long and that she wouldn't sleep. Every time a toilet flushed in the next room or a can of Coke tumbled from the top of the soda machine to the bottom, she heard it. The bed was covered in sheets as stiff as tissue paper. The space around it was small and dim, lit by a single lamp on the nightstand. The lack of light, she supposed, was meant to obscure the room's dinginess—the dark, dirty carpet, the stained grey walls.

She wanted to quiet her mind and focus, but the events of the day and evening kept returning to her. For almost fifty years, she had lived in monastic silence. When she first joined the abbey, it was deafening. But now she found that she had lost the muscles she once had—the ones that gave a person the strength to handle chitchat, traffic jams, the anxiety of calculating the taxi driver's tip as a harried businessman hovered on the sidewalk, wanting in.

The abbey was often bustling. A steady stream of visitors came to the door with concerns and grief, asking for their prayers. The guesthouses were always full. Parents brought their children every Christmas to see the crèche made in the seventeenth century. They held retreats for newlyweds and artists, for the aging, for the sick and the bereaved.

It was not as if the nuns were shut up in some castle with a moat around it. But guests came at set times. They sat on one side of the grille and she on the other and they left when they were told to. It was all entirely predictable. That was the life to which she had grown accustomed. A place where she was regarded with respect, with reverence.

She had met people who feared nuns, hated them. They couldn't believe that any sane woman would choose to join a convent. Of course, there were times in her life when she herself had felt this way. She knew Nora believed she had gone to the abbey to escape. She had said as much the last time they spoke. The truth would probably never convince her.

Eventually, she went to the phone on the nightstand. Mother Cecilia sat on the bed and dialed. It was half an hour until Compline, their final prayers of the day.

The nuns only talked on the phone when it was absolutely necessary, and never for very long—they talked to doctor's offices to schedule appointments, and to deliverymen regarding the transport of animals, feed, fertilizer. But she thought this qualified as a time of extreme need.

The portress answered on the second ring.

She asked how Mother Cecilia was faring, said they were all thinking of her. She had told them she was going to a funeral. The son of someone close to her, a friend from home.

"I was hoping Mother Placid might be free," she said.

"Of course. I'll transfer you into the dormitory."

Mother Dorothy picked up the phone in the kitchen. She asked Mother Cecilia to hold on while she looked for the abbess.

She must have left the receiver on the counter. Mother Cecilia could hear plates and silverware tinkling in the background. They'd be making preparations for dinner. Baking the bread, stirring the soup, placing pies on a cooling rack.

Every meal was of them, by them. The cheese and the butter and the milk and the bread were all made at the abbey. Whatever vegetables and fruit they had were grown in the nuns' own gardens and orchards. They ate a primarily vegetarian diet, for budgetary reasons. The only things brought in from the outside were some citrus and a bit of fish. Even the pottery they ate off of was hand-thrown and kilned on the premises.

The nuns still had to have a man there to say Mass, but it was their abbey, make no mistake. The priests rotated through each morning. During the sign of peace, the priest hugged a single nun. She in turn went into the congregation to hug the people.

When Mother Placid turned seventy-five last year, Mother Katherine made a joke during the Prayers of the Faithful. "For Mother Abbess, on her twenty-fifth birthday, we pray to the Lord," she said. Shocked and tickled, the rest of them responded, "Lord hear our prayer," with eyebrows lifted to the ceiling. Mother Abbess looked at the priest saying Mass to make sure he wasn't outraged, but he merely smiled and shrugged.

She wondered now when Bishop Dolan would come.

Contemplatives were not under the jurisdiction of local bishops like most nuns were. They answered directly to the Vatican. Since the abbey's founding, they had so rarely been bothered that Mother Cecilia tended to forget even that. The abbey was so essentially female. It seemed impossible that they should have to answer to men.

It was five years now since the first rumblings. One morning, they read in the newspaper that the Vatican had launched an investigation into all the working nuns in America. All nuns except the cloistered. All but them. The bishops said the nuns on the outside had grown too independent, advocating for birth control, homosexuality, women in the priesthood.

She was ashamed to recall how they felt relief at being excluded and simply moved forward. They already prayed for their sisters and brothers on the outside, who might not have time to properly pray for themselves. If some of them let their thoughts linger on the sisters a moment longer than usual at evening prayers, that was all.

Some weeks later, Mother Cecilia came across a story in her Catholic news bulletin. It concerned reiki sessions, which their Mother Ava had practiced for years. The bishops had issued a statement saying that reiki was incompatible with the church's teachings. This had been sent to Catholic hospitals and health-care facilities, but the directive had never reached the abbey.

"She performs this therapy on the homeless. On women who are going through chemo and poor people from the community who work on their feet all day," Mother Cecilia said when she brought it to the abbess.

"We'll consider it a warning," Mother Placid said, folding up the paper. "We won't trouble her with this. It doesn't apply to us anyway."

But not long after came an order from Bishop Dolan, handed down from Rome: Mother Ava must stop. There was no biblical justification for her actions.

Mother Cecilia wondered how Rome had learned of it. From Bishop Dolan, she supposed. He had an obsession with the abbey, with calling them out for the most absurd offenses. It was because Mother Placid had embarrassed him once, decades ago. He was a fragile, humorless man and he never could forget it.

They were forced to tell Mother Ava that her work must cease.
She wept.

When she left the room, Mother Placid began to pace.

"After everything these men have done to harm bodies and souls, this is what they choose to focus on?"

"I know," Mother Cecilia said. "It feels like something essential has been lost."

All over the world, the story was the same. The church of her childhood was in tatters. It made her heartsick to think of it.

The Vatican didn't seem to notice. They had declared it the Year for Priests.

Three weeks passed before Mother Ava came to them with an idea.

"I've looked to the scriptures and I've found this," she said, opening her Bible, turning to the page. "Mark 10:16. *And He took them in His arms and began blessing them, laying His hands on them.* A biblical justification."

"Very good," Mother Placid said.

Mother Ava resumed her work. They did not speak of it again.

Weeks passed before Bishop Dolan found out. He was raging with anger.

"Reiki is forbidden for everyone, but as contemplatives you are meant to be secluded, separate. Some of your nuns are living too close to the outside. We have been through it before."

"Yes," Mother Placid said. "And in the past, that openness was what saved the abbey from extinction."

"This is the last in a long line of infractions," he said. "We need to discuss the abbey's future. I'll come after New Year, when I'm back from Italy. I'll discuss it with Rome."

He had returned a week ago. They knew the day was imminent.

When Mother Placid came on the line, Mother Cecilia smiled at the sound of her voice.

"Has he arrived yet?" she asked.

"Not yet," Mother Placid said. "But never mind him. How is it going?"

"It's hard. Nora is so angry with me. I don't know why she asked me to come."

"Keep trying. Try again tomorrow."

"I will. But I'm angry too. Do I have the right? I still feel that if she had just done what I said, this never would have happened. It was so awful, seeing him that way."

"I'm sure."

"It makes me question everything she did. Everything I did. Ultimately, I have to blame myself."

"You're not to blame," Mother Placid said. "You did what you could do. Everyone here is thinking of you. It's quite a strange thing, having one of our own away. How does it feel, being out there in the world?"

"It feels . . . odd."

When she was young, she had dreamed of leaving, every day. Now a year or two might pass without that feeling. And when it came, she knew how to manage. She had reached an age where there was no place for her but the abbey.

Once, she thought her brother had been lucky, inheriting the family farm. But when they discussed it in their letters as adults, she realized that he wanted to leave Ireland. It was obligation that kept him home. She thought of her brother and sister now. Of the three of them, she believed she might be the only one who found happiness in the end.

Every visit she made beyond the abbey gates was at the behest of the abbey and the Vatican. But Mother Cecilia thought she had led an extraordinary life. When she was in her forties, the abbey voted to send a handful of nuns to the University of Vermont to help sustain the farm. Mother Cecilia was among them. She went back and forth to campus every day in full habit, a middle-aged nun in a rush of young coeds. She got her degree the day she turned forty-seven, and three years later, she got another. A master's in animal science and agronomy. Mother Stella Maris got a doctorate in microbiology in the end, which she applied to her cheesemaking. Mother Anne got her degree in plant science. Mother Cecilia remembered thinking of her sister then. How Nora had wanted so badly for her to be educated. How, had life turned out differently, she would have been proud.

She and Mother Placid both continued to work with young people, a passion they had always shared. Mother Cecilia was director of the internship program, which was for laypeople, some of whom ended up joining them eventually. Young adults now were more cautious than ever before. They asked her whether the abbey had insurance, whether she could write them a letter of recommendation if they did a sterling job.

The previous generation hadn't thought so much about the future. Today, she could just feel the weight on them, their strong desire to do the best thing, even when they didn't know what that was. They were living in an age of great anxiety. A young woman in a parlor told her she repeated the mantra *We are too blessed to be depressed* over and over each morning. Mother Cecilia didn't think that seemed particularly helpful. If you were, you were.

"How is Sister Alma feeling about her vows?" she asked now.

"I'm sure she'll be eager to talk to you when you get back," Mother Placid said. "She's excited, but nervous, of course."

Different parts of their lifestyle were harder for different women. Mother Claudette was an only child. Her devotion to God was never in question. But her life at its core had been a solitary one. Now she was forced to live in community with thirty-six other women. Mother Andrea had attended both Chapin and Radcliffe—she knew the ways women had in one another's close company. Her issue was the monotony of the work.

A woman of Mother Cecilia's age had never experienced all the technological advances that someone like Sister Alma took for granted in her life before the abbey. She had never had an email account, so she didn't know what it was not to have one. But some of the young ones struggled when the Internet was taken away all at once, as if it were a drug they needed to be weaned off of. She and Mother Placid had talked endlessly about the best way to handle this, and they still weren't sure.

For many, sex was the last obstacle, the thing that could not be overcome. Others agonized over giving up the idea of marriage, motherhood. Some left because of it.

She had never once told a pondering nun her own story. When they asked what her final struggle had been, she spoke about a sweater she had not been allowed to keep, she spoke about a cup of hot lemonade that had gotten her in trouble. She never told them there had been a child.

She had long ago decided that this was a lie she told for the good of the abbey. Not even a lie, but something she left out. A sin of omission. The story would only be a distraction. Now she wondered if it was wrong of her. She had asked Nora to tell the truth when she herself never had.

"Try to sleep in tomorrow," Mother Placid said. "Your one and only chance."

"No. I've set the alarm for two."

"Oh, foolish woman."

"I'm sure I'll be up anyway."

She intended to keep to the schedule as much as possible while she was here. She had always been an early riser. Her faith in God was renewed by the simple return of morning, containing the seeds of the day ahead, bringing with it new chances for redemption, for grace.

21

WHEN THE WAKE WAS OVER, Nora handed Brian a twenty. "Stop for some extra ice on the way home, will you?" she said. "Two bags."

She touched his cheek. "And don't run off again."

Being the baby of the family enabled him to disappear. When he was seven, eight years old, he'd slip under the table at big dinners and lie flat on his back on the rug, listening. No one ever told him not to. He wondered now if his parents had even noticed. By the time he was born, they were too tired to be as strict as they once were. He had an entirely different type of childhood from the others.

He went to the 7-Eleven. When he reached home, a dozen cars were parked outside the house. Brian slowed down, but he couldn't bring himself to stop. He turned the car around. He drove down the hill and then followed Nantasket Avenue to Main Street, all the way out to Pemberton Point, where Hull High School stood. He pulled the car around back to the parking lot. When he reached the baseball diamond, he shut off the engine. The sky was black and starless. Brian stared out into nothing. This was the last point of land in town. If you hit a long home run to left field, you could watch it drop straight into the sea.

He'd avoided this spot since he came home from Ohio seven years ago. It was the last place he had left still full of promise, full of the expectation that good things were coming his way. Patrick never missed a game. He drove out here all the way from Dorchester two, three times a week and stood beside Nora, the pair of them whooping and hollering, embarrassing the crap out of Brian. He wished he could hear them now.

He thought of Coach O'Leary. *I'm just waiting for you to take the reins,* he'd said. Brian told Patrick about it, expecting him to say that the job was beneath him, not the kind of thing a former pro should waste his time on. But Pat got a huge grin on his face and said, *Perfect. You've got to do it.*

Maybe he was right. The bar had nothing to offer Brian now. And he felt a little spark of something, being here again. He hadn't expected that.

He drove home after a while. He went up the walkway, bracing himself before opening the front door. Coats had been flung over the banister. There was a barrage of voices, conversations overlapping, the occasional word or eruption of laughter rising above the rest.

The neighborhood ladies were setting the dining room table. At one end were two neat stacks of plates and a basket of plastic utensils, each set wrapped in a paper napkin and tied with a bow. At the other end was the hot food—a pink ham, a steaming tray of lasagna. Every inch of the table was full. Sandwiches had been arranged in tiers, sliced cheese and crackers were spread out like a fan, cold salads had been spooned evenly into glass bowls. There was something appealing about the perfect order of it all, the abundance. They would eat their grief before it swallowed them.

Bridget's dog was under the table, waiting for a scrap to drop. Rocco glanced up at Brian, moving only his eyes.

Brian was looking back, pondering whether to give him some cheese, when Betty Joyce bumped into him on her way to the kitchen.

"Oops, pardon me," she said.

The sight of her made him stare at his shoes, even now. As a teenager, he had logged so many hours in the attic, staring out the tiny window at the top of the stairs, which looked down on the ocean in the distance and, closer to home, right into Betty Joyce's side yard. Many mornings in summertime she could be spotted there, naked in her outdoor shower after a run on the beach.

Patrick had been the one to discover it, right after the family moved in and he claimed the attic for his bedroom. Up there, sneaking one of Charlie's beers, he realized he could just make out the white orbs of Betty Joyce's breasts, bobbing up and down as she massaged shampoo into her hair. In due time, this information was passed along to his brothers, one to the next, like Patrick's old fake ID.

"Sorry, Mrs. Joyce," Brian mumbled now.

"You're fine, sweetheart."

Last night, everyone stayed at the bar until four. He slept at Ashley's. In the morning, after she and her roommates went to work, Brian found himself not hungover but still drunk. She had told him he could stay all day if he wanted. But he knew his mother was waiting. Brian sat on Ashley's sofa for twenty minutes. He let the tears fall and didn't bother to wipe them away.

At home, he had seven beers while he waited for everyone to arrive. He threw up twice at O'Dell's, before the wake got started, and vowed to slow down. But standing here now, he felt ready for another drink.

Patrick's favorite stories were always stories of drunken debauchery. There was the time they were driving down Nantasket Avenue in Pat's old Jeep and he had to stop short to avoid hitting a cat crossing the street. Pat didn't have a seat belt on. He went flying out onto the road, landing with a thud. Then he stood and shook himself off like a cartoon character, jogged back to the slow-rolling Jeep, jumped in, and drove on as if nothing had happened. There was the time Brian woke up in a bush in someone's front yard in Cambridge holding a Chinese takeout container. White rice in his hair, a purple bruise spreading across one knee. He had no idea how he'd gotten there. When he called Patrick to tell him, Patrick howled with laughter. "Happens to the best of us, kid."

Until now, all the stories were funny stories because they began and ended the same way: they had acted like jackasses, but everything had turned out fine. Occasionally it occurred to Brian that he had a problem that might need to be addressed, this thing that had afflicted his people for generations. He could choose to fight it. Or he could admit that he was one of them and carry on, leaving the problem for someone else to solve.

At work, he saw people wrestling with it all the time. Guys teetering on that blurry line between pleasure and the sick sort of need that could undo you. The ones who came back night after night kept one another drinking. Stories that might otherwise be considered tragic wake-up calls were, in their hands, just punch lines. When someone left the group to sober up, they closed ranks and never talked about that person. Or else they said he was crazy, a drama queen, that he was just looking for attention. Brian could hear in their voices how much they needed it to be true. The perfect drinker was the one who could go on all night, never getting sloppy, but never being dull either. Switching over to seltzer was considered a character flaw, but so was falling backward off the bar stool.

He wondered in those moments if there was something shameful to what he did for work. His presence, as he served them, practically pouring the liquid down their throats, gave the impression that someone was in control and would catch them before anything truly terrible happened.

Fergie had turned up wasted at the funeral home. Brian watched him wander in. He had never seen the guy in a suit before. He wondered if Fergie had borrowed it. The sleeves of the jacket fell to his fingertips. The pant legs pooled at the floor.

Fergie approached the coffin, stood over it for a long time. He spoke with Bridget and Natalie, Julia and John, and then he came to Brian. He reeked of booze.

"Well, Raf," Fergie said, stroking his chin. "I've seen him look worse."

Brian burst out laughing. It was the first time he had laughed in two days, the first time he remembered the sound of Patrick's laughter. He looked to his mother to see if she had heard, but he couldn't tell one way or the other.

Brian's buddies from high school were there, but they stood too far away, shuffling in place, eager to escape, as if death itself were contagious. The crowd from the bar came and left quickly, and he was relieved to see them go. It felt strange being in their company out of context, like running into your third grade teacher on a date at the mall.

Fergie said he wouldn't come back to the house. The family had never liked him much. Once or twice, his name came up in conversation and Bridget said, "That poor kid." Brian never knew what she meant. He supposed she thought it was pathetic that Fergie was still tending bar at his age.

Someone pushed past him into the dining room, a palm on his upper arm. Brian looked up and realized he was still holding a bag of ice in each hand. The ice was melting. Water pooled on the hardwood below.

In the kitchen, Nora stood at the stove, stirring something. She had the saddest look on her face. Then she noticed him there.

"Straight into the cooler," she said, pointing with her free hand.

"You doing okay, Ma? You want to sit down for a while?"

"Why does everyone want me to sit?"

Her tone was almost right, but it didn't convince him.

His father had joked once that he had the most important job when it came to wakes—Charlie kept the running tally of grudges, of people who had skipped out. Nora did the rest.

She turned fifty when Brian was in the fifth grade. All his friends had mothers in their thirties. Those other mothers looked to Nora to tell them how to organize a bake sale or how many chaperones they'd need for a field trip. She was a mother, even to them. He had never known her to get so much as a cold. She was up every day at six; she had her routines. She would still climb a ladder to clean leaves out of the gutters when she didn't think Brian was getting around to it fast enough.

He watched her now. The rush of all this was meant to be a defense against what she would have to feel, eventually. But he could tell from her face that it wasn't working. Brian wished he could take her away from here. She had just lost her son. She should be screaming in the streets, pulling her hair out, making a scene. Not arranging stuffed mushrooms on a plate, so that they were evenly spaced.

He wanted to ask her about her sister. But he knew she wouldn't want to discuss it, not with a house full of people.

There was a voice in the doorway. "Brian?"

Ashley.

He hadn't given her the address. The last thing he wanted was to introduce her to his mother, especially now. He had succeeded at keeping them apart at the funeral home, a small miracle.

Brian went to her, tried to guide her toward the food in the other room.

"Hungry?" he said.

But Ashley pushed her way into the kitchen.

"Ashley Conroy," she said, hand outstretched to Nora. "I didn't get to say it back there, but I'm so sorry about Patrick."

"Thank you," Nora said softly.

"We all loved him. He made so many people so happy."

"You knew him," Nora said.

"Yes. It's terrible what happened. Could have happened to half the people I know if I'm being honest. I cried all day at work just thinking of it. Of him."

It was too much. Ashley never knew when to shut up, just said exactly what she was thinking. But Nora looked grateful. She squeezed Ashley's hand. He hadn't expected that.

"Go on and get some dinner before it's all cold," Nora said after a minute. "It was nice to meet you, Ashley."

For the next few hours, people stood shoulder to shoulder, the house too warm from the heat of so many bodies packed inside. Brian rotated through them, not paying attention, with Ashley forever at his heels.

At one point, he excused himself to go to the bathroom, and when he came out, she was standing there laughing with Bridget and Maeve and Julia and Natalie. He could almost see it. A girl who would be his, connected to him on days like this one, and on good days too. Someone you wanted to keep around.

Eventually, they reached the point in the night when people had had so much to drink that they set their beer bottles down, three-quarters full, and then forgot them, opened another. The conversations grew louder. In the crowded living room, John held court at the center of a circle of work colleagues, talking about the upcoming inauguration. Eileen Delaney whispered something to the neighborhood ladies in the corner.

Lots of nights since his father died, the doorbell rang after dinner. His mother would turn to him as they watched TV, frown deeply, and say, "Eileen."

But soon after, he'd hear them laughing in the kitchen. They'd stay down there all night.

The Rafferty cousins were having a family reunion in the hall, telling stories as they balanced plates of food on their laps, the chairs dragged out from the kitchen or the dining room. On the back porch, old-timers smoked cigarettes. Years ago, they would have smoked them in the house. The memory of this seemed to keep them tethered to the door—they would travel no farther—as if at any moment the rules might be reversed again.

It was a Tuesday evening. Right now, Nora should be listening to the radio in the kitchen as she made dinner. Brian might be in his room playing a video game before his evening shift, or else doing something around the house for her. There would be that pleasant silence between them. Enough to know the other one was somewhere nearby.

Instead, the rooms were full of people. He kept expecting Patrick to come around a corner. Brian found himself wandering, then realized he was looking for his brother.

He told Ashley she should go home before the bars closed and it became impossible to find street parking, but she said, "Don't be silly, you need me here."

Just after eleven, he entered the dining room, where the table now looked like a battle had been fought on it. Cheese congealed on what remained of the lasagna. The ham was sliced clear down to the bone. A glob of tomato sauce stained the white tablecloth, a ring of grease at the edge. The salads were mostly gone. The sandwiches no longer in their tiers but picked over, put back. The roast beef and turkey had gone quickly. Now there was just the odd tuna salad, mayonnaise breeding bacteria between neat triangles of white bread.

As he reached for one of the last intact crackers on the tray, the chatter in the other rooms came to a sudden halt.

Brian heard his mother saying something, her voice too loud. A toast? A speech? It wasn't like her. He followed the sound.

"I'm sorry, but I'm very tired," Nora said. "You all need to go home now."

Their faces registered surprise, embarrassment, regret, offense. They gathered their coats and left faster than he would have thought possible. His cousin Matty offered to drive Aunt Kitty. Ashley said she would see Brian tomorrow. She kissed him on the cheek.

Only Eileen protested.

"Let me stay and help you clean up," she said.

"No," Nora said firmly. "Thank you."

Then it was just the family, standing in the hallway, looking at her. She had never brought a wake to a close.

"Mom?" Bridget said.

Nora surveyed the rooms, walking from one to the next with all of them behind her. Half-empty beer cans and glasses of wine sat on every table, and on the floor. In the rush to leave, people had abandoned their dirty plates on chairs, or under them.

Brian expected his mother to sigh and pull a garbage bag from the cupboard. But instead she said, "I'm going to bed. I'll see you in the morning."

They watched her climb the stairs.

The rest of them started picking up. In silence, Maeve loaded the dishwasher, and John soaked the pans in the sink. Brian and Julia filled three black garbage bags. Bridget and Natalie brought in everything from the dining room.

"This feels weird," Julia said. "Nora letting us do this. She wouldn't even let me fold the napkins at Thanksgiving until we'd been married ten years."

They were all silent, until Natalie said, "Should someone go talk to her?"

"I will," Bridget said.

She came back down a few minutes later.

"How is she?" Julia asked.

"She's all right. I think it just got to be too much for her."

Brian opened the back door to put the trash bags on the porch, the cold air a welcome shock. He picked up a can of beer. It had some weight to it. He looked down at his hand, rimmed in black ash. They'd been putting cigarette butts inside.

He wiped his hand on the side of his pants, reopened a bag, and tossed the can in.

He remembered a time when wakes were fun. When he was a kid and someone his parents didn't know all that well died, they'd sometimes bring him to the funeral home. Brian would wait in the car, and if he behaved, they'd go for ice cream after.

Family wakes, hosted by his mother, were even better. Especially when Nora had yet to bury anyone her own age, let alone anyone younger. Only old people, about whom everyone could say with assurance, "He had a good long life." The house would be full of revelers, boisterous laughter, his father and uncles singing Irish songs in the kitchen, two or three of them playing the bodhran, tapping out a rhythm in time with the rest. The accents got stronger when they were together.

Brian would be sent to bed at some point, but soon after he'd creep out into the hall, looking down at them through the railings under the banister, until someone spotted him and beckoned him to come back down. He'd join the crowd, bouncing merrily around, his mother taking note of him, shaking her head in disapproval, but with a smile that let him know she didn't really mind.

The next morning, he would creep downstairs in his pajamas and survey the scene. Adults asleep in their clothes on couches and carpets, their mouths hanging open. The smell of stale beer in the air. There would be bowls of potato chips and honey-roasted peanuts still out on the coffee table, and he'd swipe a handful, delighted by the small rebellion. Brian would pretend he was the lone survivor of a shipwreck, bodies strewn all around, until someone opened an eye and whispered, "Hey, kiddo. Good morning."

Three hours later, John, Bridget, and Brian sat at the kitchen table, all of them hammered. The overfed dog snored under Bridget's chair. Around midnight, Julia had taken Maeve up to bed in John's old room and never come back down. Natalie went up soon after.

They spoke of various people they had seen earlier. When Bridget started talking about the nun, her voice was louder than she realized. John shushed her, pointing upward. Nora's room.

"Did you see how Mom just ignored her?" she said, quieter now. "She didn't even invite her to come to the house. Her own sister."

Brian had been surprised when the woman stepped into the room at O'Dell's. When he was a child, he was terrified of nuns in their habits the way some kids were scared of clowns. "It's only an outfit," Nora would whisper. "Underneath they're just regular ladies." But even now, he thought that seeing a nun in habit did something to a person. You saw her, and a whole host of connotations sprang up in your head, having nothing to do with the actual woman. Just the sight of her made you feel safe or scared or angry or blessed, depending.

"Mom told Julia they had a falling-out," John said.

"But what did they fall out over?" Bridget said. "You're not even curious? I mean, what if the nun was in love with Dad or something."

"Because he was so irresistible," John said.

Bridget grinned.

"I generally assume all nuns are lesbians," John said.

"Thank God all lesbians aren't nuns," Bridget said.

John raised his beer bottle in agreement.

This was something new. A shift. Of course they all knew Bridget was gay, but it had rarely been spoken about. Even in recent years, when she brought Natalie home. Tonight at the wake, Brian had seen her take Natalie's hand in front of them all. He wondered why Bridget had chosen that moment. He looked to his mother, hoped she hadn't noticed.

John said, "Have you heard the one about the cloistered nun who took a vow of silence?"

"Yes," Bridget said, her tone discouraging.

It was an old, bad joke of their father's.

But John went on, undaunted. "She was allowed to say only two words once every five years. After the first five, she said, 'Bed hard.' After ten, she said, 'Food bad.' After fifteen, 'Room cold.' On her twentieth anniversary at the convent, she announced to the mother superior that she wanted to go home. The mother superior replied, 'Good riddance! You've done nothing but complain since you got here.'"

They laughed, even though it wasn't funny, John with that heaving sound he made, as if he were coughing something up.

For a long time, John had this voice he'd put on for work. Serious, kind of schlocky, deeper than he was naturally inclined to be. The family made fun of him for it until Patrick pointed out that John now spoke in that voice all the time. There were only rare glimpses of the old him, but he had appeared here tonight.

Bridget and John went on for a while, trying to top each other's bad jokes.

"Three-legged dog walks into a saloon," Bridget said. "He hobbles up to the bartender and says, 'I'm looking for the man who shot my paw.'"

The two of them erupted in laughter.

"How many Republicans does it take to change a lightbulb?" she said.

John raised up his hands. "Nope. Not going down that path with you tonight."

"Oh, come on!"

As he often did when he was small, Brian sat listening, not adding anything, no real stake in it, content to follow the sound of their voices. In a family where everyone had been fighting to get a word in since before you were born, you could jump into the fray or step back and let the rest of them do the talking.

Bridget and John, as different as they were, still shared an ease with each other that stretched back to the early days, something Brian didn't have with either one of them. Only with Patrick. He wondered if all families were like this, divided into teams.

When he was born, Bridget and John were ten and eleven. They were often left in charge of him, which made them eager to escape him the rest of the time. Patrick carried Brian around on his shoulders. He took him to the beach, just the two of them. When Patrick moved back to Dorchester, Brian was five. The distance only served to make Brian idolize him more. The big thrill of his week was Sunday afternoon, when Pat came to dinner and paid him to sit by the TV and turn the dial, giving him a quarter each time he changed the channel from one football game to another.

Brian was the outsider when alone with John and Bridget. In a room with just the two of them, he was always waiting for Patrick to come in and even the score. That would never happen again.

Bridget reached for a plate of sliced soda bread. The plate was covered in green plastic wrap, the holiday kind, pulled tight, one sheet over the next over the next over the next. Bridget didn't even try to unwrap it, just jammed her thumb straight through all those layers and pulled out a piece.

There was always so much soda bread at these things—dry and bland, dense and white, choking you when you took a bite, which you would anyway, hoping somehow they had found a way to improve the stuff since the last time you tried it.

Bridget bit off one small corner, then put the rest down on the table. "What else is there?"

She tried the fridge, pulled out a baking dish. Chicken Parmesan. She ate it cold, standing up, straight from the pan.

"Are those two trays with the clear plastic lids still in there?" John said. "Yup."

"Can you do me a favor and eat one of those instead, so Julia won't be pissed in the morning?"

"What are they?"

"One's Brie with dates. And the other is shrimp shumai."

"What the hell is that?"

"Dumplings."

Bridget made a face. "No can do, my friend."

"Fine. Give me the dumplings."

She handed him the tray and John sucked down five of the things.

"You like your dumplings," Bridget said.

"I like keeping the peace."

Bridget took a can of Bud Light from the cooler for each of them and set them down. The ice had melted. The cooler was a tub of water now. The cans dripped onto the table. Nora would have rushed to clean it up. But Bridget didn't even seem to notice.

"What's up with your girlfriend?" John asked.

For a second, Brian thought he was asking Bridget. But John was looking at him.

"She's not my girlfriend," Brian said.

"I like her," Bridget said. "She's nice."

"She's cute," John said. "How old is she?"

"Twenty-seven, I think."

"You're thirty-three. You're gonna have to settle down eventually. I know this is a family of late bloomers, but—"

"Speaking of," Bridget said. "I have an announcement. Natalie and I are going to have a baby."

She was trying to sound breezy, light, but Brian could tell it was a big deal for her, saying those words.

He felt stunned. He had never considered the possibility.

"Holy shit. Natalie's pregnant?" John said.

"No. She's going to be. Soon."

"So she's planning a pregnancy."

"Yes, John. Gay women don't tend to get pregnant by accident."

"Will you get married?"

"I don't think so. I don't know."

"When are you going to tell Mom?"

"Soon. Definitely by the time the kid is in high school." She sighed. "I'm planning to tell her before we leave."

"Wow."

"Yeah. But don't get too excited. I've already tried twice and failed. You two were my practice round. It didn't go so bad, right? Now. To get my mind off of that terrifying prospect, can we please go back to the nun? I don't remember ever going to a convent when we were kids. Do you, John?"

"No."

"I wonder if." She put a hand over her mouth. "Oh."

"What?"

"I almost said, I wonder if Patrick remembers. How does Mom keep a secret like this from us, all this time? We don't even know that woman, I swear."

"She tried to guilt me about how siblings shouldn't be estranged, it isn't natural, every time Pat and I stopped speaking," John said. "How's that for hypocrisy?"

Brian thought that maybe it had nothing to do with hypocrisy. Maybe it had cost their mother more than they knew, being apart from her sister for so long. Maybe she was just speaking from experience.

It didn't bother him that his mother hadn't told them about her sister. The family was built on things that went unsaid. There might be hints, whispers from another room that fell to silence when he entered. There were stories he simply accepted that he didn't know the whole of, and others he didn't even know he didn't know the whole of.

Who wanted to know everything about his own mother?

He thought about the girls he'd hung around with in college, and the ones he met in his baseball days. Dropping F bombs, wearing red thongs that stuck out above their jeans, having threesomes and then joking about it later. Lots of them were mothers now. Could their children sense it on them, this past that was anything but motherly?

He wondered what Bridget meant to get out of possessing every fact. It would never answer the questions of how or why the worst things happened. She had said they didn't know their mother. Brian knew the shape and color of Nora's underthings hanging on the drying rack in the laundry room. He knew exactly how much milk to add to her Red Rose tea in the morning, the precise shade of the liquid—still dark with a hint of sunset pink. Not too cloudy or she'd sigh. He knew that every December when *White Christmas* came on television, she'd say that *Holiday Inn* was far superior to this bit of treacle. But then she'd keep watching, forget herself and sing along.

She loved gory paperback thrillers. He had once picked up the book his mother was in the middle of, turned to a random page, and found himself reading the details of a horrific rape. Shocking to think that that's how this sweet smiling lady spent her downtime, though he supposed it was what everyone did. They read about murder and rape and scandal, or else they watched it on TV, to distract themselves from whatever was wrong with their own lives.

He knew that his mother was a bigger Red Sox fan than any of the guys he had grown up with, the kind who preferred to watch the games at home alone. When John and Julia threw a party for a Saturday game, Nora would go along, make the pasta salad and the brownies. But she got irritated when people talked over the announcers. She didn't like anyone to see how much it mattered to her, how she kneaded her hands together until they were red, how she said Hail Marys under her breath. She believed in ridiculous superstitions. Once David Ortiz hit a home run in the eighth inning while Brian was standing in the doorway to the den, saying good-bye to her before he left for work. She commanded him not to move from that spot until the game was over.

He didn't need to know any more than that, and he would never go looking.

"They said on the weather that it might snow in the morning," John said.

Brian remembered something, and for once he said it out loud, as a defense of Nora, maybe. He wanted to remind them of what was good in her.

"Did Mom stay up late with you guys listening to the school cancellations when you were kids?" he said. "I remember sitting right here, and she'd make hot chocolate and the two of us would both pray out loud for the word *Hull* to get mentioned. When it did, that meant movies on the VCR and pancakes in the morning."

Bridget looked at him and then at John, who shook his head, laughing.

"Sometimes I swear you were raised by another mother than we were," she said.

John nodded. "A mother who actually liked you."

They ran out of beer by three.

"There's Baileys and whiskey and gin in the liquor cabinet," Brian said.

Bridget said, "Liquor before beer, you're in the clear. Beer before liquor, never been sicker. Words of wisdom from the old man. Don't say he never taught us anything."

She was already getting up to retrieve the whiskey.

"I wish it wasn't too late to order a pizza," John said.

"The fridge is full of food," Bridget said.

"I hate all those sympathy casseroles. That Shake 'n Bake shit."

"Well, there's always Julia's Brie."

"I hate that shit even more."

Bridget poured them each a drink.

"He seems to have a little less stick up his ass than usual," she said to Brian, nodding toward John. "Maybe that's Patrick working his magic from the other side."

"Maybe so," John said. "Or maybe it's the forty-seven drinks I've had."

The other side. Brian wondered in earnest where Patrick was. He knew his mother believed in heaven, thought of it as an actual physical place in the sky.

"*Sláinte,*" they said. "To Patrick."

The clear, simple sound of their glasses clinking together stirred something in Brian. It was a thread, connecting every wedding and wake and celebration of his life, Patrick there for all of it.

"I want to say something," Bridget said, clearing her throat. "Just once. I know neither of you will want to hear it, and I'd never say it to Mom, but—do you think he did it on purpose?"

"No," Brian said.

She went on, as if she hadn't heard him. "Let's face it. Pat drove better drunk than sober."

"Absolutely not," Brian said, louder this time. He added, "He had tickets to the Beanpot next month," as if this proved something.

Bridget wasn't the first to say it. It had come up at the bar last night. He and Fergie were both quick to shut down even the suggestion. That wasn't Patrick. It just wasn't.

Brian looked over at John. He was crying. He didn't think he'd ever seen John cry before.

"I wasn't going to say anything, but I think I know what happened," John said. "Do you want to know about it?"

"Of course," Bridget said. "Tell us!"

Brian felt nervous. He wasn't at all sure he wanted to know.

When someone in the family died, they learned more about that person than they ever had before. It seemed unfair, since the dead were no longer there to answer for what they'd done. He didn't want to put Patrick in that position.

"It was my fault," John said.

"How could it be your fault?" Bridget said gently. "You can't blame yourself because you two weren't getting along. That's not enough to—"

"No. Wait. Listen to me. There was this article in the *Globe* on Sunday."

Brian froze. He knew what John was about to say.

"Rory McClain helped this kid he knew from Dorchester. A total mess, caught up in heroin and all that. The guy went blind in high school. He got attacked. Rory always felt bad for him. So Rory calls me today and he says Patrick is the one who did it. The one who blinded the kid. There was some kind of fight. Do you believe that?"

"That he blinded someone and we never knew?" Bridget said. "No."

"No," Brian repeated, relieved that that had been her answer. But he was thinking of the way Pat had acted at the bar on Sunday when the article came up.

"Bridget, it was right before we moved here," John said. "You remember how strange that all was?"

He wiped tears from his eyes. "Rory seemed to think the article might have set something off in Pat. And I'm the reason it was there in the first place. I pushed them to run it. I begged. I'm not saying he did it on purpose. But maybe that's why he drank so much that night. Or maybe he always drank that much, but it had him distracted and he missed something in the road, swerved just a second too late."

Bridget shook her head. Brian could tell she was concerned for John now, most of all. She looked to him. "Did Pat say anything about this article?"

Their eyes were on Brian, John's so full of hope.

"No," Brian said. "He only ever read the *Herald*."

The color came back into John's face.

"Thank God," he said. He put his head on the table.

Was it true, what Rory McClain had said? Brian didn't want to believe it. He decided on the spot that he wouldn't, he didn't.

They might never know what happened. They would each go forward, seeing it in their own ways, just as they did with all the other secrets they had chosen to share or not share with one another. He hoped Patrick had just been so drunk that he drifted off to sleep, and that despite what happened, he had somehow managed to never wake up.

"I'd better go to bed," John said. "I need to get up early and finish the eulogy."

He swallowed his drink and stood, throwing his head back. "I'm drunk," he said. He sounded genuinely surprised.

John stumbled out, and then upstairs. Brian and Bridget watched him go.

Bridget pushed her chair back. "I'm gonna head up too, kiddo. I've got to buy something online."

"For the shelter?" he said.

"Nah." She looked like she was about to say more and then thought better of it.

"You should come up soon yourself," she said.

"I will."

She paused in the doorway. "Did you see how the nun touched his hair?" she asked, more to herself than to him.

Rocco followed her from the room.

After she had gone, Brian sat alone. His glass was empty, but for a half-moon of brown liquid clinging to the bottom edge. He knew he shouldn't have any more, that if he did, he'd be unbearably hungover in the morning. But he poured himself one last small glass of Jameson.

Maybe it wasn't fair to compare, but he thought he missed Patrick more than his brother and sister did. He and Nora had loved Patrick the most. The other two had families, lives. Bridget would have a baby soon. He wondered if this would make his mother happy.

Brian had built his life around Patrick. What would he do now, who would he become?

He downed the whiskey in one swallow, then poured a tiny bit more.

After the wake, Julia and Maeve had gathered all the framed photographs and put them in a box. Brian got to his feet and found it in the hall. He took the frame on the top of the pile. Patrick's school photo. Fifth or sixth grade.

Brian carried it up to his room.

He turned on the light, stood in front of the mirror. His reflection looked troublingly normal.

One of Nora's favorite sayings was, "What would you have today if you woke up with only the things you thanked God for yesterday?" He wondered now if this had been a warning that he was too foolish to grasp.

Patrick had said that when he died, he wanted to be cremated, his ashes tossed into Boston Harbor from the back of a sailboat. Nora wouldn't allow it. She said real Catholics didn't get cremated. Brian had to stop himself from asking why she thought of Patrick as a real Catholic. But then, he was grateful too, that he would know where to find his brother.

Patrick would be buried tomorrow in the plot where their father lay. Would Brian visit him, the way his mother visited the dead, as if she were going to meet them for lunch? She swept the gravestones and left flowers and talked to the people lying beneath her feet. He thought he understood this now.

It was amazing that you did not become your grief entirely, and walk around leaking it everywhere. It could lie dormant inside you for days, weeks, years. You could seem a perfectly whole person to everyone you met. Without warning, grief might poke you in the ribs, punch you in the gut, knock the wind out of you. But even then, you seemed just fine. The world went on and on.

Part Eight

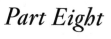

2009

22

BRIDGET REACHED OUT in the darkness, fumbled for the lamp. Her hand slammed against a wall.

Objects in the room came into focus. Slowly she remembered that she was home at her mother's house. They would bury her brother today.

Natalie was asleep beside her, the pair of them crammed onto a twin mattress.

Bridget stretched her neck, her lower back. The time spent in her childhood bed had left her sore. The booze hadn't helped. She felt like she had been hit between the eyes with a hammer. A thick, mossy taste hung in her mouth.

The sheets were flannel, a red and black plaid, pilled from wear. She had kicked them off in the night. They were too warm. Sheets for the season, which along with all the others in the house, would be replaced by a light cotton set in spring, even without the promise of anyone to fill the beds. Only faith on her mother's part that something, soon enough, would lead them all back again.

Bridget looked up at the ceiling and then at the clock. It was just after seven. She had only gone to bed four hours ago.

She considered going back to sleep, but the dog, hearing her move about, began to whine. She sat up, put her feet on the floor.

"All right," she said. "A quick one."

She stood and pulled a sweatshirt and jeans from the floor, then her coat, which hung on the top corner of the closet door.

At first, she didn't want to wake Natalie. But she was too excited to wait. Bridget kissed her cheek, and when Natalie moaned in protest, she whispered, "I got you a present."

Natalie smiled. She extended her hands without opening her eyes.

"I didn't wrap it," Bridget said. "Though in my defense, it's almost six feet tall. A hundred and seventy-five pounds."

Natalie was suddenly wide awake. "You bought the International Archeologist?"

"The full supply."

"So we're doing this," Natalie said.

"We're doing it."

They kissed and they hugged and then Bridget told her to get some sleep. She and Rocco left the room. She closed the door gently behind her.

After her mother threw everyone out last night, Bridget had followed her upstairs. She knocked at Nora's bedroom.

"It's me," she said when Nora didn't respond. "Can I come in?"

Again, there was only silence.

She opened the door anyway and found her mother sitting on the edge of the bed, staring down at her hands in her lap.

"Do you want anything?" Bridget said. "A glass of water? A shot of tequila?"

She meant the last part as a joke, but Nora just looked at her as if trying to recall who she was.

"Would you get me another box of tissues?" she said finally. "In the linen closet in the hall."

"Sure. Of course."

Bridget went to it, opened the door. Her mother had seventeen bars of Ivory soap. Ten red boxes of Colgate in two neat stacks. An unopened twelve-pack of toilet paper. When something went on sale, Nora bought ten. Usually when Bridget visited, she would ask right away, *Do you need Ziploc bags? Do you need toothpaste?* In her entire life, she had never run out of anything. It was an accomplishment.

Three boxes of Kleenex sat beside a tiny white cube, shrink-wrapped. Bridget recognized it as something Julia had given her mother for Christmas two or three years ago.

When she unwrapped it, Nora made no expression.

"That's great stuff," Julia had said. "Crème de la Mer. Movie stars swear by it."

"Eighty-five bucks for half an ounce," John said. "I'm pretty sure heroin is cheaper."

"It's a splurge," Julia said, shooting him a look. "Every woman deserves one of those now and then."

Nora held the box out to her. "You should return this. Buy something for yourself."

"Don't be silly," Julia said. "Enjoy it."

"It's a waste of money. I'll never use it," Nora said.

Apparently she had remained faithful to her word and carried on rubbing Vaseline into her dry cheeks and forehead on principle.

Bridget returned to her mother's room. Nora had gotten under the covers, turned off the light.

Bridget didn't think she was crying. Her mother wouldn't, in front of anyone. The request for Kleenex was startling enough.

"Do you want to talk?"

"I just want to sleep," Nora said. She sounded like a terrified child.

"If you want to talk about any of it, Mom, I'm here. Okay?"

"All right."

Bridget squeezed her hand.

As she turned to leave, Nora called out her name.

"Yes?"

Bridget wondered if this was the moment when her mother would say that she knew, that she loved her. Or maybe Nora wanted her to confess the truth.

Before she could give it another moment's thought, Nora said softly, "I can hear them loading the dishwasher down there. Please just make sure they know to clean the good china by hand."

The house was still. The only sounds were the sounds of morning beginning outside.

Bridget went into the hall, surprised to find her mother's bedroom door shut. Nora was usually up by now; the coffee made, bacon sputtering in a frying pan. Bridget was happy she was still asleep, that she was able to sleep at all.

On her way to the stairs, she passed John's old room, the door ajar.

John and Maeve and Julia were crowded onto an air mattress that covered the entire floor. The single bed was neatly made, a Larry Bird poster hanging above it, a plain wooden cross on the opposite wall. In the dresser, there were probably socks that had lost their form, and T-shirts, maybe an old pair of jeans. Things John no longer wanted but would never throw away because there was no need to. This house would hold their pasts as long as Nora was in it.

She had never thought to turn their bedrooms into a study or a guest room but had instead left them perfectly preserved, just as they'd been when they moved away. Their rooms were like the rooms of the dead, monuments to another time.

Bridget looked into Brian's room. The smell of cologne hovered in the air, only partly covering the stink of dirty laundry. A dartboard hung on the wall. Grade-school trophies and bobbleheads of Red Sox past lined the windowsills. He had not transformed the space with age, only added to what was already there—a queen-sized bed instead of a single, but with the same old camouflage comforter. A big-screen TV on the bureau, wedged between a CD player and boxes of baseball cards in plastic sleeves. The room was meant for a child and could barely contain all this. It was as if Brian's life had unfolded on itself and he was lost in the middle somewhere.

On the far wall, there was a small Indians pennant, the top corner flopped over in a way that depressed her. Her mother still had Indians-themed potholders in a drawer downstairs, an Indians bottle opener. There was a stack of ten or fifteen ball caps in the cellar, which her parents used to buy and give out to anyone who came over, as if they'd gotten them for free. *Our son is on the team,* they'd brag to the cable guy, or the man who came to check the gas meter.

Bridget wondered if it caused Brian pain, having to see these objects again and again. It was so easy to get mired in the past if you didn't yank yourself out for dear life.

Nora had liked them best, Bridget thought, when they were children. She imagined Nora, after they had gone, walking up the steep staircase to Patrick's room in the attic. Facing what remained of him there.

Bridget went downstairs. She put on a hat, coat, and gloves. Still, when she opened the door, the cold hit her like an object, something solid and hard. There was a sharp, crisp scent to the air. Her mother would have said it smelled like snow.

Nora's car wasn't in the driveway. She wondered where her mother would have gone at this hour. To the church, maybe. Or to O'Dell's, which wouldn't be open yet, just to be close to him.

She led the dog down the hill, past all the familiar houses of her childhood. She followed the curve of the street until she reached the bottom, where the houses sat right on the water. Betty Joyce's house was dark. At Eileen Delaney's, just the kitchen light was on.

As she walked, she thought of her mother, and of the sister Nora had never mentioned before yesterday. Now, at her worst moment, Nora wanted her back. Or some part of her did, anyway. Bridget thought of her family in terms of what they didn't know about her. She had rarely wondered about the mysteries they harbored. How could you be this close, be a family, and yet be so unknown to one another?

When she was young, it felt as if Patrick and John each commanded so much attention in his way that she was an afterthought. She dated a girl once who said this was why Bridget had gone to New York. To be seen as something other than herself in relation to the rest of them. That stayed with her. It was true. Moving to New York had saved her life. But sometimes it felt like a kind of exile. In her heart, she believed that she belonged here, among her family, in the only place she had ever thought of as home.

In her work, she saw such cruelty and injustice. She saw that people could be truly awful. But for all the sadness and the head-scratching, there was goodness to balance it out. A guy came in once with a Saint Bernard he'd found tied up, abandoned. The dog had a prong collar embedded in her neck. The guy came by and walked the dog every Saturday. After a couple of months, he told Bridget he was moving away the next weekend and wouldn't be back. He said a tearful good-bye to the Saint Bernard. But when Saturday morning came, there he was, rolling up in a U-Haul.

"I couldn't leave without her," he said. "I think she'll like Virginia."

The main drag was empty.

Out of habit, she waited for the light to change, then crossed over the road and into the public parking lot of Nantasket Beach.

She arrived at the seawall and let the dog pull her down the stairs to the sand. It was low tide. No one else in sight. Bridget let Rocco off his leash. He ran to the surf, chasing it in and out like a puppy. She pulled a ball from her pocket and tossed it into the waves. There were flurries in the air.

She missed Patrick. His sweetness, his craziness. The family looked different to her now. When one of them vanished, those who remained were transformed into something new. This happened again and again, and would keep happening, despite however much they might wish it wouldn't.

But to her surprise, she felt a burst of joy, of hope, in spite of it. Natalie's influence, she supposed. Her faith that love was everything in the end, even if it was an imperfect love, a love that depended on memory, on some former version of who they were. Natalie believed that if they let her, Nora would surprise them. Maybe there was no reason not to wish for it.

Bridget looked out at the water, the land on the other side too far away to see. She said a silent prayer for the departed, and for the ones who were yet to come.

23

TWO HOURS EARLIER, five-thirty in the morning, Nora was lying in bed, mind ravaged, thinking of what she had done. She had been up all night, on and off. Thrashing in the sheets, bolting upright, awake, and at the same time unsure of whether she had yet gone to sleep.

John had driven her home from the wake the night before. As they turned out of O'Dell's parking lot, she saw her sister at the corner, getting into a taxi. Theresa looked so alone. Nora felt something unhinge in her. She was cruel, terrible. Still, she didn't do a thing to make it right. She turned to Maeve in the backseat and asked if she was hungry for lasagna.

At the house, full of people, she thought only of the ones who were absent. Charlie. Her Patrick, whom all the wishing in the world could never conjure now. And Theresa. Nora realized it, standing at the stove, and the presence of everyone else became unbearable. Voices from other rooms were an invasion. They didn't care. Not enough.

She sent them away. Embarrassing to think about it now, but it had felt beyond her control.

In bed, at first, Nora had a strong sense that her sister had deserved the harsh treatment. Theresa could come to the funeral if she liked. They didn't have to speak. But Nora couldn't stick to her anger. Her thoughts kept wandering in another direction.

She wondered why she had made that call in the first place. She thought it was a punishment at the time. Not about her at all. But perhaps her better angels had somehow known she needed Theresa here. She had never believed that Theresa loved Patrick. Not the way she did. But standing over his body with Theresa, Nora felt it. Her sister's grief, as palpable as her own.

For some reason, she thought of Maeve in that moment, how the orphanage said someone had left her wrapped in a pink blanket in a crowded market, where she would easily be found. Diapers and coins sprinkled around her as offerings. Symbols of a mother's love, her devotion. Nora thought of Theresa running from the house that final night, leaving Patrick to her care. She thought of the medal that arrived in the mail seventeen years later, with him when he was born and when he was laid to rest.

At six, she dressed and went downstairs, expecting to find a mess. She would have fifty people here later. There was so much work to be done.

When Charlie died, she could not bring herself to make dessert. It was simply one step more than she could manage. So she cheated and went to a fancy bakery in Hingham and bought brownies and lemon squares, just that once. When they asked, in complimentary tones, "Did you make these yourself?" she sputtered, "Of course."

Last night, she had gone much further. She had let them all see the worst of her.

Now, at the foot of the stairs, peering into the living room, Nora found, with some degree of amazement, that her children had cleaned to perfection.

As she neared the kitchen, she could hear a foot tapping on the floor. She wondered if it was Patrick and then she wondered how much longer her mind would play this trick, not entirely unwelcome.

John sat there, elbows on the table, hands in his hair, a notepad in front of him.

"You're working today?"

"No," he said. "It's the eulogy."

"Oh."

He had made coffee. She poured herself a cup.

"Did you sleep?" he said.

"Not much."

John wrote something down on the page and then looked up at her.

"Did you see that article in the paper on Sunday? The one about Rory."

"Yes," she said. "Nice photograph."

"But did you read it?"

"No. I got busy with other things. I'm sorry."

"There was a kid called O'Shea. A blind kid. Do you know who I'm talking about?"

Peter O'Shea. Nora had prayed for him every night since the first time she heard his name.

She looked John in the eye. "Yes."

"You were right, you know," John said. "I should have found a way. We had our differences, but we were brothers."

She knew his list of grievances—the money, Maeve's confirmation, how Patrick had stopped him from going to Saint Ignatius. She had wondered why Patrick hadn't just told John the truth about the school: that, right or wrong, it was for John's own protection that he had done what he did. Maybe she ought to have told John herself. Someone could save your life without you ever knowing it. It happened more than most people realized.

I should have found a way.

"It's not easy," she said. "I know that as well as anyone."

John looked surprised.

"Yeah," he said. "Right. Of course."

"You should get some more sleep, John. You look so tired."

"I am."

"Go on then. I need to run out. I'll be back soon."

He looked at the clock. "Now?"

"Yes."

"Do you want me to come?"

"No thank you. Go upstairs to your family. I'll wake you when I'm back."

She was in the car by six-fifteen. In Dorchester a half hour later.

The old neighborhood had changed so much. She wondered if Theresa would even recognize it. Nowadays Edison Green had a tall brick senior center right in the middle. No more grass, no more boys playing ball. Mrs. Quinlan's house and all the others around it were full of Vietnamese people. The Irish had mostly moved on. The dance halls had closed long ago.

Dorchester had always been Patrick's favorite. So many other young people wanted to get away. He had come back, opened the bar here, of all places. He was the most loyal person she had ever known. Had he been there to see his best friend stumbling drunk into his own wake, Patrick would have found a way to excuse it.

She thought of how much Theresa had loved Dorchester too, when they were young. She thought even further back than that. To home.

Nora had told the children they couldn't afford to go to Ireland, which was partly true. But the whole of it was, she didn't want to go. She thought she would die without ever seeing home again.

John had been so proud when he surprised them with a trip. She could hardly say no. He flew the whole family over. Nora and Charlie sat in first class. She had kept the little bottles of champagne they handed out. She still had them, at the back of a kitchen cabinet.

She was so afraid that someone in town would slip. In advance of the trip, and even on the plane, she thought of just telling the children the truth—*I have a sister. We haven't spoken in years.* But she didn't do it. Time ran out. Naturally, after a long flight to Shannon and an early morning drive, bleary-eyed and on the wrong side of the road, the first person the family ran into on the High Street in Miltown Malbay was a girl Nora knew from school.

"How's Theresa doing?" was the first thing out of her mouth.

Nora startled, but then she saw that her children hadn't thought anything of it. They knew two dozen Theresas back home.

It horrified her to find the old house in shambles, as if it had never meant a thing to anyone. She supposed this was why she never threw anything away. It mattered, having something you could claim as your own.

When she and Theresa stopped speaking, their brother kept them apprised of each other. But after he died, there was silence. Charlie's brother and his wife organized Martin's small funeral. Nora didn't go back for it. Brian was only three years old then.

On the family trip to Ireland, when her brother's name was mentioned, they expected her unending thanks for what they had done. They had not even bought him a proper headstone, only a flat granite marker, while Nora was busy giving their people a king's send-off on the other side of the ocean. She stood before her family's graves for a long while, her children beside her, unable to fathom what she had lost. She thought of how hurt she had felt when Bridget moved to New York. No one else in the family had children who went away like that. She herself had gone so much farther. Never returned until now. It wasn't right that you could only understand your parents' pain once you'd experienced the things they had, and by then, in her case anyway, they were gone.

Miltown Malbay was a different place than the one she left. Cars lined every sidewalk downtown, just like in Boston. The dance hall where Charlie first kissed her was a furniture store with rows of sofas and armchairs filling the once wide and empty floor. He spun her for a turn anyway, landing them both in a recliner. A memory she would hold for the rest of her life.

She had never seen the sweeping Cliffs of Moher before, twenty minutes from where they grew up. When she went there with the children, Nora saw how beautiful the cliffs were, how majestic. John read aloud from a guidebook about the stone walls, miles of them, laid by hand thousands of years ago. He wanted to tell her the story of her own life.

There was a plaque now, not far from the house where she grew up, commemorating the site of the Rineen Ambush of 1920. It told of the blood in the streets, the children killed, the homes burned. Her own father would have been ten years old then. He had never mentioned it. Had it been too painful to say out loud, or had he spared his children the knowledge, as Nora spared hers in her way?

Nora met up with her old friend Oona Donnelly for tea. Over the years, their letters had dwindled down to a yearly Christmas card. Oona seemed happy. She was plump now, with silver hair. She looked much older than Nora did, or so Nora wanted to believe.

She had seven grandchildren already. Their photographs covered every inch of her refrigerator. Oona said three of them were being raised in Stockholm, by their father, her son, and the Swedish woman he had fallen in love with at university but never felt the need to marry. The rest lived just down the road. All Oona's grandkids were sent to the Gaeltacht on Inishmore in summertime, to learn their history. They spoke perfect Irish.

Nora was at once envious of her and embarrassed for her. There was something depressing about that country kitchen with its dim lighting, the folding chairs, a collection of porcelain cats on the windowsill. The countertops were crowded with cookbooks and circulars; newspapers and half-empty soda bottles; pans in a precarious pile. Nora felt an urge to put everything back where it belonged. There was a small television, which Oona kept switched on even as they talked, glancing over at the set from time to time.

Before they parted, Oona asked after her sister. Nora had written to her about Theresa becoming a nun, and about their falling-out, but she had never told Oona about Patrick. It was too difficult to explain in a letter. The thought of putting it down on paper seemed too great a risk.

Sitting there in Oona's kitchen, Nora considered telling her. But she only said, "We don't talk anymore. She has her life and I have mine."

She could see that the answer didn't quite satisfy Oona, but she took it no further.

The old Friel's Pub had the name Lynch over the door now, but everyone—even the Lynches—still called it Friel's. When Nora left Oona's house and found the others there, her children were in high spirits, proud of themselves for making the reunion possible. They thought having the chance to catch up over tea would delight her. They didn't think how it might stoke pain, bring back the memory of saying goodbye to Oona.

In all her years in America, Nora had never made such a friend.

She turned onto Dorchester Avenue on purpose. She didn't have to go this way. But Nora wanted to see the bar, even closed, as it would certainly be at this hour. It was the place Patrick had last been himself. The place he had last *been*.

There was nobody behind her. She slowed down as she came to the bar and saw flowers heaped at the curb. The sight of them made her cry. The grate was up, the door wide open. As she passed by, Nora could make out a figure sitting alone inside.

He made so many people so happy, Brian's girlfriend had said last night.

She was not the woman Nora would have chosen for him, but none of them would ever end up with the person she'd imagined for them. Nora thought of Bridget, holding Natalie's hand, bringing her up in line with the family. The answer to a question she had never wanted to ask, even of herself. It was crushing in its way, and yet, life went on. She didn't want to be so terrified anymore.

She turned onto Morrissey Boulevard. Two minutes later, she pulled into the motel parking lot, eager to get Theresa away from this place.

In the lobby, a boy of nineteen or twenty stood behind a desk, staring down at his phone. He didn't look up when she came in.

"Excuse me," she said. "I'm looking for someone. A guest."

"I can't give you anyone's information, ma'am," he said, trying to sound stern, looking nervous.

She realized he must think she was a scorned wife on the trail of a cheating husband. That was the sort they got around here.

"She's my sister," Nora said. "A nun. I'm here to pick her up for a family funeral."

"Oh." His face flooded with relief. "Up on the second floor. Room two zero nine." He looked back at his phone and then up again. "So she really is a nun?"

Nora went to the elevator, her hand trembling as she pressed the button.

Once on the second floor, she went to the door, took a deep breath, and knocked.

Her sister appeared, wearing a cotton nightgown. Her feet were bare. Her hair hung to her shoulders. She looked beautiful. She looked like herself as a girl.

"You don't wear the habit to bed, then?" Nora said.

Theresa looked surprised, and then she smiled.

"No," she said. "Not usually."

Nora was already imagining the two of them driving to Hull, Theresa's packed suitcase in the back. They could stop at the beach for a minute, look out at the ocean. There were so many things she wanted to tell her sister.

"I shouldn't have acted that way last night," Nora said. "Please forgive me."

Theresa bowed her head. She opened the door wider, as far as it would go.

"Nora, forgive me," she said. "Come in."

Acknowledgments

I am, as always, indebted to my editor, Jenny Jackson, and my agent, Brettne Bloom, both of whom worked tirelessly on this book. And to the friends and family members who took the time to read various drafts and provide invaluable feedback at every stage: Helen Ellis; Liz Egan; Stuart Nadler; Hilary Black; Ann Napolitano; my husband, Kevin Johannesen; and my parents, Joyce and Eugene Sullivan.

Though the words, thoughts, and actions of my characters are entirely fictional, many people helped me establish the facts of their world. For sharing stories of the ocean crossing and the Boston Irish in the 1950s and onward, I am grateful to Jack Cronin, Mary Sheehan, Kathleen Ahern, Mary McCarthy, Catherine Wyse, Caitlain Hutto, Owen O'Neill, and Ralph Cafarelli. Thank you all for answering my many questions.

In Ireland, interviews with Madeleine McCarthy, Mary O'Halloran, Patsy Jones, Kitty Meade, Charlie Lynch, Cyril Jones, and Harry Hughes aided me in painting a picture of Miltown Malbay, the town where my great-grandmother was born. Thanks to Cormac McCarthy at Cuimhneamh an Chláir and Séamus Mac Mathúna at Oidhreacht an Chláir for making it possible. And to my cousins, Mary and Pat Meade, who were so welcoming to us.

Thank you to Mother Abbess Lucia Kuppens and everyone at the Abbey of Regina Laudis, who showed me such warmth and hospitality. And to my aunt, Nancy Hickey, and Martha Kuppens for telling me about the abbey in the first place.

Two documentaries were of great assistance. *Malbay Manufacturing and Dalgais Labels,* made by Youthreach Miltown Malbay, helped me fill in the details of Nora's work. And HBO's *God Is the Bigger Elvis* transported me back to Regina Laudis after I returned home.

Thank you to Sara and Justin Pitman for indulging my medical inquiries. To Conor Yunits, who explained a lot about politics and helped me build a career path for John. To my cousin, the late Eileen Meade. To the Quinlan family: Henry, Regina, Anne Moran, Mary Jordan, and Mary and Jack McCaffrey. To Maryann Downing, for sharing her perspective on convent life, and to Scott Korb, for introducing us. To Meg Wolitzer, Mary Gordon, and Mary Beth Keane, for the last-minute words of wisdom. To Agatha Scaggiante. To Deanne Dunning. To Barry Moreno at Ellis Island, Yvonne Allen at the Cobh Museum in Cobh, Ireland, and Alicia St. Leger. Thanks to Noreen Kearney Dolan, Kate Sweeney Regan, and Kelly Coyle-Crivelli for the family recollections. And to Julianna Baggott and Joshua Wolf Shenk, for the image of Gilot having to rouse Picasso from his despair each morning, as depicted in Joshua's book *Powers of Two*.

Lastly, I'm grateful to everyone at Knopf and Vintage, especially Christine Gillespie, Helen Tobin, Anna Dobben, Sara Eagle, Zakiya Harris, Maria Massey, Amy Ryan, Nicholas Latimer, Paul Bogaards, Anne-Lise Spitzer, Carol Carson, and Abby Weintraub. To Jenny Meyer and Sara Goewey at the Jenny Meyer Literary Agency. And to Dana Murphy and all the extraordinary women of the Book Group.

J. Courtney Sullivan is the *New York Times* best-selling author of the novels *Commencement, Maine,* and *The Engagements. Maine* was named a Best Book of the Year by *Time* magazine and was a *Washington Post* Notable Book for 2011. *The Engagements* was one of *People* magazine's Top Ten Books of 2013 and an *Irish Times* Best Book of the Year. Sullivan's work has been translated into seventeen languages. Her writing has also appeared in the *New York Times,* the *Washington Post,* the *Chicago Tribune, New York* magazine, *Elle, Glamour, Allure, Real Simple, Lenny Letter,* and *O, The Oprah Magazine,* among many others. She lives in Brooklyn, New York.

www.jcourtneysullivan.com

A NOTE ABOUT THE TYPE

The type used in this book was designed by Pierre-Simon Fournier *le jeune*. In 1764 and 1766 he published his *Manuel typographique*, a treatise on the history of French types and printing, and on what many consider his most important contribution to typography—the measurement of type by the point system.

Composed by North Market Street Graphics,
Lancaster, Pennsylvania

Printed and bound by Berryville Graphics,
Berryville, Virginia

Designed by M. Kristen Bearse